R ⟍ **W9-CTL-869**

JUL 2 0 2022

GREEN LAKE BRANCH

NO LONGER PROPERTY
SEATTLE PUBLIC LIBRARY

J. Michael Wall is a lifelong resident of Washington State. Recently retired, Michael's meandering employment profile includes, but is not specifically limited to: U.S. Forest Service firefighter, steakhouse cook, bartender, electrician, lineman apprentice, meter reader, water utility technician and elementary school teacher. Mr. Wall resides with his wife, Jan, and son, Daniel, in the forested foothills northwest of Tahoma (Mt. Rainier), where he hikes, reads, writes, plays his guitar and sings, quaffs I.P.A. and finds steadfast amusement listening to out-of-state folks struggle to pronounce "Puyallup;" the little city that his family calls home.

For Jan who abided, who abides.
And for Sheila, who wears brown shoes.

J. Michael Wall

APPLETON QUARRY/
APPLETON CROW

AUSTIN MACAULEY PUBLISHERS™
LONDON * CAMBRIDGE * NEW YORK * SHARJAH

Copyright © J. Michael Wall 2021
Cover Design by J. Michael Wall
Cover Illustration by Alicia Lopez Gradilla

All rights reserved. No part of this publication may be reproduced, distributed, or transmitted in any form or by any means, including photocopying, recording, or other electronic or mechanical methods, without the prior written permission of the publisher, except in the case of brief quotations embodied in critical reviews and certain other noncommercial uses permitted by copyright law. For permission requests, write to the publisher.

Any person who commits any unauthorized act in relation to this publication may be liable to criminal prosecution and civil claims for damages.

This is a work of fiction. Names, characters, businesses, places, events, locales, and incidents are either the products of the author's imagination or used in a fictitious manner. Any resemblance to actual persons, living or dead, or actual events is purely coincidental.

Ordering Information
Quantity sales: Special discounts are available on quantity purchases by corporations, associations, and others. For details, contact the publisher at the address below.

Publisher's Cataloging-in-Publication data
Wall, J. Michael
Appleton Quarry/Appleton Crow

ISBN 9781645756347 (Paperback)
ISBN 9781645756330 (Hardback)
ISBN 9781645756354 (ePub e-book)

Library of Congress Control Number: 2020925241

www.austinmacauley.com/us

First Published 2021
Austin Macauley Publishers LLC
40 Wall Street, 33rd Floor, Suite 3302
New York, NY 10005
USA

mail-usa@austinmacauley.com
+1 (646) 5125767

Early Autumn, 1992

YOU ARE THE CROW.

YOUR SLEEK, BLACK FEATHERS CLASP UNSEEN MOTION, AND YOU ARE WINDBORNE OVER THE LITTLE TOWN OF APPLETON. TO THE NORTH, GRASSY GREEN HILLS LUMBER LIKE A FROZEN SERPENT TO THE DOORSTEP OF WASHINGTON'S CASCADE MOUNTAIN RANGES.

HERE AND THERE, JAGGED AND TOMBSTONE-ISH, RISE THE REMNANTS OF THE KENNAWACK VALLEY'S ONCE-UPON-A-TIME HEART AND SOUL; TREE STUMPS—THE DARK, ROTTING GHOSTS OF RED DELICIOUS APPLES, BARTLETT PEARS, AND BING CHERRIES. LIFE AND LIVELIHOOD TO GENERATIONS OF APPLETON RESIDENTS THEY WERE. DECADE FOLLOWING DECADE. FAMILY AFTER FAMILY. HARVEST UPON HARVEST.

NO MORE.

CROW MIND DOES NOT PONDER THIS. YOUR EYE—SHINING, LITTLE BLUE BEAD—REGARDS THE DEPTHS AND DISTANCES OF ICE-CROWNED PEAKS FLOODING THE FULL FIELD OF VISION WEST OF TOWN; THE BIRTH GROUNDS OF COLD, CLEAR STREAMS WHICH RACE LAUGHING OVER ANCIENT STONES WORN SLICK SMOOTH BY THE UNSEEN MOMENTS OF TIME. AND THIS, YOU KNOW. CROW KNOWS THE CONSTRUCTS OF TIME AND WIND. SOUTHEASTERLY FLOWS THE KENNAWACK RIVER, ISSUING FROM A NARROW GORGE WHICH EARLY NATIVE INHABITANTS CALLED THE WA-KEE-CHEE, THROUGH THE TOWN OF APPLETON—CAREENING IN JUBILANT SPRAYS OF FALLS, FOAM, AND FURY—HEADLONG IN HASTE TO MARRY WATERS OF THE MIGHTY COLUMBIA RIVER NEAR THE CITY OF WESTON.

YOU ARE THE CROW. CROW INTUITS APPLETON. CROW INSTINCTUAL-IZES THE KENNAWACK; ITS FOUNTAINHEAD AND ITS FEEDERS. CROW HAS LEANED IN, LISTENED, AND LEARNED.

AND THE SUN-BURNT SKYWAY—THAT ILLUMINATING DOME SUSPENDED OVER THESE PATIENT HOMES WITH THEIR STRUGGLING VEGETABLE PLOTS—OFFERS LIMITLESS, BLUE VOLUMES FOR YOUR FLUTTERSPUN FLIGHT. SPINNING AND GLIDING, MILES FROM YOUR ROOSTING SITE BEHIND THE OLD APPLETON QUARRY, YOU BANK HARD ON AN ARM OF PUFFY AIR, AND ALIGHT, HOP-DANCING ON SPONGY EARTH.

THE LONGLEGS IS THERE. ACROSS AROMATIC, FRESHLY CUT AUTUMN GRASS, YOU SPOT THE LONGLEGS WITH HIS GUITAR. HE IS SEATED COMFORTABLY ON THE DILAPIDATED, GREEN PARK BENCH—PAINT-PEELED AND RICKETY—RIGHT LEG CROSSED OVER THE LEFT, INSTRUMENT CRADLED LIKE A SMALL CHILD; PLAYING AND CROONING QUIETLY IN THE SHADE OF FRIENDLY, YELLOWING BROADLEAFS. IT IS SUNHIGH TIME; NEAR MID-DAY.

YOU PECK TAP AT THE DISCARDED SCRAP OF A PAPER CUP, EYEING THE DOG, INSTINCTIVELY THINKING, "THERE IS A DOG, BUT THAT IS NOT <u>THE</u> DOG." AGAIN, CROW MIND PURSUES THE TOPIC NO FURTHER. CROWDING AIR BENEATH THE MUSCLES OF YOUR ASH BLACK WINGS, YOU GARNER THE BREATH OF REMOTE ALPINE BREEZES AND LIFT YOURSELF ALOFT. INTO EXPANSES OF CLEAR SEPTEMBER LIGHT, YOU WHEEL AND SPIN, EXPLOITING AND EXPLORING A THERMAL UPDRAFT HIGHER...AND HIGHER STILL, UNTIL THE DOG, THE LONGLEGS, AND THE GUITARCHILD FUSE INTO A DARK DOT IN DISTANT BELOWNESS.

YOU ARE THE CROW.

AND YOU ARE LEAVING THE INCONSEQUENTIAL LITTLE TOWN OF APPLETON, ITS FORGOTTEN, SLEEPING QUARRY AND THE MIDDLE REACHES OF THE KENNAWACK RIVER FOREVERMORE, HAVING SPENT THE BULK OF SUMMER'S SHORT SEASON SEEKING OUT AND ASSIMILATING. YOU ARE SOARING NORTH-NORTHWEST, UPSTREAM ABOVE THE SPLASHING RAPIDS OF THE KENNAWACK RIVER...TO SOME-WHERE-ELSE (O' RAVENRILL!), AND SOME-WHEN-ELSE WITH A STORY TO RECOUNT.

*

Early Summer, 1992

"So you can pretty much imagine," huffed Kelsea, "how he must feel *inside*, even though he doesn't always show so much on the *outside*."

Erik Remarque nodded his understanding and pedaled harder. At fifteen years of age, Kelsea had a full year on him, and those longer, stronger legs were a force to be reckoned with—at least when it came to biking up steep pitches. Erik squinted in the new morning light, knitting long, blonde lashes across slit lids; a feeble measure of protection from the almost-overwhelming glare of summer sunshine. He swabbed a bony fist across his damp forehead and tongue-tipped the corners of his mouth, tasting salt.

Not even 11:00, and hot already! Yep, he was gonna like it here in Appleton just fine!

"Anyways," continued Kelsea, pumping slim, muscular legs determinedly, and breathing hard through her mouth, "his doctors were never actually able to figure out his disability. If that's even what you would call it. It just wasn't something they could put a finger on. He talks and acts pretty much like anybody else, but there are certain things that are, I don't know, just kinda beyond his ability to handle. You know, like, driving a car or maybe reading and following tricky directions, stuff like that."

Erik's tanned expression showed complete understanding, and Kelsea resumed her story. "So he kinda does odd-jobs around town, you know, like for the church an' the school an' stuff. And he has sort of a set-up bank account that he inherited, I think, that he can use as well. So he's doin' all right for himself, I guess."

"Except for when it comes to people makin' fun of his disability, right?" offered Erik.

"Yeah, but it's not even really a disability. It's more just like, well, Justin's just a little *different* from anyone else around here, that's all. Wait'll you meet him, and his dog, Kooper... with a 'K.' You'll see what I mean. What a *great* guy! And wait'll you hear him play *guitar!* Oh, man! That's the *best!*"

"Can't wait," huffed Erik. He was wishing his new friend (his *only* friend) would slow down, even just a skosh, and give his burning leg muscles a chance to stop screaming at him. Four days really wasn't much time to get to know somebody, but when Erik and Kelsea had crossed paths in front of the soda fountain—two short days after he, his parents, and kid sister had moved into town—the spark of immediate friendship had cemented them like long-lost cousins. He smiled, remembering the crisp five-dollar bill she had dropped unnoticed in the parking lot near her mountain bike. Eric had returned the money to its rightful owner without hesitation, and she had rewarded him with a lightly freckled grin so rich with unbridled appreciation that it made introducing one another *to* one another a piece of cake. The two felt like they had been best buddies for years rather than mere moments, and together they had spent the next few afternoons cycling purposefully to every corner of the community, getting everyone acquainted with Appleton's newest newcomer.

Erik was somewhere near midstream in his daydream when Kelsea braked abruptly, swerved with astonishing agility, and disappeared, laughing over the crest of a small knoll.

"Hey!" yelled Erik, "wait up Kelsea!" Slowing his bike as quickly as he could without losing control, Erik glance-checked for traffic over his right shoulder, zipped a U-turn in the middle of Frontier Street, and high-tailed it in the direction his partner had taken.

Kelsea was standing beside her bike next to three other youngsters, her arms akimbo, head cocked slightly to one side, hawking Erik as he topped the hill and coasted down the sidewalk bordering the east end of

Appleton Town Park. She scowled at her wristwatch and tapped it lightly with a forefinger, as if to say, "I was *wonder*ing how much longer you were gonna make us wait around here for you, amigo!"

Erik's heart swelled a bit at the thought of how fun, funny, and <u>easy</u> she was to *be* with. Her smiling, freckle-sprinkled face seemed to say, "C'mon, Erik! These are the some of the guys I been tellin' you about!" But the sparkle in her grayer-than-gray eyes hinted at something completely different. More like, "Ha! Out-biked ya again, didn't I boy-o?"

Erik glided to a stop next to Kelsea, gently leaned his non-kickstand-equipped bike to the ground and summoned every ounce of his will and strength to bear on the task of appearing <u>not</u> winded, <u>not</u> out of shape and, most importantly, <u>not</u> new in town.

"OK, everybody. This is Erik Remarque. His family just moved into the old Baxter place. He's gonna be a 'niner' next fall." Polite nods and smiles of welcome encircled the boy as Kelsea went on with the introductions. "So, this is Sandy and Stuart LeMaster. They're twins. Obviously enough, huh?"

Erik would never have believed that a boy and a girl could look so much alike. In both adolescents, ebony eyes peered from beneath dark, extraordinarily heavy eyebrows which reminded him not so much of facial hair as thick smudges of misplaced charcoal.

Shadowy curls of wind-brushed hair waterfalled from their heads, and Erik noticed that they were—both of them—inclined to let it grow.

"Welcome to Appleton, Erik. You're really gonna like it here!" bubbled Sandy.

"Hi, Erik," murmured Stuart politely.

Hmm. Possibly the shy type, Erik, thinking to himself, made a quick assessment of the slightly pudgy, bespectacled youngster standing next to him. *At least I won't be alone in <u>that</u> department.*

"Hey, wait a sec!" interrupted Sandy, suddenly wide-eyed. "There once lived a well-known *author* named Erich Remarque. Erich Maria Remarque, right?"

"Really?" asked Kelsea. "What books did he write?"

"'*All Quiet on the Western Front*', for one," Erik, warming, gaining some traction.

"It was a super famous book about The Great War, World War I; the war that was supposed to end all other wars forever... period."

"Ooh, are you a bookworm?" began Sandy hopefully.

"Not really. Well, kinda, but anyway my dad loves that book. It's one of his enduring favorites, and since our last name is Remarque—um, no relation to the author or anything—anyway, he named me after him. Except my name is spelled, E-R-I-K."

"... and the author's name is spelled E-R-I-C-H!" finished Sandy, broadcasting sincere personal approval of what she felt was Erik's noteworthy status in the annals of great literary artists.

"That's way cool," smiled Stuart. "Plus, you just scored some unanticipated bonus points with my pedontic sister."

"That's pe*dan*tic, Stu," corrected Sandy kindly. "But that's OK. And you're right, it's a totally trés-cool honorarium to have in your lineage."

"Pedantic?" began Erik, nurturing a hope that his fragile status as "Appleton Newbie" could *never* be derailed or compromised by his admitted unfamiliarity with the definition of an eight-letter vocab word.

Sandy laughed. "Pedantic means kind of 'student-y.' You know, 'bookish.' And an honorarium is just something you've been given by someone as a sign of appreciation. Or, um... an acknowledgment of deserved acclaim," she added. Erik took note of the fact that Sandy's pronouncement of the word 'deserved' contained three syllables.

Hmm, again. The girl seems to be very 'pedantic' indeed, he surmised.

Kelsea studied Erik with a theatrical look of dramatic appraisal. "You hang around Sandy long enough, bro-ski, and sooner or later you'll find your word power, um... *expanding exponentially,*" she quipped, sneaking a glance at the curly-haired girl.

"Well-spoken and succinctly relayed, verbal acolyte," replied Sandy, affecting an air of scholarly superiority.

Erik blew a long gust of breath through puffed cheeks. "Well, ah shure am glad ah got me a big ol' dik-shun-arry at home," he drawled comically. "Ah bleeve ahm a'gonna be needin' it _real_ bad if'n ah wanna be hangin' roun' this here smort-type gal all summer!"

With _that_ comment, the energy and enthusiasm of youthful summer laughter thumbed a ride on wafts of clean, mountain breezes lazily seeking roundabout routes to the Columbia waterways. And those very same freshets that rustled the bushy coils of dark brown LeMaster hair—moving like invisible butterfly wings across pinprick-sized sweat beads clinging to foreheads, and hiding under the arms of newly befriended bicycle riders—gave low, slow flight to the gift of sound born of vibrating guitar strings.

"WIND-VOICE-SOUND!" SO CROW OPINES FROM NOT ALTOGETHER THAT FAR AWAY.

Kelsea, the LeMasters, and Erik Remarque had, by then, wound their way a short distance past the gazebo and across the park footbridge, to gather in a rough semi-circle before a young-ish, tousle-haired fellow of the musical variety; lounging leisurely on his park seating which, in no uncertain terms, had long ago seen its better days.

"That's an 'A' minor seventh. Pretty, innit?" inquired the young man, holding the chord while it faded through its decay. "Howdy," he said at length, extending a warm right hand to Erik in greeting. "I'm Justin Bench."

Erik found himself shaking the pale, thin hand of a pleasantly smiling young man, somewhere in the neighborhood of twenty years of age. He was comfortably dressed in loose-fitting, faded blue-jeans, light-weight hiking boots, and a checked cotton shirt rolled to the elbow. A dark-green, almost black "Indiana Jones-style" Filson hat shaded medium blue eyes from noonday illumination, and his clean, unassuming appearance gave the man the honest, folksy quality that tends to invite trust and fosters a feeling of down-home belonging. Erik liked him immediately.

"C'mon, Justin!" urged Kelsea. "Finish up with the intros already, and get on with the guitar work... ya *know* ya want to!"

"Ya know *we* want ya to," amended Stuart.

"Awright, awright, try not to hemorrhage over it, people," said Justin, winking and feigning the part of a poor, simple park patron under the onslaught of a pack of ravenous music fiends craving their fix of songcraft. And he said as much, to the delight of everyone in earshot.

"Well, this here is Woody," he fondly patted the neck of the six-string guitar balanced on his right knee. "He's a steel string Yamaha, and he pretty much goes just about everywhere I go, just as sure as you're born. And down here someplace," Justin held the instrument out of his way, and leaned over to fish around for an ear to scratch, "is my good buddy, Kooper, with a 'K.' C'mere, Koop. C'mon out an' meet Erik. Kelsea says he's an awful nice guy."

A beige-muzzled, blonde scamp of questionable pedigree cracked open one sleepy eye and thumped his tail in greeting.

"I guess ol' Kooper-with-a-'K' is gonna take 'er easy today," remarked Erik.

"Ol' Kooper pretty much takes 'er easy just about every doggone day," said Justin, still grinning.

Kelsea was about to renew her demand for some afternoon guitar work when a small, green crabapple landed with a 'plump' not three feet from the circle of friends.

"Oh, no!" she groaned, "not today! Ma-aan!"

"See that, guys? I jus' damn near kerpowed *somethin'* with my little green fruit missile!"

Three thug-like looking adolescents stood defiantly around a trash container 30 meters away, watching Justin and his audience.

"Not much of a target, if you ask me," enjoined one of the boys.

"Guess yer right, my bro," countered the first. "Just an empty bench, man!"

Peals of derisive laughter ensued, and Erik was immediately surprised and sickened by the way the taunting teenagers could laugh, sneer, and glower all at the same time. Sensing trouble of the worst kind, he stole a furtive glance at Kelsea whose beet-red expression of contempt plainly evidenced a struggle to maintain control of her behavior as well as her temper.

"S'matter, Cr*owl*? You got somethin' you wanna get off yer chest? Not that there's much of a chest there for anything to be gettin' off *of!*" This from the closest boy who, though smaller by a head than the other two, communicated the unmistakable feeling of being in charge. He purposely mispronounced Kelsea's last name, making it rhyme with *"owl"*—a thinly disguised attempt at humiliation that carried all the weight of a paper clip, and bore about as much resemblance to an insult as a sofa does to a buffalo.

"It's '***Crowl***,' as in 'crow,' meat-head," corrected Sandy, "not that *you* could ever *learn* the difference, or *remember* it if you did!"

"Don't let's start up with 'em today, Sandy," Stuart, pleading; nervously adjusting his wire-rim glasses. "We always get the short end when we tangle with those freaks."

"What's their problem, anyway?" Erik, voice lowered so as not to be overheard.

"Leave us alone, Rodent. We're not bothering you… or anyone else, for that matter," Kelsea was walking a thin line; working at appearing no-nonsense, *and* non-challenging at the same time.

"Hey, Patch!" snorted the one called Rodent. "Check out the runt in the pack! Yo, Cr*owl*! (again, with the 'owl' sound) Didja pass a diaper-changin' class, and land yerself a baby-sittin' job, or did weener-boy there follow you home from the public landfill?"

The one called Patch, running thick fingers through stringy blonde hair grinned menacingly, revealing a chipped tooth lying dead center in a pasty-faced smile that reminded Erik of nothing so much as a cracked dinner plate. A two-inch vertical scar high on the left cheekbone went a long way toward accessorizing the street-tough appearance. "Hey, weener-boy!" he growled. "Git yer *be*hind over here!"

"Don't *do* nothin'. Don't *say* nothin'," murmured Justin quietly. "This'll pass soon enough."

"Atten_hut_, jerk!" shouted Patch. "Get *over* here before I kick yer butt up ta yer shoulders, an' every time ya wanna take a poo, ya hafta take off yer shirt!"

"Hey, Cr_owl_! Yer little friend there is about as dumb as a sack of hammers!" taunted Rodent.

"And about as ugly as a stump fulla spiders!" finished Patch.

"Whatcha think, Deep Thoughts," mused Rodent, scratching his chin with a rolled-up dollar bill. "I don't remember seein' that skinny-assed squirt around here before." The third kid, tall and muscular, staring a hole in Erik's skull, shook a shaggy head in quiet commiseration. Rodent moved on, "Shall we inter-doos weener-boy here to the rules of Appleville?"

Erik noticed that, alone among the boys, the one referred to as Deep Thoughts hadn't uttered so much as a syllable. And it was the nature of that silent disposition that lent an ominous air of mystery to his intimidating appearance. The guy *had* to be at least six-foot-three and probably scaled out at around 200 pounds. Erik later marveled at the idea of a monster like Deep Thoughts being led around on a leash by such a loud-mouthed scrawn like Rodent.

But at the present time, his thoughts were very much preoccupied with the same topic as everyone else, namely: *Am I about to get a scab on my beak, or is there a way to head this thing off before somebody gets bent and/or broken?*

Given a few brief moments with which to share some personal thoughts on the situation, Sandy LeMaster would be the first to remind her friends (and detractors!) that one simply never knows when fate will step in and make hell out of a heavenly situation, or vice-versa. Life on our silver/blue ball is filled to the brim with unpredictable surprises, stunning reversals, inexplicable changes of fortune, and strokes of luck. You could fill a hundred encyclopedias just documenting the mind-numbing episodes through the ages where drearily predictable outcomes had been overturned, sabotaged, or flung unceremoniously into the ashcans of history by those weirdly absurd types of events which could never have *reasonably* occurred but did.

And so…

YOU SLIDE/FLY AT TREETOP LEVEL; CIRCLING ONCE, TWICE, EYEING THE CANISTER OF GARBAGE. THERE ARE THREE OF THE LONGLEGS, AND THEY STAND AROUND IT—AROUND THE CANISTER. CROW COVETS WHAT MIGHT BE FOUND IN THAT CONTAINER, BUT THERE ARE THE THREE, AND THEY STAND TOO CLOSE.

YOU WAIT.

CIRCLE AND WAIT.

CROW'S HUNGER GROWS. THEN, THERE IS SOMETHING; SOMETHING GREEN IS IN THE HAND OF ONE OF THE LONGLEGS. YOUR DESIRE FOR FOOD MAKES YOU BOLD, AND CARVING A TURN IN A BILLOW OF SUDDEN WIND, YOU BUILD SPEED TO TARGET IN ON THE GREEN IN THE HAND OF THE LONGLEGS.

CROW VELOCITY CARRIES YOU THROUGH THE CONTACT POINT. PRACTICE, AND THE HUNGER STABS THAT ACCOMPANY PAST FAILURES, MAKE YOU ARTFUL AND ACCURATE. THE STRIKE IS CLEAN, SWIFT, AND SUCCESSFUL. THE GREEN IS NO LONGER OF THE LONGLEGS.

IT IS THE GREEN OF CROW.

TWENTY-SEVEN STROKES OF WING MUSCLE LATER, YOU END TOGETHER-WITH-WIND TIME AND COMMENCE CLUTCH-WITH-TALONS TIME ON A VEHICLE LOADED WITH THE CRUSHED BARK OF EVERGREEN TREES. EAGER ATTEMPTS TO CONSUME THE GREEN QUICKLY FAIL AND YOU BECOME AWARE THAT THIS IS CROWFOOD-NOT.

THE VEHICLE BEARING THE TREE BARK GRINDS TO NOISY, SMOKY LIFE AND BEGINS CRAWLING FORWARD. YOU RELINQUISH OWNERSHIP OF THE GREEN AND EMBRACE BROTHERWIND, WITH CROW MIND CONSIDERING THE POSSIBILITIES OF RESUMING THE SEARCH FOR CROWFOOD BEHIND THE MINUTE MARKET BEFORE RETURNING TO THE ROOSTING SITE UPLAND FROM TOWN, BEHIND THE OLD APPLETON QUARRY.

"Man, did you see *that*?" Rodent—livid, yowling. "That stinkin' crow made off with my hundie! What the hell? I mean, WHAT…THE… HELL?"

Rodent's furious rant was cut off by a rasping, excited Patch, who was pointing in the direction of the bark truck. "The freakin' bird dropped it on that pile of mulch, I shit you not!" he croaked.

Without another word, the boys leaped on their bikes and tore off after the truck which, after slowing for the *only* traffic light in town, made a creeping left-hand turn and began building speed along Sundown Highway.

"Phew, that was close!" breathed Stuart uneasily.

"A plethora of brigands!" snorted Sandy sarcastically. "Indubitably!"

"Maybe there are some minor details about little ol' Appleton that you've failed to bring to my attention…hmmm, Kelsea?" inquired Erik.

"Yeah," sighed Kelsea. "I was hopin' to spare you the *bad* news until you at *least* had a chance to learn a little more about the *good* stuff. I guess at this point, it comes as no surprise that we've got ourselves a bit of a problem here from time to time, Erik."

"An' here's another little surprise," added Justin ruefully. He was watching Rodent, Patch, and Deep Thoughts as they sped away, churning up foams of dusty sweat in pursuit of the pickup truck. "Where'd a joker like Rodent ever get *his* greasy claws on a hun'erd dollar bill? Because that's what a *hundie* is, ladies and gents. And that's what them zombies are tryin' ta chase down an' recover right now."

*

Sometime in the month of June in 1871, Emile Haufner withdrew his calloused, gnarled old hands from the icy glacial melt known as Whistle Creek. Hunkering on one knee beside those playful, clear waters racing beneath a blistering cobalt-blue Washington Territory sky, he belched noisily, yanked a not-altogether-that-clean cloth rag from the rear pocket of his threadbare overalls, and began drying his hands.

Imagine the shock and amazement that rocketed through his brittle little brain when, after closely inspecting a fingertip of his left hand, he noticed a sparkling, yellow grainy substance glinting in flawless mountain sunlight.

Gold!

Good Lord, Almighty, it was gold!

And so began the first of many (four or five) "golden" opportunities for hopeful settlers, get-rich-quick schemers, businessmen, investors, and scoundrels who were all to take their respective turns at carving a career—legal, or otherwise—out of the untamed tangles of the middle Kennawack; an area one day to be christened "Appleton."

As it so happened, those finger-tipped sun glints turned out to be the first, middle, and _last_ of the Great Whistle Creek Gold Strike. For it wasn't very long at all before the 2000-odd prospectors (and many of them were, indeed, _very_ odd) who, at the first hint of the gold rumor, had swarmed out from behind every Douglas fir in the valley like so many deer flies, only to eventually be forced to throw down their shovels, toss aside their visions of wealth, and clippity-clop cowboy-style into a pine-scented sunset.

The entire "gold dust" _mis_adventure had run itself out over the course of three short, frustrating, unprofitable years.

Scant few of _those_ hardy individuals hung around long enough to buy into (or at least bear witness to) the next phase of the tiny settlement's development. And that could be properly entitled: "The Coming of the Railroad."

Dry goods, foodstuffs, hardware supplies, clothing, and news-and-notions-of-the-world were slow in coming to the Inland Empire from factories located east of the Great Plains. Nearly anything and everything worth possessing was shipped overseas from cities on the East Coast, down around the southern tip of South America to the flourishing frontier communities of Seattle, Tacoma, and Everett.

Getting this vast assortment of sorely needed products across the purple/black spine of the rugged Cascade Mountains was the daunting problem. Construction of the first railroad line through those high, snowy passes was the solution.

Oliver Bennett is generally credited with envisioning and promoting a route through the Cascades that earmarked the Appleton area as the eastern terminus of the newly opened intermountain line. In fact, from 1890–1921, the little community was known as Bennettville; in honor, naturally enough, of the businessman whose tireless efforts and sense of commonweal had fused the political forces needed to unite the citizenry, and to bring on the railroad, along with all of its jobs and accompanying prosperity.

About that time, another mega-money-making prospect announced *its* presence with authority. In those days, gargantuan forests of Douglas fir, western hemlock, and ponderosa and white pine carpeted a nearly incomprehensible number of square miles across North Central Washington; mind-numbing in density, and inestimable in the dollar value. Lumber mills were soon constructed along the Kennawack River, which was dammed in order to provide enormous mill ponds. The citizens of Bennettville went happily and busily about the task of cutting and milling the timber which was then shipped off to the waiting world on those ready rails.

For a time (a very short time, as fate would have it), the economic and political growth experienced by the bawdy railroad/timber town made it a frontrunner in the race to establish a seat of government for newly chartered Kennawack County. It all must have seemed just too good to be true. And actually, it was, because in 1918 that same Oliver Bennett spearheaded a project which succeeded in financing the construction of a *second* cross-mountain rail over *Bushman Pass*—70 miles to the north of Bennettville… *as the Crow flies*. This, in order to solve the recurring problem of devastating snow slides and avalanches which, with clocklike regularity, wreaked havoc with the original rail line along a bedeviling 40-mile stretch of Ferguson Canyon each and *every* winter.

Of course, the older, longer line from Seattle through Bennettville, via Smithson Pass, fell into disuse, and stretches of track were soon cannibalized in order to help cover the expenses of the newer railroad being routed through the suddenly booming little town of Addersby. Bennettville-ians quickly learned that the access to limitless, easy-to-obtain raw wood products "don't cut no ice" without them "ready rails" available for the purposes of shipment to market. The community took its first staggering steps on a slow, starving path to irrelevance.

When the Great Depression suffocated the livelihood of Washington State's timber jacks, pretty much no one expected Bennettville to remain so much as a spot on the map anytime past the year 1935. But that's when people finally began to notice that old Horace Rosewood's apple and pear orchards were slowly, steadily emerging as a stable cash cow in the midst of widespread, uncontained financial floundering.

Over a bit of time, it became evident that that clever old fox had, years ago, embarked upon the simple and highly effective business strategy of purchasing real estate from desperate former railroaders and mill workers, marking up the prices as high as the wobbly land market could bear, and selling it off to hopeful horticulturalists. Crops of Red and Golden Delicious apples or Bartlett pears were, by no means, a recession-proof commodity, but the long-term prices they fetched were stable enough to secure a reasonable standard of living. And there were plenty, *plenty* of frugal, hard-working families who were willing, under those *trying* circumstances, to risk stretching their paltry savings far enough to accommodate Rosewood's requirements for a down payment *or* investment contract.

Eventually, over a bit *more* time, an increasing number of landowners began to reap the benefit of their business venture with sly old Mr. Rosewood and became independent, well-to-do fruit growers. But not before old man Rosewood had accumulated a king's ransom in inflated land prices.

And so, once again (after gold, the rails, and the timber), things began to look rosy-dozy for the little town of Bennettville. When thousands of young men returned home from the Second World War, the lending institutes of Kennawack County were there with open arms (and open vaults!) to help them stake their claims to the pursuit of happiness and domestic tranquility.

Bank loans issued for the purchase or development of orchard land skyrocketed, and the fruit-growing industry became the heart-and-soul, rags-to-riches, dream-come-true-again gravy train for the county and the tiny community.

Then on a very cold March evening in 1949, at a town meeting whose record-breaking attendance (513) wasn't eclipsed 'til several years after the turn of the century, a near-unanimous vote of the people insisted, howled, and mandated that the name of Bennett ("The brigand!" as Sandy LeMaster may well have uttered, had she been present on that chilly Wednesday evening) be forever stricken from official city association.

Henceforth and forthwith, the newly arisen "Workhorse Community of the Kennawack Valley" was to be named, rather circuitously, for its penultimate savior and providential provider; for the success and vision of the valley orchard godfather—Horace Rosewood. So...Rosewood, Washington. Right?

Huh-uh.

Appleton! And at that juncture, the populace set its collective sights on a Rosewoodish-inspired future of more-or-less-agreed-upon hardy, enduring prosperity.

The End. Le fin. C'est tout.

Except, not...

*

By the mid-1970s, it had become completely apparent to anyone and all that the Kennawack Valley's fruit industry was mid-stage in a death spiral from which it had no hope of recovering. "How can this have happened again?" the citizenry may well have asked one another.

Here's how.

Hastened by promoters of the Worldwide Free Trade Agreement (Oliver Bennett would have *loved* it!), Far East and Pacific Rim fruit producers began bombarding the West Coast with tempting, delicious, affordable, and (here's the *key*word) *durable* apples, pears, and cherries. Lengthier refrigeration life meant fresher-tasting fruit over longer periods of time. The market quickly embraced the new commodities with unbridled zeal.

In relatively short order, the fruit-production crown had been irretrievably shifted from the heads of North Central Washington growers to orchardists in China, Japan, Korea, and New Zealand. Kennawack Valley fruits no longer ruled the roosts. And the people of Appleton, who by this time constituted the fourth generation of its citizenry to experience plummeting living standards, were forced to find employment in nearby Weston. Or simply make do with whatever slivers of the local retail economy had somehow survived the fall.

My, how times change.

The town is quiet nowadays; picturesque in an old-fashioned way. Particularly during the cold months when, blanketed in snowdrifts beneath indigo skies peppered with the fire of far-flung stars, Appleton has to bundle what is left of itself against the pale, plodding, solemn weeks of winter. Then, feather-wisps of floating smoke curl (like locks of LeMaster hair) from the brick chimneys of small, sturdy, not-much-is-happening homes. The heady, sweet aroma of wood smoke bathes the air with a thin, gauze-like mist; going nowhere fast, nowhere soon.

The lovely fruit trees of little Appleton were burned for winter warmth.

*

Kelsea, Erik, and the LeMasters followed Justin out of town and up the hill to the old Appleton Quarry. Here and there, a solitary apple or pear tree emerged from the rolling landscape like a blind sentinel positioned with meaningless orders to stand guard over fields of wind-smoothed grass and alfalfa. The ditches along the gravel road were choked with morning glory, and the peppery scent of pine pollen and dust mixed with the smell of fresh sweat as the youngsters strained to keep their bicycles moving up the steep, winding grade.

Erik noticed that even Kelsea seemed winded and heat-stricken from the exertion. Not that *she* would ever *think* of hopping off and pushing her bike the rest of the way! None of them would entertain *that* notion. Justin's outline was becoming indistinct in the distance *('How does he do it on that pre-historic looking Schwinn with the balloon tires and the corny bike basket?' anyone watching, including Crow, may well wonder)*, when Stuart breathlessly croaked, "Thank God, we're just about there!"

The last 200 meters of road flattened out, and everyone gave silent thanks for stout hearts and healthy lungs. Justin and Kooper had already disappeared behind a tree-covered hill which hid the scar of the abandoned quarry from Appleton eyes. The stone pit was not so large by any standard of comparison, never having been given a serious go by its long-ago entrepreneurs. And rightfully so. A serious investment would have only added another disappointing failure to the town's history…*and* economy.

A rocky bluff formed a wall along the west end of the quarry, and a thick grove of vine maple and quaking aspen hugged the cliff, sprawling fingerlike toward the forested foothills of Chapman Butte—the highest point in the Kennawack Range of the Cascade Mountains.

Erik was surprised at the overall feeling of isolation that the quarry site evoked. Barely a half-hour bike ride from the town park—and maybe 20 or so minutes from the nearest neighbor—the jagged, rocky remnants of Appleton Quarry were seductively cocooned from the quiet concerns of the sleepy community below. He wondered if Rodent and his pals ever spooled up enough ambition to chug all the way up Quarry Road for the purposes of heckling poor Justin.

As if reading his mind, Sandy casually mentioned that "The Gleesome Threesome" never made it a practice to bother Justin Bench on his own turf. A generally accepted theory held that, minus the benefit of indignation that a watching audience provided, Rodent and his friends found little entertainment value in harassing Justin, or anyone else, one-on-one. The humiliation apparently needed the spectacle of a *public* demonstration to be worth their effort. Who knew for certain? But the tiny log cabin and its surrounding evergreen sanctuary had been a "home free" base for Justin and Kooper for a full two years by this time.

Thank heaven for small favors.

"Well, just where *is* Justin's hideaway hut?" asked Erik, scanning the jumble of stone blocks that lay scatter-strewn like huge, disorganized car bodies.

"You're not lookin' hard enough," offered Stuart with a hint of playfulness. "Ya gotta let your eyes linger longer on the grove, there, over in the Vine Maple."

Sure enough, barely visible in the shade and shadow of a thicket skirting the base of the stone bluff, the faintest reflection of sunlight ricocheted from the rectangular surface of paned glass. As the group walked their bikes closer, Justin's outline began to gain definition; slowly at first, knee crossed over knee, Woody lovingly cradled, Kooper already half-asleep beneath a pine porch swing. He was singing:

"Time slips away, and I'm here for the day,
but I'll be movin' on, come the dawn.
No turnin' back, cuz I've come to be practically sure
what I've known all along.
It's OK, no one's in my way
to keep me from singin' my song.
Time slips away, and I'm here for the day,
but I'm bound for movin' on, come the dawn."

Kelsea had been right, all right. Justin's guitar playing was to die for. Or, better yet, to *live* for! Everyone found a spot to his or her liking; Kelsea sat cross-legged, Stuart lay on a side—head in hand—supported by an elbow braced against an unstained deck of knotty-pine.

Justin reminded Sandy that the sun tea was "probably about done brewin." So she crooked a beckoning finger at Erik, and together they promptly fetched tall glasses of cubed ice, a small oak bowl of coarse, blonde cane sugar and plenty of sun-yellow lemon wedges for the group. Erik, for his part, was still laboring a bit with a mild case of the "new kid blues." Clearly, the girl knew just where to find everything, as she bustled around the kitchen and deck like it was part of her own household. Even slightly chubby, slightly shy Stuart had rethought his position and, staking a claim to a deck couch, was now contentedly massaging the toes of his stocking feet, nodding his head in time with the music. The "co-ownership" which everyone seemed to take with Justin's home, and the obvious easy familiarity they all shared with his furnishings and possessions fostered mixed feelings deep inside Erik; feelings about his place and his rank amongst these new friends.

He felt conspicuous.

Watching Erik watch the others—everyone settling in, getting comfortable and feeling at home in his cabin—Justin got the sandy-haired boy's attention. Without breaking stride in his chord work, he casually intoned, "Mi casa, su casa, Erik, OK?"

Erik smiled and relaxed a bit as an unexpected memory tickled the corners of his thoughts. He was experiencing a minor flashback to his old home in Bellevue. How he had worried about leaving the familiar surroundings of his life in the city! The family had lived right across Lake Washington from Seattle…which was just about the *coolest* place in the known universe to be! At least to *him,* it was. Born in Bellevue, and schooled in Bellevue, Erik Remarque had watched the seasons tumble quietly by as he progressed through infancy and embarked upon his pre-teen years… right there on the shoreline of an enormous, cloud-covered lake in the very heart of his beloved Puget Sound.

But Mom and Dad had wanted something different; something *more* for him and his younger sister, Peyton. Something that an upbringing in a metro setting just couldn't provide. What they sought—what they dreamed of—was often difficult to catch and hold on to in "disassociated" city surroundings. They wanted clean air, clean water, small schools, and lots of neighbors whom they could see every day; with whom they could speak with the casual familiarity of long-known friends. They wanted less traffic, less smog, less crime, and a whole lot more of the lifestyle they themselves had experienced growing up in Western Montana. They sought the opportunity for their children to grow up with the innocent, slow blooming that only small, rural towns seem to foster.

When the rare opportunity for employment arrived (for *both* of them, no less!), Phillip and Bev Remarque had wasted no time in whisking their ducklings over the cold Cascade passes to the sun-soaked slopes of Eastern Washington, to little Appleton. Erik was beginning to feel like his once-upon-a-home in King County, with its canyons of concrete and steel, had really been only a chapter in a book about his life. And that the really *good* parts of the story were only now beginning to flower.

Erik looked around the pine deck, inhaling the laid-back attitude and the uncluttered comradeship that colored the day; enriching the flavor of fun.

Good thinkin', parental units! he thought to himself. *I am so into this!*

As Justin regaled his guests with heartfelt melodies and lilting songcraft, the Appleton afternoon lazed its way unconcernedly to dusk under the watchful eye of a high roosting Crow.

O' CLEVER, WATCHFUL CROW! YOU ARE NEVER VERY FAR AWAY.
ARE YOU?

"Sun'll be down soon," mentioned Justin upon finishing his sixth song. "Maybe we oughta give Erik here a heads-up 'bout what to expect from the conduct of certain folks we know. Whatcha think, Kels?"

"Justin's correct," said Sandy, seconding him. "Knowledge is power, and there is no time like the present for the task of educating Erik about the redoubtable Rodent."

"I'm gonna take a stab and guess that 'redoubtable' means something bad," Erik arched his eyebrows, wrinkling his nose at Sandy and watching for her reaction.

"Bullseye, Mr. Remarque!" she quipped. "Your inferential skills are commendable!"

"Yeah, an' he's a pretty good *guesser*, too!" added Justin, to a gaggle of group chuckles.

"Well, for starters," puzzled Erik, "how the heck did he get a creepy nickname like 'Rodent' in the first place? Just sayin' it makes my face tighten up like I took a big bite outa one of these lemons."

Kelsea began what turned out to be a rather involved explanation of the nickname and its origin. It seemed that Rodent's full name was Rodney Neville Tattenger, and he was the only child of a Lieutenant Colonel in the U.S. Marine Corps; one seriously bad-ass dude of a dad. Rodney had a stay-at-home mom who had been under the colonel's thumb for so long that very few people who knew her (and there were very few people who actually *did* know the reclusive Mrs. Tattenger) gave her much credit for being able to think beyond or outside the limitations imposed by her control-freak military husband.

The first several years of Rodney's life were very difficult for the Tattenger family. The youngster was pale, frail, and sickly a good deal of the time, and, through no fault of his own, he became the target of his father's ridicule and criticism. His mother tried, to no avail, to shelter him from the colonel's tirades. And she attempted, without success, to bring balance to her husband's wholly unrealistic expectations for Rodney's behavior and performance.

Colonel Tattenger, disgusted by the very sight and sound of his own child whom he contemptuously referred to as "weener-boy," (sound familiar, Erik?) began spending more, and still more of *his* immeasurably valuable time self-grooming a lengthy lifetime "career of military honor." Away from home for months at a time, the man made no secret of the fact that he considered it a deplorable waste of his energy to bother with family members who struggled with issues of poor health and shaky self-esteem.

"OK. Well, a lifetime of unresolved health issues, yeah, that explains the pale features," said Erik. "But, what about this guy's bullying attitude? What the hell is *that* all about?"

"That's easiest of all to explain, Erik," Sandy pointed out. "SMC. Plain and simple."

Erik scanned his memory banks, but couldn't hit on anything helpful. And his look of uncertainty prompted a quick response from his friend.

"Small Man's Complex," Sandy went on. "Rodent is overcompensating for a humiliating father/son relationship, which is only worsened by feelings of inferiority brought on by his diminutive stature."

"Come again?" pleaded Erik with a hint of exasperation. "But this time slowly, and in *English,* Sandy!"

Stuart laughed. "He's *unhappy,* he's *short,* and he's takin' it out on *us.* See?"

Erik nodded his understanding. Sandy punched him lightly on the arm, winking conspiratorially, and he felt the color rise in his cheeks. "So, what about the 'Rodent' thing?" he pondered aloud, rubbing his "wound" with an expression of mock injury.

Erik could feel Sandy's eyes on him; smiling, kind, intelligent *(maybe, interested?).* More than *anything,* he wanted to return her gaze, but, *("Whoa! Keep it real, man! She's a whole year older than you, Mr. Remarque. And light-years smarter.")*

Erik snapped back to the conversation as Sandy's twin picked up the thread of the explanation.

"Rodent is, like, a contractive," began Stuart.

"A contrac*tion*," reminded Sandy. "But that's OK."

"'R-O-D' is for <u>Rod</u>ney, '<u>N</u>' is for <u>N</u>eville, and 'T' is for Tattenger. Put 'em all together and you got ROD…N…T—roughly, 'Rodent.' And ya hafta admit, if your aim is to inhabit an image that's as tough as you *wish* you really *were,* then a name like Rodent would likely fit the bill, yes?"

"Makes sense to me," Erik allowed. "What about Patch? Am I wrong, or does that guy routinely eat raw steak with gunpowder on it?"

"Patch is a contraction, too," Kelsea was sitting on the floor of the deck; knees drawn to her chest, encircled by her arms, left hand clasping right wrist. "'P-A-T' is for Pat and 'C-H' is for Cheney—Patch is really Pat Cheney. Isn't it just *precious* how those bouncy, fun-loving delinquents use chopped up pieces of their names to try to appear scandalously tough?"

"Well, he's the one ya gotta watch, Erik," warned Justin slowly. "Those other two're mostly smoke and mirrors, but that Patch, he's got a true mean streak, an' he takes a kinda sick joy outa makin' trouble for folks. Don't you trust 'im, even for a second."

Justin made careful eye contact with everyone present. "Fact is, we all kinda watch each other's backs, don't we guys?"

Nods of serious assent went around the deck, and Kooper thumped his tail a couple of times as if to say, "Count me in, tribe!"

"Now, Deep Thoughts is still rather somewhat of an unknown quantity," mused Sandy half to herself.

Kelsea agreed, "Nobody's quite sure *what* to think about *that* guy yet. He came to town just last September, so he's almost as new as you are, Erik. He never says much of anything to anyone, not even in class. In fact, that dark, kinda *broody* reputation is what earned him his nickname. Anyways, he just sort of fell in with Rodent and Patch, although nobody is really for sure if he even fits in with *those* jerks either."

"Well, when you're as gigantic as Deep Thoughts, you can just stay as mum as a mummy, if ya want to," offered Stu. "You're still gonna be feared by most kids just because of the *company* you keep."

"Still waters run deep," counseled Justin. "I just hope that 'Deep' doesn't mean 'Dangerous.'"

"Amen!" Erik echoed.

"I hope all that silence of his indicates 'stupidity,' and not 'hate,'" worried Stu.

"There is nothing quite so frightening as *ignorance* in action," cautioned Sandy.

"Well, even Justin has *kind of* a nickname," remarked Kelsea. "Go on, Justin. Tell 'im. He needs to know *all* of this stuff. Erik's *in with us*, now." Heads nodded in complete agreement.

"Well," semi-drawled the young man, "my first name's Justin, 'course you know *that* already. But I got *two* middle names before 'Bench' finishes 'er off."

"That's not too uncommon, I guess," said Erik.

"Not 'til you've heard the rest!" prompted Stuart. "Check it out!" he motioned Justin to continue.

"So, like I said, my first name's Justin and my last name's Bench."

"Any relation to Johnny Bench, the old Reds baseball player?" interrupted Erik.

"No! Now let 'im finish. This is sad, and true! Keep goin', Justin."

"So then, my first middle name is Michael, an' my second middle name is Thomas."

Justin finished the story and smiled wanly. Everyone sat stone-still, carefully watching Erik; waiting for it to all come together in his head.

Erik was beginning to feel like he had been *had*; set up to be the butt of some inside joke, maybe because he was the new kid in town. He squirmed uncomfortably, and the silent patience of his friends was starting to get on his nerves when—*click*—on went the "latt bubb!"

"You gotta be kiddin' me!" declared Erik with a mixture of complete understanding and partial disbelief. "It can't be for real!" he insisted.

Smiles broadened and heads went up and down in affirmation. Justin peeked sheepishly from under the brim of his Filson hat.

"Justin Michael Thomas Bench," repeated Erik, almost hypnotically. "That makes you Justin M. T. Bench! Just an empty bench!" Erik's thoughts leaped at warp speed back to the recent confrontation in the park; something that Rodent had said after he had launched that stupid apple at them. His eyes widened at the realization of what the remark was intended to communicate, and he looked at his older companion with a mixture of sad admiration and newly emerging esteem.

"Guess 'at's'a way *some* folks around here thinka me," surrendered Justin. "But ya know, it's awright, I guess. With great friends like _I_ got," his hand swept the room in a gesture of inclusiveness and gratitude, coming to rest on Erik's shoulder, "'no one's in my way to keep me from singin' my song.' See what I mean?"

"Indeed, I do, Justin," replied Erik, returning the favor with a friendly slap on the back. "Indeed, I do!"

"So say we all," said Stuart.

"Indubitably!" smiled Sandy.

*

"Kelsea! Phone call! C'mon, it's time you were up and at 'em anyway," Kelsea's mother, calling from the foot of the stairs; checking her reflection in the hall mirror and draining the last of the morning's bitter black coffee in hurried gulps.

"Lets' go, kiddo!" she repeated. "Justin's on the line and I'm almost late, oh, kee-ripes! I'm al_ready_ late!"

Scooping car keys and her handbag on the fly, Elaine Crowl speed-walked for the door to the garage. "Kels, honey, let's go! Hey! Don't forget to weed the veggie garden today, OK? Your-dad's-gonna-barbecue-tonight-so-be-home-early-gotta-run-love-ya-bye!"

She was out the door and gone before Kelsea even got to the top of the stairs.

"Mornin', Justin," Kelsea yawned, squeezing the receiver to her ear with her shoulder and rubbing snooze goobers out of her eyes with a fingertip.

"Hey, sleepy-head. Just finished mowin' the Middle School playground and I wanted to catch ya before ya took off for parts unknown."

"Well, catch me you did. What's on your mind, early bird?"

Long pause on the other end of the line. Kelsea thought at first that they may have been disconnected. But Justin cleared his throat and began again. His voice was unsteady, halting, and the timbre was unsusal; higher and almost apologetic in tone.

"Kels, I think I've got myself a li'l bit of a problem."

Wide awake now, Kelsea shifted the phone to her other ear and stopped picking at her bare toes. Justin had never been the kind of person to overreact to things, nor even be particularly demonstrative about troublesome social or emotional situations. The fear and uncertainty in his voice was as unmistakable as it was unexpected. He had her complete attention now. "What kind of problem, Justin? Is it serious?"

"Kelsea, I need to *see* ya to talk about this. Can ya come up to the cabin this afternoon? It's real important," Justin's voice wasn't much more than a whisper, now.

The stress was palpable; the anxiety as clear as the spring runoff of Whistle Creek snowmelt.

"Jeez, don't *even* worry about it, Justin. I'll be there in—oh, shoot! I forgot! Justin, I have to take care of the garden this morning. And after, that I've got about a four-and-a-half-hour babysitting job for the Maxwells. I won't be able to make it until sometime this evening, say around 5 pm—oops! No, again. Dad's firing up the 'barbie' tonight, so that's out too. Damn! Lemme think a sec."

"No, that's OK. I'll come over an' help with the garden. You'll get done twice as fast, and your place is just as safe as mine for what I need to tell ya. Any chance that Jayme might try to do some eavesdroppin'?"

"Uh-uh. Sister Sinister is long gone. But, Justin, the garden…it's a big job. It's still gonna take us 'til around 10:30 or 11:00. And you've already put in at least a coupla hours at the school, if I know you."

"S'OK by me," Justin assured her. "Jerkin' weeds isn't *really* work if you're doing it with your compadres, right? I'll bring some CDs and we can have some tunes. Music makes *everything* better, maybe even what **I** got to tell you about." Another short pause on his end of the phone, then: "Do ya think you could come up to the quarry when we've finished your chores? It's important, uh, so you'll see with yer own eyes what I'm talkin' about, when I'm *through* talkin' about it, that is."

"Deal! Now get over here so we can sort this thing out." Then, as an afterthought: "Ya know, you've got me worried. Do you think I should call the rest of the gang? Six heads are better than two, yes?" There was another span of dead air, and Kelsea giggled quietly into her fist, picturing Justin counting noses and feeling flummoxed. "I know, Justin! I *know*! You're thinking that summer vacation is deteriorating my math skills. But listen, with the two LeMasters, and we can count Erik now, can't we? Yeah, I thought so, an' me an' you, that's five, right? But c'mon, good Sir Knight! Sandy's methods of problem-solving count for *two* heads, so-oo that totals six. Am I *so right* or am I even righter than *that*?"

Kelsea was relieved to hear the tension lift from her friend's voice as he chuckled his surrender to her logic. "Awright, I gotta go along with ya on that," he said. "But please don't start makin' any phone calls, not just yet. I'd rather powwow between the two of us until I can make some kinda sense outa this. See ya in about fifteen, ya goofball, you! Oh, an' Kels?"

"Mm-hmm?"

"Thanks in advance for bein' such a great friend."

He gently returned the well-worn payphone to its soda-sticky hook. Slinging Woody's strap over his head and across his shoulder, he maneuvered the old six-string behind him like a backpack. Then he tossed a faded, frayed jean jacket into the bike basket; draping it over a boom box. Stepping lightly upon the left pedal, he pushed off with his right leg and swung effortlessly onto the seat.

"C'mon Koop," he called affably. "We got some gardenin' ta do."

*

Black is not a color; it is the *absence* of color. But were it *considered* a color, then Kelsea's stick-straight, shoulder-length locks would have to be regarded as just about a half-shade darker than Sandy and Stuart's chaotic curls. To put it into a "time perspective," if one could say that Kelsea's hair was "midnight/black," and that that of the LeMaster twins was "ten o'clock/dark," then Justin's hair would be around "half past eight/dusk." Erik, on the other far end of the spectrum, sported a close, thick crop of straw blonde "fur" that might best be described on the clock as "high-damn-noon-on-a-hot-summer-day."

Kelsea patted smooth that pillow pressed, ebony hair of *hers*, and hurried to her bedroom to get dressed for the morning. Cut-off blue jeans, a sports-bra, and her dad's old AC/DC T-shirt were quickly donned; no need for shoes—the garden earth would feel warm and welcoming under her bare feet. Seated at the vanity mirror, brushing her hair, Kelsea began to relax a bit about the nervous tone in Justin's voice. She smiled—remembering how the young man had come to be such a well-liked member of their community, as well as a trusted and true-blue friend to her, to her circle of friends, and to so many Appleton families.

He had been barely eighteen, and just out of high school when he arrived (somehow) in Appleton—quiet, and quite alone—to take up residency in the caretaker's cottage of the old abandoned quarry. News spread throughout the little town of the solitary young man who had apparently inherited the estate of his well-to-do uncle; an attorney at law known valley-long-and-wide for the fair-minded application of his professional duties, and his sympathetic treatment of the poor and underprivileged.

Justin had wasted no time demonstrating that he was genuine—the real article; intent upon upholding the behavioral standard established by his departed uncle. From his first appearances in the community, he full-on directed his mind and energy toward anything he deemed might further the interests of civic improvement and community pride. His name was always the first on every work detail or volunteer list posted at the Town Hall.

It mattered little whether the project involved re-roofing a church, making repairs around the school playground, or providing child care for busy parents who sometimes found themselves in need of trustworthy assistance with their little ones. Justin Michael Thomas Bench could always be counted on to arrive with Woody, Kooper, and a full day's worth of energy (and songs!); ready to "put the muscle to 'er" until the job was done, and done well.

As his reputation for reliability and industriousness grew, so did the offers for paid part-time labor. His difficulties grasping the intricacies of sketched work plans and designs were a recurring problem, to be certain. But Justin (and Kooper) carried on just fine, thank you very much. Certainly, Appletonians held no other citizen in higher regard, and as everyone in town came to realize over the months: a generous heart far eclipses the attribute of intellectual prowess.

What a sweet guy!

But the event that had done more than anything to elevate Justin's status to "hometown hero" occurred two years ago when Jayme Crowl (Sister Sinister, as Kelsea would playfully aver) and her then bosom buddy, Livy Baxter (remember the old Baxter house?), accidentally locked themselves in the trunk of an abandoned automobile. Justin had been shade sheltered beneath an ancient elm that afternoon, relaxing on "his" park bench, playing guitar when Kelsea had zipped her bicycle to a wild-eyed halt in front of him, breathlessly inquiring if he had seen her kid sister anywhere that day.

"She's over two hours late for lunch, and it's *just not like her* to not follow the rules!" the girl, implored, almost feverish.

Justin and his canine companion had immediately joined the hunt; Justin agreeing to comb the northern part of town while Kelsea continued west on Fender Street. It was while cruising alongside the alfalfa fields bordering the north side of Mitchell Street that Justin had become aware of the distinct, discordant sound of crow clamor. The rasping, distressed bird cries drew his immediate concern (though at the time, he could not have told anyone why), and he wheeled his bike in the direction of the noise; dog buddy hard on his (w)heels.

Turning north on Schoolhouse Road and following his *instincts* as much as the sound of bird ruckus, a vision of what truly may have happened began to take shape in his imagination.

"I've seen those two playin' around that old barn and car a coupla times," he had later commented. "And once I headed down that dirt track offa Schoolhouse, I had a pretty strong suspicion that they'd somehow let their explorin' get 'em in *way* over their heads."

Employing a bit of locksmith legerdemain with a piece of baling wire, Justin managed to free the sobbing youngsters in a matter of moments. And following numerous reassurances that, despite their fears to the contrary, neither of them was going to be "killed by their parents" when he got them home, Justin propped *both* seven-year-olds on the mid-frame bar of the old-fashioned Schwinn bike, and escorted them back to their grateful families.

Later that afternoon, the young man was seen back up at the barn; working steadfastly in the midday swelter, removing the trunk cover from the body of the derelict car, and laying it carefully in the dusty brown grass beside the _car_cass.

YES, SEEN HE WAS—INDEED...BUT ONLY BY <u>YOU</u>... NOISY, SOLITARY CROW. AND YOUR RAUCOUS, PARAMOUNTLY UN- IGNORABLE CRIES OF DRAMA AND ALARM COMPOSED A

DISSONANT, LURING SQUAWK-FEST FOR A BICYCLING ONE-MAN SEARCH PARTY ON A MISSION OF MERCY.

EVEN FOLLOWING THE RESCUE, NOT FOR ONE MOMENT WAS THE LONGLEGS AWARE OF YOUR PRESENCE AS HE PATIENTLY AND SKILLFULLY WENT ABOUT THE BUSINESS OF DISMANTLING AND DEFUSING THE POSSIBILITY OF A RECURRING KID SAFETY HAZARD. CROW SCRUTINIZES... CROW LEARNS... CROW INTERVENES.

Kelsea Crowl placed the hairbrush gently on the vanity, and regarded her reflection momentarily. She was anxious to hear what was on Justin's mind; anxious *and* worried, because she knew him to be the solid kind of guy who never permitted himself to become overwrought. Kind, and soft-spoken almost to a flawless degree, he was possessed of an earthy approach to life that made him just sort of, well, one to take things as they come.

A lesson in living that more grownups *should pay attention to,* thought Kelsea.

She smoothed her bedspread, just enough to pass the "parent test," and hurried downstairs to find something to eat. A yellow burst of early dayglow filled the roomy kitchen; sunlight flooding from the sliding glass door, an adjacent bay window, and the skylight overhead. True to form, her mother had left a cranberry bagel on a small china plate with a napkin on the breakfast bar. Next to it lay an unopened tub of cream cheese, a butter knife, and a large glass of orange juice. *Thanks, Mom!*

Kelsea quickly prepared her light morning meal. Then she placed the tub in the fridge; the knife, plate, and empty glass in the dishwasher; and made for the washroom door and the garage. She was scavenging about her father's tool bench, looking for gardening gloves and a trowel, when something occurred to her, something about a dream she had had the night before. Unclear and unshaped in its imagery, it was like she couldn't quite decide if she had actually *had* the dream, or if she was just trying to recall something else altogether. Curious...the uncertainty of this feeling.

Well, it would finally either become clear to her, or, it wouldn't...*wouldn't it?* Better to apply Justin's methodology, and just let the chips fall where they may.

And yet, something about birds? A blackbird? A crow, again?

*

The Classic Rock station broadcasting from Weston pounded out Queen's *'Fat Bottomed Girls,'* following it up with Warren Zevon's *'Lawyers, Guns & Money.'* Next came Springsteen's *'Born in the U.S.A.,'* Lynyrd Skynyrd's *'Free Bird,'* and Dire Straits' *'Money for Nothin.'* No doubt about it: If you were into fossil rock produced in the '70s and '80s, your money, and your dial, had to be on 101.3 KIST for your midday music fix.

But all that free-spirited, guitar-drenched energy essentially fell on deaf ears as Justin and Kelsea solemnly went about her gardening job, with the story of her friend's dilemma unfolding in the process. With every handful of crabgrass and dandelion she tugged from the topsoil—clumps of damp, sandy loam clinging stubbornly to the root clusters—Kelsea became more grim-faced and concerned.

This *was* serious.

Justin did <u>indeed</u> have a problem. And what was even more disturbing was the fact that the more her friend spoke of a strange and threatening event that had occurred at his cabin in the early morning hours of that very day, the more crystallized and focused became the recollection of *her dream*; the dream which had sown its seeds in her sleeping thoughts just prior to Justin's telephone call to her.

She was remembering that it <u>had</u> been another "CrowDream" similar to the others she had experienced more or less regularly over the past two years, ever since the backpacking trip with her father. The hiking accident. The Silver Creek Fire. Things almost best left un-remembered. "CrowDreams" were always ill-defined and too difficult to understand, let alone explain to anybody. But they always possessed a quality, or feeling of premonition or prediction; of teaching and guiding. And of…what?

Kinship/cousin-ry(**?**)

Very strange, and *very* beautiful.

They finished the job, tossing the last of the weeds into a compost bin in the corner of the fenced back yard. Silent, now—thought-burdened and pre-occupied with the challenge of making sense of a most puzzling start to the day—Kelsea and Justin hopped on their bikes and coasted side-by-side…mute, down a gently sloping street toward Quarry Road and that long, taxing pull up to the quarry. Kelsea's "CrowDream" somehow dovetailed with Justin's mystery; she just felt it, just *knew it*. Although precisely _how_ the connections actually fit together was, as usual, more a matter of intuition than something densely concrete or even revelatory in its nature.

What to think of it all!

*

People may be thought of as creatures inhabiting duel existences; one, in the waking-world we think of as reality, and the other in the MindWorld of unwakened dreams.

Look!

Sleeping Justin's eyelids flutter, almost imperceptibly in dawn's slanting, filtered light.

And, see?

Kooper's paws and leg muscles twitch comically; a dance-in-the-dark to the irresistible rhythms of unknowable doggie dreams. Wakened or un-awakened, it seems we are always preoccupied with alternating mental designs of one kind or another; concrete or conjured. Practical or perceived.

At first, Justin imagined that the plaintive tapping sound was born of his dream. His physical, sleeping body was blanket curled and at rest in the old caretaker's cabin of Appleton Quarry, and inside his

DreamDrifting mind, he was duteously nailing down a strip of carpet trim at Rosewood Elementary School.

Tap-tap, tap-tap, nailing the dreamworld carpet trim.
Tap-tap, tap-tap, wakingworld sounds slipping into his slumber.
Tap-tap, tap-tap, dreamworld.
Tap-tap, tap-tap, wakingworld.
Which one is real?

Justin squinched open one reluctant eye. He furrowed his brow; channeling all of his concentration into processing only the sensory information which was auditory. Did he *hear* something or *dream* it? He held his breath, hoping to listen more acutely, but it only made his heart pound harder, and he already felt as if a river of blood was rushing through his eardrums.

Tap-tap, tap-tap. An unnamable fear sank its roots deep into Justin's imagination, deep enough to penetrate the strongholds of reason and logic, and he began to feel the stirrings of helplessness; an inability to shield himself against those things which cannot be understood in rational ways.

THIS is *no dream!* Justin lay with his back to the sound. As his thoughts began to crystallize and his attention became focused, he identified the sound as coming from an object made of glass. Yes! That was it! Something or someone was tapping on his bedroom window. The noise was rhythmic and repeated, unvarying; almost hypnotic. It wasn't some*thing*. It was some*one*!

Maybe it's Kelsea, or the LeMasters, thought Justin, struggling to slow his breathing and control his accelerating pulse rate. *Those twins can be playful, and jokey sometimes. Why, hell! It's probably all of 'em, yeah, 'at's it. It's the bunch of 'em, just havin' a little sport with ol' Koop and me. Whew! They really had me goin' for a minute 'r two there. Just wait'll I get my hands on those rascals, sneakin' up on a body before the sun's even up an' all.*

(?!)

Virtually <u>no</u>body in Appleton moves about in the pre-dawn hours, and <u>well</u> he knew it. Especially youngsters like Kelsea and Company. Whoever had wakened Justin with this subtle and slightly scary early morning antic was obviously mucking about when decent folks were all snoozin' and was therefore probably up to no-damn-good.

Tap-tap, tap-tap.

Kooper's head shot up; ears erect, *instantly* awake. He glowered through dull quarter-light of the faintly illumined bedroom window, and growled softly.

"Shhh," whispered Justin. "Shh, easy Koop. 'S'OK, boy. 'S'OK. Lay down, fella. Good boy!"

The old dog did as he was told, but a low rumble continued from deep in his throat, and his trembling muscles betrayed his difficulty in obeying his master's command.

One more, Justin, carefully considering. *C'mon, just one more.*

Tap-ta—

With catlike agility, Justin flung the blankets away from the bed, wheeling his body in the direction of the window and hitting the hardwood floor at a dead run.

Momentarily stunned by his owner's unexpected "explosion," Kooper took less than a millisecond to recover, and he shot to his side, teeth bared and barking.

Together, they went flying past the shadow shapes of desk and dresser, flying over dim piles of boots and books, of jeans and jackets, flying to that dark, translucent glass slate; where Justin pressed his face against the smooth, cold window in a frantic, heart-pounding attempt to see below the sill. A dark face behind the windowpane had been visible for the thinnest slice of a moment as it ducked below view. But not before time, space, distance, and all dimension had locked rigidly into a freeze-framed memory image, and sealed itself within a secretive corner of Justin's recollection.

What was it he had just seen?

Nothing(?). Quickly he scanned from right to left, east to west; his eager eyes hoping to catch a telltale sign of movement in any direction. But the close proximity of thick vine maple and brushy undergrowth, which for so long had lent a cozy reclusiveness to his woodland home, now clinched and closed; swallowing the trespasser who had delivered wonder and worry to Justin's pre-dawn hour. The unknown intruder had simply evaporated into the quarry's shapeless, still-dark wilderness.

What was it he had seen?

Hoisting and buttoning his jeans as he rushed about bare-chested and barefooted, Justin whistled for his dog who, completely Kooper-like, was already waiting for him at the rough-hewn cabin door, paws prancing and tail twirling in energetic anticipation of a chase.

"Stay close now, partner," cautioned Justin urgently. "Heel up, boy. *Heel*, Kooper!"

Together they gingerly stepped outside the old quarry cabin precisely as the last vestige of star-fire began to flicker and fade into the smeared rose blush of new morning light.

"'S'no use tryin' to follow 'em through the brush," Justin spoke resignedly.

"So le's just listen a spell, an' see if we can hear any cracklin' or mashin' about goin' on anywheres out there. Later on, we can look for clues proper-like."

He hunkered down close to the damp-smelling earth; left knee up, right knee straight forward with half-a-buttock resting on his right heel. Kooper lay down with a thick sigh beside the young man, and the two of them remained motionless for long minutes—straining to apprehend the slightest vibration that didn't jibe with the familiar and well-understood NatureMusic of Appleton Quarry. Justin broke off a slender, dry stem of summer brown grass, slipped it between his teeth, and chewed thoughtfully.

Chewed and listened. Listened and thought. Thought and chewed.

What <u>was</u> it he had seen?

*

43

SUN-SEE WIND IS PREFERABLE TO MOON-SEE WIND IN THE MID-ELEVATIONS OF THE KENNAWACK RIVER VALLEY. THICK, COOL BREEZES RENEW EACH APPLETON DAY, LENDING THEMSELVES SPLENDIDLY TO TOGETHER-WITH-WIND TIME, AND YOU ARE SKYBORNE WITH THE FIRST SHARDS OF HEAT THAT GLEAM OVER THE EASTERN RIDGES.

YOU ARE THE CROW.

FAULTLESS AND UNAPOLOGETIC, YOU PURSUE HERE-NOW-IS TOWARD UNFATHOMABLE POINTS OF SOMEWHEN/SOMEWHERE. THIS, AT THE IRRESISTIBLE URGINGS OF YOUR LIFE'S ETERNAL HEART LOGIC AND HARMONIC DIRECTIVE:

CROW STUDIES, CROW LEARNS,

CROW INTERVENES, CROW RECOUNTS.

(O' RAVENRILL!)

MUSCLE, MIND, LUNG, WING, BLOOD, EYE, AND SPIRIT ALL ORCHESTRATE; BEND AND BLEND TO THE COMMONTASK, AND YOUR TOGETHER-WITH-WIND TIME REAFFIRMS A GIDDY REASSURANCE OF CROW MEANING AND PURPOSE. WITH ASTONISHING ABRUPTNESS, VERTICALLY YOU DIVE THROUGH THE PALE, FROSTY BREATH OF NEWBORN DAYLIGHT.

BELOW YOU LIES THE SILENT, BLACKENED BLANKET OF THE UNLIT QUARRY FOREST.

AND THEREIN, RAPIDLY MOVES THE HORSE AND THE LONGLEGS RIDER YOU SEEK. YOU ARE THE CROW. REMEMBER...SO AS TO ACCURATELY RECOUNT.

CARVING SHARP ARCS—AN ONYX BLUR OF SYMMETRY WITH THE SHADOWSCAPE OF STONE AND TREE BARK—YOU CAREEN EFFORTLESSLY; BUILDING YOUR MOMENTUM AND REVISING YOUR FLIGHT PATH. SHARP PINE SCENTS RISE THROUGH COLUMNS OF SLOWLY WARMING MIST, AND YOU PIERCE THE PRE-DAY HAZE LIKE A DOLPHIN WEAVING GRACEFULLY THROUGH OCEANIC DEPTHS OF SPLASH AND FOAM. IN JUST UNDER 300 BEATS OF WING MUSCLE, YOU ESPY AND OVERCOME THAT FOR WHICH YOU COMMENCED TOGETHER-WITH-WIND TIME. THE HORSE AND THE LONGLEGS ARE CAUGHT UNAWARES, BUT IT WOULD MATTER LITTLE EVEN IF THEY HAD KNOWN YOUR WHEREABOUTS OR YOUR INTENT.

CROW IS SWIFT.

CROW IS SILENT.
CROW IS PRECISE.

Erik would have marveled at your ability to utilize no more than an instant of measurable time in shifting from patterns of glide to dive. Kelsea would have been stunned by the projection of fearlessness embodied in your attack. Sandy would have drawn everyone's attention to the 'adroitness of your maneuverability.' And Stuart would have scratched his head in disbelief and simply uttered "Holy crap! Did you see <u>that</u>?"

Justin, habitually chewing a tasteless stem of dry grass, would have tickled Kooper behind a scabby ear and thought to himself, 'Have I seen that very same Crow before?'

A SINGLE, PROLONGED 'SKRAAA-AAWWW!' ISSUES FROM YOUR THROAT AS YOUR BODY SLINGSHOTS MERE INCHES OVER THE NECK AND HEAD OF THE HORSE AND THE LONGLEGS WHO SITS ASTRIDE IT. THE TRUNK, SHOULDERS, AND ARMS OF THE LONGLEGS JERK INSTINCTIVELY, PROTECTIVELY AT THE UNEXPECTED ASSAULT. BUT THE JOLT OF SHOCK AND SURPRISE ENDS AS QUICKLY AS IT BEGINS, FOR, ACCELERATING THROUGH WHAT AMOUNTS TO LITTLE MORE THAN A CONTROLLED CRASH, YOUR CHIPPED BEAK SAVAGELY SLICES THE BROWN EAR—TALL, WIDE, STRAIGHT, AND VULNERABLE—OF THE HORSE.

REARING IN PAIN AND PANIC, THE BEAST BELLOWS ITS CONFUSION; A REVERBERATING COMPLAINT THAT RESONATES ECHO-LIKE AMONGST THE HILLOCKS AND HOLLOWS OF APPLETON QUARRY'S FOREST LANDS. THE RIDER—THE LONGLEGS—GIVES TEMPORARY FREE REIN TO HIS STRICKEN ANIMAL; THE ONLY RESPONSE WORTH CONSIDERING WHICH WILL SECURE AN EVENTUAL REASSUMPTION OF CONTROL. WET FOG SWIRLS AND CLOSES BEHIND THE HORSE AND RIDER WHO VANISH INTO THE APPARENT NOTHINGNESS—ENRAGED AND UNCERTAIN ABOUT WHAT, EXACTLY, HAS JUST TRANSPIRED; PONDERING AND PUZZLING OVER A SUDDEN, UNEXPECTED, WHOLLY UNPREDICTABLE OCCURRENCE THAT CAN ONLY

SWIM ABOUT THE FRINGES OF HORSE (AND HUMAN) INTELLIGENCE, BEREFT OF EXPLANATION.

YOU EMERGE, UNSELFCONSCIOUSLY, ABOVE THE TOWERING CROWN OF SUN-TINGED EVERGREEN TREES, AND SET A COURSE FOR THE ROCKY, MOSS-COVERED SHORELINE OF THE KENNAWACK RIVER—600 BEATS OF WING MUSCLE SOUTH-SOUTHEAST OF APPLETON.

MORNING HAS BROKEN.

A NEW DAY HAS BEGUN.

*

None of the embittered curses spat by the rider succeeded in audibly penetrating the collapse and collision of quarry underbrush. Nor did they endure long enough to waft their way across the winding, shallow gullies to Justin Bench's awaiting ear. But the strangled, dry cackling cry of a Crow followed by the thin, high wail of a beleaguered Appaloosa were duly noted by the solitary young man—shirtless and shoeless in the newborn day's anemic glow—precisely as his gaze settled upon a handwritten message.

One which an unknown horseman had scrawled haphazardly across his bedroom window in the wee small hours of the morning.

Justin Bench deliberated deeply upon that far off, easily identifiable sound of horse fear as he studied the window scribblings, and the frightening possibilities of their meaning. He chewed and listened. Listened and thought. Thought and chewed. And he wondered, over and over and over again:

What was it he had seen?

*

"Whaddaya make of it, Kels?"

Justin stood beside his younger friend, hands shoved deep into the pockets of his trademark denim jeans; thumbs hooked through the front belt loops, watching Kelsea for a hoped-for sign of understanding.

Kelsea Crowl, left fist resting against her hip, stared worriedly at the message that had been left by the trespasser. Her hands were still filthy from the long morning job in the vegetable garden, and when she tweaked her lower lip pensively between her thumb and forefinger, she left a thin, brown smudge of dirt.

"I dunno, Justin," she remarked slowly, shaking her head and furrowing her brow.

"This looks like, what's it called? *Hasslement?* And that kind of thing is against the law. I think you should report this to the police, as in *right away,* if not *sooner!*

"The word you are looking for is *harassment.* And Kelsea is absolutely right, Justin!"

The couple quickly turned and were surprised (not!) to find Sandy LeMaster, along with her twin brother and Erik Remarque, quietly observing the scene from just a few meters away.

"Good thing ol' Koop's asleep in the cabin or you'da never snuck up on us that way," grinned Justin. "What brings you renegades up to my neck 'o the woods, anyhoo?"

"Process of elimination, my dear fellow," quipped Sandy. "That, and top-flight deductive reasoning. We all rode by Kelsea's place in order to procure, nay, *enforce* her accompaniment in our safari to the Swimming Hole."

"When she wasn't there, we decided to make a list of places where we could begin an ingenious, fool-proof, bound-for-success 'Search and Find' mission," added Stuart.

"Yeah, Justin," quipped Erik. "And after *your* name was mentioned upfront as the starting place, we figured the list was probably pretty much complete. So! Whooza smart kiddos, Jussie? Whoooooza smaaarrrrt kiiiidooossss?"

Chuckles and high-fives in the brightening air of Appleton Quarry. But Sandy was intent upon getting back to the problem at hand. Running her fingers through acres of thick, curly hair, she emphasized the seriousness of what "must indubitably be construed as a crime of malice."

"Well, maybe somebody's just havin' a little sport at my expense," Justin, in a trial-run of 'let's-try-an'-be-reasonable-about-this-thing.' "Just 'cause the writing _seems_ bad doesn't mean I've got enemies, or that someone's out to get me. I mean, what've _I_ ever done to rile folks up enough to, to..." he faltered, and the thought was left hanging.

Erik picked up the slack. "...enough to threaten you, Justin? Because that's exactly what this is. It's a threat. And you don't need a law degree or a police badge to get the meaning out of _this_ message," gesturing toward the cabin window.

Justin regarded each of his friends in turn; registering the concern and sadness, as well as the affirmation of every individual. As usual, the group was in complete agreement. This was no laughing matter, and some important decisions were going to have to be made.

"Still, in all," insisted Justin, "I'd kinda like to cool my jets, just for the time bein', an' see if this whole thing just blows away by itself. A bruise ain't necessarily a sign of a break, ya know."

"Very well, my good friend," surmised Sandy with a Shakespearian wave of her arm. "But allow us to at least engage in a bit of 'Een-vay-stee-gay-see-own a la LeMaster.' Let us leave no stone unturned. Let us be vigilant in the pursuit of the truth in all matters pertaining to..."

"I bet it was Rodent and his cesspool gang of half-wit morons!" blurted Stuart.

"Half-wit morons is a redundancy," advised Sandy gently. "But that's OK. However, it is decidedly _not_ OK for us to presume to cast blame upon _anyone_ in the absence of iron-clad evidence which is of a truly compelling and condemning nature."

"Sorry! But I'm with Stu on this one," argued Erik; the tone of his voice gaining everyone's attention with its quiet, forced delivery. "I think the half-wit morons did it!"

"That makes _three_ of us who are for sure certain that _this_ is the work of the half-wit morons!" enjoined Kelsea, shaking the locks of her indigo hair and pumping her fist in the air like a crazed vigilante on the manhunt of the century.

"Hang 'em from the highest apple tree!" yowled Justin.

"There aren't any apple trees around here anymore, buddy," reminded Stuart. "They all disappeared years ago."

"It's jus' as well," mused Justin aloud. "We ain't got no rope neither. Man, it's gettin' hot. Let's go on inside an' get ourselves some of that sun tea."

Together they trooped back to the cabin deck; loyalties strengthened by a sense of necessary, self-imposed merriment. A merriment which belied an undercurrent of dread which was anything *but* invisible. As everyone retreated to the comfort and familiarity of the shade-embraced cabin, and those tall, frosty tea glasses, Kelsea alone lingered; nursing an indignity that welled up inside her over the bullying assault on everybody's—*all* of Appleton's—mutual friend.

The whites surrounding those sea gray irises of hers pinkened; waxing to the color of Bing cherries which, in a time long ago, used to cling plump-ripened to sun-dappled Kennawack Valley trees. The kind of lovely, luscious trees whose sturdy trunks and branches had been born of dreams far too courageous to simply die; Crow-like dreams which were strong-willed and too defiant to admit when their time had begun and ended.

Even after it already had.

And though her pretty eyes glistened with the moisture of sentiment and grief, they did not fill to flowing. Kelsea Crowl was deeply—almost *mortally*—offended as she reread the grade school-ish handwriting on Justin Bench's bedroom window: **"justin mt bench if your gonna stay your gonna pay!"**

*

Laarkin's Soda Queen was pretty much the place to be if (A) you were between the ages of ten and eighty-eleven, (B) you happened to live within or near the confines of Appleton, Washington, U.S.A., and/or (C) you and a couple of friends were fortunate enough to have in your collective possession some assorted bits of spare change *and* some parched "Jool-Eye Throats."

That's how Oskar "Pops" Laarkin *always* greeted the youngsters (the *oldsters* too, for that matter) who shuffled in and out of his combination drug store/mini-mart/gas station/post office/hang-out in a more or less steady-as-she-goes fashion.

Pops' soft drink confections started with the *real* thing; sweet, sticky, genuinely flavored syrups *to which* was added the effervescent magic of cold, clear carbonated spring water. The blend was spilled over half a dozen clinking cubes of sparkly ice, then lovingly mixed with a thin, long-handled silver spoon and served in a fat, frosted mug with a red-and-white-striped bendy straw and a plump, bobbing maraschino cherry.

Throw in a double scoop of Champion-brand vanilla ice cream with perhaps a few pinches of rainbow sprinkles and, o-wee, humanoids! You had yourself a bubbly thirst-quencher that'd put to rest *anything* shamefully marketed in containers so crass as, say…plastic bottles or aluminum cans!

Season to season, the scene was the same.

Watch.

Listen.

There's Pops yelling, "Got yerself a Jool-Eye Throat there, young feller?" *Or, there's Pops bleating,* "Howdy, Scalawags! (Pops' self-invented nickname for Kelsea and Associates) Ya look like yer meltin' down with a right bad case of Jool-Eye Throat!" *And sometimes, there's Pops lamenting,* "Mother of Mercy! Is it ever *hot* today! Betcha I got just whatchu all need fer them there Jool-Eye Throats o' yours!"

Even in *mid-January,* with four and a half feet of fresh white powder hiding the hills and hushing the valley, a spate of red-cheeked residents could be seen tracing squeaky snow steps across town to Laarkin's place for, whatever, a book of stamps or a box of tissue. And once inside, almost no one could resist the hypnotic temptation to shrug off the snow-dusted overcoat, slip into a vinyl-covered booth and order up fries and a cola while Pops held forth on world events or community gossip. A Kennawack Valley landmark was the Soda Queen, and a lovely, likable old gentleman indeed was Pops Laarkin—with a fringe of ivory hair ringing his bowling ball of a skull, those impossibly ice-blue, mirthful eyes and a ridiculous pair of Superman suspenders stretched dangerously over a somewhat-more-than-ample 65-year-old belly.

Kelsea and Erik sat across from one another, contentedly contemplating the inexpensive pleasures of youth, summer vacation, and Pops' delicious, wholly non-nutritious snack food.

"That Sandy is somethin' else, isn't she?" mumbled Erik around a mouthful of greasy French fries.

"Yep. And in a lot of different ways, too," Kelsea agreed, reaching for the ketchup bottle. "Did you have something particular in mind?"

"Well, for one," gulped Erik, studying the maraschino cherry floating in his soft drink, "the way she was able to figure out that whoever bothered Justin yesterday was riding an unshod horse. That's a pretty fine piece of detective work when you think about it."

"True dat, Erik-san. Lucky for us she and Stuart have been horse owners off and on, so they knew what to look for. Let's just hope their survey turns up something more, cuz right now the horse and the lipstick are about all we've got in the way of evidence."

"Pretty slim," agreed Erik. He slurped thoughtfully on his plastic straw, and secretly permitted himself the indulgence in a short-lived daydream revolving, in no small part, around Sandy LeMaster's dark curls. Kelsea, taking note of his half-smile and thousand-yard stare, feigned indifference and said nothing. She turned her thoughts to the incident.

There was the lipstick message. The hoof prints. That was Saturday. Yesterday.

Here's what had happened—then and there—at the quarry site when the Scalawags began to brainstorm in earnest; just before they swarmed the woodlands east of Justin's cabin, and began to search the area for clues:

*

Three jokes (two funny, one dumb), four guitar songs (two original, two Beatles), one pitcher of iced tea (extra-large, with lemon slices), one riddle ("Too easy!" complained Justin), 57 general statements, six questions (with five answers, and one educated guess), one petty complaint, 16 tail thumps, and a stomach growl after the think-tank session on the deck, Sandy led her group-mates back to the scene of the crime in order to (_her_ words, mind you) "commence an exhaustive investigation into the _heinous_ act which has been perpetrated against our mutual confederate."

Upon close examination (sight, scent, texture, and taste), the sleuthing Miss LeMaster concluded that the brownish-looking stuff, which had been used in writing the threat-rhyme upon Justin's window was, lipstick. An odd choice, both as an instrument for inscription, _and_ as a color option.

"Who th' hell wears _brown_ lipstick?" demanded Erik.

"Wackos who write misspelled hate slogans on people's bedroom windows at four in the morning," grumped Kelsea, glumly referring to how 'your' should have been written as 'you're.'

At Sandy's well-conceived suggestion, all of the etchings were washed from the window, save for a two-inch high letter 'J' which was carefully covered with three transparent strips of scotch tape, and overlaid again with a small, taped square of cardboard.

"This will protect it from precipitation and sun fade," Sandy advised. "If we are fortunate enough to recover any lipstick evidence of a suspicious nature, we can compare _its_ color to the one we saved here. A match, while not conclusive, may well assist us in narrowing the focus of our inquiry."

Next, Sandy had everyone fan out equidistant from one another in order to search the vicinity of Justin's home in ever-widening circles. It was hot, exacting work—taking up a good portion of the afternoon—and only after the better part of 70 meters in all directions from the cabin had been painstakingly combed was she satisfied that nothing in the way of helpful artifacts was going to be uncovered.

But it was on a barely visible game trail a full ten minutes east of Appleton Quarry that mopsy-headed Sandy LeMaster astounded her friends with her detection of the hoof prints. Clearly outlined in the moist, loamy soil—and obviously fresh, even to the eye of a novice—the evidence corroborated itself well with Justin's recollection of the sound of a whinnying horse on that memorable morning. There was no sense in trying to follow. The direction the rider had chosen led across shale slopes and into numerous creek beds where tracks could too easily become chaotic and ultimately lost.

And although Sandy was no tracker in any true sense of the term, her discerning eye managed to uncover one more piece of the puzzle before everyone called it a day.

Kneeling beside the trail, bending at the waist and scrutinizing the hoof print with the patient fastidiousness of a CIA agent, she slowly lifted her round, brown eyes to everyone, and smiling with satisfaction, declared, "This animal is unshod. I'd swear to it! If we can talk to the nearby farriers—and I believe there are only two or three of them in the valley—we may well find out who owns a horse who, for any reason, has been without metal shoes for the past couple of days. Alright, then! Stuie, let's get cracking!"

*

The feasting finally finished, Erik and Kelsea were still sitting at the window booth inside the Soda Queen when the LeMaster twins came hurling down Frontier Street, jammed their mountain bicycles into the bike rack, and hurried in to join their friends.

"Holy cow!" yelped Pops at full lung capacity. "Now _here's_ a couple of overheated, soon-to-be-tenth-grade-Scalawags if ever I seen 'em! Got yerselves some Jool-Eye Throats there, I betcha. Right, twinsies?"

"Double indubitably!" sang out Sandy. "I'll take a large cherry cola!"

"Tall green river here, Pops!" echoed Stuart. "Muchas grawchas!"

"It's 'GRAH-see-ahs,' Stu. But that's OK." Then, turning to the others: "You aren't going to _believe_ what _we_ found out this morning!"

Kelsea glanced quickly about the room. "All right, let's have it," she murmured.

"But let's also try to keep it to ourselves. You know how Justin feels about this getting out—at least for the time being."

Nodding in agreement, their voices were lowered accordingly.

"Here ya be!" bellowed Pops, seemingly materializing from out of thin air, and startling the living bejeebers out of four suddenly very security-minded adolescents. "On the house, fer doin' such a great job mowin' an' trimmin' aroun' my place last week!"

"But Pops," Stuart, in corrective mode, "you already paid us for that job. Don't you remember?"

Pops feigned surprise at the statement. "What! Ya never heard of gettin' _tips_ on top of yer wages?" The old fellow rolled his eyes, and wandered off, whistling and wondering quietly to himself whether he should wash some glassware, or to continue badgering some of his other customers.

"Remind _me_ to leave a tip for the colas and fries," urged Erik.

"Will do," promised Kelsea. "Now! What'd you guys find out today? Are we _on_ to somethin', or what?"

"Well, for starters," whispered Sandy secretively, "I was correct in my assumption that there are only three farriers in the valley; two in Chapeeka, and one all the way down in Weston. Now, most, but not all of the horse owners in the upper valley are going to secure the services of horse-shoeing tradesmen from Chapeeka because 'drive time' is figured into the billing, and Chapeeka is at least half an hour closer to

Appleton than Weston is. That fact notwithstanding, Stuart and I elected to hop one of those cool, new ValleyTrans buses and visit *all* _three_ of the area's blacksmiths; leaving *nothing* to chance, as it were. What we found, while very speculative and totally inconclusive, is nonetheless quite interesting."

She paused to quaff her spritz-y soft drink. The bubbles tickled her parched Jool-Eye Throat, and she swallowed hurriedly as Kelsea squirmed with anticipation for the rest of the story to unfold. In the meantime, Stuart's attention had been diverted to one Debbin Ramsay who had just "slinked in the door," (as Sandy would have put it) and was being assisted by Pops over by the cosmetics.

As a silence ensued, it slowly became increasingly apparent to *all* that poor Stuart was losing touch with reality as we understand it, and was evidently slipping into some kind of glaze-eyed goo-goo land; a dumbed-down netherworld of shape and form, but clearly devoid of much functional context.

"Jeez, Stu," chided his sister, "use a napkin! You're drooling!"

"Wha—huh?" began the boy, obviously embarrassed at the thought of being caught gazing with worshipful reverence at the attractive blonde-haired girl.

"We *know* she's a *cheerleader*, Stuie," admonished Kelsea, affecting a motherly tone to the grinning delight of everyone seated. "But she's 17, Romeo! She's got a driver's license. She's a _senior_. Earth to LeMaster. Earth to LeMaster. If you can hear us, tap three times on your wooden head!"

Stuart smiled, red-faced—acknowledging the innocent ribbing he had brought upon himself. "Well, ya gotta admit she's pretty much a _hottie_."

"Stuart LeMaster!" scolded Sandy under her breath. "Doth my ears deceive me? While admittedly attractive in a *visual sense*, do you fail to recognize the fawning pretentiousness, the preening presumptuousness—" she left the thought floating and unfinished. "Boys!" she managed. "Who can *fathom* them?"

"Pretty weird that _she_ should pop into Pops' right about now," offered Stuart, floating gently back to reality from PlanetLove.

"How so?" wondered Erik, stealing a surreptitious glance of his own in Debbin's direction. _She is cute, but not as cute as Sandy!_

"I'll cut right to the chase," stated Sandy, suddenly very businesslike. "A farrier in Weston identified a horse that's being stabled up Triple Creek as currently being unshod due to a hoof infection. That's way too far away from Appleton Quarry to have been ridden there that morning, especially under the circumstances."

"And, anything turn up any closer to home?" persisted Erik.

"Just one," offered Sandy. "Identical situation, actually. One of the smiths in Chapeeka mentioned an appaloosa that was plagued with a minor hoof ailment requiring the temporary removal of her steel shoes. Furthermore, the animal's owner lives just a short riding distance from Justin's cabin."

Erik and Kelsea exchanged astonished glances, and commenced a mad, frantic dash through their memory banks; a futile attempt to flush out the answer for themselves.

"C'mon! C'mon! Whose horse do you think was ridden over to Justin's yesterday?" pleaded Erik.

The silence was thick; stifling. Unbearable.

The twins looked at each other knowingly, if somehow skeptically. They fixed their good friends with the kind of gaze that seemed to assert, "OK, but you may not understand this any more than _we_ do."

Sandy drew a heavy sigh as Stuart rolled his eyes in the direction of the make-up rack, where Debbin Ramsay was completing the purchase of some recently ordered cosmetics.

"The unshod horse belongs to her," was all he said.

*

"Woh, woh, woo-ohh! Slow down, everyone! Lemme see if I got this straight!"

Justin Michael Thomas Bench threaded slender fingers through the coarse fur behind one of Kooper's scabby ears, and waded contemplatively back into the thick of the discussion.

"Now, unless I'm misunderstandin' all this hullaballo, what yer tryin' to tell me is that *Debbin Ramsay* was the one who rode that horse over here an' wrote that love letter on my window." Here, the young man paused while he took measure of his own words, and studied the expressions of each of his friends in turn. "Nothin' against her, mind you, but I bet I've never piled up more'n a hundred words with that gal in the, what, 'bout almost three years now that I been here? It just doesn't make any sense that she'd hold some kinda grudge towards the likes o'me."

Four excited voices burst into a clamorous, collective explanation—jolting Kooper out of a light snooze, and prompting Justin to poke his fingers into both ears in a comical plea for order.

Kelsea produced a single, sharp, hawk-like whistle between her front teeth, bringing everybody into compliance with a long agreed-upon Scalawag rule: 'One-at-a-time-or-nothin'-gets-done.' "He's right," she admonished. "Let's let Sandy do the talking. She and Stuart are the ones who did the footwork and pieced it all together. Agreed?"

No dissenters, and Sandy began, "Well, like I said, Justin, we completed on-site investigations at each of the valley's three farriers in order to ascertain which horses in the area would be, or *could* be, currently shoeless."

"Didn't that arouse any suspicions? Comin' in an' askin' a lot of questions an' all?" reasoned Justin.

"Not really," said Stuart. "We just told them we were gathering some information for a project we wanted to do at school next fall. We asked a *ton* of stuff before we actually got around to quizzing them about the horse we were looking for."

"It was Stuie's idea—very well-conceived, if I may say so—and it worked like a charm! Ben Jorgenson, the outfitter in Chapeeka, was the gentleman who supplied the information about Debbin Ramsay's shoeless appaloosa, the one which is stabled about a *three-mile ride from the quarry*, Justin! And in *exactly* the direction in which those hoof prints were found to be heading."

Justin held his palm up, politely asking for silence while he rolled the news over in his mind. Finally, shaking his head grim-faced, he was forced to admit that if any of this made any sense, *he* certainly wasn't able to shake the meaning out of it.

"Allow me to position the last piece of the puzzle into place, mon ami," said Sandy. "Then we can commence some serious brainstorming as to the 'whences' and 'wherefores.'"

The dark-haired girl sat cross-legged on the living room floor, her mahogany eyes suddenly bright with anger and excitement. Everyone followed suit, and momentarily they were all seated in a circle, leaning forward in rapt attention as Sandy LeMaster held forth regarding the last portion of what had happened at the Soda Queen just three hours earlier that very day. Her retelling was succinct, concise, and to the point.

But here's a longer version:

*

Start with four measuring cups of '*uncertainty,*' poured into a large pitcher.

Add eight to ten ounces of pure '*disbelief.*'

Stir in a dollop or two of '*extract of confusion.*'

Season with a bit of authentic '*surprise*' (just a pinch will do).

Top with a frothy swirl of '*outrage,*' '*ire,*' or '*infuriation*' (according to personal preference), and serve to your guests in tall tumblers filled with ice cubes of '*utter befuddlement.*'

A baffling beverage, to be certain. But that's how Sandy *would* have summarized the incident at Pops' place had she chosen to rely exclusively upon a "Soft Drink Recipe Metaphor." Now, they had *all* been drinking deeply of said aforementioned "brew" when Debbin Ramsay sashayed past the booth where they all sat frozen and unblinking.

Debbin 'I-dare-you-to-try-and-not-look-at-me' Ramsay—her hair, a coquettish flounce of sun gold ringlets—was looking nonchalant, and at the same time *exquisitely* self-aware; trailing otherworldly scents of bath salts, expensive colognes, and dramatic 17-year-old-ness.

There she goes, man, thought Stuart to himself as she glided ethereally out the door. *Wrapped like a gift for your slobbering, worshipful eyes. Adorned in snug, bone-white designer shorty-shorts, a clean, freshly ironed cotton T-shirt, and name-brand sandals… the whole, sweet package exuding a delicious, casual elegance or, what my sister would quickly amend to: "A depraved caustic arrogance!"*

"Yessiree, Bob!" barked Pops as unexpected as a thunderclap. "There goes one of the purtiest little cheerleadin' gals ever born of Apple-burg!" He was wiping down the fountain counter, and peering over the tops of his John Lennon-type eyeglasses. "Gotta hand it to 'er, too. She ain't afraid to spend top dollar on her make-up supplies!"

"And she wears it so well," murmured Stuart. *Well, the silence engulfing the window booth had been starting to feel like a suppressive bubble,* Stuart, thinking in his own defense. *Hell, somebody needed to burst it.*

"Crime-in-Italy, Stu," whispered Erik. "Get over yourself, will ya?"

"Oh brother, brother!" mourned Sandy, who stared dejectedly out the window; elbow on the table, and chin in her hand.

Just then, something flickered in Stuart's eyes. And although later he was honest enough to admit that he had really only been following a subtle instinct, and stabbing around in the dark, he decided to follow the feeling.

"Wha'ja *mean* about Debbin's taste in cosmetics, Pops?" he asked.

Over Kelsea's muted groan, Pops began a rather lengthy explanation of the girl's impeccable knowledge of beauty aids. As Pops saw it, Debbin pretty much knew *all* there was to know about the secrets of soft, clear skin, and how that understanding was boosted by a refined knowledge of cutting-edge herbal moisturizers, milk baths, aloe-vera ointments and blah blah with their *all-natural ingredients* (Pops—

reading from a label, now) blah-blah which yields lustrous blah-de-blah and more-blah and will-somebody-please-wake-Kelsea-when-this-is-finally-over-etc.-etc., and so forth, blah-blah!

A triviality was rushing right by, *almost* unnoticed; slipping out of, and right back into a cloak of invisibility while the Scalawags temporarily had their collective "radar down," so to speak.

Now.

Here's what happened at Laarkin's Soda Queen just as afternoon's shadows began a slow, seventh-inning stretch eastward toward the city of Weston.

Look over there. Can you see that?

Sandy—her bushy brown hair all wind-shaped and wonderful, is quietly brooding; staring out the window at, well, at pretty much nothing.

Kelsea's rainy-sky-colored eyes are closely inspecting a freckle on her forearm, wondering if girls like, oh, say, *Debbin Ramsay* deal with skin pigment issues too.

Erik is staring a hole in the magazine rack, hawklike; expertly disguising the fact that he is furtively wishing that he was a year older, and could be in Sandy LeMaster's homeroom at school come September.

And Stuart, alas, poor Stuart is still scalding in the juices of a boiling vat of 'I-wish-I-hadn't-asked-that' soup, clinging desperately to a thin hope for redemption, *when* "...an' that makes her nearabouts the only gal I know of who special orders stuff like that there mocha lipstick." Pops has concluded his skincare spiel, and is returning a glass banana split boat to a tall shelf.

There! Did you hear that? *Didja?* Well, the Scalawags did!

Watch what happens next!

Look at how Sandy's head whips from the window to the fountain counter at "warp-speed." Pretty remarkable, huh? And Kelsea. Ever see a kid snap to attention that fast in your whole life? I doubt it very much!

What about Erik? You couldn't have put a timer on *that* reaction and come out with readable information. Not a chance!

"Stuff like that there mocha lipstick." Amazing how much power and weight could be packed into a simple phrase fragment. More amazing still, the ability of kids to pick up on minutiae; to pay attention to details, even when they *aren't* paying any attention at *all*.

Stu sat stone still.

"Mocha lipstick?" he finally inquired quietly. "That'd be some shade of brown, wouldn't it, Pops?"

"Yepper," agreed Pops. "Expensive stuff, but it's supposably top o' the line. Leastwise that's what Miss Ramsay herself tells me, heh, heh, heh. And she's the only customer I got who wants it, so, it's a special-order item. But, then again, a *lot* of the stuff she uses is."

By now, *everybody* was aware of just what it was that Stuart had stumbled upon. The implications were far-reaching; *enormous,* really. And no one... *no one* wanted to blow it all at *this* point.

Kelsea finally regained her presence of mind, and seized the opportunity to broaden the subject with Pops.

"Well," she admitted, feigning a yawn and trying hard to appear only *moderately* interested, "I suppose Debbin really *does* know a bit about stylin' and profilin.' Most of the *boys* sure seem to think so anyways. (A sidelong look of slight disdain toward Stu, who squirmed noticeably.) Which brand and color did you say she uses, Pops? Let's have a look at it."

"Beatrix brand, mocha shade," Pops declared amicably. "But ya can't check it out, 'cause I special order 'em one at a time, an' the only one I had in stock just got carried out the door by the only customer who requests it. See?"

All eyes were on Kelsea Crowl while she struggled valiantly to concoct a plausible fabrication out of sheer nothingness in zero seconds flat. Which was just about how much time she had left before Pops would begin to wonder just what the heck she was up to.

"So anyways, um, how much would it cost to order a stick of that Beatrix Mocha?"

Pops eyed Kelsea quizzically over the tops of his specs. "Kelsea Kathleen Crowl takin' to wearin' lipstick these days? I figgered you fer a backpackin' bike rider fer the next coupla years at least!"

"Not for me, Pops," corrected the girl. "It'd be for my cousin in Port Murrey. She's so much like Debbin Ramsay, you wouldn't believe it. Anyways, I think she'd really be surprised to get a little gift like that from, you know, from me!" Kelsea was warming to the weaving of her fiction, and her friends were smart enough (and quiet enough) to let the charm blossom and bloom unbroken.

"I see," said Pops. "Well, that makes more sense than the idea of Ms. Kels dollin' up to go ridin' out to the Swimmin' Hole with her Scalawag buddies!" He winked at the kids in the booth, who smiled at the well-worn joke and watched to see what would happen next.

"Now, that'll be $17.95 when it arrives next Thursday."

"Seventeen ninety-five! For a stupid tube of *brown lipstick?*" Stu blurted, incredulous.

"Well, I told ya it was top 'o the line, now," soothed Pops.

Beneath the tabletop, Stuart began quietly rubbing the spot on his leg where his sister had just kicked him, not-so-gently, in retaliation for 'endangering the mission.'

"No problem," Kelsea countered, "she's worth the price. And I'll just bet she gets a double kick out of knowing it came from *me*. She's sorta like you, Pops. She thinks I'm still too busy bein', ah, bein' a tomboy to have, um, good taste in, uh, things."

"Okey dokey, then! One Beatrix Mocha lipstick fer ya. Like I said, it'll likely be here on Thursday. Come to think of it, I may as well just order another one fer Debbin. That last one she bought only lasted her a few days, an' she was right back in here orderin' another. Makes a feller wonder what in tarnation she's doin' with that stuff, writin' letters or somethin'?"

Kelsea thanked the old man for his help with the lipstick order. Returning to the window booth, she left a substantial tip for the cokes and fries, and hurried to hook up with the other Scalawags, who were assisting Stu out the door; the apparent victim of an unexpected coughing fit.

*

A watched pot never boils.

All good things come to those who wait.

Patience is a virtue.

And so on.

Summer days floated by Appleton's youngsters like dry wood drifting serenely in a high mountain lake.

From Sunday until Thursday (the day the mocha lipstick was due to arrive at the Soda Queen), the gang made three trips to the Swimming Hole together. Stuart skinned his knee doing a stunt dive, and the Tuesday trip was shortened considerably as a result.

Kelsea cleaned and swept the garage, for which she was paid ten dollars by her appreciative father. Erik was invited to the LeMasters for a barbecue picnic, after which they took a ValleyTrans bus to the cinema in Weston where he and Sandy held hands.

Well, almost.

Actually, Erik's hand brushed hers accidentally as they were taking their seats.

Well, almost accidentally.

The first days of July began to take on all the attributes of soon-to-be August as the days grew brighter, hotter, and shorter. Yet, longer. Mostly longer. Because that's the way time feels for you when you are in a terminal waiting mode. Lawns are mowed. Songs are written and sung. Dognaps are taken. Sunburns are gingerly treated, while the waiting continues.

And threaded through those daily activities of small-town living was the endless speculation: Why did this happen to Justin? Who was responsible? Was this as serious as it appeared? Will the mocha lipstick match that smudge on the window?

Thursday finally came. (It always does.)

So did the Beatrix Mocha lipstick.

And no one was very surprised when, gathered shoulder to shoulder before the cabin window, Kelsea uncapped the lipstick, swiped its tip on the window beside the tape-covered letter "J," and with that one short stroke removed all doubt about the nature of the medium used to write the note. It was a perfect match. As Sandy stated: "Indubitably."

The evidence of the hoof print and the lipstick now pointed directly to Debbin Ramsay, and with clues becoming more concrete, the discussion began to turn to motivation. What was Debbin's problem with Justin Bench? Was it just a one-shot prank, or did she harbor some deep personal resentment of some kind (making a future violation a distinct possibility)?

Tom Petty was right. The waiting **is** the hardest part.

Later that evening, Justin pulled Woody onto his knee, pressed a chord, strummed, and softly sang to the empty woodlands; sang to fiery stars floating the infinite ink above him.

Justin...playing and singing, singing and thinking...continually, quietly puzzling over it all: *"What was it he had seen?"*

*

REVERENTIAL CROW...

YOU RIDE THE CUSHIONS OF THERMAL UPDRAFTS INTO THE HIGH, THIN AIR SWIMMING IN DIZZY DISTANCES ABOVE APPLETON. FROM THAT COLD, WHIRLING VANTAGE POINT YOU WHEEL WITHIN UNIMPEDED VISUAL RANGE OF KENTSWORTH, DEERFIELD, CHAPEEKA, AND WESTON; SPLOTCHES OF HUMAN SPRAWL ZIG-ZAGGING DOWNSTREAM ALONG THE KENNAWACK RIVER.

UPSTREAM—WHERE UNCOUNTABLE, CRYSTAL CREEKS FEED THE STREAMFLOW FROM ANCIENT SNOWFIELDS—YOU SOAR THROUGH A STAB OF SUNLIGHT REFLECTED FROM

YOUNG'S LAKE; ONE AMONG THE HUNDREDS, STREWN JEWEL-LIKE IN THE CREASES AND FOLDS OF THE MIGHTY MOUNTAIN RANGE.

CROWLOGIC REMINDS YOU THAT IT IS TIME TO COMMUNICATE ANOTHER PORTION OF YOUR CHRONICLE. AND YOUR FLIGHT WAY INSCRIBES AN ARC—NORTH, NORTHWEST—WHERE, IN JUST OVER 1,100 WINGBEATS, YOU WILL SINK, SLIDE AND SETTLE INTO LOW, FIR BRANCHES BRIMMING A REMOTE MILE-LONG HANGING VALLEY KNOWN AS RAVENRILL.

THERE, TO DECLARE YOURSELF.

IN PART, <u>THIS</u> IS WHAT YOU OVERHEARD THE VOICES OF THE LONGLEGS SAY AS YOU OCCUPIED YOURSELF SCAVENGING THE GRASSES OF APPLETON PARK THAT MID-MORNING.

IT WAS EXACTLY TWO DAYS AFTER JUSTIN'S PROPERTY HAD BEEN VANDALIZED.

"You're <u>sure</u> he saw the message? I haven't seen any reaction from <u>any</u> of them."

"They're scared. They're groupin' up, tryin' to decide what to do."

"Well, I have to admit, using that horse for the getaway was pretty smart. It's fast and quiet. And it's probably left them with a lot of unanswered questions as well."

"Thanks. I thought the lipstick was a pretty good idea, too. I saw that trick used in a movie once. It just kinda adds to the tension; to the mystery, ya know?"

"Fine. Whatever. As long as that moron gets the picture. Now, I want him <u>out</u> of that shack by the end of the summer, no excuses. You hear? And you'd better be <u>damn</u> <u>careful</u> about covering your tracks. If <u>any</u> of this even sniffs of leading back to me, I'm gonna be on you like ugly on an ape!"

"I know, I know. Um, how about the money?"

"It's in the envelope. Don't be flashy about showing it off. It'll attract attention that we don't need at this time. Now, don't bother filling me in with what's coming up next. I'm not interested in the details. I just want <u>results</u>. That's what I'm paying you for, so I suggest you get on with your next steps...you <u>do</u> have another plan in place, do you not? Good. Then go make it happen."

And wouldn't Kelsea Crowl just give a boatload of garden-weeding income to know what <u>you</u> now know, stealthy Crow? To have overheard the conversation that <u>you</u> overheard? But she'll have to wait it on out before <u>that</u> kind of information sees the light of day. And the waiting is always the hardest part.

Isn't that so?

*

"Well, his hopes and dreams are slimmer than a whisper;
he's inconsequential as a puff of wind.
And I would not make a joke,
but a feather wisp of smoke
is more likely to reveal where it has been.
He's a product of his own imagination;
insubstantial in his self-deceptive way.
Partly truth, and partly myth;
like a spider's thread adrift
on a stream of air, above some foamy bay."

Kelsea's tar-black hair riffled ever so slightly, as a vagrant Cascade breeze pushed its way past her in search of wings *(Crow wings?)* to inspirit. Justin sat nearby; cross-legged and drowsy, playing and singing his newest composition while the girl sprawled in the shade of a jumble of vine maple.

Goose feather gray eyes serenely closed. The back of her T-shirt pressed upon cool, green grasses. Enveloped protectively in the living green of Washington woods surrounding the quarry cabin. Not a bad way to spend a lazy summer afternoon.

"Do what you will do. Do anything you're able to.
He will only do just what he can.
Always pale and always frail, but somehow never failing;
the here and there Imaginary Man—
the now and then Imaginary Man."

Kelsea found it remarkable that someone as unassuming and earthy as Justin Bench could express himself so eloquently in his lyrics. He typically did *not* speak using the same colors of articulation with which he composed his music.

Oh, well. Life's little mysteries.

Sighing with contentment—stretching and smiling—she abruptly dismissed any more serious contemplation in favor of an emotional surrender; giving herself over to the innocence of original songcraft…delivered in unconditional friendship by a gentle-spirited human being. It occurred to her, on some kind of semi-conscious level, what a non-arrogant and wholly tolerable world this might be if everybody acted like, or at least *had a friend like*, Justin Bench.

"He's diaphanous as gossamer at daybreak;
translucent as the wings of butterflies.
Not a lot that's held inside,
not a single thing implied;
the myopic prophet of his own device.
Well, he moves through time and space so unencumbered;
just like laughing waters—dancing over stones.

And you cannot pin him down,
and you cannot spin him 'round,
for the halcyon has stilled his killing storm."

The song was so full of sweetness and frank sincerity that Kelsea understood at once that it was destined to be one of the favorites amongst their circle of friends. Despite the serenity of the moment, the 15-year-old suddenly felt a twinge of impishness. She decided to play a wild card.

"Hey, Justin," she yawned, "what's 'halcyon' mean?" She was, truth be told, far more interested in *how* he answered the question than *what* the definition was.

"Well, Kels," drawled Bench wistfully, "the halcyon was a made-up bird that got oceans to settle down when it sat on 'em."

Kelsea erupted into fits of giggles.

"I say somethin' funny?" inquired Justin, eyebrow arched; the suggestion of a smile.

"Oh, Justin, no," smiled Kelsea, regaining control of her composure. "I was just thinking about how differently you *write* as opposed to, you know, the way you *talk* to people."

"I do?" smiling more expansively, now. He knew exactly what she was getting at, but he wanted to hear her explanation all the same. They were such good, *good* friends.

"An' just *how* would I have given ya _that_ pertickler definition…in a song, I mean?"

"Well, for starters," she informed him, "in a *song,* you would have sounded more like Sandy LeMaster. You would have said somethin' like, um, 'The halcyon is a mythological fowl popularly thought to secure a sense of tranquility to oceanic environs of its liking.'"

Justin cradled his right elbow in the palm of his left hand; his arm lying flat against his stomach. Thrusting his thumb under his chin, he began lightly tapping the side of his nose with his forefinger; a mock-studious pose of analytic preoccupation. "Hmm," he offered reflectively, "the way I got it figgered, if I *talked* the same way as I *wrote*, I'd hafta change my darn name."

"Change your name?" She didn't get the connection. At all.

"Yup. Hafta go from Justin M. T. Bench to Justin Other LeMaster."

The forested hills of Appleton Quarry rang with laughter.

*

Pat Cheney. Seventeen years of age. Poised to enter the tenth grade.

"Held back" in grade three.

"Retained" in grade six.

The beneficiary of Cascadia School District's policy of 'social promotion' in all other grade levels.

Pat Cheney. "Patch." Feared by many students, reviled by most—mistrusted by all the rest. A full two years older, three inches taller and a *good* 20 pounds heavier than anyone in his class. Second in size only to Deep Thoughts. Lots of leverage there.

Oodles of dark opportunity for an outcast adolescent whose singular purpose in life, from all appearances, seemed to be the ongoing refinement—to the point of perfection—of a 'scorched earth' policy toward anything and everybody...pretty much all of the time, and everywhere.

Patch slammed the door behind him—*hard!*—and strode noisily across a bare, linoleum living room floor in a single-wide, moss-and-mold-covered mobile home; currently on blocks in a weed-choked corner of Paxton's Mobile Park. Frequently referred to as "Hell's Half-Acre" by the citizenry of the Mid Valley, Lawrence Paxton's clattered collection of aluminum abodes resembled not so much a trailer park as a junkyard, and even the meter man from the electric company winced at the thought of making his rounds through the maze of derelict kitchen appliances, rusted car bodies, and yawping, foaming pit bulls. Patch's calloused hand swept angrily across the light switch.

Nothing!

My old lady probably didn't pay the bill again. Nothing new here! A boatload o' bills go unpaid in this rat's nest. Hell, I haven't even seen good ol' Mom for, what, two weeks now? Patch—pacing, angry, red-faced. *She'll be back... eventually. Probably drunk and disorderly. But with a little cash to get us to the month end. Who cares anyway?* **Nobody! *That's* who!**

He stomped, scowling, to the breakfast bar and jerked the telephone from its hook, carelessly chipping a plastic shard from its cradle. Jamming the receiver to his ear, Patch confirmed what he had already guessed; the phone company had disconnected the service to their residence as well. He dropped it where he stood, and walked away, leaving it to dangle—abandoned and ignored—exactly like his father (whoever the hell **he** was!), and his mother had pretty much done with him.

OK. **Fine!**

No phone, no lights. No lights meant no TV or radio. It also meant no stove, no oven, and no refrigerator. He decided to take care of as much of the perishable food as he could before it started to all go bad. Flinging open the door with such force that it bent the hinges and sent colorful stickup magnets flying, Patch stared—cruel and embittered—at its meager contents: half a jar of dill pickles, one Vidalia onion, an unopened stick of butter, some kind of spoiled meat and three cans of Schaeffer's lager laced together with plastic six-pack loops.

Patch raised the onion to his mouth and bit down—gripping it in his teeth like a child bobbing for apples, snagging the pickle jar with one hand, and the three-pack of beer with the other. Mumbling unintelligibly (even to himself) he returned to the living room, darkening now with the close of another Appleton summer day, and sagged himself into a sad armchair which squatted sullenly before the lifeless, glass face of a portable TV. No power. It was just as well. The reception on that piece of shit was always rotten anyway!

He was swashing down half-chewed chunks of peppery/pungent onion with huge, noisy gulps of cheap beer when the thought occurred to him: he couldn't even take a shower! For Christ's sake, there was no freakin' electricity to heat the water!

Patch felt the heat begin at the base of his neck; over, around, and through the muscles of his wide shoulders. He was aware of its rapid ascent through his jaws (the clenching of teeth), his cheekbones (a burning sensation ensuing), arching over his brows—turning his vision reddish and waver-y, and inflaming the scar tissue under his left eye.

It was when the fury/fever reached his temples that reason finally broke and bled from Patrick Cheney. Slowly, he stood erect—body trembling with the tag-end remnants of an emotional restraint which was fading out just as surely and completely as an old prospector's dream of riches in a panned-out highland stream.

Swearing violently, Patch fired the empty pickle jar through the TV screen, sending glass fragments flying in every direction. He downed the remainder of the beer, emitting wet, bubbly belches that were wiped away with the back of an unwashed hand.

"Who cares?" he howled to the ceiling. The chipped paint gave no response.

"Nobody! That's who! That's who! No-gawdamm-body!"

Patch had no filter for the nature of his own unbridled hatred. Possessed no coping mechanism which could assist him in controlling his desire for destruction and revenge. Had no way of targeting his pain, nor of identifying his tormentor. For Patch, everything, everybody, every time, everywhere had become loathsome; had become that which isolates, betrays, mocks, represses, and condemns.

He swaggered to the door, half-blind with rage and indignation; slightly stupefied from the effects of alcohol swirling in a stomach not nearly enough filled, and reeking with unfit, raw food. The boy plucked a grimy sweatshirt from the back of a wooden chair and slipped it on over his head as he banged out the trailer door and headed for the town; arrogance and angst swelling with every step.

"Somebody's gonna pay!" he snarled to himself. "Tonight, somebody is totally gonna *shittin' __pay__!*" He wiped his fingertips across the embossed letters of the heavy, hooded sweater, and spun off into the Appleton night. Across his chest, the shirt bore a question in large, sun-faded red letters:

"What's That Smell?"

And across his back, blazed the written response:

"It's Life. And Life Stinks!"

*

Lieutenant Colonel Harding Corbett "Hard-Core" Tattenger was like a grown-up version of Pat Cheney, with a military uniform. The colonel had muscled his way to the top of the Marine hierarchy in a "take-no-prisoners" kind of career that spanned the better part of 30 long, uncompromising years. Best known for his unflinching sense of personal responsibility and an unshakeable credo of strict discipline bordering on outright brutality, "Hard-Core" was well-steeped in the conviction that the vast majority of Americans were 'spineless worms,' unfit and undeserving of the freedoms secured for their sorry carcasses by real men of The Marine Corps.

Most folks in and around Appleton did not much care for the colonel. He made no effort to conceal the fact that he despised them, one and all—regarding them as rabble and vermin. And were it not for the fact that he was away on military business for the better part of ten months of every year, most people would not have been able to stomach the indignities and sarcasm with which he completed his social and business transactions, up and down the Kennawack River Valley.

Colonel Tattenger ruled his family with an iron fist. His wife, Lauren, a poor shell of a creature, might have been good-natured—happy, even—at some point in her life. But any hope for a life balanced with healthy prospects and pursuits lay buried under years of scornful mistreatment at the hands of her inflexible, demanding husband.

Mrs. Tattenger did her best to raise her son on her own. In the absence of a husband's influence, bringing up a child turns out to be an arduous task. This, she learned slowly and inexorably. Being a very small woman, Lauren was rather frail, and not necessarily gifted with inordinate amounts of courage, energy, or strength. And Rodney no doubt owed his diminutive stature and pale complexion to the genetic inheritance he received from his tired, tiny mother.

During the early years, Rodney and Lauren co-existed in a reasonably peaceful and conventional world. They went grocery shopping together, saw movies, took walks in Appleton Park; all very simple, unassuming, and normal. But the colonel's military career mushroomed, cancer-like, and over the years his attitude toward his wife and son became increasingly inflamed with an overt sense of disrespect and disdain. He began to perceive character flaws—imperfections and weaknesses—whenever he returned from his billets for a short leave of absence. It was reflected in the faces of the people of the community in which he resided. He discovered it in the attitudes of store owners with whom he traded. He was appalled to uncover what he perceived to be a substantial amount of "laziness" and "incompetence" in the congregants of the church he attended.

Bewildered and bedeviled, Colonel Tattenger was forever tormented by omnipresent hometown images of (in *his* estimation) apathy, inferiority, and impotence. But nowhere, _nowhere_ did he experience more irritation at the "feeble deficiencies of substandard human behavior and bearing" than when he intermittently hung his hat at 2112 Prescott Street, Appleton, Washington; home.

Lieutenant Colonel "Hard-Core" Tattenger was home on leave the week before Justin Bench was threatened with a message written with a mocha lipstick. Rodney and Lauren remember the time well enough, if for different reasons than Mr. Justin Bench did; they had a full plate of their *own* to deal with. And they *both* fervently wished they could forget about most of *that* week altogether.

"Did you complete the assignments you were charged with, weener-boy?" Colonel "Hard-Core," growling. He was seated behind an enormous, well-polished walnut desk; hands folded, fingers laced businesslike and motionless beside an expensive-looking set of pens.

"Yes, sir."

"You didn't muck 'em up, did you? You didn't let your well-documented reputation for screwing things up get in the way of carrying out my orders, did you?" The man possessed the quality of a block of concrete, rising to his feet, spreading stiffened fingers, and leaning upon their tips across the desk.

"No, sir."

"That punk, hood-of-a-friend of yours—Pat Cheney; if I didn't dislike him with such singular intensity, I'd give _all_ these chores to _him_. Why in hell he hangs out listening to an incompetent runt like _you_ is utterly beyond me. Look at me when I'm talking to you, weener-boy!"

"Yes, sir."

The colonel moved rigidly around the desk; hands clasped behind him, standing with his back to his son—studying the wainscoted wall decorated with dozens of framed military photographs. He removed one from its hook, exuding an expression of cold, prideful recollection; the curl, that passed for a smile at the corners of his mouth, more closely resembling a reflection of gas pains than of pleasure. "At least _he's_ got spunk. _That_ kid's gutsy," he continued. "He isn't afraid of any_thing_ or any_one_. And that beats the living shit outa hangin' around with that _Crowl_ (rhyming it with **owl**) kid, like _you_ used to do. You're lucky she didn't turn you into a syrup-headed hippie, just like the crap crowd she runs with..._and_ those limp-wristed parents who pathetically attempt to raise her!" Without pausing for breath, the man bore on: "I'd like to know exactly what you were thinking about when you went through _that_ phase in your Nancy-boy life. Or maybe I'm better off _not_ knowing!"

"Yes, sir."

"It's too bad she and her old man didn't go up in smoke when that fire took out the Silver Creek drainage two years ago. The world would be a centimeter closer to perfection if all the pale-spirited, mental cripples like them—and that geek, Bench—would just burn up and blow

74

away. And how _you_ were _ever_ able to save _your_ sorry butt from _that_ inferno is _another_ one of life's great mysteries!"

"Yes, sir."

"You get the garage attic straightened up?"

"Yes, sir."

"How about that load of firewood that was delivered two days ago? Is it stacked and covered?"

"Yes, sir."

"Very well. But don't forget...you've got plenty of other assignments on your docket. You'd better triple-check and make damned sure that everything has either _been_ done, or is in the process of _being_ done, and I mean _exceedingly_ _well_! Understood?"

"Yes, sir."

"Dismissed!"

Rodent wheeled smartly and exited his father's study. Colonel Tattenger did not see the thin, clear streak of a tear etching its way down his son's cheek. If he had, he would have beaten him within an inch of his life. Not with a belt. Not with a paddle. Nor even with his hands or fists, but with demeaning, poisonous, humiliating remarks. For well did his father know that wounds of the flesh all heal in time; that cuts, abrasions, punctures, breaks and bruises all scab over, eventually, leaving the beleaguered combatant intact, and none-the-worse-for-wear. But _inside_ pain—hurts of the heart—can grieve one everlastingly. Forevermore.

Returning the photo to its place of honor amongst the others on the "wall of fame," Harding Corbett Tattenger crossed the room; plush, olive-drab carpet cushioning his footfalls. He perused an eye-level shelf of books, sliding his forefinger along the edge, and muttering the names of titles and authors as he continued to search. His personal library was extensive—the culmination of years of collecting and culling—and the bookshelves were built floor to ceiling, extending from one end of the wall to the other.

Finally settling on a selection of Machiavelli's *The Prince*, the colonel retired to his executive-style swivel chair behind the massive, orderly desk. Slipping on a pair of Marine-issue, black-rimmed reading glasses, he gave himself over to the literature, and its remarkable ability to sweep away the distasteful remnants of his colorless domestic existence.

Meanwhile…

Rodent was dog-trotting down the tree-lined sidewalk; wiping tears, and doing his best to shore up and restore some semblance of his dignity and self-esteem. He had long ago given up wondering why his dad hated him and his mother (everyone!) so much; speculation of that nature was a study in futility. Jogging north along Prescott Street, he flashed briefly on his mom. And for a selfless second, he worried that maybe he should go back and be with her. Misery loves company, so the saying goes, and he knew that the colonel would be on her about *something*…just as soon as he finished whatever self-absorbed and self-promoting thing he was currently engaged with in his study. Poor Mom! The whole damn thing was just…so…un-frigging fair! But one of the lessons his father had repeatedly pounded into his brain was that "you can't save somebody who's in trouble if *you* die in the attempt." **That** was what had spared *his* so-called "sorry butt" when walls of flame had nearly claimed three lives two summers ago.

And *that* was the lesson he was going to repeat right now. Rodney "Rodent" Tattenger was one of the walking wounded—unraveling inside-out from gross neglect. That, and from an unrelenting, years-long assault on his sense of self-worth.

He was running to save his own skin.

Sorry, Mom, he thought to himself—legs picking up the tempo, lungs working double-time to put distance between him and home. *You're on your own with the colonel, today. Best of luck.*

One thing you can*not* hide is when you're crippled inside.

*

Who exactly was Chase Reed?

That was probably the $100,000 question up around Appleton way those days. It was almost certainly on the minds of many of the 198 students (give or take a kid or two) who attended class at Snow Creek High School—just a hop, skip, and proverbial jump from Appleton Park.

Chase's family moved to town from who-knows-where and took up residence in the old Shaw place. The Shaws (a nice family, a good bunch of kids, Pops often observed) had finally given up trying to make of go of their little hardware store on Fuller Avenue.

Mr. Shaw reluctantly took up his brother's offer to work for him in a metal fabrication plant near Seattle, and the family bid a reluctant good-bye to quiet, quaint Appleton forever. It was bad enough for the town to lose yet another of its small business owners; folks had to make the trip to Chapeeka or Weston for pretty near all their shopping needs, short of groceries. What was _really_ tough for the little town was losing _the Shaws,_ for they were well-liked and universally respected in the community.

It's hard to find replacements for wonderful neighbors who, for financial reasons, are forced to relocate outside the Valley. And the repetition of the theme down through the decades does not make it any easier.

Life goes on, however, and the good people of Appleton welcomed the Reeds to the Middle Valley, just as they had been (infrequently) welcoming new families for as long as anyone could remember. In general, departing residents were _not_ replaced by newcomers on a one-to-one basis. Since the floor had collapsed under the fruit industry, the trend had been more consistently like four-to-one; for every _four_ families leaving Appleton, there was, on average, a _single_ family coming in to call it home. As more and more businesses folded, and the opportunities shrank beyond tolerable limits, struggling parents packed their kids and cares into their cars, and solemnly struck out for greener pastures.

It was a slow process, this death spiral. A very sad process to bear witness to. Now, what the Reed family personified was a new wave of "commuter residents," an idea which was gaining acceptability with a younger, more mobile-minded generation of adults, and was finding favor up and down the twisty Kennawack Valley. Jobs could be found in Weston, all right, sometimes even in Chapeeka. But although those towns held out the lure of restaurants, shopping malls, and employment, many people simply did not wish to *live* there. Not when sleepy, laid-back little Appleton was just a 65-minute jaunt upstream. In fact, by the late '80s, a sizable number of Appletonians was opting to maintain a permanent residence in Mid Valley while earning a living somewhere else.

First off, there were the Crowls: Tim and Gayle. Trim and boyish, Kelsea's father was an insurance adjuster, and his bubbly, energetic wife worked at the county courthouse; both in Weston. Born and raised in Appleton, they had entered school together, graduated in the same class, and held their marriage ceremony in Appleton's historic old Methodist church on Marshall Lane. Kelsea and Jayme were both brought into the world at Good Samaritan Hospital in the city of Weston, but that was only because Appleton's Pioneer Memorial had been, by then, reduced to operating solely as a day clinic.

Then there were the LeMasters. Daniel owned and operated the Riverview Steak and Chop House in Weston. His wife, Paige, commuted with her husband every day to her studio—located in the Columbia Mall just four blocks south of the restaurant. They, too, were natives of the Middle Kennawack—though not of Appleton proper. And they, too, had graduated from high school together, two and five years after Tim and Gayle Crowl, respectively. The twins were born in Seattle (on a shopping trip, surprise!) but, like Kelsea and Jayme, Appleton was the only home they'd ever known.

Fulfilling a longtime dream to "get out of the city and re-sink some rural roots," Phillip and Bev Remarque quickly readjusted to small-town living (they were both originally Montana folk, remember?). It was especially satisfying from their shared adult perspectives to note how well Erik had adapted to the change, and to watch him bond up with well-adjusted, good-natured kids like Kelsea and the LeMasters. Phillip "lucked into" (as he oftentimes put it) the assistant editor position for the *Weston Ledger*, located in Weston, of course, while Bev secured a good job managing the OfficeWorld store in Chapeeka, midway along the rushing Kennawack River between little Appleton and the city of Weston.

A tightly interwoven network of global military obligations kept Colonel Tattenger out of town for the lion's share of each year. A *very mobile* commuter indeed was he!

His wife Lauren, of course, was locked securely into place executing airtight responsibilities as "military spouse/domestic engineer." She, and not many others, could be properly regarded as one of the select few permanent, *non-commuter* residents of the village…like it or not.

Even the unknowable Rita Cheney, Patch's mom, was another individual who had to be added to the list of traveling employees, since she regularly vanished into the aether for unpredictable lengths of time; returning with just enough earned income to maintain her largely vacated address at Paxton's junk hole.

Now, Dave and Dawn Reed, along with their two children, Chase and little Erin, were Appleton's newest community members—next to the Remarques. Dad and Mom Reed were both employed by Kaplan's Feed and Grain in Chapeeka. All of the aforementioned which, taken together, probably makes it sound as though lovable Pops Laarkin was the only guy around who lived where he worked and worked where he lived.

Such was not the case, in the strictest sense of the idea. But commuter employment *had,* by then, become a viable, growing lifestyle of choice in rural central Washington state. And if earning a living in

Weston while maintaining a residence in Appleton helped to mitigate the population drain on our favorite little town, why then, so much the better.

At any rate, the Reeds were embraced by their "next-doors" as full-fledged Appletonians in fair short order. Not _because_ they radiated any degree of social charm or warmth, but rather _in spite_ of the fact that they _didn't_. You see, it was never actually important, or even necessary, to be "Mr. and Mrs. Congeniality" in order to get along with Appleton's easy-paced villagers. Not everyone in town was _expected_ to embrace and engage in the social interaction of each other's company—like the Crowls, the LeMasters, Justin Thomas Michael Bench, and, more recently, the Remarques were typically wont to do. All that was really expected for full-circle acceptance by the slow-going people of the Middle Valley was a modicum of politeness, a neatly kept property frontage, and any/all of your dogs to be kenneled and quiet at night.

The Reeds kept pretty much to themselves—complying with all of the generally understood requests for civility—and were regarded as quiet, unobtrusive, slightly strange good neighbors. One would be happy to have them living alongside on the same block, but one would also probably only know them well enough to say "hi" whenever they were spotted out working in the yard. That went for their son, Chase, as well (but with a slightly _different, darker_ spin to it, shall we say?).

Now, the notable exception to the demeanor of _this_ particular family was the youngest Reed—Erin, age ten—whose effervescent personality had won her instant recognition as an indispensable member of a _new_ legion of Scalawags, or as Pops winkingly referred to them: The "_Scalawaglings_." For Erin Reed had found plenty of frolic and friendship in her new surroundings by linking directly up with Kelsea Crowl's super-charged little sister, Jayme.

And _that_ high-octane-fueled team became even more energized with the addition of (did you guess it?) Peyton Remarque! Go, Grr-rrrlz! Go!

Dramatically opposed to Erin's striking likeability, was the smoldering persona that inhabited her big brother, Chase. Big, _yes!_ The boy was alarmingly tall for his age; a *monster*, really. Dark complexioned, with dark eyes, permanently possessed of a solemn, intense expression, everything about him seemed to swallow light; to drain energy and activity into an un-illuminable black hole of uncertainty. Chase Reed was indeed endowed with more than a modicum of what Sandy LeMaster would insist, using 14 syllables, was *incontrovertible unintelligibility*. Not so much broadcasting chaos as simply demonstrating **no** identifiable characteristics, Chase did not so much move, as drift; did not so much speak, as communicate; did not so much live, as exist.

Chase neither watched nor observed. He just *looked*.

He was never heard to laugh or complain, never seen to smile or frown. A walking riddle. A living, breathing mystery—*that* was the embodiment of Chase Reed. He and his family had arrived in town a year before the Remarques, and in the span of four seasons, no one could claim to know very much about him, with the exception of two things— items which only deepened the speculation about his character and motives:

One: He tended to hang out, off and on, with Rodent and Patch. *Definitely not good!*

And two: He was often spotted at the public library checking in and out tall stacks of thick books. Odd.

People did not know quite what to make of him. Running in a pack of losers lent him an ill-defined quality that brought him across as somehow vaguely shadowy, or threatening. But the sheer literary tonnage through which he continually plowed kept everyone guessing as to just what was going on in those deep thoughts of his. So, that's who Chase Reed came to be known as by so many residents of the Middle Kennawack Valley:

"Deep Thoughts."

*

Officer Carlos Santiago eased his green and white police cruiser from northbound Ketelle Street onto Oregon Avenue and drove west. Being the only Kennawack County sheriff's deputy assigned to the Appleton area had its benefits, as well as its drawbacks.

To begin with, Carlos was pretty much on his own. No *immediate* supervisor or boss; *they* were located at the headquarters in Weston. No partner. Just his cruiser, his equipment, and the Middle Valley routes to run. And for a man of solitary persuasions, working *solo* was a very comfortable and gratifying situation in which to find himself.

Having lived his childhood in the squalor of a poor barrio in East L.A., Carlos Santiago had spent every living moment of his youthful years sharing, dividing, sacrificing, and compromising. Beds were shared, food was divided, privileges were sacrificed and personal space (read as *individuality*) was always compromised if you grew up in a poor neighborhood with nine brothers and sisters. It was *nice* to be *alone*.

And as to the *drawbacks* of his duty assignment—what exactly might *those* be?

Well, Deputy Santiago was pretty certain that they existed. He just hadn't been able to identify any of them as yet.

Back in Southern California, his Madre had taken in laundry, while his Padre labored in the blazing vegetable fields. This, to support a proliferating family that eventually included Tio Luis, Tia Maria, and Abuela Rosa; long-lived family members, ancient and worn well beyond employability. Being the eldest of his brothers and sisters, Carlos was the first fledgling out of the nest.

And far away he did fly.

He graduated from the police academy, third in a class of 44 rookies, and within a fortnight he was packed and headed for Washington state and a job with the Kennawack County Sheriff's Department.

Deputy Santiago was given jurisdiction over the Appleton unit; an area which ran north to south from Grass Lake to the Silver Creek Gorge, and west to east from Smithson Pass to Chapeeka. Nearly 1,500 square miles of solitary, scenic, lightly populated patrol routes. For a single man 32 years of age who had propelled himself out of the slums of Los Angeles, the deputy and the assignment comprised a marriage made in heaven.

Santiago received orders and checked in regularly with HQ via the two-way radio in his cruiser. He also completed a daily log accounting for his time, routes, check-in points, and record of occurrences using a portable word processor which had been supplied by the Sheriff's Department. Other than that, Carlos' only other requirements for his position were to make punctual Wednesday trips to Weston for paperwork completion, and to be in attendance for any and all training, continuing education, and professional development exercises.

It was a great job! A great life and career for a competent, young officer who valued his "alone time" every bit as much as he did his oath to serve and to protect. Violent crime and unlawful activities of a grisly nature were virtually foreign to the insulated valley of the Kennawack; that kind of filth and horror were hallmarks of city life in places like the home he left behind—places like L.A.

Petty theft, minor vandalism, maybe an auto accident now and then, those were the kinds of calls to which Officer Santiago was asked to respond. He performed his duties with competency and compassion, and he mailed one-third of every paycheck to a tiny, impoverished house in East Los Angeles at the end of each and every month.

Middle morning breathed a blend of cut grass and floral scents through the driver's side window of Santiago's automobile. He stopped the car and inhaled; eyes closed, a small smile emerging at the corners of his straight, thin lips. Motionless, the cessation of moving air brought immediate sun warmth to his round, brown cheeks. It was gonna be a hot one! *Pops would love it! Plenty of "Jool-Eye Throats" converging on the 'Soda Queen!'* There was the sound of a lawn trimmer down the street. An assortment of birds made their presence know. Somewhere, a dog barked.

Es un dia muy bonito. Verdad! he thought to himself. *OK, Let's see what nuestro malo muchacho, our bad boy, was up to last night.*

"Why Ossifer Santiago! Whadda nice surprise! An' how're you doin' this most excellent summer morn?"

Patch sat, legs outstretched, his back leaning luxuriously against the thick trunk of an elm tree in the middle of Appleton Park. Deputy Santiago had pulled his patrol car over, parked and locked it, and was striding in an easy-going manner toward the reclining figure; a look of resigned understanding painted across his features, thumbs hooked over the tops of the wide, black belt from which was suspended his service revolver. He stopped five paces from the boy, and removed his sunglasses; shaking his head and smiling—a tightlipped surrender to the sheer avoidable, unnecessary _waste_ of it all.

Patch took a long pull on the enormous "ThirstyMan" cola cup straw. The last half-ounce of soda sklorked loudly across the shards of ice as he finished it off with a noisy, sucking gesture of contempt.

"Dude! You looked stressed! Alla bad guys skip town an' leave ya with nothin' to do but patrol the park?" Patch laid the empty plastic cup on the grass beside him, crossed his legs at the ankles, and flashed Santiago a cold, chipped-tooth display that passed for a smile.

"Naw," the deputy played along, "most of the dirtbags who have been workin' so hard to get themselves behind bars have been successful." He held Patch's gaze evenly.

"That frees me up to look after the 'wannabes'—you know—the small-time toughs who waste my time _and_ theirs practicing for a shot at _making it_ as a, you know, counter-culture criminal-slash-hero archetype. Haven't seen any around lately, have you Patch?"

"Well, goodness no, Ossifer Sanfranciso!" sneered Patch with mock alarm. "But if there's _anything_ I can do as a civic-minded youth, why, I'd be just pickled tink to lend a helpin' hand...especially to a law enforcer ossifer such as yerself." He watched Santiago carefully, trying to gauge his reaction to the sarcasm. But the lawman gave away nothing, and Patch continued. "Anything pertikaller troublin' the community this fine day?"

"Only about forty garbage cans that were tipped over sometime in the middle of the night last night," replied Santiago. "But you probably wouldn't know anything about that, would you Patch?"

"Gee whillikers, no, Ossifer! That's terrible! Why, I bet that made an awful mess for everyone." Patch picked his nose and regarded Santiago with cold detachment.

"Your mom gone again this week, Patch?" inquired Carlos. His voice was gentle; almost fatherly.

"Where my ol' lady is, is nobody's stinkin' business, Ossifer Sanitation!" Patch erupted. ***"You got somethin' to say to me, why doncha come out an' say it?"*** The boy suddenly throttled back, lowering his voice, and fixed his gaze at an invisible point 200 feet in front of his eyes. "Otherwise, donchu have a garbage gremlin to be bringin' to justice?"

"When was the last time you had a hot meal?" offered Santiago.

"When's the last time you brushed yer teeth?" seethed Patch.

Carlos studied the boy in silence for a moment. "I know what it's like to go without," he said finally. "I came up poor—just like you, Pat. But there are still *choices* to be made. Choices that can deliver you to a decent, ordinary life, and ones that can bring you more misery than you can possibly imagine."

"Puh-leeze!" moaned Patch. "Spare me the sales pitch on how *I, too* can someday turn out bein' a big ol' hornkin' success story…like you fr'instance. Whadda _you_ know enough about _anything_ ta be givin' _me_ advice on life options?"

"I know this," countered Carlos. "Whoever dumped those garbage cans all over people's driveways last night is probably the same person who spray-painted the elementary school last month. Probably also the same guy who went around slashing garden hoses and bustin' up county signs last summer, too."

"Awww, somebody runnin' amuk, an' makin' you look bad in yer perfession, Marshal SanDiego?" Patch, oozing; his tone dripping with affectation.

Deputy Sheriff Carlos Santiago chewed an ear hook of his sunglasses and shook his head again, weighing his thoughts carefully before continuing. "Somebody's causing a considerable amount of damage around here, Patch. Somebody's angry about something, and he's taking it out on just about everybody in the whole of the Middle Kennawack area. That *somebody* is running between the raindrops, so to speak. He's gonna get caught, partner. That much is for a certainty. He's gonna get caught. And when he does, he's gonna be 'sent downstream.' Do you know what that means? I think you do."

Patch continued to glare into the near distance, stone-faced and silent as the deputy continued.

"It won't be a short trip, and it won't be a pleasant trip, I can tell you that. And I wouldn't want to be that guy. Not for all the badges, money, or success in the world."

He replaced his sunglasses, pushed them snugly up the bridge of his nose, and turned to leave. Taking two steps toward the cruiser, he stopped and half-turned toward the boy—venomous, lying in the shade of the park tree.

"If you ever think you might like to have somebody to talk to, someone you can trust, even with a secret that is hurtful, or if you ever even need a couple of bucks, or maybe something to eat. I want you to know that I'll do whatever I can to help you out. I mean that, Pat. Just give it some thought."

Patch watched the police car drive out of sight. He laughed suddenly, derisively and kicked the empty plastic cup across the grass; scratching his ribs and heading for Main Street.

"What a complete jerk!" grousing bitterly to nobody there. "What an absolute moron! That cop couldn't catch a wallet thief, even if the dude had his hand inside the hip pocket of his damned uniform. And all that crap about lending a hand? What kind of a feeb does he take me for? Man! What a _load!_"

WITH THE EXCEPTION OF THE TWO LONGLEGS, THE PARK IS EMPTY THIS MORNING; IT SEEMS THAT EVERYONE IS BUSY WITH OTHER THINGS…ELSEWHERE. BUT <u>YOU</u> ARE THERE, AND <u>YOU</u> OVERHEAR THE GRUMBLED MUTTERINGS OF THE YOUNG LONGLEGS. FROM NOT SO VERY HIGH ABOVE THEM, IN CLUTCHING-WITH-TALONS TIME, YOU DISCERN AND INTERNALIZE EVERYTHING THAT TRANSPIRES. EVERYTHING. SECRETIVE CROW!

Patch had had a busy night, all right—quietly going about the twisted business of making innocent people pay for a rotten life that he in no way invited upon himself. But "Ossifer Salmonella" had been right about one thing, at least. It _is_ good to have the ear of a confidante when it comes to imparting secrets of the soul. And since he had a full night's worth of secrets to share, he reckoned it was about time to uncover the whereabouts of someone worthy of his tales; someone who understood and valued the actions and reactions born of pure misery.

Time to go find Rodent.

*

"If we give ya a buck, will ya _slow down_ on some of this school building work?"

Kelsea and Jayme Crowl had tiptoed up behind Justin who was happily humming his way through a downspout repair job on the sunward side of Rosewood Elementary School.

The young man broke a wide grin and countered, "Well, now. A whole _dollar,_ you say. Hmm. If yer willin' to part with money of _that_ kind, I'd say there must be a darned good reason for you wantin' to see this work order come to an end. Now, what might _that_ be?"

Kelsea nudged her sister with her elbow, barely suppressing a giggle.

"Well, if you'd work a little slower, Justin, maybe school wouldn't have to open until, um, let's say, half-past October! How about it?" Jayme laughed. "Will a buck do it for ya?"

"Gotta better idea," Justin, in full-on, ear-to-ear smile mode, extending a fistful of hand tools. "I'll give _you_ a buck to stay here an' finish this job whilst me an' Kels make a beeline to the Swimmin' Hole before the good spot on the beach gets taken. Deal?"

Jayme rolled her eyes in theatrical exasperation. "I _knew_ it!" she complained. "I just _knew_ it. He's holdin' out for _more money_! Fine! I'm going over to Erin's house. Maybe _she's_ got some cash she'd like to throw into my very own, _personally made-up plan_ for makin' summer vacations _longer_. An' I'll be back if she does, Justin. So don't you go raising your prices while I'm gone now, y'hear?" With that, she hopped on her bike and raced, laughing, across the playground toward Water Street.

"Keep him talking, sis!" she yelled over her shoulder. "Maybe ask him to sing one of his new songs for you. Just stall 'im 'til I get back!"

Kelsea and Justin stared at one other, wide-eyed and gape-mouthed; on the verge of disbelief. "If that don't beat all," Justin finally surmised. "We're gonna hafta start callin' that little gal 'K.J.', I reckon."

"'K.J.?'" repeated Kelsea.

"Mm-hmm, 'Kelsea Junior.' There ain't hardly a _hair's_ worth of difference between the two of ya!"

"Why Justin Michael Thomas Bench, what_ever_ do you _mean_? Everyone knows that Jayme Crowl—a.k.a. _Sister Sinister_—is the _scourge_ of the neighborhood while I, _myself_, am widely known to be a young lady of manner and taste—quiet, sensitive, and thoughtful—the very—"

"Kels?" interrupted Justin, looking her straight in the eye. "I'll give ya a buck if you'll go tell it all to someone else."

Kelsea punched him playfully on the arm and Justin feigned _serious_ injury, requesting an immediate phone call to the school district for a substitute custodian. "I'm thinkin' maybe some water therapy'd be good for these damaged arm muscles," he moaned. "I'll meet you at the Swimmin' Hole 25 minutes after my replacement gets here."

"I've patched you through to the district office, sir," said Kelsea, holding her left hand to her ear, faux-phone-like.

"Please don't use the word 'Patch' around me, madam," winced Justin.

"Sub Services wants to know the exact nature and extent of your injury, sir."

"Tell 'em it's serious, life threatenin', maybe even epidemic on a world scale."

Kelsea repeated his instructions word-for-word into her "handphone."

"Tell 'em I'm bleedin' all over the playground," wheezed Justin. "Tell 'em my tongue's hangin' out, an' my face is ashen an' sweaty. Tell 'em my dog is lonesome for me, an' I ain't even dead yet—but I soon _will_ be if they don't…"

"Justin?" quipped Kelsea. "Sub Services says to quit your belly-achin', and get back to work."

"Oh."

"And Justin?"

"Yeah?"

"Sub Services says they're docking your paycheck a buck for bothering them."

*

Justin went whistling back to work under the dome of a fabulous summer sky the color of lapis lazuli. Kelsea hung around for a while, half expecting Jayme to return with Peyton Remarque, for a joint assault on poor Justin's work project. But they never did, and it was pretty evident that the two of them had found adventure (or mischief) in some other corner of their fourth-grade world.

"Oh, hey. I almost forgot why I came out here today." Kelsea handed a Phillips-head screwdriver up the ladder to her friend. "Mom and Dad want you to come over for a barbecue tonight. And they said to tell you to be *sure* to bring your guitar. You *can* come, can't you?"

"Sure! Sounds like fun. Who all's gonna be there, an' what else should I bring along besides Woody?"

"Well, there'll be you, us, the LeMasters, um, the Remarques will be there for sure—it's sort of a welcome-to-the-neighborhood kinda thing anyways, right? So that's (she counted in her head) 'bout 13 I guess. No, better make that 14. Erin Reed'll show up for sure, even though the rest of her family will probably pass on the invite again. God, can't you just see Deep Thoughts playin' *badminton* in our back yard?"

"That's some pretty frightening imagery, Kels," agreed Justin with a chuckle. "*That* guy'd know how to put the 'bad' in 'badminton' for sure!"

Kelsea laughed. "So are you on it? It'll be really cool! Dad got out the Chinese lanterns, and there'll be lawn darts, and croquet, maybe a little volleyball, lots of burgers, steaks, whatever you like."

"OK! You bet. What time should I show up? Oh, and can Kooper come along? Or is Mr. Jinks still bent outta shape from the mistreatment he got the *last* time a dog invaded his kitty kingdom?"

Kelsea smiled. "Naw, he's OK now. Bring Kooper along, and we'll make sure that Jinksy is kept in my room where he can rule in safety. Um, does 5:30 sound good for you?"

"Yep. I'll be done here 'round about 4:00. I can head home, take a quick shower an' be back with Woody and Kooper just about the time the burgers hit the grill. Oh, hey! I made up a big bowl of my special potato salad last night. Haven't even dipped into it yet. Would ya like me to bring it along, too?"

"*Would* I? Are you kidding? That potato salad of yours is to die for! Good timing, Justin. You must have known that a big potluck was in the wind. Tell you what. I've got some errands to run for Mom, so I'll scoot along and let you get back to work. But I'll swing by, say, about 3:45?

We can ride up to the quarry together, and while you're getting cleaned up, me and Koop can pick some salmonberries for tonight's dessert. That way I can help you carry all of your stuff down to my place for the feast."

"Kelsea Crowl, you are *'indubitably'* a lady of 'manner and taste.'" Justin stepped off the ladder and bowed deeply.

"Good Sir Justin," she preened coquettishly, "you are *only* saying that because it is so undeniably true! Later, skater!"

*

CROW KNOWS ABOUT SOME EVENTS THAT OCCURRED PRIOR TO THE START OF THE CROWL BARBECUE. DON'T YOU, CROW? EVERY-HEARING, EVERY-SEEING WINGED WATCHER!

Justin temporarily parted company with Kelsea and Kooper, who had both trotted off across an incline of tinder-dry grass in the direction of a copse of salmonberry bushes at woods edge. *That'll keep 'em busy for an hour or so*, he thought to himself. *Enough time to get myself ready for the shindig.*

It was shade darkened and cool inside the quarry cabin, with a thick, green-leafed overgrowth embracing the structure on all four sides, spilling across the roof to break and block the heat-light of Appleton's summer inferno. Justin slipped off his hiking boots, leaving them next to a pair of cowboy boots and some tennis shoes on a woven mat beside the heavy wooden door.

Crossing the bare hardwood floor in his stocking feet, Justin stripped off his T-shirt and absently gathered up another one which had been left lying on the arm of the dusky-toned, overstuffed sofa. He'd do the laundry and cleaning tomorrow. For the time being, he'd have to make do with a quick pick-up, so he could shower, shave, and shove off.

He straightened the deep burgundy wool carpet so that it lay squarely beneath a hexagonal oak coffee table, upon whose surface was strewn magazines; mostly hiking, camping, and cross-country skiing. Colonel

Tattenger would have appreciated the décor of Justin's tiny living room, if only for the ceiling-high bookcase that covered the right wall, and was filled to brimming with a generous assortment of literary genres.

The other walls, to the left and beside the door, were windowed and contained framed artwork. The still life paintings and landscape photos that were favored by the young man had been purchased for next-to-nothing at the Goodwill store in Chapeeka. Those, and the books which he displayed on the carefully dusted shelves (also purchased at Goodwill), reflected the tastes of a soul whose life energy was simple and earthy; never showy or pretentious.

Behind the sofa, to the right of a matching armchair and ottoman, stretched an eight-foot-long, waist-high dining counter which separated the living room from the kitchenette. Overhead, a row of cabinets were arranged over the bar, allowing plenty of chat space across the countertop between the adjoining rooms. An unadorned reading lamp sat upon an end table situated between the sofa and armchair. And beside the lamp was a double-framed photo holder; on one side, the picture of a well-groomed man—on the other, a young woman who looked a lot like Justin.

Notably absent from an otherwise normal, if modest, household arrangement was the apparent lack of a cathode ray tube; that is to say, a television set. It wasn't that Justin was opposed to TV programming in general. It was just that, to him, it all seemed so insipid, and there were few things that Justin disdained more than a waste of his time.

Movies? Maybe…sometimes with friends at The Odeon near the park. But game shows? Sitcoms? A soccer match? All interspersed with legions of mind-numbing infomercials and insufferable sales pitches? Ix-nay on *that* it-shay. Life is too damn short, and he *far* preferred hiking, biking, swimming, and cross-country skiing over, under, around, and through the middle and upper reaches of the Kennawack River Valley to sitting, frog-eyed, in front of a glowing box of fake imagery.

Justin's little cabin did, however, feature a rather stylish home entertainment center. Shaped like a jukebox from the '50s, the glass-door in front opened to reveal shelves housing a turntable, tape deck, CD player, and receiver. Beside it rested two large wooden cabinets containing no fewer than 300 long-play record albums and at least as many CDs and cassette tapes. It was common knowledge that the only things in the *world* that Justin M. T. Bench loved more than listening to music (rock, blues, jazz, funk, classical, you-name-it!) was playing Woody, goofin' with Kooper (with a 'K') and hangin' out with his friends. Although you'd have to consider the day, the circumstances, and, for that matter, possibly even *the wind direction* if you wanted to correctly arrange the order of *that* particular list. At the near end of the armchair was a guitar stand, and a small ceramic bowl containing a capo, a tuning fork, and an assortment of picks. Close to the door was a hutch with a dozen open shelves displaying knick-knacks and hand-me-downs from his childhood days with his uncle—his foster dad, in the city of Weston. Justin had benefited and blossomed from the steady guiding hand of his mother's brother; the man who had unselfishly nurtured his progress from a child to a young man of 18. The quarry estate, where he now resided, had come into his possession upon the passing of his uncle/father, and his simple financial needs were adequately managed through honest labor requested in exchange for honest labor provided. That, and a trust fund that more or less guaranteed against Justin Bench's inadvertently falling into a state of fiscal ruin.

Justin's Uncle Thomas was actually much more than simply his benefactor and role model. Thomas had been, in the truest sense of the word, his *father*.

Past the kitchenette was the storeroom on the right, his bedroom to the left, and the bathroom at the end of the hall. The entire interior was paneled in knotty pine, giving the place a soft feeling of warmth and drawn-together coziness which, particularly during the long, snowy months, induced guests to imagine they were sitting inside a Norman Rockwell painting.

So, the rustic quarry cabin and all its homey contents provided sanctuary for Justin Bench; a quiet retreat into which he could simply dissolve and disappear at the end of the day; ripe with remembrances of good times happily spent with the people he loved, and who loved *him*— Appletonians. Of course, Justin acknowledged to himself, as well as to everyone else, that the *real* heart and soul of the quarry cabin resided in the atmosphere of friendship and sea-deep trust that blossomed most fully in the presence of that pack of high school comrades known valley-wide as the Scalawags. For although he understandably, and justifiably, had earned the allegiance and respect of an entire community, the degree of freedom with which Kelsea and the others were permitted to come and go was a testimony to the breadth and scope of that ironclad relationship.

Justin stacked a couple of dirty plates in the sink, and ran some water over them. He swept some toast crumbs into his hand and deposited them in the paper bag under the sink. Reminding himself to grab the potato salad (*and* Woody!) on the way out, he glanced around the cabin with semi-approval (*Close enough for now*) and headed for the bathroom at the end of the hall to shower off the day's dust.

Time to get ready for some music, and some fun!

*

From birth to death, everyone participates in the process of creating his own memories. Good/bad, happy/sad, funny/scary, enlightening/perplexing; they are all interwoven within the tapestry of shared experiences. And the richness, purpose, and meaning of those life experiences will surround you like a blanket in your old age. They are the keys—the determinants—of just how warm you will remain when your life story draws to a close, and your energy force diminishes, commencing the slow, cooling return to its wellspring.

Some _great_ memories will be born in, amongst and around that covey of neighbors and friends during the night of the Crowl barbecue. At one point during the long evening of relaxed merriment and laughter, Justin will be asked why he is holding his hands in front of his chest, arms extended and palms out, smiling for all the world like a man in possession of the world's most ancient, open secret. "Why, I'm warmin' my hands in the glow of this neighborly friendship," will be his smiling reply.

What a generous statement! What a memorable summer night this will be!

Justin and Woody start the ball rolling by leading the entire entourage in a sing-along. The song is called *Dead Skunk in the Middle of the Road*—an oldie by Loudon Wainwright III, and a favorite at this type of get-together.

Tons of songcraft swirl skyward from the backyard potluck party on Meadow Street this night. *'Bring Somethin' Round, And We'll Have a Ball'* leaves everyone clasping their sides, gasping for air between peals of laughter. Justin's newest composition—*'Imaginary Man'*—brings moisture to the eyes of all who hear it. The guitarist moves through 15 or 20 more originals, and well-known tunes alike; caressing the melodies from Woody's well-worn frame while a sliver of a moon climbs through the black vault of stars wheeling overhead; steadfastly marking the passing of time well spent.

At one point early on, Kelsea and Jayme's dad, Tim, is seen limping away from the volleyball net. He is smiling gamely, as everyone knows he is inclined to do at these gatherings. But those who have watched closely know that, in diving for a save, he has re-injured his hip; the one that was broken two years ago in the Silver Creek blaze that nearly took his life.

In his youthful years, Tim was an all-star athlete at Appleton's Snow Creek High School, and he often openly admits to missing those bygone opportunities to express himself in physical exercise. But he knows better than to push the envelope too far, and brushing off his bruised ego, he wisely (if painfully!) relegates himself to the duties of the barbecue grill; shifting gears smoothly and without complaint. He has, in his possession, enough sporting memories to keep him warm for the rest of his life.

Erik affords little mercy in manhandling all comers in the Third Annual Crowl Bowl, which is not actually a football game (as it may sound), but a croquet match. His dad, Phillip, jokingly speculates that his *own son* "may have enhanced his game performance via the illicit use of steroids," and he threatens to expose the abuse in an upcoming editorial in the Weston Ledger. Erik, rabid as a badger in the defense of his sterling silver gamesmanship, insists that he is in no need of muscle drugs, because he has been bequeathed the "body of a Greek god" through genetic gifts inherited from his "ripped" Mom, who just happens to weigh in at a willow-slim 98 pounds.

And then there is Stuart, who—although arriving a bit late—labors diligently, confidently through the consumption of three—count 'em, *three!*—'LeMasterBurgers.' He builds 'em *big*, Stuie does. As Sandy somewhat skeptically points out, "He is serious enough about these barbecue affairs to insist upon demonstrating to everyone that his culinary expertise is a valid form of self-expression; an art form which should not, nay, *must not* be underestimated!"

"I eat, therefore I am," Stuart states flatly.

"Don't worry," Erik later adds playfully. "He won't make himself sick. He's a *true artist*, and he understands his medium well. Get it? Burgers? Medium-well? Mwaah-ha-ha-ha-ha!"

Hmm…well, at some point during the festivities, Deputy Santiago stops by—kidding around about "seeing smoke, and hearing a lot of noise; following up on a complaint of public rowdiness; making an investigation into possible criminal activity," and so forth. He cannot stay very long because, technically, he is still on duty. But while he is there, he regales all guests with a lovely Spanish tune on good old Woody before gratefully accepting one of Stuart's unspeakably enormous 'LeMasterpieces' in a take-out paper bag. He promises everyone to drop back when he is finished for the day, and he does!

The "Scalawag*lings,*" for their part, are omnipresent; everywhere at the same time.

Look at 'em go!

"*No one* has the right to have *that* much fun in life!" remarks Paige LeMaster, shaking her head in wonder.

Always together, Jayme, Erin, and Peyton never seemed to waste a moment's time in their rush to find creative new ways of conquering small-town boredom. The cyclone of giggles, squeals, and whoops constitutes a sustained state of perpetual motion; *miraculously* averting near-spillages, near-breakages, and innumerable near-body injuries with the deftness, dexterity, and balance of a well-choreographed ensemble. Their whirlwind activity amounts to little more than what Sandy defines as a "non-stop, no-fault, no-holds-barred, near-catastrophic, marginally controlled wreck-fest."

To repeat: Look at 'em *go*!

Freckle-nosed Kelsea, and coily-haired Sandy become caught up in the heat of a badminton match (one-on-one) in which they duel to a grueling draw. After helping the collective moms tote a metric ton of snacks from the kitchen to the picnic tables, they attempt to drum up some frisbee interest in Kooper who, with half a vanilla shake and two burger patties in his scruffy, round belly, is *clearly* more interested in finding a place to lay down! Preferably, a spot where he can keep an eye on Jinksy, who is only too happy to engage himself in a stare-down with a dog, as long as a thick pane of glass is in place to separate the contestants.

Those are among, but not limited to, the many happy 'photographs,' captured and heart locked for all the years to come by some of the neighbors in and around Meadow Street.

Appleton, Washington. Mid-summer, new-ish-ly in the 1990s.

And as the slow-motion, expanding stain of lavender and apricot evenly smears its crown upon the western ridges of the Cascade chain bordering town, Kelsea asks for and receives parental permission to accompany her friend, along with his guitar, his dog, and some empty salad bowls back up Quarry Road. It *is* getting a *little* on the *late* side…sort of. But that's OK. They both have bike lights, and reflective shirts. After all, it's *only* Appleton. And *all* are safe from hate and harm here.

Aren't they?

*

YOU WANDER—WIND LIKE, JUST <u>LIKE</u> THE WIND—AT YOUR OWN PLEASURE...IN YOUR OWN TIME, FOR YOUR OWN PURPOSES. AND YOU, CROW—HIDDEN BLACK SHADOW IN ENCROACHING PURPLE NIGHT—BORE WITNESS TO WHAT OCCURRED EARLY THAT EVENING.

DURING THE PARTY. AFAR FROM ALL THE NOISY FUN. UP AT THE QUARRY SITE.

They knew that something was wrong when they first noticed that the cabin door hung open a crack. A pale slice of yellow light penetrated the darkened woods, spending its feeble energy within a stone's throw of Justin's log home. He had seen it first, halting in his tracks, and staring in mute disbelief. He was a man who always locked up before going anywhere. *Always.* Tonight was no exception, and full-well he knew it.

"Uh-oh," murmured Kelsea to herself.

"Uh-huh," echoed Justin, "I've got a bad feelin' about this."

They did not recall, hours later, dropping their bicycles right where they stood. They had no recollection whatever of racing up that crackly slope; ankle-deep in sun-toasted wild grass. No memory of warm, 'Jool-Eye' night air, scented lightly with the aromas of earth, stone, needle, and leaf. Of cricket call and frog song broadcasting simple summer-long messages of contentment to any and all who are, for one moment, willing to place their distractions on 'pause'…to listen with their hearts, and dare to wonder. Like a kid does.

What they *did* remember could be retrieved for years to come; with the clarity of a precisely cut diamond. They remembered reaching the cabin door at the same time; to stand, gasping in heart-thumping silence, before the ruins that *used to be* Justin Bench's living room. Everything experienced or endured in the past, everything anticipated or striven for in the future qualitatively *dissolved* at the speed of hate into a thousand shades of numb, leaden *now*ness.

How long did Kelsea and Justin stand, wide-eyed and stiffened with heart shock, in the doorway of the old caretaker's cabin at Appleton Quarry? How long did it take them to process the grief they spontaneously shared on a soul wide scale? How much time passed in the creation of mental constructs meaningful enough to allow them to assimilate the waste and utter humiliation of random, senseless destruction? It could be said, with *some* degree of truthfulness and accuracy, that they are standing there still. To this very day.

"Well, there's where he/she/they got in…in through that window screen," said Justin, hooking a thumb toward the bathroom. "And out the front door when playtime was all done." Grim-faced and quiet, Justin solemnly began moving about the room, picking up broken articles, righting overturned furniture, returning items to their proper places; straightening, correcting, replacing, sweeping.

Kelsea continued to stare transfixed at the spectacle of chaos and disorder. When she finally broke the reverie of her silence, she marched purposefully to the telephone.

"*That* tears it!" hissing through her clenched teeth. "I'm calling Carlos Santiago *right now!*"

"Don't, Kels," Justin stood, holding the remnants of the table lamp. "Please don't do that."

"*What!* Justin, you are the victim of a *crime* here. Don't you *realize* that? This isn't just some message scribbled on a window, this goes *beyond* the level of a…some kind of *sick* prank! This is *vandalism*, Justin! It's breaking and entering! Look over there! They tore up your window screen to get in here…and rip everything up! You need to get Carlos involved with this, and if *you* don't, then *I* will!"

"Just don't, Kels. I'm askin' as your friend. *Please*, just…don't."

"Justin, I can NOT _understand_ why you're taking this position. You can't just permit yourself to be…" the girl groped for words, "repeatedly _victimized_," she finally blurted.

"It's degrading, it's inhumane! It's…it's _against the damn law_, Justin! And if Sandy or any of our troops were here right now, they'd tell you the same thing. You need to _move_ on this before it gets any _worse!_"

Justin eased himself into the old armchair. Sighing with weariness and disappointment, he reached for his guitar and began lightly strumming; following a series of chord progressions with no particular pattern or sequence.

"Kelsea," he began slowly, "there's quite a bit about my past that you don't know about. Things that happened when I was your age that helped to shape me; made me who I am today. Not _what_ I am, but _who_ I am."

The girl felt a rush of emotion, swelling from distant points deep within her, and she wrestled to keep control of her tears.

"Justin, I," she stammered, "I don't care about—"

"I'll try an' tell ya more about it sometime, Kels. But for now, just try to understand that I don't wanna draw any attention to myself. I just wanna fit in, as much like everybody else as I possibly can. People _like_ me, Kelsea, mostly because _they_ know that _I_ know the difference between right 'n' wrong, and that I'll always make the right choice when it comes down to decidin' between the two." He paused, looking the girl straight in the eye. "Let's face it, Kelsea. I ain't exactly the sharpest tool in the shed. But I don't want anybody's charity. I don't want anybody feelin' sorry over me for any reason at all. And I don't need _anyone_ to help me out of a jam when I'm able-bodied enough to solve my own problems. I may not _be_ much or even _know_ much, but I've gotta prove to folks that I am _not_ a burden for someone to hafta tote. I can stand on my own two feet, like, well…like I was taught."

He picked up the double-framed photograph of the handsome man and the pretty young woman; tracing his fingertip over the cracked glass and gently placing it back upon the righted end table. "Can you understand what I'm sayin', Kelsea Crowl?"

Kelsea slowly lowered the receiver and regarded her good friend. She was dangerously close to coming apart at the seams, and when she finally spoke, her tone was paced and deliberate.

"I'm not even gonna *begin* to tell you how much we all care about you, Justin. How much this whole *town* cares for you," she began.

"With a few notable exceptions, I reckon," he rebutted.

"This is bad skoobies, Justin. Seriously bad skoobs. I understand your need for privacy with your personal life, and maybe we can talk about it someday, if you think I can help you. But if you won't let me call Deputy Santiago, then the least I can do is call my dad."

The young man shook his head and studied his boot tips.

"Justin, I won't let you stop me this time."

More body language, indicative of an unspoken disagreement.

"Hello, Daddy?" she already had her father on the line.

Justin looked evenly into Kelsea's frost gray eyes and mouthed a single word; softer than a whisper—inaudible, really—yet understood with more clarity and certainty than could have been rendered possible with an ear-searing scream.

"Please," he lip-shaped.

"Yeah, I'm up at the quarry now. No, no, everything's all right, well, *kind of.* But, um, I've got somethin' I need to ask you."

"Please."

"It's just that, uh, just that, well, Justin's place has been—"

"Please."

"...been...um—"

"Please."

"...been wrecked by...a bunch of raccoons. No, well, we think through the bathroom screen window, but they really made a mess. Yeah. Uh-huh. Yep, and I was wonderin' if you'd give me an extra half-hour to help him get things straightened up? Uh-huh, sure, Dad, thanks a bunch. Yeah, I'll be home in about 45 minutes. Uh-huh, yeah, no problem. Thanks again, Daddy! I love you, too."

"Thank you!" said Justin, still soundlessly mouthing the words.

"Oh, and Dad? Justin says 'thanks a boat-load!' Mm-hmm. Bye!"

She hung up, smiling weakly and looking around the ravaged cabin for a place to begin.

"I'll start with the living room if you want to do the kitchen," she offered. "But first maybe you'd better scout around a little and see what the rest of the place looks like."

It was a good idea, in more ways than one, and Justin was back just inside of five minutes with the welcome news that most of the damage had been confined to the big room—the combination kitchen/living area. So while he slipped in an Elvis CD and goofed good-naturedly about guitars, music trivia, and anything else in the way of prattle that he could use to detract from the event which had scarred the evening, the two slowly set about the task of putting the cabin back together.

They finally parted company at 11:00 that night; hearts heavy, but heads held high.

And hooking pinky fingers in their patented show of solidarity, they agreed to chase down Erik and the LeMasters, first thing in the morning, for a brainstorming powwow.

The cabin at Appleton Quarry would be safe until then, for it was unlikely that the perpetrator(s) would be willing to run the risk of returning to the scene of the violation so soon.

However, each of them—Justin and Kelsea—retained a bit of information, each from the other that evening. Kelsea's secret, which she never divulged to her friend, was the fact that she rode her mountain bike home that night at speeds which were _far_ from safe; given the road conditions, and the poor visibility. That, and the fact that she cried every foot of the way back to town.

Justin's secret was a bit of evidence he'd discovered (and subsequently withheld) in the bathroom while assessing the damage to his cabin. Correctly judging that Kelsea's capacity for dealing with any more tough news had to be pretty much *maxed out* for one day, he wisely restored the bathroom to its former condition, vowing to produce his finding and broach the subject at tomorrow's meeting with the Scalawags. He could already guess what the reaction would be when he showed them the message that had been scrawled across his bathroom mirror.

One that read: **"ARE YOU <u>STILL</u> HERE?"**

And that had been written using that same damn mocha brown lipstick.

*

What emerged from the stars and scars of Friday night was a Saturday morning that could have been culled from a collection of Michael Hague illustrations. Sunny and splendiferous; bees buzzing about their business in green and purple carpets of wind-wavering clover; it was the picture-perfect day in which you would expect to find Justin Bench—guitar in hand, Kooper at his feet—strumming and smiling on the pine deck of the quarry cabin.

And in fact, that's exactly where they *did* find him, just a Crowl Freckle past 9:00 am on the morning after the barbecue. Kelsea had already taken the time to fill everyone in on the misadventure of the night before. But of course, the question on their collective minds was: "Had Justin uncovered any new clues in the meantime?"

"As a matter of fact, I have," Justin articulated, slowly, uneasily, as if he was about to break new ground, and he wasn't at all sure how to go about it. "But before I get into *that*, I promised Kelsea here that I'd explain a little about my upbringing, so as to give her...an' *all* of you, really, a better understandin' of the way I *am* about things. Especially in light of what's been goin' on around the quarry lately."

He paused, carefully noting the expression on each face. Finding the quiet patience and unspoken affirmation he sought, he continued. "Anyroads, I figured that, well, anything I can say to Kelsea, I can pretty much say to all of ya. We're pretty much in this together, more or less anyway, and I know you wanna stick with me until we get to the bottom, and sort the whole damn business out. It's the way we *are* about one another."

"I don't mean to barge in, but I saw something late yesterday afternoon that may have a bearing on Justin's problem," inserted Stuart suddenly.

A nudge and a glance from his sister told him that whatever he had could wait; it needed to be subordinated to the story Justin was laboring to unfold. Stuart nodded his agreement, and made a mental note to speak his piece when the time was right.

Then…three darned-near tenth-graders, one almost-ninth-grader and a mild-mannered mutt of mixed heritage settled in for what proved to be a lengthy story of desertion and redemption.

THE AUDIENCE WAS JOINED BY A LARGE, BLACK CROW—IN CLUTCHING-WITH-TALONS TIME—HIGH OVERHEAD ON A PINE LIMB. ALMOST OUT OF SIGHT, BUT WELL WITHIN EARSHOT, THE CROW WAS (YOU WERE)—HOW SHALL IT BE DESCRIBED?— ATTENTIVE, AND AT THE SAME TIME SEEMINGLY OBLIVIOUS TO THE BANTER AND BUSTLING OF HUMAN ACTIVITIES JUST A FEW METERS BELOW.

YOU…CROW. THIS IS THE STORY *YOU* OVERHEARD, AS IT WAS IMPARTED TO HIS COMPANIONS BY A SAD, STRONG, SIMPLE YOUNG MAN WITH THE IMPROBABLE NAME OF JUSTIN M. T. BENCH.

YOU PREEN YOUR BREAST FEATHERS…CAREFULLY REGARDING THIS NARRATIVE.

IT SEEMS THAT…

He was born in a small, rather backward logging community in the highlands of Northeastern Washington 21 years ago next month. His father, like most other men 150 miles in any direction of that area, made his living in the logging industry. Fallers, truckers, equipment operators, mill workers—nigh on to 60 percent of all employable males—worked in one way, shape, form, or fashion in the brutally dangerous, economically unpredictable timber industry.

Foster Falls was a town which, unfortunately, could best be described using an assortment of rather *negative* adjectives. The words "dull," "poor," and "desperate" come to mind. Average incomes were small; opportunities for improvement or advancement were poor. And, as a result, many people lived in what must surely have been viewed by wealthier outsiders as lives of quiet desperation. If one considers for a moment the plight of little Appleton—the steady degradation of her industries and livelihood—and then multiplied *that* by a factor of two or three, *that* might provide a workable construct of the powerlessness and vacuum visited upon the hardy survivors of calloused little Foster Falls.

Justin was born at 1:56 am, on a Saturday night, in the third week of August. It was four minutes before closing time at the Spar Tavern, which was where Samuel Hoskins, his father, was holding his own in an arm-wrestling match with one Delbert "Dirt Bag" Phelps. Sam labored in a most dedicated fashion at securing and maintaining a reputation for being the toughest tree-faller, and the hardest drinker in Ferry County. And after handily, if inevitably, dispensing with the aforementioned Señor "Dirt Bag"—as well as half a pitcher of beer (straight from the pitcher)—he navigated his way home; sloshing audibly, and listing badly to starboard.

The news of his son's birth was waiting for him on the telephone message machine. In fact, several messages had accumulated over the course of the last few days, as Sam continued plowing, without respite, through the repetitive nature of his life cycle: Out of the sack at 4:00 am; *inhale* a fast breakfast of ham, eggs, and black coffee; load the truck and get on the road, unshowered and unshaven by 4:40 am; drive 38 miles of steeply curving, dimly lit mountain road to the timber camp; make stumps—six feet across—out of as many Ponderosa pine and Douglas fir trees as the fuel and oil would allow in a 12-hour period; drive home and drop the saw on a gas-and-oil-soaked sheet of newspaper by the door on the kitchen floor; lock things up and walk two blocks to the "Spar Pub 'n' Grub" for another cheap, greasy, meal washed down with inordinate quantities of cold, foamy beer.

It was the way things had always been, long before Sam Hoskins had ever met and married young Miss Suzanne Bench. It was the way things had, unfortunately, remained after the birth of the little boy, whom his mother named in homage to her three brothers: Justin, Michael, and Thomas. And it was, not surprisingly, *exactly* the way things forever *would be* with Sam, even after he walked out on his family, and disappeared into the remote, forested hills of northern Oregon…eight months after the arrival of what turned out to be his only child.

Once, just once (upon one time), the yellow/orange sunset of another working day cloaked and closed about Sam's blocky physique, silhouetting him in the doorway of his tiny house. He stood there—pine-scented, work dirty, chainsaw fisted—in the doorway, staring at Suzanne, holding the baby; rocking gently, and holding the baby.

Suzanne—smiling weakly, rocking gently, and holding the baby.

Sam set the saw down on the newspaper rectangle. Crossed the room uncertainly, wiping his big hands on his work pants; logging boots making heavy thuds on the wood floor and leaving prints of caked mud in his wake. He crossed that room, Sam did; a room filled for the first time in days with the aroma of home cooking, and the fragrance of Suzanne's lightly perfumed hair; crossed through subtle drifts of baby powder and clean laundry hung upon wobbly, wooden drying racks set before a cracking, spitting wood stove; crossed to gaze with fear and wonder into those new, blue eyes—the eyes of all futures, the eyes of his son.

It was the only attention Justin ever received from his father; the only acknowledgment given for the long, difficult labor his mother endured in the solitary drama of birthing. It was the only time Samuel came directly home from work and *stayed* there, all evening, and all through the night. It was the only time, evermore, when he quietly went through the motions of being a provider. And it was the only time he remained hushed about his feelings regarding the unfamiliar and unpracticed obligations of a first-time father.

Sad to say, Justin was such an unhappy baby. And for good reason. As truly bad luck would have it, his inner ears had become inflamed soon after his arrival home (perhaps even prior to birth?), and the poor child was in such excruciating misery that his crying continued non-stop—day upon day, night after night. Regional physicians—30 miles away in the larger town of Mt. St. Anne—were at a loss to explain the cause of Justin's malady. And though they did the best they could—times being as they were—smaller town medical clinics simply did not possess budgets up to the task of acquiring modern, sophisticated diagnostic equipment.

The infection, as it was discovered a short time later in Justin's life, had been *behind* the eardrum, and therefore would not have been visible to attending physicians unfamiliar with the use of tympanometry techniques. The inflammation left the youngster with something in the range of 80 percent of his total hearing intact and was responsible for a delay in the development of his speech and early learning traits. It was the reason why, even in his adult life, Justin spoke slowly and with much deliberation. He was habitually concentrating on *hearing his own voice* and, at the same time, making every effort to *not talk too loudly* because of his own hearing impairment.

Prior to the eventual diagnosis and subsequent treatment, baby Justin's squalls of sickness and pain confounded medicos who prescribed antibiotics of every category and potency—to no avail. Doctor bills *piled up* while the logging contracts *dried up*. Samuel handed over those interminable, hours of nerve-grinding child care to the brave, determined, slowly eroding Suzanne, while he himself took up near-permanent residence at the Spar Pub. When word of work opportunities in Oregon found its way into Foster Falls, Sam and his good buddy "Dirt Bag Delbert" packed their chainsaws and a Redbone hound into his truck, and were 200 miles down the road before Justin and his exhausted mama returned home one afternoon with a small, sad, brown bag of groceries.

What a somber, lonely Sunday *that* was.

Three summers came and went, and nothing much changed in the little town of Foster Falls. Justin continued to struggle with serious bouts of ear infection, and many, many nights were passed in the arms of his worn, worried mother who valiantly championed the cause of bringing whatever comfort she could to her tiny, ailing child. The delays in his hearing, speaking, and learning were becoming increasingly evident, and Suzanne was gently warned that her baby may *also* be, in fact, suffering from a mild to moderate form of mental retardation.

Alone in life, barely able to make ends meet, and utterly spent from the effort of caring for a feverish, disabled toddler, Suzanne's spirit finally gave out in early autumn of Justin's fourth year. Even then, she would not relent to the temptation of outright abandonment. Too grief-stricken and heart-heavy to muster tears, she painstakingly completed all of the required legalities in order to deliver her son into the care of a foster home.

It could not have been an easy thing to accomplish. In truth, if Suzanne had possessed even a shred of remaining hope or strength, she would have held out for the possibility of a miracle. And it was such a shame indeed because, within a calendar year of her exhausted surrender, Justin's trial by fire began to ebb and subside. His eardrums began to heal and his hearing was partially restored. He *heard* his first words.

He *uttered* his first words.

He began to learn.

Those happy, remarkable, important first steps occurred in the absence of his truant father, who was stumbling around half-drunk somewhere in the woods of Oregon, and his psychologically ruined mother, who had boarded a northbound bus—soul crushed—leaving behind a forwarding address: Canada.

Justin was given trial adoptions by four different foster families in the year following his mother's departure. His longest stay was at the home of Wilfred and Emily Tarver; a very loving couple—elderly, and therefore rather grandparent-ish—who were strong and capable enough to withstand Justin's non-stop howling, for a full ten days and nights.

Then it was back once more to the State Adoption Center in Mt. St. Anne, where he lay shivering in confusion…and fearful of life's next anxious, hurtful moment.

This might have gone on forever. The hopelessness of Justin's undiagnosed and painful infection, along with the accompanying learning delays had all the hallmarks of a death spiral—a losing cycle of unsuccessful fostered home care followed by a return to the adoption agency. But the darkest hour is just before the dawn, so goes the saying.

Things probably could not have looked bleaker for the little boy when two extraordinary events occurred: First, Justin's painful ailment began to improve; God alone knows why, and he ain't tellin.' And second, he was fostered to a moderately well-to-do, middle-aged bachelor from Weston, Washington named Thomas David Bench.

Second in line of Suzanne's three brothers, and the *only* one with whom she had maintained any *real* correspondence throughout the years, Thomas had learned of his sister's desperation via the infrequent letters she had written since Justin's birth.

Saddened by the breakup of the Hoskins family (but in no way surprised, given Sam's reputation for irresponsible behavior), Suzanne's favorite brother had observed her plight from a distance; had held her thorny trials at arm's length, hoping upon hope that she would corral her fears, and somehow transform them into the kind of strength and self-forged luck that she and her son would need to weather the storm, and make it through the troubled times.

And while *that* had been, more or less, the way things had worked out in Thomas Bench's world—an up-from-the-bootstraps, captain-of-his-own-fate kind of success story in law (and, to a lesser extent, in real estate!)—a happy ending to the tale simply was not in the cards for Suzanne Hoskins.

Her eldest brother, Justin, resided in Florida with his wife and their four children. Despite the closeness of their relationship during the years of their childhood—Suzanne was second born, scarcely 11 months younger than her older sibling—time, distance, and the events which shape people's lives had taken their toll. If it was never admitted in so many words, it was generally accepted as unconscious information that a slow and steady drifting apart had, across the divide of years, made strangers of them.

Her youngest brother, Michael, was a kind and well-intentioned individual who nonetheless had fallen through the cracks of the American social fabric. Michael lived, for the most part, in a small town in Colorado where he marked time by alternately gaining and losing entry-level positions with a wide range of low-paying employers.

Honest and likable to a fault, Suzanne's little brother unfortunately labored with issues of dependability, employability; frankly, just plain *ability*. And that made him a *liability* for any potential job prospect short of seasonal labor of the most menial types.

Michael Allen Bench was a nice enough guy. But he limped through life like a three-legged dog in a locked tin barn; going nowhere at all, and getting there very slowly. So, then…

It was Thomas David Bench—financially secure, emotionally stable, confirmed bachelor—who graciously offered his home, his guidance, and him*self* to four-year-old Justin; the only son of his only sister. Thereupon, things began to brighten up. But trials lay ahead for the both of them, and who could tell just how much the power of love could influence the outcome?

When, on a windbitten November day, social workers introduced the two to one another, Uncle Thomas leaned over, placed his hand on the lad's shoulder, and gently inquired, "Well, well…what might *your* name be, my little cowboy?"

"Jussen Myka Tomma Hossins," replied Justin politely. Thomas raised an eyebrow in modest amusement. Then smiling broadly, he took his nephew's tiny hand firmly in his own and led him to his automobile, parked in a corner stall of the State Adoption Center in Mt. St. Anne.

"Come along, son," he said simply. "We've got a lot of work to do."

*

"The Work" began with a full medical examination performed by Thomas's personal physician—a knowledgeable and skillful practitioner with many years of experience who, coincidentally, had access to some of the very latest equipment and techniques. It was during these evaluations that Justin's previous inner ear problems came to light. Dr. Pennington astutely surmised that the boy's speech impediment had been a direct result of his inability to hear properly. He further reckoned Justin's permanent hearing loss to be 20–25 percent. Taken together which meant that with therapy, practice, and patience, he should be able to recover the use of most, if not *all* of his communication skills. Virtually no one would be the wiser. Dr. Pennington also ordered a battery of I.Q. tests, and here the news was not quite so encouraging. While performing well enough to dismiss mental retardation or any of the easily identifiable learning delays, the results showed that Justin was nonetheless processing and comprehending information at a level in the bottom quartile. Academic achievement was going to be elusive and, most likely, not without its challenges.

Would he graduate from high school? **Don't know.**

Will he eventually be employable? **Not sure.**

Can he one day take care of himself? Stand on his own two feet? **Uncertain.**

Thomas Bench thanked his physician friend. Then, throwing young Justin a mischievous wink, he hoisted him up over his head, planted him firmly on his shoulders, and strode jauntily out of the clinic.

"Mo wukk to do, Unca Tomma?"

"That's right, my boy!" beamed the man confidently. "More work to do!"

This time "The Work" took the form of speech and language therapy, three times a week for the better part of six years. It took the form of private tutors—six in all—who tracked and trained Justin from the age of three-and-a-half years until the time of his high school graduation (Yes, graduation! 52nd, in a class of 244!) 15 years later.

It took the form of uncountable hours of shared reading; innumerable hours attending and discussing the performing and visual arts; inestimable hours of trial and error, days spent on trails, evenings spent do-it-yourself-ing, and home-repairing; practice and patience; labor, loss, laughter, and love.

Absolutely inseparable (minus the restrictions of school and job), the bond between Thomas and Justin was a thing of beauty—a Hallmark TV Special celebrating the victory of selflessness and unconditional trust over the far too familiar forces of "I-me-my-ism." They were the toast of Weston; an example to, and for, inhabitants of the entire valley.

AND FOR ANYONE ELSE PAYING AS CLOSE ATTENTION AS <u>YOU</u> DID, CROW!

Even so, Justin always had to struggle to fit in; always had to work doubly hard just to blend in with the crowd, and *not* draw attention to his 'differentness.' And right around the time of his stint in junior high school—the critical period in a kid's life when the perceived necessity of 'fitting in' with his peers takes on its sharpest color—Thomas bestowed (or in *one* case was *preparing* to bestow) three important gifts upon his foster son; gifts which were to profoundly change the life and character of the youngster in ways that no one could have possibly imagined.

The magic, as well as the *benefits,* of the first gift, were made crystal clear from the get-go. Its influence *resonated through* Justin's awkward adolescence exactly as it now *radiates from* his young adulthood. It *def*ined his personality, it *ref*ined his search for self-expression and it *rev*ealed the gentle nature of his uniqueness to other people in a language that could be lost only on the most calloused and forbidding listener.

That language was music. And the *first gift* was Woody.

The *second* gift was less conceptual; more pragmatic, though still heart-connected and directly traceable to family, roots, history, and values. Thomas asked Justin to become his legally adopted son, and Justin—delighted beyond measure—eagerly accepted (Embraced! Bear-hugged! Immediately inhabited!) the offer. Thenceforth, Justin Michael Thomas Hoskins became, in the eyes of the law (and the world!), Justin Michael Thomas Bench.

Suzanne would have been the first to appreciate, applaud, and approve!

The *third* gift was made known to Justin only after the death of his adoptive father, just five months after the young man's 18th birthday. Attorney Thomas Bench's real estate transactions had enabled him to acquire several parcels of land and homes up and down the Kennawack Valley; land parcels, the eventual sale of which, provided a capital cash flow directed, for the most part, into a trust fund of which Justin was the sole designated beneficiary. Though not exceedingly large in any sense of the word, the trust fund established by Thomas Bench in Justin's behalf was adequate for the purpose of ensuring the young man a lifestyle that would want for none of life's necessities. Moreover, and of perhaps greater importance was the fact that Thomas had employed the services of his lifelong friend and attorney, Jefferson Greenwood, to administer the funds in such a fashion as to obviate the necessity for Justin to ever become entangled in the paperwork that comes with such financial matters. Jeff was also the chief executor of Thomas's will (for Thomas trusted him implicitly). And as such, he was authorized and charged with the responsibility of handling *all* matters—legal, financial, and otherwise—in regard to a particularly large piece of property that had been purchased with one specific purpose in mind. It was a semi-secluded residence; a large, wooded tract of land where the soul of his life—his beloved son, Justin—could spend the rest of his days self-contained and at peace with nature while, at the same time, living in close proximity to the amicable and accepting citizenry of small-town Appleton.

The parcel of land which Thomas had purchased, and which Jefferson Greenwood quietly and unobtrusively administered, was the acreage including the old Appleton Quarry. And a massive heart attack that claimed the life of his uncle/father was the unfortunate event which triggered the process of putting it into Justin's possession. Well-known as a man of sensible, intelligent behavior in all of his living habits, the shock of losing Thomas Bench with such cruel abruptness, and at such a relatively young age (51) sent scores of friends and supporters spiraling into dismay. Justin, himself, may *never* have gained a toehold on recovery from that blow had he not been aided and encouraged, by Mr. Greenwood, to take up *immediate* residence in his newly inherited quarry land cabin.

Jeff also made certain that Justin introduced himself to the community of Appleton, rather than languishing in self-imposed solitary seclusion. "Plenty of folks out here are in *real* need of a helping hand, Justin," insisted Jefferson, his wide hands firmly embracing the shoulders of the broken-hearted youngster. "And there are still more folks with problems way bigger than yours, son. Thomas, himself, would tell you the same if he was here right now; now, you just tell me that he wouldn't…hmm?"

Justin could not. And gathering his flagging spirits—along with Jefferson Greenwood's advice—Justin Michael Thomas Bench went about the daunting task of creating a new home for himself, establishing a reputation worthy of his father's name, and healing his heart the best way he knew how.

The tract of land comprising Appleton Quarry was an investment with a substantial heart-and-soul value attached; that much was true. But the *hard dollar* net worth of the quarry woodlands was of little interest to Justin and his easy-going lifestyle. He didn't care, or even *know* what the quarry lands were worth on the open market.

Until somewhat later.

*

SOMETHING CATCHES YOUR EYE; SOMETHING SMALL, BRIGHT, IRREGULARLY SHAPED.

HUGGING TOGETHER-WITH-WIND TIME, YOU TUMBLE EARTHWARD, AND PULL YOURSELF INTO A PARALLEL GLIDE, MERE INCHES FROM THE YELLOW DEAD GRASSES OF APPLETON QUARRY...JUST OUTSIDE JUSTIN'S CABIN. WITHOUT MISSING A WINGBEAT, YOU PECK-STAB THE OBJECT IN MID-FLIGHT, RISING TO TREETOP LEVEL WITH ASTONISHING SPEED, AND VEER OFF FOR THE NEAR-IMPENETRABLE BRUSH LAND—235 WING STROKES WEST-SOUTHWEST OF THE QUARRY.

THE REMAINS OF A WEATHERED ROOFTOP ENTER YOUR SCAN OF VISION, AND YOU RECOGNIZE THE TRAITS OF ABANDONMENT. THE ONE-ROOM SHACK HAS BEEN UNINHABITED FOR MANY LONG YEARS; PERHAPS IT NEVER WAS INHABITED, OR NEVER WAS MEANT TO BE. NO TRAIL EXISTS TO DIRECT THE FEET OF ANY OF THE LONGLEGS TO ITS WHEREABOUTS, AND IT SITS UNNOTICED AND UNKNOWN FAR FROM PLACES YOU KNOW THEM TO FREQUENT.

SOME OF THE TALL GRASSES OF THE CLEARING HAVE BEEN SPLIT; PUSHED APART, LEAVING A BARELY DISCERNIBLE, CROOKED WAKE THROUGH THE MEADOW TOWARD THE CABIN. A DEER, MAYBE? AT ANY RATE, CROW DISCERNS NO SENSE OF DANGER, AND THE STABILITY OF THE SHANTY ROOF INVITES CLUTCHING-WITH-TALONS TIME; AN OPPORTUNITY TO CLOSELY INSPECT THE "LITTLE SHINE" WHICH YOU DISCOVERED LYING IN THE DRY GRASSES NEAR THE QUARRY CABIN.

SUDDENLY—VICIOUSLY, AND WITHOUT WARNING (THAT'S THE WAY IT IS WITH A SONIC BOOM)—THE HEAVENS CRACK APART, AND THE IMPACT OF SOUND AND CONCUSSION THRUM THROUGH YOUR BODY. REFLEXIVELY MANEUVERING INTO A FLIGHT MODE OF TACTICAL DEFENSE, YOU RELEASE THE "LITTLE SHINE" FROM YOUR BEAK, AND IT SLIPS TO THE FOREST FLOOR TO LAND MERE FEET FROM THE PADLOCKED DOOR OF THE DERELICT SHANTY SHED.

YOUR SURVIVAL TENSION DISSOLVES IN THE SPAN OF A HEART PULSE, AND WITH THE RETURN OF THE SENSATION OF DANGER-IS-NOT, YOUR INSIGHT INTO YOUR CONNECTION WITH, AND TO, THE "LITTLE SHINE" BLOOMS TO NEAR FULLNESS: "LITTLE SHINE" BELONGS NOT IN THE DRY GRASS NEAR THE

QUARRY CABIN. "LITTLE SHINE" <u>BELONGS</u> IN THE TALL GRASS OF THE MEADOWLAND...NEAR THE SHANTY SHED.

SOMEBODY, SOME LONGLEGS, WILL FIND THE "LITTLE SHINE," LYING THERE IN THE DIRT JUST OUTSIDE THE OLD ABANDONED SHACK, AND WILL THINK OF IT AS SOMETHING OF A MINOR MIRACLE. CROW DOES NOT BELIEVE IN MIRACLES. CROW BELIEVES IN WIND, WING MUSCLE, AND—WHEN NECESSARY—PURPOSEFULLY DESIGNED, AND PRECISELY (SURREPTITIOUSLY) IMPLEMENTED MEDIATION. (O' RAVENRILL!)

THE MATTER IS DISREGARDED; NOT SO MUCH FORGOTTEN AS 'DELETED,' AND YOU GIVE YOURSELF OVER TO THE ANCIENT, RHYTHMIC BALLET OF FREEFORM FLIGHT.

CROW IS ALIVE.

CROW IS FREE.

<u>CROW</u> <u>IS</u>.

EVERYTHING ELSE—IF NOT THE COMMONTASK, OR THE ONE-NESS—EXISTS AS...CROW-NOT. EXISTS AS...THE OTHER-ING.

*

"So that's pretty much it in a nutshell, guys," Justin, wrapping up his story, crossing his legs and stretching the cramps out of his trunk and arms. "I *understand* what's been happenin' to me up here lately. But what *you all* hafta understand, as friends of mine, is how *long* I've worked at *acceptance*. As far as *I* know, I've never done *anything* to *anybody* to rile 'em up enough to make 'em hate me. An' I *still* say that if we wait this damn thing out, we'll find a way to patch it up...*without* the need for me to holler an' point an' get folks starin' at the weirdo who lives up in the rock pile."

As he scanned, hope-hearted, about the pack, it was plain as rain that Justin's friends were concretely *in his corner* on the matter, even if his strategy-of-choice was "a bit of a struggle to bite off and chew" (Eric, at a later date, admitting). A long, thoughtful, quiet spell ensued, and Kelsea was the first to crack the ice.

"I'm..." Kelsea, glancing left, right, "<u>*we're*</u> so sorry about your dad, Justin. We had no clue, actually, about your upbringing...your recent, um, history…we—" fumbling now, ashamed *not* to have known what she/they could not *possibly have* known. And embarrassed about being ashamed. "He just…had to be a one-in-a-jillion kinda guy." A mini-pause, here, while it sinks in with every warm soul in attendance.

Kelsea haltingly, pianissimo, "You must miss him something terrible."

Justin nodded, mute. But a thumbs-up, half-smile of semi-confidence left little doubt that he had come to terms with his loss, and had settled with it in an embracing and mature manner.

"Have you had any contact at all with your mom or your, uh, biological dad?" Erik inquired cautiously.

"Not a bit. An' to be honest, I don't expect any either." A sigh, here. "Though I s'pose it might be kinda nice. In a way. I guess."

"Well, we'll all support your pacifistic approach to solving the problem, Justin," Sandy offered. "Especially after understanding where you've been, and what you've been through…*before* we ever met you." Now, frowning slightly, the presence of saltwater lingering yet in those dark brown eyes. "But the larger questions still remain: 'Who is committing these criminal acts?' And, moreover, 'What *reason* do they have for persisting in this heinous behavior?'"

"Yeah," remarked Erik glumly, "I'd love to pin the whole thing on the 'pinhead trio,' and just start tracking their every move. But the fact of the matter is that all the information we've collected so far points to *Debbin Ramsay* as the bad guy, and that just doesn't make any sense." Raking ten fingertips back through his hair, and across his scalp in exasperation, "Anybody got any fresh ideas?"

Cue the crickets. Not a word was spoken. None, that is, except from one Stuart James LeMaster.

"Guys," he began earnestly, "hold on to your sombreros. Here's the tidbit I started to tell you all about just before Justin began his story. *This* oughta give you something to think about while you're power-munching your cornflakes!"

Quizzical looks spread from face to face, but the confident assurance with which Stuie spoke told them that he might just be about to impart something of genuine importance.

"Remember how I was late to the barbecue last night?"

"Sure," butted in Erik with mock cynicism, "late, but as I recall, you made up for lost time by eating a metric ton of hamburger meat, *and* downing a 50-gallon drum of cola!"

"So speaketh the weight-conscious Croquet King of Kennawack County," laughed Sandy. "Only a *couple of dozen* burgers for you that night, am I right, Sir Carnivore?"

"All part of a rigorous training program, sports fans," Erik, honking, boastful. "Must keep up my strength if I am to compete on the triple-A level of the 'Crowl Bowl.'"

"Do you people want to hear this or *don't* you?" warned Stuart. He was becoming impatient with their apparent lack of interest in his personal contribution to the investigation.

"Course we wanna hear it, Stu," drawled Justin. "We're all just gropin' aroun' for a little comic relief from all the damn 'mise*ray*,'—spoofing on Hollis Greenwood, a street-hipster-talking mutual friend of the Scalawags. We don't mean to make you feel ignored. Honest, man."

"Yeah, c'mon, Stu. We're listening. Sorry."

Stuart LeMaster paused, hoping to shape his remarks with some dramatic effect, in order to (*maybe, finally!*) be able to hold forth with an *attentive* audience.

"Well," he re-began, "I was late for the party *because* I just happened to _be_ biking around the Quarry Loop _with_ Mr. Hollis Greenwood. Him_self!_"

"Oh, man!" blurted Erik. "Hollis is a cool guy. You shoulda brought him along to the get-together."

Stuart stared hard at his new friend. He was starting to get pissed.

"Sorry," mumbled Erik, the pink rising up his neck and giving his ears a rosy flush.

"Sorry, go on."

Stuart's expression reflected a growing reluctance on his part to tolerate the rudeness of any more interruptions. *One more time*, he thought to himself.

"So, right about the time everybody was beginning to show up at the picnic, that's right *about* the time that Justin's home was broken into, and *that's* just about the *exact* time when Hollis and I saw a car, *up close and personal, mind you,* come driving out of the entrance to the quarry site. Now, I'll give you *three guesses* who was driving that car, and the first two don't count."

An explosion of simultaneous conjectures, speculations, theories, and accusations followed. Even Justin, normally prone to under-reaction and understatement, joined the throng of voices all trying to be heard at the same time. The cacophony rang through the wooded quarry site; over the stone relics strewn haphazardly across the landscape, into the heart of green-black timberland, where it startled the starlings and antagonized the squirrels before disintegrating inside bottomless, acoustic wells of verdant foliage.

Stuart sat—stoically waiting.

As quickly as it had begun, the madcap jabberwocky subsided; leaving everyone breathless, and electric with suspense. It was only then, when the buzz of high-pitched conversation had dissipated, that it finally came to their collective attention that the 'Answer Man' had been watching everyone for long moments; a mixed look of injury, exasperation, and urgency etched upon his features.

"So, well, Stuie?" stammered his sister, suddenly remorseful over her participation in the verbal stampede that had (yet again!) left her twin trailing at the rear of the pack.

"Oh, yeah, jeez. Stuart! Finish up, man," insisted Erik. He was every inch as embarrassed as the others. "Who's car did you see leaving the quarry last night?"

Silence, thick enough to cut with a cutlass, and spread with a soup ladle.

"C'mon, Stu!" encouraged Kelsea. "Don't keep us hangin.' Who was up here at Justin's house while all of us were at the party?"

Stuart shot a toxic look in the general direction of his friends. "You're so damned smart," he admonished. *"You figure it out for yourselves!"*

"But we don't *know,* Stu," remarked Kelsea. She felt a little sick to her stomach.

"You saw the whole thing. We need *you* to tell *us*."

"Well, *Hollis* was there too. Why don't you all just up and go find Hollis *Greenwood?* He's got the lowdown on Justin's little visitor, same as I do. Only I'll bet you'll *listen to him!"*

That said, Stuart LeMaster about-faced, and stomped indignantly down the hillock to the mountain bikes. Locked, loaded, and in 'full-on pissed mode.'

"Well, I guess we sure enough had *that* comin' to us," lamented Justin. "Whadda we do now? Go get 'im an' smooth things over, or what?"

Sandy was quick to answer that question. "We'd better give Stuie a bit of space for the time being," she advised. "In the meantime, I guess we'll have to just settle for doing the next best thing."

"Meaning?" Erik wondered.

Sandy shrugged her shoulders philosophically. "I guess we'd better go find Hollis Greenwood," she said matter-of-factly.

*

It was immediately decided that the search for Hollis Greenwood would be "expedited" (Sandy's word) by splitting up, fanning out, and covering all the most likely hang-outs first. The afternoon was still in its infancy; a lot of daylight hours remained, and a plan was devised to swarm the greater Appleton area in the smallest possible amount of time.

Justin was to check the basketball courts at the elementary, middle school, and high school, for, it was a well-known fact that Hollis was a 'hoop fool' to the to the absolute max.

Kelsea would partner with Justin by first looking in at the 'Soda Queen,' and then hooking up with him as he canvassed the town Park.

Erik drew Sandy as his partner (putting a swagger in *his* step that he tried hard not to betray). His job was to see if Hollis was doing any work down at his father's law office.

Yes. Hollis Greenwood was Jefferson Greenwood's son. Yes. Greenwood owned a law firm located in Weston. But he commuted from Appleton, where he resided and co-managed his 'satellite' office.

Yes. Justin knew that Jeff Greenwood organized and administrated his inheritance affairs for him as requested by his late adoptive father.

No. Justin knew neither the extent of the landholdings nor the dollar value of his trust fund. And it would not have interested him much if he did. Right?

Connections, cross-connections, and synchronicity. Simple as that.

Sandy would be responsible for scouting out the Swimming Hole, and then making a beeline for Greenwood Law in order to "rendez-vous avec Monsieur Remarque." By that time, Kelsea and Justin should be right across the street in Appleton Park. It sounded like a sound plan to the Scalawags. A small town like Appleton should be pretty well scoped out by four people on bikes in just under, well, in virtually no time flat! Even a Crow, on the wing, might be inclined to agree, but…

Nope.

Nobody anywhere had any knowledge whatsoever regarding the whereabouts of a ninth-grade lad of African-American ancestry who lived right there in Appleton, and answered to the none-to-common name of Hollis Greenwood. It was frustrating. It was annoying. It was downright "stultifying" (Sandy's word, again).

Everyone gathered around Justin as he slumped, disheartened, upon his favorite old park bench. Stuart LeMaster, of course, was *very* conspicuous by his *very* absence, but it was all for the better. For at just that *very* moment he, Stuart, was stumbling (quite by accident) across yet *another* set of clues which would muddle *everyone's* understanding about *everything* to a considerable degree. But meanwhile…

"Now what?"

"Beats the hell outa me."

"Did anyone notice that Stuie left his bike at the cabin?"

"Yeah, what's *that* all about?"

"Probably just took off hikin' in the woods to blow off steam, and think things over."

"Probably. He'll be all right."

"Anybody wanna go to Pops' for a while?"

"Naw. Too close to suppertime. Besides, I'm broke."

"What time *is* it, anyway?"

"Just shy of four."

"Already? No *wonder* my stomach's yowlin.'"

"Where'd Kooper go?"

"Look behind you!"

"Oh! Hey, Koop. C'mere, boy. *Good boy!*"

"Where the hell can he *be?*"

"Who?"

"What do you mean 'who?' Hollis! *That's* who!"

"Oh. He's right up there in the window of the library."

"<u>What</u>! He *is?* He *<u>is</u>!* There he *<u>is</u>!* He's right ***there!*** "

"What's he doin' up *there*?"

"Who knows? Who cares? *Ándale!*"

And so they did, lickity-split, and on-the-dad-blamed-double: the four of them—Kooper, too. Across the street, single file into the City Hall building—constructed in 1922, and never once been remodeled—up two flights of noisy, echoey, wooden stairs, around the corner and into the musty, varnish-smelling-y, cob-webby, dim lit-ly, silent, sequestered sanctuary that was the Appleton Public Library.

Miss Hobbes, the octogenarian librarian, didn't even bat a wrinkled, hooded eyelid when Kooperdog casually strolled, accompanying Justin and company, into her hallowed halls of literacy and learning. But she *did* raise a bony finger to her lips; peering semi-sternly over the tops of the tiny, rectangular, coke-bottle thick lenses of her granny glasses and go, "Shh." She then pointed authoritatively to a faded, yellow, metal sign—which had not been replaced since it was hung there in (again) 1922—bearing a two-word imperative:

"QUIET, PLEASE."

Justin and company and canine reverently crossed the large, airy library entry to the arched window, whereby sat the widely sought Hollis Greenwood. Looking up from his reading, young Master Greenwood registered pleasant surprise at the unexpected appearance of his school chums plus Justin plus Kooper-with-a-"K."

"Yo! Jus*tan*, Koo*pare*! S'goin' on, mah frenz?" he said, extolling a lavish salutation replete with the lingual decor of a downtown L.A. streetster.

"*Hollis!*" Kelsea hissed under her breath, so as not to incur the wrath of the vigilant fossil-brarian. "We've been looking all <u>over</u> for you! What the heck are you doing *here?*"

Hollis's eyebrows arched in authentic astonishment at the question posed. He peered reflectively out the second-story window at the grassy park below, noodling his possible responses. Then swiveling his head back in the direction of the black-haired girl, he calmly announced: "What am I doin' *here?* Yo, baby dudette! Dig! Man, <u>*every*</u>body got ta be *some*where. An', I...am...*here!*"

*

Turns out, Hollis Greenwood was a more deeply layered individual than most people gave him credit for. On the surface, it was, like, basketball *this,* and basketball *that.*

123

Run, pass, dribble, shoot, screen, cut, rebound; basketballs, basketball magazines, basketball jerseys, you know the type. Don't *nobody* <u>not</u> know somebody like Hollis.

True dat!

And everyone knew that he worked a couple of days a week at his father's law office downtown. But very *few* suspected that he was developing a genuine *interest* in that profession. And it shouldn't come as any shock when you think about it. Here was a bright kid—with a top-notch attorney dad, and a talented legal assistant mom—who devoted a portion of his 'off-court' time working in the town legal office. There would probably be a natural inclination for one to become involved in and with the profession of American law and order; at least on some level.

The situation acquired some comical undertones when, trooping down the well-worn steps of the City Hall building—foot-thumps overlapping one another all down the narrow stairwell—the Scalawags tuned in attentively as Hollis spouted an almost unintelligible blend of legalese and high school/college/pro hoop jargon. He had been reading up on the subject of his *current* preoccupation (*outside* of b.b), which was 'insider trading' when the group had finally found him.

"Whatchu got ta 'preshee-ate," exhorts Hollis, gushing newly acquired knowledge, not unlike a ruptured fire hydrant, "iz that, dig, purcha*san*' or, like, in any damn way *at-tall*, complee*tan* any transact*shans* involvin' like, securi*tays* on the basis of special knowledge or informa*shown* which is, like, unavailable to the pub*leek* as shareholders is, dig, way ill-damn-legal, my very fine dudes, dudettes and doggie."

"Uh-huh," goes Justin.

"An' that's why we got the securi*tays* an' exchange commi*shown*, dig? To, like, supervise the exchange of stocks and bonds so as to, like, you know, protect invest*orz* from malprac*TYCE* in the free market. Dig it."

"Uh-huh," goes Erik.

"Uh-huh," goes Kelsea.

"I see," says Sandy.

"Now, gainin' ac-SESS to confidential informa_shown_ is, like, not technically ill-damn-legal, you dig? But to **use** said informa_shown_ in order to gain mone_tary_—"

The Scalawags had led Hollis across the street and into Appleton Park, "uh-huhing" every step of the way. Mr. Basketball had made it abundantly clear how his "picture-perfect-profound-professional-plan" was going to reap him the double rewards of a double career: All-Star NBA point guard for the Portland Trailblazers on the one hand, and agent/attorney/financial advisor on the other. That way, he could have total legal and financial control over every aspect of his illustrious basketball career. Awesome athletic ability, combined with astounding academic aptitude. A success story of epic proportions!

Dig?

Hollis took the middle portion of 'Justin's Bench,' dribbling his basketball on the grass, switching from hand to hand, pausing occasionally to spin it adroitly on the tip of his forefinger. Kelsea and Justin took up positions on either side of the boy, and Erik and Sandy sat cross-legged on the ground facing the others. (Erik was aware that their knees were touching, but he focused on the conversation; bravely, if only barely, suppressing the not-at-all unpleasant presence of handfuls of colorful butterflies flitting merrily around inside the hollow of his stomach.)

"Well, Hollis," smiled Kelsea, "sounds like you've really given a lot of practical thought to this, uh, stuff."

"I guess if anybody could pull off a plan like that, it'd be you, all right," Justin added.

"But the reason we've been looking for you (all damn day!) is that we have sort of an important question. And you're really the only one who can provide the answer."

"Legal or athletic?" inquired the boy.

"Hm?"

"Is the quest*shown* of a *legal* nature, or of an *athletic* nature? Dig."

"Oh. Uh, actually, neither. It just has to do with somebody who may have gone up to the quarry yesterday afternoon, to, uh, well, visit Justin, or something."

"You mean when I was ridin' 'roun' the loop wich yo twin bro?"

"That's right, Hollis," exclaimed Sandy. "Did you notice any cars going in or out of the quarry when you and Stuart were up there?"

"Sure we did. I c'n tell you 'zactly who was comin' out the quar*ray* when Stu and I was loopin' da loop."

You could have heard a pin drop on a cotton ball. Justin leaned forward. Kelsea grew round-eyed. Sandy reached for Erik's hand. Erik fought the feeling of spin-headed jubilation and held tight to the moment for all he was worth. Kooper gave pursuit to the apparition of a dream squirrel and yipped muffled-ish-ly in his dog sleep.

Hollis pounded the basketball into the turf; hand to hand, hand to hand. Bounce, bounce, bounce, bounce. Then up on the fingertip; spin, spin, spin. Back to the ground; bounce, bounce, bou—

Kelsea's hands snaked out with almost invisible swiftness, snagging the ball in mid-air. "Hollis, if you don't mind terribly," her tone was controlled, measured, "could you please tell us who you saw driving out of the quarry yesterday? We kinda…need to know…"

Hollis slowly, warily retrieved his ball from the thin, strong hands of the girl; eyeing her with guarded uncertainty.

"Yeah, yeah, OK I gotcha. The car we saw up there at Jus*tan's* place was a navy blue, '82 Honda Civic, dig?"

Non-un-anti-comprehension bathes the air of Appleton Park.

"Belonging to whom?" insisted Sandy politely (syrupy?).

"Shoot, girl. On'y but one blue '82 Honda Civic in the *en*tire Mid-*dell* Val*lay*! Dig. Lady who own *that* fine ride be none other than sweet, sweet Debbin Ram*zay.*"

You could have knocked every last Scalawag flat over with a Crow feather.

"But, yo. Twin-dude Stu*art* was up there wit' me. Man, he saw every*thang* I saw. Why dintcha jus' ask *him*?"

"He's not talking to us at the moment," Sandy said almost absent-mindedly.

"Well, yo. Here's da news: Y'all seem to listen to *me*, all right…sayin.' But may*bay* y'all jus' don't lis-*san* to *him* enough."

"So we've heard," said Erik, staring holes in the toes of his sneakers. "Dig the word."

*

RECKON THE NUMBER OF ALL THE FAR-FLUNG STARS IN ALL OF EVERY-NESS.

QUANTIFY ALL THE SAND SPECKS—CURRENT-SWEPT, TIDE-PILED, STORM-STREWN, AND WIND-SCULPTED—ACROSS THE WATER-BORDERING SHORES OF TIME AND SPACE.

COUNT EVERY LEAF…ON EVERY TREE…THAT EVER LIVED—ALL-WHERE-WAYS.

ALL POSSIBILITIES FOREVER-ISH-LY WEIGH AGAINST ALL IMPOSSIBILITIES—THE SAME WAY THAT EVERY BEACH LINE EMBRACES EVERY WATERBODY; THE WAY NIGHT DRAINS DAY TO QUIET BLACK; THE WAY YIN BLEEDS TO YANG.

IT IS THE WAY THAT THE WAY SURELY AND MOST CERTAINLY IS… "THE WAY."

THE EVER-WAY. THE ALL-WAY(S).

THE WAY THAT YOU, CROW, MIGHT JUST AS WELL HAVE BEEN ANY-SOME ELSEWHERE; INHABITING AN ALTERNATIVE THERE-AND-THEN, INSTEAD OF BEING PRECISELY HERE-AND-NOW.

BUT, PRECISELY HERE-AND-NOW…IS.

IT IS.

CROW IS.

LISTEN, CROW…

…LISTEN…

"You finish the next part of your job?"

"Done and done."

"Well, I still haven't heard any *complaints* from any of 'em. And that makes me wonder if things are going according to plan."

"Don't worry. I messed it up real good. Left another message, too."

"There's been no *reaction*, though. You'd think the news would be all over town by now. What's he holding out for?"

"He's a freak. That's why he acts the way he does. I say we're going to have to up the ante if we want to put the scare in him."

"Listen. This whole thing depends a tremendous amount on timing. You could screw the whole thing up in about a nano-second, so don't start thinking too damned highly of yourself!"

"Sorry."

"Just remember to stick to your plans. Keep it simple, keep it to *yourself and* we'll all come out of this in *really* good shape. Botch it, and I'll boil you in oil. There's a *lot* at stake here, and I'm counting on the fear factor to bring him to the bargaining table."

"No problem. The next step is ready to go; the next two steps, actually. And trust me, he'll be ready to listen by the time this is over."

*

"Think, Justin! There *must* have been *something* you said or did to make her *this* mad."

Kelsea paced back and forth; a furrowed look of focused concentration wrinkling her forehead. The knotty-pine deck of the quarry cabin squeaked with the rhythm of her footfalls. Elsewhere about the balcony, Sandy sat on her bottom—knees drawn up, encircled by her arms—staring at a stand of Douglas fir with the distant expression of ironclad dead-end-ed-ness in those bear brown eyes.

Erik was watching Sandy, and his prolonged gaze might easily have been mistaken for the lost look of the lovelorn. In fact, however, he was wrestling with the Debbin Ramsay debacle; the same as everyone else, and he really couldn't have told you what (or whom) he was staring at, even if you had asked him. Dead-end-ed-ness, redux.

Fuming Stuie was still M.I.A. from the confederacy; presumably still nursing wounds sustained after being taken for granted by his dearest friends. (*Inside* pain hurts much more than *outside* pain. *And,* it takes longer to heal.) Sandy's advice was still being diligently, if reluctantly, adhered to: "When he decides he is ready for our apology, he will come looking for it. *That* is when we should offer it, and *not* before."

Kooper was napping comfortably under the porch swing. Justin was quietly strumming, but his demeanor reflected more of what could only be described as 'absolute elsewhere-li-ness.' Pondering and strumming, he sang:

"You say they been unkind to you, but it's all relative.

You couldn't take a perfect life, and still say that you've lived.

You say you only seek to know how freedom you can find.

But you'll never know it 'til you learn that freedom, freedom's in, freedom's in your mind."

Kelsea stopped pacing, stopped chewing her nails, and turned to her friend. "Didn't you catch Debbin throwing snowballs on the school grounds one time?" she asked hopefully.

A plethora of subtle eye rolls greet *that* line of inquiry.

"That was three years ago, Kels," Justin replied wearily. "She was in the ninth grade then."

"But didn't you turn her in to the principal? *Some* people might hold a grudge…(quieter, now) over something like that (sotto voce, now) for, um, quite…a…while," Kelsea waved the white flag of surrender over her own anemic suggestion.

"Sorry, Kels. But I never turned her in for snowballin'. I did the 'Santiago' thing and let her off with a first offense warning," he laughed lightly. "Besides, I'm just a part-time maintenance man. I don't keep an eye out for kids bendin' the rules a little."

"Really, Kelsea," Sandy interjected testily. "Busted for snowballing is *not* the kind of thing which would drive a *sane* person to destroy property—especially three years *after* the fact."

"Well, *excuse me all to pieces*!" retorted Kelsea hotly. "I *thought* we were trying to brainstorm possible explan*ations* for what's been goin' *on* around here lately. And since we've got so *little* to go on—aside from Rah-Rah Ramsay's involvement—it just seemed to *me* like we ought to check out *every detail*…no matter *how small* it might appear. My mistake all-the-hell-together for attempting to think…*out*side the damn box!"

Sandy looked startled. She and Kelsea stared at each other as if seeing one another for the first time. Erik said nothing, but the unexpected 'stand-off' had suddenly constricted and frozen his thought-waves. He was *definitely* no longer concentrating on the problem du jour. Kooper perked his ears, uncertain, but instinctively aware of the fact that there was something *new* in the air, and that, whatever it was, it was anything *but* business as usual.

A rift! Ha! This will <u>never</u> do! Justin, bursting suddenly, and *very* loudly into song:

"Come sailin' over the aqua foam bubbles.

We'll forget all about all our troubles,

and pack it all in for a pirate's lifestyle.

And you'll love it!

Believe me, there ain't nothin' above it.

Just tell all the stuffed shirts to shove it!

You're gonna come sailin' with me!"

Kelsea smiled, conked the side of her head with the heel of her hand and mouthed the words "I'm sorry!" while Justin finished his summertime sailing song.

Sandy rose from her spot in the corner of the deck and hugged her friend tightly.

"We're *all* getting jittery about this thing, Kels. And now with Stuie holding a grudge and everything, oh, shoot! I'm really sorry, too!"

The two of them hooked pinkies (like *good* Scalawags), and had a belly laugh at themselves while Erik blew a puffy sigh of relief. Justin Bench, refusing to let a melodic moment go half-finished, promptly launched into one of his homemade rockers:

"Well, the first trimester's over, and everyone's done his best.
Now it's time to take that winter break. Time to give those books a rest.
Forget all the snow, kick up a tune,
laugh at yourself, and bark at the moon (aahhh-ooooooooo!)
Have a rockin' rollin' Christmas, and a groovy New Year, too!"

"Justin!" moaned Sandy. "It's only *July*, for crying out loud. We're not ready for school *or* winter! Or even Christmas break…not by a *long* shot!"

"Sing, ya durn fool!" yodeled Justin, not missing a wrist stroke across Woody's birch blonde soundboard. "Who asked *you* what time of the year it was, anyways?"

Cecilia, Patroness Saint of Music, once declared to the third-century world: "He who sings, prays twice." That being the case, Justin, Kelsea, Erik, and Sandy spent the rest of the afternoon in joyful, uninhibited, throat-shredding prayer.

Amen to that.

Now, Justin Bench may not be Albert Einstein when it comes to conceptual thinking.

And he wouldn't be confused with Jimi Hendrix regarding his guitar work. But he knew how to multi-task without giving away his private thoughts. And even as he slyly devised those slick melodic tricks he sometimes used to maintain law and order amongst the Scalawags; even as he Pied Piper-ed them *all* through the tomfoolery of another summer day's "prayer meeting," and even as the songcraft was performed, in reverential respect, for the ever-present Saint Cecilia (as well as the musical edification of a nearby, semi-secluded *Crow*), Justin was thinking to himself—turning the question over and over in his mind:

What was it he had seen?

*

Stuart was shooting hoops with Hollis Greenwood at Rosewood Elementary when Justin swung by to pick up some power tools he needed for a job at the high school.

"I think two days is about enough time to get over a little issue of unintended rudeness, don't you, Koop?" Justin plopped a circular saw and a 50-foot coil of extension cord into his bike basket and hunkered down beside his shaggy companion. "But I don't know as ol' Stuart is quite ready to make up with the likes of me just yet. Sandy says he's been mighty standoffish ever since the blowup."

The young man watched Stuart from the shadow of the building entrance for a bit.

Stu was nowhere *near* the same caliber ball player that Hollis was, but Hollis was very sporting; cutting him plenty of slack, and stopping to give advice and point out mistakes.

Yessir. Hollis Greenwood was a good kid. Probably Stuart's favorite buddy—outside of his twin sister, and the rest of the gang. And Justin pondered for a moment why Hollis had never found *his* way into their close-knit association.

"Well, old partner," shrugged Justin. "Guess it's up to you to break the ice for us. Go on out there and *bug* Stuart. Go on, Kooper! Go get Stuart!"

Kooperdog broke into a gallop, but soon enough throttled back into the lower-paced *gallump* that was his trademark gait of choice. Tongue lolling, and tail scrolling invisible sketches in all directions at once, the old dog inserted himself enthusiastically between the boys again and again until, laughing in surrender, they traded their game of 'one-on-one' for Kooper's request for a little 'four-on-one,' meaning *four* hands all over *one* dog.

Justin grinned to himself, watching Stuart and Hollis roughhouse with his canine companion. It was darned hard to stay angry about anything when old Kooperdoodle was in the vicinity. The young man waited and watched for a full minute, then…

"OK, I reckon right about now!"

Justin began pedaling his bike across the schoolyard just as Stuart removed his face from Kooper's coat. The boy instantly spotted him, and his smile along with an energetic wave o' the hand spoke volumes to Justin, who correctly interpreted the gesture as signifying the 'truce' he had been hoping for was in the works.

"Yo Jus*tan,* the maintenance *man!* You gots da aces mutt-buddy, dude, but, dig. He don't know *squat* 'bout 'one-on-one!' Doggone dog *fouled* me three times, man. An' the on'y dribblin' *he* know how ta do is off the end o' that sloppy, pink tongue o'his!"

"I know. I know," Justin countered with good humor. "I tried to tell 'im to stick to chess, but he won't listen to me."

Six minutes of small talk followed; a little bit of "what's up/not much." Then Hollis excused himself and headed off for his father's legal office, expressing his regrets to both of them with a near-English farewell that sounded a lot like "gotta-go-man-dig-ya-*lay*tah!"

At that point, a rather awkward quietude smooshed its way in between Stuart and Justin; not at all *unlike* the manner in which a semi-overweight mutt dog squooshes himself in between two half-grown NBA wannabees.

"Listen, um, Justin," Stuart began. Words failed him and the silence crept back in.

"Every darn one of us is sorry we took you for granted, Stu," allowed Justin. "We all make mistakes from time to time. Us, me, you, everyone."

Stuart looked like he was about to cry. But he didn't. He just listened, mostly with his heart which, as everyone knows, is the purest path to understanding.

"Mistakes'll prob'ly be made in the *future*, too, amongst the group. But that doesn't mean we do it on purpose. Basically, we love us, one and all. Now ain't that true?"

Justin held his little finger up, and Stuart hooked it with his own, faster than you can say, "Gotta-go-man-dig-ya-*lay*tah."

"Indubitably!" quoted Stuart happily. "I can *dig* it!"

The three of them—dude, dude, and dog—trekked across the athletic field together. It was high time for Justin to get his *be*hind over to the high school. After all, it *was* Monday, and he *was* on the clock for the district. Before they shook hands and parted company, Justin brought Stu up to speed regarding the conversation with Hollis over the weekend.

"So we've got a *lot* of 'probably's' pilin' up on this thing," Bench remarked. "It was probably Debbin's horse that was used as the 'getaway vehicle' a few weeks ago. It was probably Debbin's expensive lipstick that was used to write those message*s—both of them*, come to think of it. *And*, it was Debbin Ramsay *herself* who was seen drivin' out of the quarry on the evening of the barbecue—the night my place was torn apart."

"Pretty convincing evidence, I'd say," Stuart sported the look of a man who had his mind made up about things. "Believe it or not, I've got a couple of *more* facts to throw into the pot. Have you got time to hear about 'em, or do you need to get to work right away?"

"As a matter of fact, Stu, I *do* need to get on over to the high school. They're probably wonderin' what's holdin' me up. But, more importantly, we need to be *all together* to hear what you turned up. That's just the way it should be, an' I know for a *fact* that's what the others'd say, too. OK?"

Stuart beamed and nodded his agreement. "At the 'Soda Queen,' then?"

"Yep."

"What time?"

"After dinner, 'round about 7:00."

"Got it. I'll tell my sister, and she'll get ahold of Erik. You tell Kelsea, all right?"

"I'm *on* it! See ya tonight."

"Hey, by the way…Justin, this is off the subject and all, but have you noticed anything, like, *weird* around Sandy and Erik?"

"Weird? Weird in what way?"

"I dunno. Sometimes they just seem kind of, um, it's hard to put my finger on it, actually," Stuart realized that he had absolutely no idea what he was trying to say. "Aw, never mind," he bailed out of his own dilemma. "It's probably just me."

But for a long time, he wondered about that "knowing" little smile that his older friend had left him with on that hot afternoon, in the month of July, at the schoolyard.

*

And right about that same time…**Somewhere,** very much elsewhere…

Somebody was getting *very* angry because a door had been left unlocked. **Someone Else** was being defensive by insisting that *nobody* ever came up there *anyway;* that no one even *knew* there was a cabin there *at all*; and that even if they *did* know, they wouldn't know how to get through all the Nootka rose, stinging nettle, and all that other clinging, stinging, sticking, stabbing stuff that kept the shack so isolated from nosey day hikers in the *first* damn place!

Somebody then insisted that *that* was no reason to go off and forget to replace the stinkin' *padlock*. **Somebody** *also* expressed discontent with clambering over half a mile of rocks (in order to skirt the nightmare of the bramble thorn thickets) only to find the door to the hide-out wide open for *anyone* who might happen to feel like dropping in, looking around, you know, maybe putting two and two together, and ***messing up the whole freakin' works!***

Someone Else decided to remind **Somebody** that the shack door was *not* left wide open—it was just goddamned left unlocked.

Somebody *then* became *very* vexed, and asked **Someone Else,** *"What's the goddamn difference?"*

Someone Else said, *"Fine!"* **Someone Else** also said that it would probably be a good idea if **Somebody** took the keys—*both* of them—so that **Somebody** could thus have *complete-ass-control* of the padlock, because **Someone Else** didn't feel like being chewed out over this shit anymore!

Somebody thought that was a *magNIFicent* idea, since **Someone Else** hadn't shown a whole lot in the way of responsi-damn-bility where padlocks were concerned.

Somebody then asked **Someone Else** to hand over the keys. Whereupon, **Someone Else** dug around in a pants pocket and produced...a key.

Somebody inquired where the *other stinkin'* key might be, and **Someone Else** began digging through *all kinds* of pockets, hurriedly.

Thereupon, **Somebody** became *increasingly* agitated, and demanded that **Someone Else** better have that other key on 'em, *or else* he, **Somebody,** *might* just have to resort to twisting **Someone Else's** keister!

Someone Else shrugged his shoulders, and attempted to remind **Somebody** that it only took *one* key to open the stupid padlock, and so what was the big damn deal?

Somebody then got almost *too pissed off* to articulate coherently. At which point, **Somebody** snatched the key out of **Someone Else's** hand, jammed it into *his own* pants pocket, and crushed the padlock closed, barking something like, ***"See how that works…Morris Ronald?"***

("?")

"Morris Ronald…***MO-RON! Moron! Jayzuz!"***

Finally, **Somebody** and **Someone Else** tromped angrily up a short rise of waist-high grass that masked their passage to and from the hidden meadow, wherein lay the newly-relocked ramshackle shed. On the way out, both of them—**Somebody** and **Someone Else**—inadvertently stepped over the *other* key to the shanty padlock; the key which had been dropped there just a few days ago by a trinket-loving bird *(you, Crow!)* who had skittishly coughed it up, so to speak, after being startled at the unexpected sonic boom of a low-flying jet.

Remarkable. Yes?

*

They were lucky to find a booth at 'Laarkin's Soda Queen.'

"Never in all my born days seen so many folks with a 'Jool-Eye Thirst' like I been seein' the last coupla weeks," squawked Pops, hustling every which way with armloads of burgers, shakes, sundaes and tall, frost cold sodas. "What're you Scalawaggers gonna be havin' today?"

Having spotted the 'body-press' inside the Queen, everyone had lingered outside long enough to put their heads together, and make up a snack order in advance. Anything to save old Pops some time on a busy day like this. He'd definitely appreciate not having to stand around with an order book in his beefy hands while everyone went "Uhh, let me see now, what do I want today?"

It came down to three colas (make one cherry!), a Green River, and a Graveyard.

Ahhh. 'The Graveyard.'

A most unusual concoction consisting of equal parts cola, lemon-lime, orange, root beer, and creme soda. Not something that *everyone* necessarily found tasty, nor even thirst-quenching. But it was a bad boy blended beverage with a definite cult following among many of Appleton's more experimental soda freaks. Like, for instance, Stuie.

"Anything to chaw with that, kiddos? MegaBasket of fries to pass around?" urged the old man, wiping his hands on his starched white apron.

"I don't think so, Mr. Laarkin. We've all eaten already," Justin said. "But if you'll put all the drinks on one tab for me, I'll take care of the damage."

"Ah-**HA**!" Pops bellowed, walrus-like. "*At last,* I know what day old Justin Bench gets his paycheck on! I'm a'gonna mark my calendar *right now,* so's I can commence to squeezin' this here rich custodian for cash ever time he stops by on a payday!"

Of course, just about everyone in the 'Queen' heard Pops' pronouncement of Justin's jackpot 'wealth.' There followed a series of whoops and yells for him to "buy a round for the house," and to "spread a little of that over here," much to the young man's amusement. And Pops? Oh, there was nothing *that* old boy liked *better* than a roomful of _noisy_ customers in his establishment. *Folks sittin' around in a soda fountain parlor hang-out a'bein' all quiet just ain't right! It jus' ain't!*

Pops Laarkin eventually got on top of the early evening rush, and soon enough everyone was chatting, slurping, and munching contentedly. When he returned with the order for Justin's table, he hesitated momentarily (more for the desired effect than from any kind of *real* uncertainty) before delivering every soft drink to its proper customer.

"Lessee here," mumbled Pops, trying to appear as if he'd just consulted his crystal ball, when, in fact, he was a just a savvy drug store/hang-out owner who *really knew* his customers. "Here's a Green River. That goes to Mr. Big Money Justin hisself, heh, heh. An' then here's a cherry cola, why that'd be for Miss Kelsea, am I right? 'Course I am. An' I got a coupla regular colas for Erik and Miss Sandy, how'm I doin' so far kids? An' this here bubblin' cauldron of lighter fluid and battery acid which, by-the-by, requires specially licensed gloves just to safely handle…why, this 'un was brewed up special for none other than Master LeMaster, an' good luck to ya son. Be careful. It's flammable. Also toxic, so be sure to not get any on yer flesh. Oh! An' here's a MegaBucket of fries for the bunch o'ya!"

"Oops, we never ordered any food, Pops," Kelsea cried. "This must be somebody else's. We're not really very hungry."

"Yes ya'are! Ya jus' don't know it!" chimed the bespecktacled old duffer. "An' don't even *think* of arguin' with me, 'cause I've never been wrong a day in my life, except for that one time back in '69 when I *thought* I was wrong, but I was actually *right*, so I was, well…wrong, I reckon…come to think of it, aw, quit pesterin' me with yer tail-chasin' pretzel logic. Can't you see I got customers to *bother*?"

"There he goes," mused Stuart, taking a long tug on his Graveyard, and keeping an eye on the old shopkeeper's antics, "the unstoppable Pops Laarkin. One. Of. A. Kind!"

"Indubitably!" seconded Sandy, who then added, "Ye gods and little fish, Stu! How can you drink that noxious concoction? It's positively disgusting."

Stuart dismissed the criticism with a wave of his hand. "I *totally forgive* those of you who weren't fortunate enough to be born with a discerning palate loaded to the max with gourmet-level taste buds. (Stifling a yawn, for effect) It's not your fault."

Plenty of eye-rolling, head-shakes, and groans after *that* one.

"'Course, I'm not terribly wise in the ways of soda-guzzlin', mind you," prodded Justin, studying the streamlined curve of a fat, greasy French fry. "But *I* think that stuff you're drinkin' could probably scald the chrome offa trailer hitch."

Laughs and elbow jabs go around the table.

"Yeah, Stu*arto*!" offered Kelsea in a warning tone. "I've watched my dad use that stuff to degrease his tools *lots* of times. Says it's better than sulfuric acid for the really *tough* jobs."

Stuart held the large, frosty glass under his nose and waved it in a circular fashion, lightly inhaling, as if it were an expensive glass of rare, vintage French wine.

"Note the bouquet," he insisted. "Playful, with just a few hints of oak and berry. No, my fellow Scalawags, this is a *heady* elixir; full of mischief and brashness, which only a true connoisseur of refined tastes and world-class experience could possibly—"

He stopped right there, glaring hypnotically across the table; straight over the backrest of the booth where Justin, Kelsea, and his sister sat watching him with sudden concern. Erik was next to pick up on his enigmatic matter, and he too became very still, looking for all the world like a deer in the headlights. Then he began slowly shaking his head from side to side as if to say: "Do *not* turn around. Do *not*!"

The three of them—with their backs to 'whatever it was'—played along, and did their best to maintain an air of casual chattering; biding their time, and wondering what the hell the hush was about.

"So-ooo, the movie turned out *way* dumber than all those reviews would have you believe," Erik stated flatly. That sentence fragment had nothing to do with *anything*, and the look of near-absolute blankness on his face meant simply: "Guys, hold on just a few more seconds. Be cool. You are _not_ gonna _believe_ this!"

Indeed, the Scalawags could not have been more surprised if Elvis had walked by, decked out in that fetching, cloud-white Las Vegas cape and pantsuit. They could not have been more knocked off their collective feet if Napoleon Bonaparte strode through—hand stuffed inside his jacket, with that sideways military hat perched upon his arrogant little head. They could not have been more cataclysmically *rocked* if Bargog—Inter-Celestial Flesh Harvester from the Pan-Neural

Prefects of the Thirteenth Dimension—particle-beamed to life directly in front of them, asking for directions to the Swimming Hole.

Remember? The whole reason for that 'meeting-of-the-minds' at the 'Soda Queen' was to discuss new evidence that had been uncovered by Stu*arto* LeMaster. That, *and* to review The Debbin Ramsay Issue, in toto.

Debbin Ramsay.

The Debbin Ramsay—the *very* one—who was, even now, sauntering up to the fountain counter, leaving five young Appletonians in her fragrant wake; each staring mutely at the others; fidgeting nervously with their soft drink straws.

Sandy continued to keep her eyes on Stuart; no longer radiating Ramsay-esque heat waves of *Amour,* but who presently looked like nothing so much as a man marking time on 'Death Row.' Erik's gaze averted everyone else's, as he dispatched his nervous tension by mini-sucking hundreds of thousands of hummingbird-sized sips of his cola.

Justin and Kelsea stared at one another's soft drinks, and you could almost hear the gears commence a simultaneous grinding as their mental motors engaged, full throttle, in a manic attempt to seize upon *any* opportunity—however small!—for information or evidence which might come to light in the next successive moments.

"*I* say we *confront* her," Stuart whispered finally. "*Right here! Right now!* Let's find out once and for all what this whole butt-ugly thing is about!"

The briefest of glances from Justin told them all that *that* was *not* an option.

Never was, and probably never *would be.*

"Shh," warned his twin, "listen up. We're close enough to maybe hear what she's saying."

"Hi, Mr. Laarkin," Debbin, honey-voiced and chirpy. "I'd like a medium cola, please, and guess who needs to order some more Beatrix."

That brought a jumble of hands-over-the-mouths mumbles from the Scalawag table!

But with the 'Soda Queen' being busy and buzzy on this particular early summer evening, Debbin Ramsay would have needed the built-in radar of a fruit bat to have heard and understood the content of the hushed, hyper-excitable conversation that ensued just a few feet away.

"My goo'ness," exclaimed Pops in amazement. "You certainly go through a lot of that stuff. Now, I *know* it's mocha, sweetheart. But yer *not* s'posed ta *eat* it, ya know."

The girl laughed brightly. "Well, like everything else, it's just not *lost-proof.* With some people, it's their sunglasses, or their car keys. With me, it's my lipstick."

"Hmmph. Pretty spendy item to be losin' an' replacin' all the time. Not that I'm complainin', mind ya. A sale is a sale, and I got a *big mouth* to feed, namely, my *own*! But maybe you oughta try drillin' a hole in the casing, drawin' a string through it 'an' wearin' it around yer neck, so's ya always know where ya c'n put yer mitts on it."

Debbin laughed again, "Not a bad idea, Mr. Laarkin. I'll certainly give it some thought. In the meantime, it's a good thing I landed that job at the City Pool. Between trying to *save* up for college, *and* pay up for my *personal* excesses, I need every paycheck I can get."

It was Pops' turn to chuckle. "Well, Debbie-Lu, we *all* got our little ways about us. It's part o'what makes the world go 'round. You jus' stick with that there 'high-society' make-up 'cause it looks real purty on ya. Just remember to leave the drugs, an' booze an' that old stuff alone, an' don't you worry a skosh 'bout *what* ya pay fer lipstick <u>or</u> how often ya manage to misplace it. Ain't nobody's business but yer own, anyways."

"Thanks, Mr. Laarkin. I'll be back in a few days for the Beatrix. Well, I've gotta get back to the pool. How much for the soft drink?"

Pops knocked twice on the countertop; his way of indicating that the 'house' was buying. "Can't allow a lady to let herself go *totally broke* in here, can I?" he asked cheerfully.

The tall girl turned to go, and found herself locking in on Justin Bench; passive and pensive at the window booth with his friends.

"Oh, hi Justin!" she bubbled. "I'm glad I ran into you today. You're just the person I wanted to talk to."

The Scalawags were very, **very alert**, now!

"I went up to your place last Friday, but you weren't around."

Stuart coughed a couple of times, but got himself under control. Sandy watched Debbin for telltale signs of criminal admission, or at least *guilt*. Kelsea watched Justin in hopes that he could play the cards he was being dealt without tipping his hand. (She needn't have worried.)

Erik went sipsipsipsipsip.

"Really?" asked Justin innocently. "About what time of the day was that?"

"Oh, about 6:30 or 7:00 pm. I'm not sure exactly."

"Yep, I was down at the Crowls' right about then. Burnin' steaks an' bangin' on Woody," Justin was cool as a cucumber. "What brought you up to the quarry, if I may ask?"

"Glad you *did* ask that, Justin. I talked Mom and Dad into letting me have a pool party at our place. It's by invitation only, because we really don't have the room for the whole high school. Anyway, I was wondering if you'd come and play some music for us. Whattaya say?"

"Well, sure. Sounds like a good time, all right," Justin's voice was reserved, but polite. "I've known most of the kids in those classes since they were in, let's see… must be about eighth or ninth grade, I guess."

"OK, then! It's next Saturday afternoon, say, from noon until around 6:00 pm. Can we ink it?"

"Why not? I'll torture yer ears as long as there's a good supply of two things."

"Like what?" she smiled.

"Well, I can probably eat my own weight in cheeseburgers."

"That's easily taken care of! What else?"

"I'll be needin' a more or less non-stop stream of complimentary remarks regarding the quality of my scabby voice."

Debbin's delight was apparent. "I'll give all the guests a number," she giggled, "and I'll make certain that they continue to schmooze you in a rotating order *all day long,* OK?"

"Got yerself a deal, ma'am." They smiled and shook hands, but before she left, Justin had one further question. "Um, you didn't happen to see anyone *else* up at the cabin that day, did you Debbin? Anyone comin' or goin', or even just lingerin' about the quarry site?"

Debbin looked genuinely puzzled. "Why no, Justin. There was just me and some friends, let's see, there was Nicki, Taylor, and Evan. But nobody even got out of the car except me. Is something wrong?"

"How long were you there? Did you wait around to see if I'd show up?" Justin was being *very* tactful, despite the tricky nature of the questions.

"No, no. We just wanted to invite you to play for us, that's all. As soon as we found out you were gone, we took off for the theater in Weston," Debbin eyed the five of them suspiciously; they were acting a bit strangely. "Justin, is there a *problem* of some kind?"

"Oh, somebody bar-soaped my windows that evening. You know, just goofy kid-stuff. No harm done, really, but I just wondered if you had seen anyone around during that time of the day."

"Hmm. I see. Well, sorry about the soap job, but there wasn't anyone else around when *we* arrived. And all I had with *me* was a bunch of mighty, mighty seniors! *Far* too mature for that kind of 'trick-or-treat' stuff! Now," she became cutesy and impish, "we might be inclined to toss you, fully clothed, into the *swimming pool* next Saturday. But soap your windows? I don't *think* so."

Then, dazzling them all with a 200 million-dollar, ivory-white smile, Debbin 'Rah-Rah' Ramsay bounced out the door of the 'Soda Queen,' exactly like the peppy, preppy cheerleader she was.

"Whew! Whaddaya make of that?" breathed Erik.

"I wish I knew," remarked Justin. "I really wish I knew."

*

144

"Hey, where'd Kooper run off to?"

The band of allies had just stepped outside the 'Soda Queen' and Erik was looking around apprehensively.

"No worries, good buddy," Justin reassured him. "That old dog o'mine tends to wander off from time to time, especially when we're in town together." Justin swung his leg over the seat of his bike, and waited for the rest to saddle up. "Fact is, he's gotten to be such a roamin', gypsy-dog lately that I'm startin' to think maybe he's got a girlfriend stashed around hereabouts someplace." He smiled at the idea, and added, "Shows up at the quarry cabin around ten, ten-thirty lookin' real smug-like. Whatcha think, Erik? Think ol' Koop's in love?"

Erik threw a quick glance in Sandy LeMaster's direction. She was watching him—a look of mild curiosity in her soft expression. *Well, Erik?*

"Um. I really wouldn't know anything about that, um, Justin," he managed.

"Uh-huh," countered his older friend. "Well, what say we head down to the park, and put our heads together for a just little while more?" *(Yes! Erik Michael Remarque—deftly dodging yet another schoolboy confessional.)*

A peach yellow sun was slowly easing its way down behind Tamarack Ridge when Justin's clan finally got around to squatting, sprawling, and lolling around the bench where the young man sat, one leg over the other and hands behind his head.

"I still say *she's* the one who did it," declared Kelsea. "The shoeless hoof prints we found on the day the message was written—that horse *had* to belong to Debbin. And the mocha lipstick that was used to write the message."

"*Two* messages," corrected Sandy.

"*Two* messages," agreed Kelsea. "Both written with a mocha brown lipstick that *nobody* buys, or *uses,* except for her. *And* me. Sorta'"

"And don't forget that she *was* up at the cabin just about the time *somebody* unloaded on Justin," Erik offered. "Only a coincidence? *You* make the call."

"Well, she seemed to have a plausible explanation for her visit," thought Sandy.

"Yeah, but maybe that's just what she *wants* us to think," Erik doodled with an oak leaf while he tried to construct a case for criminal genius. "Maybe she's dumb like a fox, know what I mean? Maybe she and her buddies showed up at the cabin, made sure no one was around—maybe posted a guard down by the entrance—then messed up the place good, and drove off sayin' 'Oh, we didn't see *anything*. We were just looking for a *guitar player for our pool party*.'"

"That's true," agreed Kelsea. "The story about being absent-minded and losing her lipstick and all, that could be just blowing smoke, and covering her tracks."

"Same goes for being all nice to Justin—inviting him to play at the party next week. It could just be a clever diversion. You know, act real nice to his face, and run roughshod over him behind his back," said Sandy.

"It just doesn't make any sense," complained Justin. "No darned sense at all. There's no reason in the world for that gal, or anyone else for that matter, to wanta come down on me like this."

"That's exactly the point, I think," insisted Erik. "Hate crimes, bullying, pushin' people around, none of that crap requires a *logical* reason to occur. It just *happens*. It's random, rotten behavior…without good cause of *any* kind. And it puts me right in mind of Rodent, Patch, and Deep Thoughts every damn time I think of it."

"But we haven't seen those guys for weeks."

"That's what I'm getting at. Where have those jokers been lately, and what…have…they…been…up to?"

"Well, I don't know where they been *or* what they been doin'," Justin drawled. "But smart money wouldn't be bettin' on their participation in a bake sale for the new hospital wing."

That brought a chuckle; well-timed because it was sorely needed.

"As if we don't have *enough* to worry about at the moment, how's about I tell you all what *I* ran across when I went out 'strolling' the other day?" Stuart cracked his knuckles and waited. He wore a self-satisfied expression that made him look a little like the Cheshire Cat from Alice in Wonderland; very sly and *chock full* of secrets.

CROW, WHERE ARE YOU? AND WHY ARE YOU NOT HERE TO HEAR THIS? THEN, AGAIN, THERE ARE SO FEW APPLETON SECRETS THAT ESCAPE YOUR ATTENTION. AND, NO DOUBT, YOU ARE ALREADY WELL AWARE OF WHAT HAPPENED TO STUART ON THE DAY OF THE BIG ARGUMENT.

PROBABLY JUST 'YESTERDAY'S NEWS' FOR CROW. TO WIT...

*

"You're so damned smart! *You* figure it out for *yourselves*!"

"You're so damned smart! *You* figure it out for *yourselves*!"

"You're so damned smart! *You* figure it out for *yourselves*!"

Sometimes a block of words gets stuck in your head. Like, for instance, the way a song sometimes does (especially a song that you find particularly repulsive). And no matter where you go, or what you do, the words to that song just keep ricocheting through your imagination, ad nauseam. Doesn't that just drive you sideways?

Uninvited, unwanted brainwave phenomenons—those obsessive mental grooves into which people can sometimes haphazardly slide—can even be *contagious*. Like when you hum a couple of bars of some obnoxious little tune and !*bingo*! right away, it pinches down like a vise inside the poor, helpless mind of some innocent by-listener, who then *hates* you for it, and wishes you would take a long walk on a short dock because you didn't have the common decency to keep your vile, little head rhythms to yourself.

Stuart was thinking as much, as he set off alone to blow off his frustration and try to settle himself down. He wished his friends had not heard those last words—the ones that were resounding inside his *own* head without let up; words he had lashed out at them with such ferocity. He wished he hadn't uttered them—acid dripping from every syllable—without giving some prior thought to the possible consequences. He wished for *their* forgiveness, for *self*-forgiveness, for some kind of…clarity.

But *visual clarity* is not possible when the saltwater wells up faster than it can be blinked away. And *clarity of purpose*? Well, that would have to languish in the shadows; waiting for the heat and the passion of fury to subside. No creative light could strike until it did so.

As for *mental clarity*, would that be a reasonable thing to wish for when your head is yet throbbing with the echoes of hurtful words; spoken in haste, and remembered with such regret? Asking for mental clarity before you've burned the desire for revenge out of your heart is like trying to shovel smoke…with a pitchfork…in the wind. It's like trying to nail jello to the wall, with a flyswatter. Like trying to push an oyster through a keyhole.

Stuart had been wounded.

And Stuart had *inflicted* wounds *in return*.

And in so doing, he, himself, had been wounded *further*.

And inside pain hurts the worst.

"You're so damned smart! *You* figure it out for *yourselves*!"
"You're so damned smart! *You* figure it out for *yourselves*!"

The boy crushed his hands over his ears as if the very act of muffling his hearing could somehow squeeze the sound of those reverberating denunciations out of his consciousness forever. Or maybe he could compact them; crush their dark quality into discreet packets which he could then simply *will away* into the small, still, deep place inside everybody, where forgiveness, when humbly sought, is readily given. Where second chances are handed out without reservation to anyone possessing a heart large enough to admit to having made a mistake for which one is truly sorry.

Stuart LeMaster was only 200 meters into the underbrush when he realized, with a massive degree of relief, that he had already forgiven his friends for the misunderstanding. Step one on the road to reconciliation had been successfully completed.

He also knew, in his heart of hearts, that Justin, Kelsea, Erik, and his sister would grant him amnesty—without trial—the split second he rejoined the group. It's the way they _were_ about each other. It's the way they'd always been…and, it was the way they'd always be.

That was step three.

But wedged between them was step two; arguably the most difficult piece of the equation. Because in order to deal with his ego, and to acquire closure to the incident, Stu had to wrestle with the harshest critic of all; the one whose favor was infinitely hardest to curry. Stu was going to have to find a way of forgiving *himself*. Not as easy a task as it may initially seem.

That was the fever, and that was the fury that scorched and tortured poor Stuart as he thrashed his way through the brambles and briars of the quarry nether quarters. He would mangle his way through that tangle of intense, unchecked growth. He would sweat, swear, fight, barge, and *hack away* with his body against the physical impediment of this wild barricade; the same way his heart/mind/spirit would clash and collide with the petty character flaw of pride…silly human pride.

This, all of it, to be *thrashed through* and *struggled with*—yard by brush choked yard—endured and overcome, that he might through sweat, muscle, and invective laden self-examination, reclaim his rightful place amongst his friends; might initiate the beginnings of an identity reflective of truer self-knowledge and self-assurance. Might inaugurate the development of more polished, more mature, and more civil behavior.

To go, and be, back home. Where he belonged.

*

Just how long did 15-year-old Stuart LeM pound and pummel at his almost impassable wilderness wall? More than two hours. Almost three, actually. The bristling claws of wild rose bit through his clothing and into his flesh. Blackberry vines, like ropes of barbed wire, snagged his jeans and tried to hold him—groaning—in their puncturing embrace. The toothy, jagged ends of broken branches revealed themselves from out of nowhere, abrading his shins and causing him to tumble face-first onto coarse-grained granite boulders which ground at his elbows and bruised his forearms.

This heaving, lung-searing 'dance-with-the-devil' left the boy soaked in perspiration, which bled from his body in tiny rivulets; across and down the dirt-and-pollen-stained raceways of his skin, where it lit up miniature stinging fires in scores of scrapes and scratches.

The punishment went on and on, and Stuart, filled to overflowing with adrenaline and self-pity, seemed incapable of exhausting the wellsprings of his disappointment. His ribs began to ache with the effort of delivering more fuel to his heaving lungs. But he continued to inhale enormous gulps of air, and to flail, half-cartoonishly, half-psychotically at the wreckage of chaotic vegetation—remorseful, but unrelenting.

When he finally exploded from the curtain of trees, his initial reaction was to burst into fits of laughter. There was no gradual tapering or thinning from the middle brush to meadow. It was like a line had been drawn in the forest; distinct, specific, and well defined. On one side of it, he was standing upright—tall and free limbed—in a quiet meadow of breeze blown grass. On the other side, he had been stooped and ensnarled; racing and ranting against absolute nothingness in a directionless, green hell.

It was comical, in its own weird way.

The meadow itself was rather ovoid; roughly 30 meters across and 40 meters up and down its grassy slope. The wider part of the egg-shaped field was nearer the top, where an enormous slide of talus rose steeply up the side of the mountain. The rest of the opening was completely encased by the same dense woodland through which Stuart had come thrashing, crashing, and crawling just moments before.

And then there was the shanty. It sat there, in serene isolation, in the center of the clearing. Stuart noticed that the roof was intact, although that was about *all* you *could* say about it. It was sturdily built, but it was difficult to guess just how old it actually was, or what it's intended purpose had originally been. It didn't have the appearance of living quarters; at least it was not the kind of structure which one would think of being inhabitable by today's standards. And it was bigger than a storage shed, much bigger, although its boxy, seemingly one-room construct gave it a kind of multi-purpose quality.

It was plain. It was simple and unadorned; fashioned from fitted logs and designed with a function—rather than beauty, or form—in mind. There was no chimney, no porch, and no windows.

There was a single door. With a padlock on it.

*

YOU ARE THE CROW.

YOUR WING MUSCLE POUNDS A WINDSONG THAT IS THE MELODY OF YOUR STRUGGLE; YOUR RISK-FILLED, FREE LIFE. PERIL ABOUNDS IN CROWWORLD. DANGER LIES HIDDEN— MASKED AT EVERY LEVEL—AND YOUR EXISTENCE HANGS BY THE THREAD OF FORTUITOUS MOMENTS. SOMETIMES YOU EAT. SOMETIMES YOU ARE EATEN. SUCH IS THE PRICE YOU PAY FOR YOUR FREEDOM; FOR THE UNPARALLELED JOY OF CROWFLIGHT—RAPTURE BEYOND THE RECKONING OF MORTALS WHO LONG, LONG AGES AGO COLLECTIVELY AGREED TO EXCHANGE THEIR WILD, NATURE-GIVEN LIBERTY FOR A CLAUSTROPHOBIC AND IMPOVERISHED KIND OF PALE SECURITY.

SOME THINGS ARE MUCH WORSE THAN DEATH. BUT ONLY LONGLEGS WOULD KNOW ABOUT THAT.

YOU GLIDE WITH GRACE AND GLORY; REVELING IN UNTAMABLE OCEANS OF MOUNTAIN WIND—SKIRTING THE MID-SLOPE OF THE TALUS RUBBLE WHICH STRETCHES, FROZEN-TUMBLED, ABOVE THE SHANTY MEADOW. YOUR AERIAL

BALLET IS THE SYMBOL—THE EMBODIMENT—OF COLD HUNGER; OF INCESSANT, UNCONDITIONAL VIGILANCE, OF STARK, LIVING FACT AND INEXPRESSIBLE, LIMITLESS JOY.

YOU ARE THE CROW. AND YOU ARE AT-ONE-WITH-ALL.

YOU SEE THE YOUNG LONGLEGS, ALONE AND LONELY, STANDING AT THE PERIMETER OF THE CLEARING FAR BELOW YOU. HE IS STUDYING THE SHACK. THE DOOR, OF WHICH, APPEARS TO BE OF PARTICULAR INTEREST. HE IS MOVING TOWARD THE DOOR OF THE SHACK. YOU CONTINUE TO FLY ACROSS THE BOULDER-STREWN SLOPE OF THE MOUNTAINSIDE; BACK IN THE DIRECTION FROM WHICH THE LONGLEGS HAD EMERGED—SWEAT-STAINED AND WILD-EYED—FROM THE TREE LAND. BACK TOWARD YOUR NEST HOME AND THE QUARRY.

YOU CALL TWICE; PLAINTIVE-SOUNDING UTTERANCES WHICH NONETHELESS DENOTE CROW EXHILARATION; CROW EXUBERANCE.

THE LONGLEGS HEARS YOUR CRY, AND PIVOTS HIS ATTENTION HEAVENWARD; TAKING NOTE OF YOUR SKY PATH BEFORE RETURNING TO HIS INVESTIGATION OF THE OLD SHED. THAT THE LONGLEGS WILL DISCOVER AND MAKE USE OF THE LITTLE SHINE IS SUDDENLY PART AND PARCEL TO CROW COMMON TASK; INTEGRAL, NOW, TO AT-ONE-NESS WITH CROWKNOWLEDGE. PRECISELY HERE AND NOW—IN THIS VERY SPOT, AT THIS EXACT MOMENT—CROW TRANSCENDS SENTIENCE...BECOMES PRESCIENT. AND YOUR EYES—THE LITTLE GRAY BEADS—GO BLUE.

(O' RAVENRILL!)

NINE MORE STROKES OF WING MUSCLE AND YOU ARE GONE FROM SIGHT.

*

Stuart approached the rough-hewn timber door cautiously, warily; coming to a full stop every few feet in his advance to scan the edges of the field for signs of movement.

He strained his hearing—breath suspended for long seconds—striving for awareness of the tiniest of tell-tale sounds which might indicate the presence of any "anti-Stuart entity."

The sad, high squawk of a Crow drew the boy's attention cloud-ward, and he watched the bird in flight until it became a black dot, and until the dot had disappeared behind towering columns of tan-brown bark and feathery evergreen needles.

That way—over yonder—*that* was the *best* way into and out of the shanty meadowland; a judgment influenced, in no small part, by CrowCry, CrowWingPath, and Stuie's own conscious decision to believe what his eyes and ears told him.

Picking one's way over and amongst the enormous avalanche of boulders was infinitely preferable to hurling headlong through that dark forest fortress. North, across the rocks, probably over that finger ridge and back down into Appleton Quarry: *that* was his return-of-choice.

Stuart continued inching his way to the strange little building—eyes darting in all directions, keeping to the grassy ground in order to safeguard against stepping upon a dry branch that may snap and reveal his presence...to whom? *The door is* padlocked, *big guy. No one is in there unless they are* locked *in there, man.*

He was beginning to acclimate to the self-soothing notion that "prob'ly nobody's home," and, further, he was pondering the idea of (guy-ish dream of grandeur, here) maybe springing open that beguiling padlock, when, carefully attending to foot placement, lo and behold...a key! ***The*** key...lying in the grass...right beside his sneakered left foot, and only meters from the meadow shanty.

"Well, I'll be..." Stu, aloud to himself. "I dunno who dropped *this* here, but I'll just freakin' *bet* that it fits that lock... Right. Over. There!"

Sneaking one more glimpse around the meadow perimeter, Stuart slipped the key up inside the heavy, silver padlock; twisting his wrist to the right, and popping the locking mechanism. Drops the lock and key into his pants pocket, presses his ear to the door of the shack; holding his breath. Quietly, *ever so quietly,* leans in on the stout wooden door, an inch. A sliver of a suggestion of a crack in the opening of the doorway is too eensy to reveal anything about what may lay a'wait inside. *Well. This is it then, laddie. Far bay-tar, ar far warse.* Stuart **Mc**LeMaster, in his finest Scottish internal monologue. *Nothing more can be known about this unlikely, little discovery wi'out openin' 'er up all the way, matie. M'kay...one last good, hard gander around my behind-ers, for security's sake, and then...*

The door swung open easily; hardly the hint of a sigh escaping its rusty hinges.

There were two sleeping bags tossed haphazardly upon the plank floor near the walls of the structure. They were worn; old-fashioned, and lacking modern insulating design and detail. These bags weren't brought here for the purposes of sleeping comfortably through long nights of cold mountain air. (And besides, there were no pillows.) Clearly, they were hauled all the way up here just so Somebody (or maybe **Someone Else!**) could have something to put between his ass and a hard wooden floor.

In the center of the room were two wooden apple boxes; still sturdy, even these many years beyond usage as a durable container for consumable products of a dead industry. They were probably substituting as chairs, Stu guessed.

Crumpled potato chip sacks, and crushed soda cans littered the floor. A calendar was tacked to the wall; a different South Sea island in full color on each page. A deck of playing cards, a roll of toilet paper, a short stack of old Rolling Stone magazines, a large canteen of water. This was a meeting place, Stuart deducted; a clubhouse (or something) for who-knows-whom. Unknown, unnumbered people were making a long trek over the broken stone highway—whenever, and for whatever reasons—to convene here, where the ears and the eyes of any valley folk would not intrude.

Stuart was feeling very clever indeed, after having pieced together as much of the mystery as he felt he had a right to. After all, there was no contraband to be found, and if this hut was somebody's cool, little get-away in the woods, well, who was *he* to come barging in, and begin mucking about?

He had just turned his back on the minor mess of the cabin floor, and was extending his hand for the metal doorknob when something flat and white entered the field of his peripheral vision. It was a 12-inch square chunk of that particular kind of material from which school whiteboards are made. A mini-whiteboard. Stu read the writing on the slate, puzzling over the possibilities of meaning and replaced it gingerly on the floor where he had found it.

Then he trotted hurriedly up the meadow slope to the rockslide where he picked, hopped, and scrambled from stone to stone for 40 minutes in the direction of the quarry site and his bicycle. He had remembered to replace the padlock upon the door hasp. And he had diligently and dutifully remembered to snap it shut. Alas, he *had not* snapped it *completely* shut.

There *is* a qualitative difference.

*

Ice cubes clinked contentedly in tall glasses filled to the top with tart, freshly-squeezed lemonade. Scalawags sipping; absent-mindedly—almost robotically—as if the only way Stuart's tale could unfold was drop by drop; like a cold summer drink trickling down a 'Jool-Eye Throat' in the heat of the summer-vacation-month-of-your-choice.

The idea of an old, abandoned shack lying so close to the quarry in a hidden meadow was interesting, *more* than interesting. It was downright intriguing. Practically *irresistible* (at least to a *couple* of the Scalawags). And whaddaya wanna bet that *they* were already thinking about checkin' out that there shanty? When the time was right.

"That's somethin'," mused Justin, strumming his way through some random chord changes. "This's been my home for the better part of three years, an' I never had an inkling there were buildings of *any* kind up around here, other than the caretaker's cabin."

"Well, Appleton goes back pretty far," offered Kelsea. "Lots of pioneers tried to make a go of it up and down the valley, so I imagine at least *some* of those houses and barns and sheds are gonna stand up over time."

"Yeah, I remember you telling me about miners, railroaders, um, orchardmen. All kinds people who took a turn at making a living here. It makes sense that when folks give up on their dreams and move on, well, the land, and the forest, and all just kind of reclaims itself. Whatever is left behind could easily stay hidden from sight for who-knows-how-long."

"Makes me wonder if there are other buildings scattered in the woods."

"Wouldn't surprise me in the least. It's not like folks could take their buildings *with* 'em when they moved on, or would just burn 'em to the ground when they were finished with 'em."

"And with more people *leaving* than moving in, there were probably plenty of places that couldn't be *sold* off, so, there they sat, and there they sit."

"I wonder if any of these old buildings have anything *valuable* left in them," mused Erik with a cheesy look in his eye. "Maybe there's a profit to be made here."

He was clearly baiting the others, and they *knew* it.

"Hey, Justin," announced Sandy playfully. "Our Financial Officer and Chief Investment Analyst, Erik 'The Pirate' Remarque, informs me that there is a veritable *fortune* to be made by ransacking the remaining rat_holes of Kennawack County."

Kelsea quickly joined the dog pile. "I say we storm that castle **_now_**!"

"And take no prisoners!" echoed Stu.

"Careful, citizens!" warned Justin with mock gravity. "According to Stuart's report, that stinkin', broke-down dump might still have people hangin' around it off and on. They may not cough up their treasures without a fight."

"If fight we must, then fight we, um, we uh, *must!*" yodeled Erik. A theatrical look of unleashed mania reddening his eyes. "Quickly, brethren, and sis-tren! Join the bloody fray!"

"For king and country!" wailed Sandy.

"For cash and currency!" bawled Erik.

"For pancakes and syrup!" whooped Stuart.

"For ever and ever!" yelled Kelsea.

"For cryin' out loud!" hollered Justin.

"Did somebody shout something about a 'cistern?'" demanded Sandy.

A free-for-all ensued which *included*, but was *not limited to* the following exercises in random mayhem: unrestrained laughter, noogies, loud/discordant guitar playing, dog barks, shrill whistles, animal calls, a couple of throat searing belches, bad jokes about "storming the castle," dramatic posturing, and minor civil disobedience.

Many things may be said, in varying shades of truth, about those Scalawags. But chief among them is this axiom: They know how to have a good time.

*

The third week of July—a Wednesday—floated by, warm and lazy (not unlike the Quarry Gang, itself). It wasn't really a day for swimming. It really wasn't a day for bike riding. It was a day to hang out, be loose, and listen to the telling and retelling of Stuart's brave tale of forbidding forests and hidden surprises. It was a well-known fact that *nobody*, at least to anyone's recollection, had ever penetrated that part of the woods which sprawled south and southwest of the quarry corner. It was just too intimidating—thick, tangled, dark—with nothing compelling to entice or tempt an investigation of its remote recesses.

The idea of ascending the finger ridge and skirting the landslide to the meadow shanty was fascinating. Everyone was curious about its secluded nature. Everyone loved 'the strange new secret.' Everyone wanted to be on the *inside* of a bit of information that only a select few were privileged to possess.

But it was for that very reason that Justin cautioned them all to resist the urge to explore the area.

"Somebody *else* wanted to have a secret," Justin instructed. "And they *found* one *before* Stu did. So I think we oughta let 'em have their hideout and not be botherin' 'em."

Group agreement thus assured, Kelsea added, "We've kind of got *our* spots staked out around town—the bench at the park, the big rock at the swimming hole. Most people assume that it's sorta *our* territory, and they respect that. We can do the same for someone else."

"The fact that Stuart explored their meeting place can be forgiven," continued Sandy, "because he came across the shanty by accident. He had every right to investigate it in order to ascertain its possible usefulness to his friends. He didn't know it already had 'owners.'"

"That reminds me of a little something I forgot to mention," advised Stuart, tunefully jingling the remaining cubes of ice in his glass. *A frosty melody for a warm day*, he thought to himself with a smile. He quickly double checked to make certain that he had the full attention of his audience. He did *not* want to be blown off again, and although he really needn't have worried about a recurrence of *that* nature, he was aware of the possibility, and he *did* worry about it all the same. Once bitten, twice shy, as it were.

"Just as I was getting ready to leave, I noticed a small square of whiteboard, like school whiteboard, ya know? Anyway, it was lying on the floor with bits of scrap and stuff, and I picked it up 'cause it had some writing on it."

"And?" Kelsea, urging.

"And it said five things, like a list—one word above the other."

"And?" Sandy, insisting.

It said:

"Glass

Trash

Float

Wood

Bark."

"Glass, trash, float, wood, bark," repeated Justin, rubbing his chin. "Wonder what that could mean?"

"Could be a code of some kind," offered Erik hopefully.

"Sure. If a club meets there sometimes, maybe it's part of the secrecy that only the membership would know about."

Sandy's head was working overtime. "Maybe the first letter of each word represents something, like the first or last letter in each member's name."

"Maybe it stands for something they want to bring to the shed, or the first letter of each word in a list of things they want to remember."

"Or a list of things they are going to do."

The brainstorming luxury liner hadn't even left the dock when Stuart let the other shoe fall.

"I'm not for sure what the words on the list mean," he murmured quietly. "But I can tell you *one* thing that's *very* important to us at this time."

Eight eyes, eight ears, four hearts, and four minds *all* locked onto Stuart, and his concluding remark about the meadow cabin.

"That list," he stated evenly, "was written using a mocha lipstick." The boy continued whirling ice cubes around the inside of his empty glass; a tight-lipped, twinkly eyed smile on his tan, round face that said, "Interesting, don't you think?"

*

Here's something strange:

Thursday afternoon. Light breezes, warm sunshine—puffy clouds suspended in a pond of blue air. It had been a short workday, and Justin had the rest of the afternoon to himself. Himself, his dog, his guitar, and his park bench.

Seizing the rare opportunity to snag some solitary kickback time, Justin slumped onto his bench—slit-eyed from the heavy heat—the brim of his Filson hat shading his forehead from a narrow gap of sunlight leaking through the shade of an enormous, spread-limbed oak (planted well over 100 years ago, and still snaking its crooked arms skyward like a frozen octopus).

Kooper was fast asleep beneath the legs of his owner; partially shaded by the wobbly, green bench. Gettin' ju-ust enough sun to keep himself warm, and ju-ust enough shade to keep himself a' snoozin.' Justin knew that the ol' guy was plumb tuckered out, because he hadn't show up at the cabin until nearly 10:00 pm last night. *Oh, Kooper, you bad boy. What do you find to occupy your doggy time away from home?*

Ol' Koop was keeping it to himself. Keeping everybody guessing about the kinds of canine Scalawags that *he'd* been running with. Justin watched him lying there. Why, it almost looked like he had a trace of a smile on his dreamy face, didn't it?

Well, whatever it was that he'd been up to, he didn't seem to be getting into any trouble over it. Because if he had been digging up vegetable gardens, or chasing cats, or knocking over garbage cans, Justin would have heard from Carlos Santiago by now. No, Kooperdog was licensed and up-to-date with all his vaccinations. He was street-legal and street-smart, and Justin—as well as all the other Appletonians—had jointly concluded that doggies who minded their P's and Q's should be left to quietly go about the business of attending to their sundry duties without meddlesome interference from human beings.

Justin sighed. Kooper sighed. What a day!

Then, from outta the blue, Woody 'hopped up' on Justin's knee, (Imagine that!) demanding attention of the melodic type. Eager to comply, as always, Justin glided into song while uncountable, tiny, park birds supplied rhapsodic counterpoint in 4/4 time:

"Simple Man—simple dreams,
a simple life, or so it seems.
Day to day—nothing new.

Who'd have thought your dreams would all come true?"

You wouldn't know it to watch him—sitting alone in the mottled half-shade of splendid tree cover—but Justin Michael Thomas Bench was 'multi-tasking,' coveting some quality solo time with the things he loved best in life: his dog, his park bench, his guitar, and his music; his friends would be along soon enough.

But simultaneously, he was very carefully considering a multitude of options, choices, and alternatives—along with their possible ramifications—in regard to certain mysterious and wholly unpleasant events which had recently transpired. He was playing and singing; singing and thinking; thinking and *hugging the moment.* Laying claim to time—*Crowlike*—with the clarified absoluteness of untainted self-respect. Justin continued to sing:

"Were you born, times ago,

a mountain man? Well, I don't know.

If you were, it's long forgot.

Little things mean such an awful lot."

Justin thought: *We need to keep goin' slowly on this. Slowly, at all costs. Now, we all know that the evidence is startin' to pile up. We're gettin' more clues…well, almost daily. An' that's good! It means we're steadily buildin' up a buncha information that can support the truth. It also helps us to whittle away at ideas that take us down the wrong road; that might make us start pointin' fingers at the wrong people. Not good!*

And a bad move now could easily undo everything we've come to know about what's been goin' on around here. The 'bad guys'—and I'm gonna hafta think there's mor'n one, on account of the stuff found at Stuart's woodland shack—now, they're smart an' wary. They'll be twice as savvy if we slip and tip our hand too soon. We'll never pin 'em down if they start gettin' any more cautious than they already are.

Justin sang on:

"And as you go about your simple ways,

you'll take a blessing with you all your days;

your simple days,

oh Simple Man."

Justin, still pondering: *Stuart already told us that to his way of thinkin', there wasn't anything of interest in the shanty except for the message on the slate. OK...that's* big *news; very important, I'll admit, because it might just put a, what? An enemy camp right outside my own back door. I dunno if that brings us any closer to puttin' a face on the person, or person_s, who are out to get me. But if we go pokin' around that shack, sooner or later we're gonna be found out. You can take* that *to the bank, an' live off the interest ya get for it.*

More internal brainstorming, as if rehearsing what he wanted to confess to his friends: *Now, I'm not sayin' we shouldn't make a visit or two to the meadow shanty, especially now that Daniel 'Stuie' Boone knows the way in an' outta there. And I know how much this ploddin' along of mine is drivin' everyone* crazy. *But I'd rather use the fullness of time to get to the bottom of this; once and for all, and with dead* certainty—*than play a hunch—however strong—and come up with a big ol' pocketful of empty!*

Justin finished his song, sparrows and chickadees continuing with harmonic vocals, as he put the cap on his thought processes: *Whoever it is we're up against has got the second most important weapon of all, right in hand: the element of surprise. But,* we *have somethin' even more valuable than* that...*if* we learn how to use it. We have time *on* our *side.*

As it was soon made clear, *two* of the Scalawags simply could *not* come to terms with Justin's plea for continued, unwavering patience. And *that* bit of imprudence brought them a peck—though not a bushel basket full—of trouble.

*

162

So, *that's not* the <u>*strange*</u> part. Here…<u>*here's*</u> the <u>*strange*</u> part. Or as Hollis Greenwood very well might have been inclined to put it, "Yo! Dig <u>*this*</u>."

Justin had just finished 'multi-tasking,' and was giving due consideration to launching himself into another song, when…

"You're pretty handy with that guitar, young man. Mind if I sit with you a while, take a load off?"

Without waiting for a response, Colonel Harding Corbett Tattenger slipped into the space on the seat beside Justin.

"Hmm. Yamaha, eh?" the colonel plucked Woody from Justin's hands leaving him blinking in unexpected disbelief. "Mmm-hmm. Birch soundboard, rosewood fretboard. Generic machine heads. Fairly well-crafted instrument, I'd say. Nothing extraordinary, mind you. But in the hands of a troubadour such as yourself, quite equal to the task of bringing forth some very pleasurable sounds, eh? Heh, heh."

He handed Woody back to its owner, and let his gaze drop to the old dog, resting comfortably below them.

"Now, I see *this* rascal all over town. Answers to the name of Kooper, does he not?"

At the sound of his name, Kooper acknowledged the recognition with two un-energetic tail thumps before continuing the pursuit of his dog dreams.

"Yes, he's a good ol' guy, this Kooper is," continued the colonel. "I sometimes see him with a pack of kids, sometimes he's just trotting along all by himself. Never causes anyone any trouble, though," he reached under the bench and scratched behind an ear. "Yep. Good ol' boy. Smart, too, I'll bet."

Justin nodded in quiet agreement, but the man didn't leave an opening for a reply.

"I'm Colonel Harding Tattenger," announced the colonel. Years of military training had ingrained a rigid kind of formality into his introductions. The smile flickered briefly from his face; a businesslike expression of stark seriousness flashed and faded, and he extended his hand stiffly. Justin took it, and the two of them shook with all of the warmth that the younger man would later liken to momentarily holding a refrigerated trout in your palm.

"And you, of course, are Justin Bench," the colonel took it upon himself to complete the cordial. "You may or may not have heard my name about the community. I'm, uh, Rodney Tattenger's father. You know Rodney, I'm sure. He'll be a tenth grader this fall. You work for the school district, am I correct? Yes, yes, I thought so. So you probably know every youngster in the whole town pretty well. Heh, heh."

Justin blinked.

"Yes, my career demands a great deal of my attention. Military, you know. Gobbles up a tremendous amount of my time and energy. I travel all over the world on a regular basis. Heh, heh. Mostly the Orient these days."

The colonel certainly loves to hear himself talk, Justin thought.

"Yes, I may begin my day with breakfast in China, and watch the sun go down over dinner in Japan. The rigors and challenges of military life are not for the squeamish, no sir. But the rewards are considerable. To serve one's country at the highest levels of diplomacy and confidentiality is an honor entrusted to few individuals, a *very few individuals,* and I take *great* pride in my accomplishments on behalf of my President and my nation."

Justin blinked, breathed, and listened.

"But nothing lasts forever. 'Nothing gold can stay.' So saith the poet. I'll be resigning my commission soon, within the year, as a matter of fact." At this point, his tone softened—became almost wistful—as if he had suddenly fallen victim to a flood of years sweeping him into non-relevance. Awash in reminiscences, Colonel Tattenger's shell-like expression grew visibly pale. And for a fraction of a moment, the glistening armor of an aging knight-errant was replaced by a cardigan sweater hanging loosely on the shrinking frame of a worn-out old man.

Tattenger gave a little jerk, and his eyes, just seconds ago fixed and distant, retook their piercing, hawklike quality—ice-blue and focused.

"This old soldier," the colonel tapped his chest, all five fingers laced tightly together like a weary salute that had slipped from his head to his heart. "This old soldier has carried out his final assignments. There will be no more top security orders to give. Or to receive. The torch is ready to be passed to a new generation of leaders. And I? I will soon be coming home…*to* a home about which, sadly, I know very little."

Justin fingered a small, deep scratch in Woody's soundboard and waited, seam-lipped.

"Oh, sure. Appleton has been my residence for the past couple of years," recalled the colonel. "My wife and I handpicked this community—*handpicked it,* mind you—with an eye toward the golden years of my retirement. Of all the cities and towns and hamlets we've encountered in our many wanderings, this place—the Middle Kennawack—was simply *destined* to be the final resting spot for this tired warrior and his little family. Unfortunately, this lovely village has been little more than a mailing address for a man such as I, what with jetting off to all points of the globe in a more-or-less nonstop fashion for all these years. And Lord knows it's been tough on Lauren, that's my dear wife, and uh, the boy. It's hard to sink roots and grow strong when the head of the family is off on business for ten months out of the year."

I can see how that could be a problem, thought Justin.

"But my heart has always been with them," insisted the colonel. "I have *always* had their best interests in mind. Yes, yes, yes, my every conscious moment; in fact, my every top-level decision was always arrived at with due consideration for its impact and import upon my loved ones at home. What's good for my family, in particular, is good for the nation as a whole. And vice-versa. It's an inescapable law by which a man may live his life with faultless certainty; and by which he may, with only exceptional *rarity,* make an error in judgment."

Poor Lauren, thought Justin. *And poor Rodent. I mean Rodney. I mean _Rodent_!*

"And as the day of reunion approaches, I am driven to the overwhelming conclusion that I have (short pause for effect, here) fences to mend, as it were. I need plenty of quality time with my wife and son; time which has not been so much stolen from them as (slight clearing of the throat) *borrowed* on a long-term basis, while I fulfilled my pre-ordained obligation to my country, and to the Marine Corps. Very soon, they are, both of them, going to be richly reimbursed for all that lost time. Paid back with interest earned, I might add. Paid back for domestic heroism beyond the call of duty in keeping the home fires burning, and for keeping a candle in the window during the long intervals between my, ah, brief, um, infrequent homecomings."

The man has answers to his own questions, and solutions to his own problems, marveled Justin to himself. *How does he do that?*

"All I really *need* to make my dream a reality is a new start, a new *beginning* in a new *home*, one that is, hopefully, shall we say: *semi-secluded*; where I may conclude the work of my life peacefully sequestered. I am speaking, of course of the arduous yet compelling task of writing my memoirs. For, I could not consider the story of my life to possess a fitting conclusion without that *perfect, particular* piece in place. Heh-heh. A home *outside* of town will also grant me the very private and personal time with which I may reacquaint myself with my wife and son. Long overdue though it is, it is never too late. *Never.*"

Justin Bench stared straight through the colonel's forehead and, metaphorically, right out the back of his skull.

"No, I simply could not abide life in town, however comfortable or even elegant the neighborhood; no matter how opulent the dwelling. I realize that *now* (with a butterfly-brief glimpse at Justin). If I had only understood that about myself earlier, I would have insisted on a *rural* address when we moved here two years ago. But no, then again that's not true either. It was important for Lauren and, er, Rodney to be in town where they could at least mix a bit and socialize. With me overseas so much, it just wouldn't do for them to have been secluded away in some nearby forest all the time."

Good luck, colonel. Let me know how your plans work out for you, thought Justin.

"No sir. I am happy to say that I have a full, clear vision of family life for the Tattengers starting in just a few short months. I have invested my life savings very well, thank you, and I am going to build a good solid house on a large plot of wooded land, and I am going to spend the rest of my days writing, *and* being the kind of man to my family that I was to the Corps: heroic, deserving, selfless, *and* distinguished by service. My world will not be inhabited by the sound of lawnmowers or leaf blowers. No sir! No truck traffic, no bus noises, no car alarms, nor even school bells...er, no offense intended, young man. Just the sound of wind rustling through tall pine limbs, and the call of birds and squirrels arguing over who-gets-to-build-a-nest-where."

I think we're coming to something here.

"So, my guitar-playing gentleman! I am going to allow you to get along with your afternoon! I am going to plant a seed of a thought in your noggin, and then I am going to move along, because I do not, repeat, *do not* want you to respond to my proposition (index finger, straight up in front of him), not...right...now. I want you to *think* about what I have to say to you...very carefully, very critically, and *then* we can converse more when, well...when the time ripens, yes? This could be a very important decision for you, my lad, so be sure and take your close friends into your confidence, and weigh their words well. Opportunities of the kind I am about to offer you occur once in a lifetime—sometimes not even *that* often. Heh, heh. I should know. I've been around the planet a hundred times, and I feel like I've seen and heard it all. Heard it *all!*"

OK. Here it comes...whatever it is.

"Whatever the quarry land is worth, the total acreage, I will give you market price plus 20 percent. It means *that* much to me. Trust me, when the colonel sees what he wants, he knows it right...on...the spot! And mark me here, as well. With the price you fetch from this old fool—heh, heh—you'll be able to set yourself up in just about any kind of lifestyle you could want.

"No. No! Not a word, lad! Either way, you may end up saying something that you could regret for the rest of your born days. Just think. Think long and hard. Then talk with the people you love and trust the most. Then, *think some more!* The offer will still be good when you've had *plenty* of time to look at all sides of the issue."

Here, the colonel gave a sly, confidential wink and lowered his voice to near whisper level; cabalistic. "Just between you, me, and old Kooper here, I'm betting that an intelligent man such as yourself will quickly come to the inescapable conclusion that, well, you really can't afford to *not* take this offer, if you know what I mean." Justin did *not* know what he meant.

Colonel Harding Corbett 'Hard-Core' Tattenger checked his wristwatch. "Holy Hannibal! I have *got* to get going!" He rose smartly, brushing down his slacks, and straightening the tuck of his starched and immaculately pressed short-sleeved shirt.

"Carry on, Mr. Bench. I will be in touch with you in the very near future."

The colonel issued a starched and immaculately pressed smile, saluting professionally and striding smartly across the street to his automobile.

Then, and *only* then did Justin finally find his voice—uttering just ten short, syllables:

"Wait'll we tell the Gang about *this*, Koop!"

*

Justin *did* exercise an opportunity to broach the subject of his 'conversation' with the colonel. And popular Scalawag opinion held that the old boy was unquestionably *barking mad* to entertain a notion that Justin would ever even *consider* parting with the Quarrylands…at *any* price!

"Case closed," confirmed Justin.

"Hallelujah," echoed Sandy.

"Done and done," remarked Erik.

"Locked and sealed," quipped Kelsea.

"What's for lunch?" Wondered Stuart.

Well, that took care of *that*…didn't it?

*

"Jayme, honey, would you run out back for me real quick and let your sister know she's got a phone call? Tell her it's Justin, sweetie."

Gayle Crowl laid the receiver on the breakfast counter, turned the radio volume down a bit, and returned her attention to the family 9 AM-isms; sipping her coffee, buttering toast, reading the headlines in the "Ledger" and watching her girls grow up right before her very eyes.

"Kelsea! Justin's on the phone for ya!" Jayme, shouting through the sliding screen door. Thence, like a scalded rabbit, spinning a 180-degree turn with *blinding* speed, and darting for the hall which joined the kitchen with the foyer.

"Jayme Crowl!" sputtered her mother. She was trying to get the coffee cup away from her lips fast enough to snag a 'teachable moment' with her younger youngster.

"That is _not_ what I…"

Too late. Kelsea's "Sister Sinister" was already gone, out the front door, onto her bicycle and rocketing down the sidewalk; a crusty shingle of jelly-smeared toast clenched between her teeth, and a purposeful look in her eye that said: "Let's get this day *started*!"

"You've gotta be faster than *that* if you want to stay on top of fourth-graders these days." Tim Crowl poured himself a cup of strong coffee, carefully avoiding the studious gaze of his wife. "*I* would **_never_** have allowed that little bandit to engage her forward thrusters in the kitchen like that. Just look at the scorch marks on the linoleum."

Gayle cupped her chin in her hand, tapping her cheek in a sugary display of faux-concern and fawning attention. "OK, Dr. Know-it-all—child psychologist extraordinaire—tell me, s'il vous plait: Just how

169

would *you*, in your infinite wisdom and paternal experience, have handled the situation? But before you wax eloquent, oh learned scholar, could you let me know the precise reason why <u>you</u> didn't snag her *for* me, as she ran *right by you* down the hall? I prithee, for I wouldst learn at the feet of 'The Master.'"

Tim cleared his throat several times, warming to his impromptu role as a stuffy, elitist, professorial guru, preparing to hand down tablets of knowledge from high, airy places located well beyond the understanding of mere mortal men and women.

"Well, to begin with," he huffed, "I am *not* a LeMaster. If you want to learn at the feet of a LeMaster, why I just happen to *know* one, and I can give him a call immediately, if not sooner, and see if he could schedule some time for you. Would you be interested?"

Gayle rolled her eyes, slowing shaking her head from side to side. "Oh, *brother*."

"Nope," countered Tim without a second's hesitation, "he is *not* my brother. No relation whatsoever, actually. But he <u>is</u> a close family friend, and I, therefore, consider him *somewhat akin* to a brother, if you see what I mean."

Gayle began to giggle. Her husband correctly read *that* as a full-on green light, and continued to goof his soulmate relentlessly.

"Second of all, my split-second analysis of this morning's escapade *instantly* revealed to me the paramount importance of allowing...nay, *insisting upon* <u>you</u> solving your <u>own</u> dilemmas. If I should intervene in an attempt to fix all the little problems you create with our children (now on the receiving end of a well-aimed thump to the shoulder from his wife; round-eyed with indignation at the suggestion of ineptness. *Ouch, Gayle!*) and stamping out all the little fires you appear to be unable to keep from igniting *before* the day even gets *started*... "

And *here*, Monsieur Crowl got the full-on assault of kisses and tickles (the old 'One-Two') which pretty much ended *that* particular guru's lecture for the day. And *that* was the way Kelsea found them both as she scurried into the kitchen for her phone call.

"Hi, Jus!' What's up?" Kelsea, aiming a quick, 'parent-like' glance at her mother and father, still horsing around in a warm, yellow patch of morning sun beside the dishwasher.

"Oops. Sorry," apologized her father. "Overseas business call," he advised his wife. "Probably something to do with that Arabian oil interest she's been yawping about. We'd better pipe down. We could mess up the whole deal. Send billions of petro-dollars fluttering wildly into the clutches of the _wrong_ hands."

Gayle Crowl slipped a buttery slice of toast into her husband's mouth. Sliding her hand under a tray containing a plate of biscuits, a jar of jam, and two cups of coffee, she quietly ushered him through the sliding screen door and onto the deck for breakfast.

Parents, smiled Kelsea to herself. _Too weird for words._

"Sorry, Justin. Had to provide some compassionate discipline for the 'old folks.'"

"_Again_?" laughed Justin. "You've got yer hands full with _those two, Kels!_"

"You don't know the _half_ of it, my non-Eskimo friend," Kelsea chimed. "Anyways, what's up?"

"Two words. Gimme two words to define the day."

"Um," Kelsea, deliberating only briefly. "'Kelsea's cool?'"

"Nope," answered Justin.

"'Girls rule?'"

"Definitely _not_!"

"'Think pink?'"

"_What_!"

Kelsea laughed. "It's from a cartoon I was watching this morning. Never mind. Anyways, I give up. What're the two words for the day?"

"You quit too easily, Kels. It's as plain as the nose on Kooper's furry face. C'mon! Look outside! Take a good, long gander at that sunshine an' tell me you don't know what two words grabbed _my_ undivided attention right as soon as I finished up my mow job at the middle school."

"'Where's breakfast?'" teased Kelsea.

"Aw, fer cryin' out loud," he's mumbling now, barely audible, owed to the fact that he is clutching the receiver at knee-level; covering his eyes with his free hand, shaking his head—his patience running thin.

"Just kiddin', Justin," chuckled Kelsea. "Whew, where's your sense of humor? For your information, I happen to know *exactly* what two words are bangin' around in your brainpan on this most auspicious 'Jool-Eye' August day."

"Do tell. Are you clairvoyant?"

"Naw. Just incredibly intelligent."

"Well. I'm waitin' for the *proof* of *that*. What two words am I thinkin'?"

"Elementary, my dear Mr. Bench. Elementary. The words on your mind have *gotta* be 'Swimmin' Hole.' Am I right?"

"Give the little lady a cigar!" announced Justin. "You are truly a wonder of the modern age. Must rub off from the kind of people ya tend to run with!"

"Indubitably," Kelsea, employing her sincerest Sandy LeMaster vocal imitation.

"Hey, do you need to run back up to the quarry…get some stuff before we head out?"

"Nah, I was so set on the river this morning that I brought everything to work with me. Left the cabin at 7:30, got done at 11:30, and stopped by Pops to give ya this here call to arms. Thataway, if you couldn't make the trip, I wouldn't have to double-back and waste all of Koop's leg power."

Waste your leg power, Kelsea internally corrected. "Well, I am all for *that* idea, let's go hug some water!"

*

Standard operating procedures were observed. That is to say, Kelsea got on the phone to Erik Remarque, and Justin called to notify the

LeMaster twins of the plan in progress. Everyone being "in," a rendezvous was made at the Appleton Park bench for the purpose of entertaining alternate ideas and fleshing out the details.

At first, Erik hedged a little, appearing uncertain about the whole idea. He explained that he and Hollis Greenwood had 'headed for the Hole' the last three days running, but had always ended up either catching sight of some or all of Rodent's group of McNasties on the way there, or had arrived to find them already on the beach. It would appear that the dog days of August had been bringing out the water-lover in *everybody* lately.

"There's no way I'm sharing any body of H2O with those 'benthic organisms' (a term surreptitiously snagged from none other than one Sandy LeM)," he remarked firmly. "I'd sooner go to the town pool."

"Yeah, that way we wouldn't have to swim through any oil slicks, either," said Kelsea, wrinkling her nose. "What a slimy bunch of carbon-based life forms!"

"I hear the view is very nice at the town pool, too," offered Stuart helpfully. Referring, of course, to the fact that Debbin Ramsay was newly employed there as a lifeguard. Debbin's swimwear—like her choice in makeup—was top-notch and, well, it could be summed up by re-mentioning that "she always wore it well."

"Listen, before you get too enthused by the enchantments of chlorinated water and deeply tanned, curvy lifeguards, let me just inform you that the rumor mill has it that 'Patch' is also employed there on a part-time basis," Sandy half-admonished her brother whom she suspected (even now!) of harboring some immature fantasy of, oh, say, diving into those sterilized, public pool waters, and somehow *rescuing* Dazzling Debbin from a near-drowning; perhaps selflessly performing some life-saving *mouth-to-mouth* resuscitation. You know, the old *"Oh, Stuie! My hero!"* bit that _some_ boys cannot *help* but *obsess* over.

"Patch? Work?" asked Erik incredulously. "Don't those two words constitute, like, a mutually excluding term?"

"It's *mutually exclusive*," corrected Sandy gently. "And you're right…to a certain degree. But remember, his mom is not exactly the perennial winner of the National Provider of the Year Award. For all of Patch's faults and flaws, he's still got a tough row to hoe. And employment—at the very *least* on a part-time basis—is probably not so much an option for him as it is a *necessity*."

"Pick yer poison," claimed Justin. "If we're gonna cool off today, we may as well resign ourselves to sharin' the wet stuff with the weirdos—one way or t'other. And remember," he added as an afterthought, "if we wanna take Kooper with us, we're gonna *hafta* go to the 'Hole.' Last I heard, Hoskins Memorial Pool took a dim view of furry, four-leggers dogpaddlin' around in their pond."

"Yeah," agreed Stuart. "Koop really looks like he could use a dip. And it's always been more fun swimming *with* him than *without* him. Let's take our chances, and hit the river."

"Everyone's already packed to go. I vote for the Kennawack over the pool," decided Kelsea. "All in favor?"

"Aye! Oops, almost 'aye,'" Justin, stalling out, here. "Gotta run across the street to the drug store an' get me some sunscreen. You guys wanna wait a sec for me here?"

"Nah, I'm comin' with… I could use some more myself."

"Let's get a coupla cold sports drinks, Stu. It's gonna be a scorcher!"

"I need to buy some gum so's I can break this 500 million dollar bill I got in my wallet," said Erik, looking serious as a bad haircut.

"Better keep that weekly allowance of yours for a rainy day, Mr. Bankroll. And afford *me* the small pleasure of springing for your chewing gum!" Sandy LeMaster, all smiles and curls.

"Well, let's go on over, get back an' get goin.' We're burnin' daylight, goys and birls!"

And so across the main street of town, they paraded. *Goys, birls,* doggie, and all.

*

174

WHAT HAPPENED IN APPLETON PARK DURING THE INTERIM—BETWEEN THE PROCUREMENT OF SUNDRY BEACH SUPPLIES AND THE DEPARTURE FOR THE KENNAWACK RIVER—MAY HAVE BEEN WITNESSED BY ANY NUMBER AND VARIETY OF HOME-VERSION WILD WASHINGTON BIRDS; TO NO CONSEQUENCE. BUT <u>YOU</u>, NEWLY BLUE-EYED CROW, NOT ONLY TOOK NOTE OF THOSE PROCEEDINGS, BUT DEVISED AND IMPLEMENTED A PLAN-OF-ACTION FOR REMEDIATION. YOU INTERVENED.

AND THE NATURE, CONSTRUCT, TIMING, AND DURATION OF CROW INTERVENTION IS A THING OF LEGEND; BORN OF FAR-FLUNG OTHERWORLDS, AND CARRIED TO EARTH BY THE DISPERSAL VESSEL, 'ARKADAS,' ON A SEEDING MISSION THAT SPANNED CENTURIES OF EPOCHS ACROSS LEAGUES OF LIGHT-YEARS. A SAGA IN A CLASS OF ITS OWN.

YOU OBSERVE THE TWO LONGLEGS AS THEY SWIFTLY APPROACH THE BICYCLES LEFT BEHIND IN THE PARK BY THE OTHERS; THE ONES COLLECTIVELY REFERRED TO AS 'SCALAWAGS.' ONE OF THE TWO ADMINISTERS SOMETHING TO THE REAR TIRE OF A BICYCLE, THEN ROTATES THE WHEEL—JUST SO—SO THAT THE AFFECTED PORTION IS DIRECTED DOWNWARD, AND RESTS PRESSED AGAINST THE GRASS. THAT DONE, THE TWO SIMPLY JOG OFF ACROSS SUNRISE HIGHWAY, IN THE DIRECTION OF THE TOWN POOL.

CROW WAITS, AND IN SHORT ORDER, THE SCALAWAGS-LONGLEGS COMPLETE THEIR TRANSACTIONS, DEPART THE DRUGSTORE, AND CROSS MAIN STREET TO RECOLLECT THEIR BIKES. THEREBY, YOU ENGAGE IN SOME ATTENTION-GETTING BEHAVIOR.

EXPLICITLY COMPLEX.

CONCEPTUALLY NUANCED.

INFINITESIMALLY INFINITE.

O' RAVENRILL...HOW CROW DELIGHTS—AND <u>EXCELS</u>—IN HIS TASK WORK!

"Well, don't that beat all?"

"Don't *what* beat *what*-all? And please, be specific."

"Hold up, guys...stop. *Stop!* Will you lookit that?" Justin, staring— nonplussed.

The Scalawags are all scrunched up at the edge of the park. Justin has his arms in a spread-eagle position, holding them all back—group-like, his back to the focus of his attention, head and neck screwed around as far as he can wrench them in order to keep an eye on what has him transfixed.

"Woh!" Now, Stuart sees it. "Lookit that crow! What the hell does he think he's _doin'_?"

Erik, squinting, "He looks like he's pecking a damn hole in Justin's rear tire. Ya know, I've learned a lotta new things since I moved to town, but a rubber-eatin' crow is one for the books!"

"Watch 'im careful, Justin," Kelsea's turn to cut-up. "He may decide he wants your bike basket for dessert!"

"All seriousness aside," Sandy, wading in; providing a sense of balance. "The bird is no doubt pecking at something that is _underneath_ the tire. Maybe a bit of candy, or gum...?"

"Well, while the illusion of a tire-eating crow is not as harrowing as a fire-eating dragon, maybe we should send him on his way and head river-ward before I fry any more well-done than I already am."

YOU CONTINUE TO PECK-TAP AT THE BICYCLE TIRE UNTIL THE SCALAWAGS-LONGLEGS BREACH THE SEVEN-METER CIRCLE. WHEREUPON YOU LOOSEN A SINGULAR, PLAINTIVE VOCALIZATION, AND RISE SHARPLY SKYWARD. IF ASKED TO COMMENT, KELSEA WOULD HAVE SWORN THAT YOU LOCKED EYES WITH HER, NOT THREE WINGBEATS INTO YOUR RETREAT. BUT...NO ONE ASKED.

"Well, if _this_ don't beat all as well!" Justin lifts the rear half of his bike off the grass, looking for anything that might pass for 'crow food.'

"_Now,_ what? Don't tell me that bird was actually dining on your tire, man. What? Justin..._what is it?_"

"Nope, no gum or candy crow food to be found. An' no crow fang marks on my tire, either," Justin paused, then raised his rear wheel slightly, tilting it to expose the carpet tack that was deeply embedded in the tread. "Tire still has a good amount of air in 'er. But I'd guess about halfway out to the Swimmin' Hole, she'd go flat as a 33 rpm vinyl record. An' it'd be a long, hot ol' walk back to town to get 'er fixed, now wouldn't it?"

"A stroke of good fortune, indeed, my fine Mr. Bench," the ever-optimistic Sandy.

"The day is not lost, it's just been momentarily sidetracked. Let's ride over to Custer's Shell station; you're still inflated enough to make it that far."

"True enough," agreed Stuart around gulps of Gatorade. "Shorty'll have us back on our wheels in 45 minutes tops. Probably won't cost more than two-fifty."

"Well, thank Crow-Almighty…what're we waiting for?" Erik, embodying the spirit of Scalawag undefeatability. And then, employing his absolute *worst* French accent: *"Allons-y, mes amis!"*

To which *everyone* responded with a friendly intended head-shake or eye-roll.

Everyone except Sandy, who smiled broadly. Anyway, just like that, they were off riding and/or dog-trotting.

*

The cold, clear stretches of the Kennawack River take their headwaters from a long, deep, blue-black lake by the same name. That water mass is fed by two rivers—the Powderflake and the Trask which, surging lake-ward, swell with the spillage of a hundred thousand silver rills; etching deeply and steeply into the breastbone of the purple Cascades Mountains of North Central Washington.

Past the mirror face of the mountain lake itself, the Kennawack River drains the lake; twisting and turning, tittering and talking its way to a narrow, winding gorge 40 miles to the southeast. There, the stream ceases its meandering, muttering slosh…and gets an attitude. Choked and channeled by walls of sheer vertical granite, the river dives and accelerates with sudden, unexpected ferocity. The tirades of those abruptly enraged waters are audible a mile away; far from the flash and fury of their free fall descent down the precipitous canyon.

A foaming, cacophonous water storm of unforgiving flood and fury it now becomes. Deafening, billowing, turbulent troughs, and crests of wave and furious current relentlessly pound the stone riverbed—whiting out sight and sound and subordinating generic human feeling to the angry beauty of nature and its raw, incomprehensible power.

Then, almost as suddenly as it begins, the River Kennawack issues forth from its frothy tunnel of clash and collision; spitting and spending the last of its tidal energy by tumbling over a small, picturesque cataract near the mouth of the gorge—Patterson's Falls. The river slows, broadens, and deepens—turning about on itself in horseshoe-shaped loops and oxbow lakes; as if attempting (anthropomorphically) to get a good look behind from where it came, and exclaim: "All that ragged, roaring, threatening, noisy confusion…was that really _me_ back there?"

Hard to believe those two stretches of river are part of the same watercourse, so diametrically opposed in temperament they are. Upstream, near the lake, is a haven for fishermen, and light recreationists. The canyon is for kayakers and other risk-takers who dream of volumes of heaving, snow-white breakers, and the velocity with which they career from boulder to pulverizing boulder. The rest of the Kennawack, from Appleton to its confluence with the Columbia River near Weston, is for, well, for everyone _else_.

But the _middle_ stretches of the Valley shoreline, _they_ belong to the young of Appleton, who know, so well, that it is their fortunate birthright to possess the premiere swimming hole of the entire known universe (ask Bargog, _he'll_ tell ya). That would be the wood-hidden, sandy beaches behind the farmhouse of the Gunnar Heinrich family.

*

Back in 1957, summer it was—cool mountain air mitigating the burn of a glorious sun fired afternoon—Gunnar and Hilda lost their only son to the whirling whitewater above Patterson's Falls. Grieving deeply though they were, the Heinrich family forthrightly consecrated part of their landholdings—a section of property on both banks of the Kennawack River—in remembrance of the life and the love they had lost, and as a provision for future generations of water-lovers.

The youth, Francis "Frank" Heinrich had been, himself, a certified 'water hound' of the first degree; gliding through those half-lit green volumes of filtered sunlight with the ease and grace of a dolphin. His strength and endurance was legendary, and though not generally regarded as foolhardy in any sense of the word, he nonetheless fell victim to one of life's ultimate lessons (unforgiving and fatal): that those churning rapids above the Falls possessed a reckoning power in abundance to his own considerable skills.

He was 14 years old the day a Kennawack River undercurrent proved him fundamentally in error with regard to the depth, width, and scope of his mettle. Into the washing swirl he went: suntanned, muscular, cavalier, and laughing. Out of the unforgiving maelstrom he came— faraway downstream—pale, cold, rigid, and unblinking upon a rock-strewn beach near Chapeeka.

His elder sisters, Elena and Elois, were the two who promoted the plan to create a permanent, enduring memorial to their unlucky brother. Children and adolescents of all ages (even a smattering of youngish adults) had always been drawn to the river during the short-lived, sun-soaked months of sweet, sweet summer. And this should come as no surprise, really. The Kennawack River was the Blue Ribbon natural resource of the entire valley. It was *meant* to be shared by all, for a *multitude* of practical and recreational purposes.

"Why not," the sisters asked, "take the shoreline and island acreage comprising the oxbow lake, and set it aside for swimmers, tubers, picnickers, and the like?"

"Furthermore," they argued, "why not allow passage across our north field, along the fence line, for access to the wood-enshrouded beach site? Better yet, let's *build a trail* along the property line and *actively* _encourage_ public use of the area as an open invitation...to attract river use *away* from danger zones like the Falls that took the life of our brother and the others?"

Gunnar and Hilda accepted the suggestion with the serene yet joyful sense of purpose that comes from the knowledge that something truly unique and *good* can rise from the ashes of burnt away dreams and unfulfilled promises. Gunnar straightaway fired up his backhoe and cut a walking path four feet wide and a third of a mile in length alongside the barbed wire fence separating his property from the Van Arnesses.

Out front on Foxx Road, just about a hundred meters from the Heinrich farm was a wide, flat, open area that was owned by the county and had served as a staging site for an old construction project. Kennawack County Roads officials agreed to allow public use of the lot for the purposes of parking their vehicles while folks visited the Heinrich Swimming Hole. They even took responsibility for a bit of the maintenance; filling the potholes when it became necessary, and occasionally leveling it with a grader.

Mr. and Mrs. Heinrich then took the matter two steps further by providing a refuse container for the parking lot, as well as a portable toilet at the beach itself. Actually, the costs incurred by the sanitation equipment were generally offset by donations provided by the Chamber of Commerce's fundraiser—the annual Fourth of July Pancake Breakfast in Appleton Park. But, overall, the undertaking was initiated and promoted by the surviving members of young Frank Heinrich's caring family.

As for the Swimming Hole itself, well, it was simply *the best* summertime place to be if you happened to be an Appleton kid in 1992.

Hands down!

First of all, it was an oxbow lake. Rivers surge and race down *steep inclines*, but they meander sleepily, sluggishly across the flatlands. Appleton was nestled, cup-like, at the head of the long Kennawack River Valley—midstream between the river's source at the lake and its confluence with the Columbia, near Weston. The Kennawack—issued from the lake and, subsequently, *exploded* from the gorge—made its sweet, unobtrusive way through town on terrain as level as a ball field.

The result? River flow, having no clearly defined slope to inform its direction, loops its way back and forth across the landscape; seeking out the easiest route to take it from the higher ground to the lower—from up thither to down yon. At some points, the looping becomes so dramatic that the flow of the river *nearly* rounds about upon itself in a full circle before changing directions yet again; winding, snakelike, its way across the tableland, loop-by-loop.

So, what happens at the locations of those near-circular loops of water path, is that narrow necks of land are all that separate the backwinding currents of the river; around which bends the slowly zig-zagging water.

Sometimes a particularly arrogant storm event occurs. This may cause the isthmus—that fragile, narrow neck o' real estate—to collapse and wash away; effectively completing the *circular shape* in that portion of the river loop, and creating an island as a by-product. The flat terrain, whereupon that portion of the river unhurriedly meanders, makes for some pretty leisurely currents, slowing even *more* so after the formation of an oxbow lake. And as the drift pace continues to decelerate, more sand and sediment settle out of the stream feed to carpet the riverbed; making it *ever* so nice for the tender feet of river lovers!

Slower currents also mean that the sun has more time to warm the water before it is eventually flushed from the river circle; thence to continue its nonchalant search for the Columbia River, and the open sea.

Even though just such an oxbow island—as well as the landlocked acreages to the north, east, and south of it—was owned by Gunnar Heinrich, there was really no practical way to put that piece of land to agricultural use without building a bridge to it. It was, therefore, pretty much given over (as part of the entire Swimming Hole package, as it were) to the young people of the community who, in their inventive and experimental ways, had been building forts and trails, hide-outs and hang-outs across its wooded breadth since the summer of '57.

A 15-foot-deep pool of clear blue-green, sandy-bottomed river-water lay in a serene reservoir beneath a suspended two-inch manila 'Tarzan Rope' at the Swimming Hole.

Three 'diving boulders,' ranging roughly in size from a small sedan to a small school bus, more or less equally divided two full acres of beaches on *both* sides of the river; its sand the color of elephant hide—fine as silt and scorching to the touch. Kid paradise, it was, just as sure as you're born.

It was on this beach, one warm September evening, that Gayle Woodbrooke got her very first kiss from a boy whose impossibly green eyes shine as brightly today as they did on that once-upon-a-night long ago. The boy's name was Tim. And Gayle eventually replaced her own last name with his, which of course was Crowl, and you know the rest of *that* story. It was in these tepid waters that Daniel and Paige LeMaster taught their little twin children how to swim. It was *also* here that Justin Michael Thomas Bench gave his goofy-dawg, Kooper (with a "K"), the same kind of instruction. Now, *that* was a lesson in aquatics that *everyone* will remember in perpetuity!

It was *also* on this very same sandy shoreline three years ago, that Kelsea Crowl met and befriended a new boy in town—kind of shy, a bit sad, even, but very nice—named Rodney Tattenger. The slow-blooming, innocent exchange of kindnesses and camaraderie bled some of the misery from Rodney's young life, but it was not destined to endure. And the severing wedge that was finally, and nearly *fatally*, driven between the two young people is, perhaps, worthy of another story.

Meant for another time.

*

FROM AN AGED, DYING POPLAR TREE—STRESSED WITH DISEASE AND THE INFESTATION OF INSECTS WHO BUSY THEMSELVES WITH THE TASK OF RENDERING WOOD INTO SAWDUST—YOU TAKE CLUTCH-WITH-TALONS TIME. YOUR EYES

ADROITLY SURVEY THE SECTION OF THE STREAM JUST UPRIVER FROM THE POINT WHERE IT SWINGS AROUND TO BACKWASH ITS OWN WATERS—20 OR 30 BEATS OF WING MUSCLE ABOVE THE OXBOW LAKE.

YOU CANNOT SEE THE YOUNG LONGLEGS AT THE SWIMMING HOLE; IT IS FURTHER DOWNSTREAM, WHERE THE SLOWLY MOVING CURRENT FIRST BEGINS TO ENCIRCLE ITSELF.

BUT EVEN THROUGH THE DENSE FOLIAGE OF MIXED DECIDUOUS AND EVERGREEN TREES, YOU CAN HEAR THEM; LAUGHING, PLAYING, SHOUTING, SPLASHING, LEARNING, AND LIVING. ALL WELL WITHIN THE SCOPE OF CROW UNDERSTANDING.

CROW LEARNS.

THAT WHICH IS LEARNABLE IS ENDURING; IT LASTS. AND ITS USEFULNESS IS UNIVERSAL AND FOREVER. CROW LEARNS; AND IN SO DOING, GROWS TO MORE DEEPLY INHABIT THE COMMON TASK; THE AFFIRMATION OF CROWLIFEPLAN WITH RESPECT TO THE CONSCIOUS, BREATHING PRECEPTS; EVER-EVOLVING FROM THAT-WHICH-IS: FROM RAVENRILL.

NEWLY BLUE-EYED—IN YOUR EMERGING/EVOLVING PRESCIENCE—YOU STEALTHILY EXAMINE THE SOLITARY LONGLEGS WADING THE SHALLOW RIFFLE OF THE KENNAWACK RIVER. HANDS ARE MAKING SMALL, REPEATED GESTURES AS PIECES AND PARTS OF OBJECTS COME TOGETHER TO MAKE A COMPLETED WHOLENESS OF.

CROW REGARDS, CONSIDERS. BLUEEYES CLOSE; MINDEYES OPEN, AND YOUR FIRST-EVER REMOTE LINK WITH RAVENRILL IS ESTABLISHED AND CONFIRMED. KNOWLEDGE IS TRANSACTED; CROW UNDERSTANDING OF HERE-NOW-IS BECOMES MARGINALLY COLLATED WITH EXPERIENTIAL UNDERSTANDINGS THAT HAVE BEEN MELDED AND FUSED OVER SCORES OF MILLENNIA. ACROSS THE IMMEASURABLY EPIC DISTANCES WHICH CLEVE AND ISOLATE THE DISTINCT, DISPARATE REALITIES OF UNKNOWABLE WORLDS.

SUCH IS YOUR BURGEONING UNDERSTANDING, CROW, OF THAT-WHICH-IS.

THE LONGLEGS FINISHES, STANDING WITH HANDS UPON KNEES, BENT SLIGHTLY FORWARD AT THE WAIST; RELEASING THE OBJECT—A TINY RAFT—TO THE WILL AND WHIM OF THE KENNAWACK CURRENT'S LETHARGIC CENTER STREAM.

THUS REASSURED THAT 'THE REST WILL FLOW,' YOU BREAK INTO THE SKY LIKE A BLACK DART SUDDENLY FLUNG INTO THE VERY HEART OF ALL-SURROUNDING, ILLUMINED NOTHINGNESS.

Downstream, past the shuffle and flux where the river meets itself coming and going; past the overhangs of shore brush around which sluggishly crawls the blue-green water; to the sunny, sandy, curving beach of the swimming hole. Justin Bench and Appleton's Scalawags are approaching.

*

"Bat crap!" said Stuart, practically spitting the words. "They're here!"

Across the glassy water face to the island side of the oxbow sprawled Rodent and Deep Thoughts; the beach towels, sunglasses, and styrofoam cooler broadcasting disheartening evidence of their every intention to 'make a day of it.'

"Could be worse," offered Justin, darkly philosophical. "I don't see Patch anywhere around, an' he's by far the worst of the litter."

"He's probably finishing a shift at the town pool," moaned Stuart dismally. "I'll bet he shows up sooner or later."

"Well, there's quite a few people here already," observed Kelsea. "I say we stake ourselves out a spot while there's still some spots to stake."

"Say that really fast ten times in a row," challenged Erik in a less-than-inspired attempt to lighten the mood.

"Whatever," said Sandy. "I second the motion that we settle in while we can, and just ignore the Ratpack for the afternoon. They only bother us when there is a *small* group of bystanders. In a crowd of people, they're basically cowards."

As if to add his own agreement to the proposal, Kooperdog bounded pall mall into the water, barking happily and snapping at phantom fish. Justin and Stuart join the ruckus, and soon there was a throng of younger children surrounding them, petting Kooper and throwing sticks which he tirelessly returned to their eager hands; splash laughing at the world in general.

Sandy's prediction seemed to be holding true (as many of her predictions usually *did*), for Rodent and Deep Thoughts paid scant attention to the activities of the quarry crew. Although undoubtedly *aware* of their presence on the opposite beach, the boys seemed engrossed in a world of their own design, which consisted chiefly of carefully monitoring each and every movement made by a purple-bikini'd Debbin Ramsay, performing a well-choreographed version of Swimming Hole beach volleyball.

"Wonder who's minding the pool while *she's* away," mused Kelsea, hooking a thumb in the direction of the blonde-haired girl.

"Maybe they gave the afternoon shift to the 'Patchman,'" suggested Sandy, fully allowing more than a *hint of* sarcasm to color the tone in her voice.

"Naw," Erik disagreed, "he'd be fired for holding little kids' heads underwater."

"Or for pawing through girls' purses looking for something to steal," countered Kelsea. But there was something about her own statement that made her stop and consider for a moment…

…the CrowDreams, something so strange about them. Real and unreal at the same time, like dreams surrounding/encircling other dreams. No, that wasn't quite the way to describe them. They were more like cascading dream events; cocooned or layered, like the overlapping pleats of a glass onion. With the imagery of each and every sleep terrain so rich—untainted and independent of the others—but still fused into an otherworld kind of uniformity that was as complex as it was cohesive.

It was kind of like seeing a hundred thousand things going on simultaneously. But through the eyes of someone (or some<u>thing</u>) else.

Theft, betrayal. Then, now. What other elements? What more?

A bag. (A pouch?) Water. Chaotic sensations. Can you feel in dreams? Faceless people. (Those were the dream pieces that were obscure and lacking focus). Vivid mind scapes—slightly frightening—but punctuated throughout with reassuring themes of wind, flight, air, space. All of that, and a breath-taking, heart-soaring sense of reclaimed lost innocence...and freedom! On a scale that was impossible to grasp with the waking mind.

Kelsea shook her head and blinked her eyes. The volleyball game was over, and its participants had broken out in different directions; some heading straight for the refreshment of the river, others for shade and sandwiches. It was then that Debbin noticed Kelsea and Sandy sitting cross-legged on blankets, applying generous layers of sunscreen and chatting amicably.

Dancing deerlike over the sand, flashing that hundred-thousand-dollar all-American smile, Debbin deftly slipped onto the beach blanket beside Kelsea, and slid her arm around the younger girl's shoulders like a long-lost big sister.

"Kelsea Crowl! However, in the *world* did you *know* that I *wanted* to run into *you* today?"

"Um—" began Kelsea uncertainly.

"Listen, girlfriend. You know that my pool party is next Saturday afternoon, right? You know, the one that Justin is going to bring his guitar to?"

"Uh-huh. I—"

"Well, we were thinking that it would be really cool if we had a couple of next year's tenth-graders at the party to serve sandwiches and drinks and help out and stuff. You know a kind of good-natured way to sort of 'initiate,' well, not really initiate, but sort of 'highlight' your last year of 'underclassman-ship' and, more or less, mentor your beginning steps into 'upperclassman-ship.' You know what I mean!"

"I, uh."

"So *we* thought..."

Who is this we, anyway? Kelsea, wondering weakly.

"...well, who shall we ask? Who's nice, who's popular, who'd be dependable and fun and want to do it and everything?"

"Gee, I—"

"And we thought..."

We who? Who are we? Kelsea's head was now whirling in doubt.

"...the LeMaster twins would be fun. But then we thought 'No...can't limit this to just a brother/sister team,' am I right, Sandy? Thought so."

"Well, you—" Kelsea began.

"And Erik is nice, and he's *really* cute, too, don't you think? But he won't be a tenth grader this fall, will he? And we really decided that for it to be fun *and* kind of meaningful at the same time, it would need to be a couple of tenth graders, right?"

"Well, actually, Erik and I already *have* some plans in place on that particular evening, so..." Sandy, letting the statement float downstream without resolving the thought.

"So, you, and Justin, and Stuart then, right Kelsea?"

"I guess, um..."

"Oh, please say you'll do it for us, Kelsea-kins. *Please*! It'll be just, so...rilly rilly *fun*! We're going to dress you in white togas, like Roman servants. It'll be great! And with Justin there to sing and play, why, everybody'll just have such a cool time, don't you think? Just say 'yes,' OK? And I'll go and talk Stuart into being there with you, OK? What do you say, kiddo? Hmm *please*? Deal?"

She took Kelsea's head in her hands and wobbled it up and down, laughing and babbling on about the sheer 'fun-ness' of it all. Despite the surprise ambush, and the 'semi-hard-sell' approach, Kelsea had to give herself over to the bubbly, superficial pomposity of it all.

She *and* Sandy just *had* to laugh...*in spite* of themselves!

"All right, all right...you win, Debbin. I'm in!" giggled Kelsea breathlessly.

Sandy was definitely _not_ helping the cause with her pronouncements of "indentured servitude," followed by a brief, faux-terse monologue about "Appleton maid and butler services." Debbin squealed, hugged Kelsea tightly, and bounded down to the river to talk with Stuart.

"Run, Stuie, run!" laughed Sandy. "Save yourself, boy!" But her words were loud enough for Kelsea's ears only.

"He's gonna _kill_ us," tittered Kelsea, watching Stu closely, so as not to miss his initial reaction to Debbin's proposition.

"Are you kidding? No way!" corrected Sandy, trying to regain some composure as Debbin approached Kooper and the boys, now knee-deep in river flow. "The lad is smit-smit-smitten, I tell you. He'd show up to serve sandwiches for Debbin Ramsay even if all she gave him to wear was a zebra-print speedo."

A short-lived reprieve here, while the total impact of _that_ visual imagery took full effect in their collective imagination. Stuie. Slack-jawed and glassy-eyed, standing with a plateful of tiny sandwiches beside Debbin's pool, wearing a zebra-print speedo; looking as masculine and virile as a wet tabby.

The girls howled at the hilarity of the thought.

"Wait! Wait!" gasped Sandy, drying tears of laughter with the heels of her hands.

She could barely talk, and she held her aching ribcage to stem the pain of mirthful overkill. "She's hitting him up now. Watch this, Kels! Let's see how Don Juan handles his lady!"

They were too far away to hear Debbin's offer or Stuart's response, but from the shape of his mouth, _his_ end of the conversation seemed to go something like this:

"Huh? Wha? Huh? Umm. Uhhhhhh. Uhmm. Duuuhhhhhhhh. OK."

"He looks like he's been struck by lightning," wheezed Kelsea.

"He looks like someone who just peeked down and discovered that his own kneecaps have switched places," yowled Sandy.

"He looks like someone who's just been told that he oughta start rotating his teeth more often," crowed Kelsea.

"He looks like someone who just saw himself in a mirror and discovered a beer bottle growing out of the middle of his forehead!" cackled Sandy.

"He looks like," gasped Kelsea, running dangerously out of breath, "looks like someone who just got handed a zebra-print speedo by a pretty cheerleader who said, 'Wear this for *me, __sugar__!*'"

Poor Stuie.

Too giddy to be embarrassed—too embarrassed to be cool.

Sandy regarded her brother for a moment before turning to her friend and subversively chirping, "Wet tabby, *girlfriend!* We-e-et tabby!"

*

The boys returned to their beach towels, shoving and jostling and making greedy grabs for sandwiches and sodas. Kooperdog lay in the sparkling sand, warming his underbelly and panting his clear intention to be up and moving again just as soon as this *brief, unnecessary* rest stop was over and done with.

"Um, Kels," muttered Stuart around a startlingly large mouthful of tuna fish sandwich, "about this pool party job."

"Relax, Stuie. You *think* too much," the girl replied reassuringly. "Look at it this way: You like Justin's music, right? OK, we're there for the music. And I'll bet Justin would like to see a couple of us around that night, just for general purposes and to feel more at home, am I right, Jus?"

"Darn straight about that, Kels-eroo!" Justin allowed.

"What she's trying to tell you, in her own Crowl-y way—" began Erik.

"*Inimitable,*" amended Sandy.

"In her own *un-copy-able* way," scowled Erik, full of artificial indignation, "is that Debbin is *still* a prime suspect in the quarry mystery, and she wants to snoop around the Ramsay place, right inspector?"

"Indubitably, Baron von Remarque," Kelsea admitted. "Your powers of observation are equaled only by your ungentlemanly appetite for tuna sandwiches lightly dusted with beach sand."

"Crap!" muttered Stuart under his breath.

"No really, Stuie. It'll be fine, you'll see."

"No, I mean: Crap! Look who just showed up!"

All heads turned in unison in the direction of Stuart's gaze. It was Pat Cheney, and he was striding directly toward the Scalawags, a look of unrepentant contempt on his face. The boy stopped in front of the group with his back to the sun, forcing everyone to shield their eyes to look up at him. For a moment, he just stood there—greasy hair, greasy smile, greasy voice—oozing venom in an undercurrent of barely concealed threat.

"In the park or at the beach, it's still 'Just An Empty Bench.'" The words rolled off his tongue like a salamander sliding off a slick stone.

That was it.

He turned his back, belching noisily, walked brazenly to the river, and swam across to join his cohort.

"Why is it," wondered Sandy coldly, "that every time I even _look_ at that guy I experience the *overwhelming* desire to take a scalding hot shower?"

"He makes me wanna go get a tetanus shot," grumbled Justin.

"More like a distemper shot," revised Erik.

"That guy makes my skin crawl," said Stuart.

"Makes my mind itch," lamented Kelsea.

"Makes my bones bend and fold," moaned Sandy.

"Makes me wanna scrub my entire body with a stiff wire brush!" complained Justin.

"Makes me want to ease myself down into a 50-gallon drum filled with battery acid and soak overnight!" claimed Erik.

And so it went.

For the next half hour, the Scalawags were left alone to entertain themselves. The "creeps across the river" paid them no mind, and the afternoon began to unfold in merry ways that allowed them to forget, for a bit, the circumstances in which they involuntarily found themselves from time to time.

Half an hour...give or take a couple of minutes.

Half an hour of sunny laughter and sandy Sandy sandwiches and chasing Kooperdog and frisbee contests and getting buried in the beach and then...

Stuie spotted the raft first.

The sun was in his eyes, and the glare from the surface of the water momentarily fooled him into thinking it was just another piece of driftwood; something that kids upstream had been playing with and had eventually lost to the pull of the river.

Hmm, he thought to himself, *that's not driftwood. It's something that's been put together...that's been built. It's a boat or a kind of a raft or something.*

He made a waving motion to Erik, who was standing 50 meters upstream, and had immersed himself in an animated discussion with a little boy about who-the-heck-knows-what. Erik understood the signal and, spotting the floating object not far upriver, dived in to check things out.

By this time, pretty much everyone on both shores had taken notice of the odd, little raft moseying lazily around the river bend. Even the Ratpack had sat up and was registering a kind of detached interest in the unexpected event. Erik swam out to midstream, and circled behind the raft. Then, gripping it with his hands, he held it at arms-length in front of his body and kicked his legs, using the gentle current to assist him in steering it toward the beach.

Even before Erik was able to push it—and himself—into waist-deep water, the girls could see a look of deep concern clouding his expression. Once he made it into shallow water, the boy let his feet drop to the smooth riverbed, and he clung to the raft while a small crowd of curiosity-seekers gathered around.

Justin picked up a flat, square, whiteish looking object from the raft; staring hard at it for an instant before tossing it back down and heading for the beach. Stuart and Erik looked at the object, looked at each other, and watched Justin return to shore. Then Erik picked up the plaque and, after exchanging grim glances with Stuart, flung the little flotation device upon the shore.

"I wonder what the heck *that's* all about," breathed Kelsea.

Justin reached the spot where the gang had been picnicking and, barely breaking his stride, he swooped up his towel and the remains of his personal belongings; heading for the footpath back to Foxx Road.

"Sorry gals, gotta go! Erik'll explain. C'mon Koop!"

With that, he was gone, leaving two *very* confused young ladies in a state of utter befuddlement.

They weren't perplexed for very long at all, for the boys arrived, stone-faced and silent, and they too began getting ready to leave the beach.

"Hey, guys! What's going on? Where's everybody going in such a rush?" asked Kelsea worriedly.

Erik held the plaque up for the girls to see. It was a square piece of classroom whiteboard material—the same kind that Stuart had found in the meadow shanty.

"Oh, no!" whispered Sandy. She was afraid she was going to start crying. "Not again!"

Kelsea was completely speechless, but she immediately fell to helping her friend collect their things in readiness to leave.

Eric's attention was fixed in the direction of Debbin Ramsay and her beach buddies.

He swiveled his head across the river to the Ratpack and watched carefully, looking for telltale signs of foreknowledge of the raft incident. Back and forth the boy alternated his gaze, hoping for something, anything! A gesture, a mocking stare of contempt, derisive laughter, something that would tell him that *somebody, _anybody_* on the river today was responsible for releasing that raft, and its threatening message, onto the Kennawack and into their hands.

"Does anybody know anything about this?" yelled Erik suddenly, holding the plaque high in the air. Anger shook his voice, and his arm muscles trembled with the effort to maintain self-control.

"Eric, man. That won't help matters any," Sandy soothed, tossing a tube of sunscreen into her backpack. "Whoever put the raft into the water and sent it on its way was upstream from us all along, and is *long-gone* by now."

Erik knew she was right, of course. Everyone, even Patch, had been on the beach for quite a while, and it wasn't possible to be in two places at the same time, was it?

"Alibis all around," he said hotly. "Can't even blame it on the Ratpack this time."

"Nor Debbin Ramsay," added Kelsea.

Erik read the message again, and scanned the former suspects once more before the rest of the quarry gang turned their backs, and headed for the footpath. Nothing…absolutely *nothing* seemed out of place, or even the least bit fishy.

He read the message a third time before shoving it into his pack, and slipping on his sandals. There were seven words written on the square. Including the misspelling, it read:

"Have you checked the kwary cabin lately?"

It was written using a Beatrix Mocha lipstick.

*

The warning which had been written on the slate and released into the river was no hoax. But it _did_ turn out to be a false alarm, of sorts. And an hour later, when everyone was reasonably certain that no harm had been visited upon the cabin, the Scalawags 'saddled up'—with sadness, but also great relief—for the ride back to town.

In the meantime, a quarter of the way to the quarry on their way from the Swimming Hole, Erik and Sandy had doubled-back to the Kennawack with the sudden, overwhelming compulsion to comb the brushy river banks above the swimming hole in hopes of turning up clues to the puzzling raft episode. Kelsea and Stuart had arrived at Justin's place just about ten minutes after he and Kooper did. A quick, but thorough swarming of the house and property had revealed nothing out of place; nothing stolen or broken, and the unspoken feeling amongst the three was that Erik and Sandy would probably fare no better in their search along the stream.

Stuart had insisted upon calling home and asking permission to spend the night, but Justin had demurred.

"They've made their point," he said solemnly. "He, she or *they*, won't be back until it suits 'em. Until the time is ripe, and we *least* expect it."

"It's like the whole idea of the message on the raft was just to let you know that they have the power of surprise *all* the time," remarked Kelsea glumly. "They don't actually have to *cause* any damage. It's enough for them to simply be in a position to *remind* you of that power from time to time."

"It's eerie," said Stuart, "it's so well-plotted and executed. It's…"

"It's *demented!*" accused Kelsea suddenly. "*And* it's about time we got Officer Santiago on the case, don't you think, Justin?"

He winced lightly; stung by a comment which implied, among other things, that he was not thinking clearly about a serious-enough problem. Kelsea noticed the reaction, and immediately changed the tone of her voice.

"Oh, Justin! I didn't mean that the way it sounded" The girl placed her hands on the young man's shoulders, and gave them a gentle squeeze. "Just promise me that you'll keep thinking it over," she amended. "And don't worry. We won't say anything to anyone unless you give us the word." Then with a coy smile, she added, "But hurry up and give us the word, OK?"

Justin released a tight smile, doing his best to buck up under the strain of it all.

"I'll keep it in mind, Kels," he remarked, his voice a mixture of concern, forgiveness, and reflection. "I'm startin' to think you may be right about that after all. Just let me mull it over a little more."

Justin glanced at his wristwatch, and regarded his two good friends. "You guys better hit the road," he said. "It'll be dinner time soon."

Kelsea and Stuart mumbled in agreement, and mounted their bikes.

"How's about everybody comin' up tomorrow evening for a barbecue?" he offered.

"You can help me pick out a set list for my big performance on Saturday night."

"Right on!" agreed Kelsea. "It'll also give me and Stu some time to collaborate on our gig as 'galley slaves,'" she laughed.

By that time, the sun was being chased behind western ridges by innumerable elastic shadows; lengthening by the minute, and pointing a fingery way east, to Weston. In a last-ditch effort to claim sovereignty over the day, and to draw some closing attention to its own flame and splendor, that celestial ball of fire had annihilated the western heavens of Appleton; crushing the juice of peaches, grapes, tangerines, and huckleberries into a splendid visual narrative; surrendering itself to colorless dusk, and finally bleeding down to black.

Another day had come and gone. And Justin's concerns began to grow.

*

Sandy and Erik had beaten the brush along the shoreline from the entrance to the oxbow lake to a point nearly 200 meters upstream. Expanding the search much further along the Kennawack would have probably been futile since, from that distance, the raft would have run the risk of drifting too close to far-stream, and possibly bypassing the oxbow lake altogether; thereby missing the intended target.

"Couldn'a been Debbin," mused Erik. "She was there before we were."

"Couldn'a been Rodent or Deep Thoughts," countered Sandy thoughtfully. "*They* got there before we did, too."

"Coulda been Patch…he arrived a little late."

"Coulda been somebody working on Debbin's orders."

"Coulda been somebody else working on Rodent's orders."

"Coulda been someone else *entirely*. Man! Every clue we uncover *raises* more questions than it *answers*! This is makin' me *nuts*!"

"Me, too. Think how *Justin* must be feeling," Sandy hunkered down. "Well, I don't know… I just don't know, but it doesn't look like we're going to turn up anything of interest around here. Let's head up to the quarry and join the others."

"May as well," said Erik, eager to keep moving, if not progressing.

From a thicket 50 meters away, a pair of eyes watched the two of them; watched them leave the way they had come, and make their way back through the brush to Foxx Road.

They were *not* the eyes of a Crow.

*

"What do you mean, you watched them upstream from the 'Hole?' Are you expressly <u>trying</u> to get caught? And what if they get tired of trying to work this thing out on their own? What if their fear finally gets the best of them, and they go to Santiago about it? What if he dusts those message slates for prints? Did you ever think of that? That your fingerprints are all over every damn thing you've touched?"

"What <u>difference</u> does it make? Let 'em think and do whatever they want. So, what? They know about the lipstick and the stupid horse, too. SO. WHAT? Every clue they find points in a different direction. The whole thing is just a bunch of garbage that they can't even come close

to understanding. And I used <u>gloves</u> for <u>everything</u>. The only prints anyone can find anywhere are the ones left by whoever handles it after me."

"All right. I'll give you credit for being careful. But we're going to have to heat up the production, understand? And that means we can't afford to start getting lax. Now, when's the next step?"

"The next one's a good one. It's gonna bend that guy's way of thinking right back on itself!"

"I didn't say <u>what!</u> I said <u>when!</u>"

"Saturday. This Saturday night."

*

Stuart lowered the barbecue spatula, and squinted through the billowing haze wafting aromatically about him like a mouth-watering cloud. An intellectual argument was being waged on the topic of "smoke categories"; Erik firmly supporting the notion that *hot dog* smoke was, by far, the most delightfully sniffable barbecue by-product known to mankind.

Head chef, Stuart James 'Daniel Boone' LeMaster provided a lively and animated counterpoint as he flipped, prodded, and shuffled a dozen sizzling dogs and meat patties about the well-worn grill.

Dang, thought Justin. *He's gettin' pretty good on that thing!*

"Yes, I suppose," blustered Stuart, "that the *untrained* olfactory of an *amateur* might fall victim to the *brash fumes* of the Great American (pausing right about now to wrinkle his nose in regret and disdain) *hot...dawg,*" he finished, pronouncing the phrase as two distinct, well-spaced words as if pushing them past his vocal cords and off his tongue was somewhat of an uncomfortable chore which nonetheless *needed* to be done in order to complete his oral dissertation.

Sandy LeMaster munched on a celery stick, and eyed her twin with amusement.

Kelsea busied herself with paper plates and condiments, but she smiled knowingly at the snatches of conversation that drifted to her through the sweet-smelling haze. Justin tuned his guitar, and fussed with a list of songs; ordering and reordering the sequence in which they should be sung at tomorrow's pool party. Every so often, he stopped what he was doing; peering up at Stuart, standing there in grill fog, making sweeping gestures with his arms like a college professor pontificating on some obscure metaphysical proposition.

Clearly out of his element, Erik was smugly satisfied with his own ability to have 'put a quarter in Stuie's slot,' so to speak, and 'start him up!' He settled himself in with a sack of potato chips to enjoy the oratory.

Stuart was *full of it.* Everybody knew that.

Everybody *loved* it.

Stuart, resuming: "But the learned (two syllables, *'learn—ed'*) gourmet *refuses* to be reeled in by the naïve, sophomoric…"

"Easy, Stuarto…high school sophomores present, here."

Stuart, resuming after throwing a short, side-long glance, communicating exhausted condescension, "…the *sophomoric* aroma emanating from (scowling slightly) *seared weeners.* Or <u>even</u> that of *The Celestially Conceived and Highly Hall-ow-ed* (three syllables) omm-boor-zhair (Stuart's fake French pronunciation of 'hamburger'). The *real deal,* where barbecue smoke is concerned, comes only from grilling up a thick, juicy slab of…"

Sandy groaned, "Oh, Stu, if you wanted a steak why didn't you just say so when we went to the store?"

The boy directed his long-handled spatula accusingly in the direction of his mussy-haired sister. "And just who among you," he quipped (point, point, point!), "would have been willing to crack open his savings vault in order to purchase a lip-smacking sirloin? Not you, sis! Nuh-Uh. Nor Erik, nor any quarry-person but me, I'm thinkin.' I just didn't wanna be the odd-man-out, that's all."

"Well, mowin' lawns and babysitting doesn't exactly supply *any* of us with extra spending money, Slick," Kelsea countered. "I'd say a weekly barbecue together is about as far as my purse'll stretch."

"Too bad," sighed Stuart with weary resignation, "but I guess I'm the only person in *this* crowd who can think well beyond the old-fashioned idea of greasy, ketchup-y, sesame-seed-bun-y—hey! Isn't that Carlos Santiago coming up the drive?"

"Why, yes it is," verified Justin, easing Woody onto a guitar stand, and rising to his feet. "Better throw on another patty, Stu."

"Better make it two, Stu," echoed Erik. "The grill chef who can't *afford* a steak should ease his own misery by doubling up on the burger intake. Whatcha think?"

"Great idea. Glad I thought of it!" remarked Stu, thereupon flopping two more patties on the wire grill. He was grinning ghoulishly, not at all unlike an undernourished vulture hovering over a dead jackrabbit.

"Uh-oh!" warned Sandy, her voice thick with good-natured alarm. "I just *knew* all this greasy smoke would be in violation of County Air Quality Standards. Now look what you've done, Stuart. Your blatant disregard for outdoor cooking regulations has run us afoul of the law again."

Stuart said nothing. Instead, he extended his arms, wrists together, to Officer Santiago who had approached the cabin deck with a clownish pair of enormous purple plastic handcuffs. The man was obviously ready to "make the arrest."

"I've got rights. What about my rights?" complained Stuart as Carlos slapped the cuffs on his wrists and snapped them shut.

"OK. Sure thing, citizen scofflaw," the sheriff complied. "You've got the right to choose between these cuffs, a set of leg-irons, or an ox yoke."

"Stay with the cuffs, Stu," advised his sister. "They'll make a nice accessory to the orthodontic braces you're due to get next month."

"Leg-irons say 'tough guy' to me," offered Erik. "You'd come across *muy macho* in a clinking, clanking set of leg-irons, my non-Egyptian friend."

"An ox yoke would build up those puny, flaccid shoulder muscles of yours, Stu," prompted Kelsea helpfully. "Us girls just *love* guys with big, strong shoulders."

"Puny?" asked Stuart in a small voice.

"As a sworn officer of the law, sir," Justin intervened, "I don't suppose you'd be interested in the offering of a small, um, bribe?"

"Flaccid?" repeated Stuart weakly.

"Bribes of any and all types and sizes will be given due consideration," responded the deputy. "However," he warned, "if the offer presented is found to be insulting to my dignity as a public servant, or is unacceptable due to its total *uselessness* to my particular needs, well, I'll just have to take you *all* downtown and book the *lot* of you."

"What would be the charge, sir?" inquired Erik.

"Section 1204 of the Penal Code, Chapter Four, paragraph six, line three and I quote: 'Anyone who cannot offer a *proper* bribe to a hard-working cop should be held without bail, with all rights of citizenship suspended indefinitely—without hope of legal representation—in a cramped, damp, moldy, lightless prison cell until such time as he, she, or they can produce an illegal bribe worthy of consideration.'"

"Give him the burger, Stuie. It's your only hope."

"Puny, flaccid shoulder muscles?" wondered Stuart, staring despondently at the comically *huge* handcuffs. They were big enough to go around his upper thigh without pinching.

"You are free, for now, delinquent," warned Santiago. "But I'll be watching for you to step outside the bounds of justice again." He dutifully removed the toy wrist restraints, allowing Stuart to scoop up a sizzling patty, plop it onto a fat bun, and hand over to the smiling police officer.

"May the mustard stain your tarnished badge," Stu muttered with mock disrespect.

"Crime doesn't pay, citizen waste-oid," remarked Officer Santiago, applying plenty of condiments to his sandwich.

"What's new, Officer Santiago?" asked Kelsea, steering the conversation away from the good-natured goofiness. "What brings you to the quarry today? Besides the alarming smell of burnt LeMasterpieces, I mean."

She stole a quick peek at young master LeMaster, still pushing meat around in circles over the flame, and muttering to himself about shoulder muscles.

"Well," Santiago came right to the point, "word is out around town that the Scalawags intercepted a message of some kind out at the Swimming Hole." He enjoyed a moderate-to-large mouthful of succulent sandwich, and studied the bite mark in the bun.

Things got very quiet very quickly.

"Folks who were there and saw what happened said that every last one of you took off like a swarm of killer bees was after you. *Superb* burger, Stuie! Truly an *objet d'art!*" Carlos praised the smokey chef, and rotated his burger, inspecting it from every angle like it was a museum-quality sculpture worthy of critical assessment.

Justin tuned an "A" string up and down. Someone coughed quietly. Erik shifted uneasily in his deck chair, making a little metallic squeaking sound that caused Kooper to jolt awake suddenly, before drifting unconcernedly back asleep.

Officer Santiago scouted the small circle of faces, charting the depths of the silence and making mental notes. "Uh-oh. Did I touch a nerve?" he asked mildly.

Various unconvincing gestures; shoulder-shrugging and head-wagging punctuated by a flawed-sounding "search me!" Kelsea made furtive attempts at gaining eye contact with Justin, who steadfastly refused to look at *anything* above the level of Woody's tuning keys.

It was surprising to discover how thick, how viscous a period of time could become. There, in the absence of any sound, oxygen became compressed, congealed; crushed and compacted to the point where the simple inhalation of mountain air was as audible as the sweep of tide flow over a pebble beach. Space was gathered and fused; dense with the suffocation of inescapable confinement. Discreet human feelings synchronized—of their own accord—and all organized modes of thinking converged to one involuntary blend of shared ideas: *Does he know? How much does he know? Should we tell him what we know? What is it that we really do know?*

And all that while ('*while*' being rich, affirming measurements of heart-rhythm and wingbeat for Crow, but, at the same time, ungovernable intervals wedged between "begins with" and "ends at" for humans)...all that while, the fluency and fluidity of decision-making faltered and failed as individuals wrestled with consciences over what was the 'right thing to do' at that precise moment in time.

Another throat cleared, the sole of a sneaker scuffed across the dusty deck floor, making an abbreviated 'shuufff' noise, and Carlos Santiago dabbed at his mustachioed lips with a paper napkin.

"Kiddos," he declared softly; kindliness and concern showing in his dark eyes, "I *know* how Rodent and Patch lean on you all from time to time. That's just unconscious knowledge. But, to what extent they are abusing you, and to what extent Deep Thoughts has become part and parcel to the harassment is very questionable. Mostly because you have all chosen to pretty much keep that information to yourselves."

A flurry of exchanged glances, proffering no reply.

"Whatever happened, or whatever *is* happening, remember this: Don't try to handle too much by yourselves. Don't let things go too far before asking for help." He walked to the steps and turned, smiling the smile of a father whose love and respect for his children restrain him from assuming *too much* control over their lives, but who worries about their hidden dilemmas just the same.

He touched his napkin lightly to his silver deputy's badge. "I believe I got a bit of mustard on my star," he winked. "Thanks for the lunch, everyone. You're a *great* group of kids. And Justin, you're a heckuva good guy. You all take care, now, ya hear?"

He turned and walked down the hill to his patrol car.

"You're a heckuva guy too, Carlos," whispered Justin hoarsely.

And he wondered even more just what the hell he was supposed to do.

*

Saturday.

August fifth.

The afternoon of Debbin Ramsay's pool party.

Two very important things happened that day—at two very different places *near* the little town of Appleton. *Near,* in that neither event took place *inside* the town limits.

But both occurred *near* the quarry site which, as you know, is up the Quarry Road and just outside of town.

One occurrence involved Justin and, to a lesser extent Kelsea and Stuart, who were at his side more-or-less all afternoon and evening as toga-clad party servants.

The other involved Sandy and Erik who had bilaterally taken it upon themselves to disregard Justin's explicit wishes, and do a little unauthorized snooping around.

As it came to pass, *nobody* was destined for a particularly *fun* ending to that evening.

In fact, things got downright uncomfortable. And *Crow* was there to bear witness to snippets from *both* of these occurrences, as two scared Scalawags found themselves *trapped*—in harm's way—just before an explosion brought Debbin's pool party to an abrupt end.

*

YOU, CROW...

YOU <u>KNOW</u> THEY ARE APPROACHING BEFORE YOU HEAR THEM.

YOU <u>HEAR</u> THEM APPROACHING BEFORE YOU SEE THEM.

YOU <u>SEE</u> THEM APPROACHING RIGHT AFTER YOU DISCOVER THAT THE LITTLE SHINE (THE KEY), WHICH YOU HAD DROPPED NEAR THE SHACK WHEN SKY CRY (THE JET) OCCURRED, IS NOWHERE TO BE FOUND.

LITTLE SHINE IS-NOT.

ARE THE APPROACHING LONGLEGS THAT-TO-LEARN? TIME LENDS LEARNING, AND TIME KNOWS.

SO, YOU WAIT AND WATCH IN LEARNTIME.

AND YOU SEE HOW...

Erik and Sandy crept cautiously over the hardscrabble; between and around dwarfing boulders of mind-splitting magnitude. Sizes, masses, and volumes of confused, shapeless weight sprawled expansively in a bizarre, three-dimensional jigsaw puzzle saturated in a thousand shades of chalk.

The daylight was beginning to fail, and so was Sandy's strength. It had been a hard climb. Relatively short, but a *hard* climb all the same. It had taken them the better part of an hour and a quarter—with few stops along the way for resting—to climb the hill in the southwest quarter of the quarry site, to top the crest of the finger ridge tapering from the shoulder of Tamarack Mountain to the Quarry Road, and to begin a long, slow traverse of the difficult talus slope, to the meadow.

Justin would *not* have been happy, had he known of their whereabouts. But he and Woody were, at that moment, energetically engaged in a self-styled version of 'Can't Buy Me Love' for an appreciative collection of party people.

"Phew!" Sandy exhaled exhaustedly, and plopped down on a chair-shaped block of granite. She raked her fingers through springy spirals of sweat-dampened hair, and smiled weakly at her friend. "Sorry, Erik," she apologized. "I know I'm slowing you down. You could've been to the shanty and back in the time it's taken you to wait up for me."

"Who are you tryin' to kid, kid?" Erik dismissed her entreaty with a wave of his hand as he scrambled up the side of a wide, flat boulder for a look-see. "I'm only a step-and-a-half ahead of you for appearance's sake. I've got my newly emerging male ego to protect, in case you didn't know it," Erik winked at the girl before hunkering down to survey possible paths amongst the ruins of rock.

"Hard to believe that the way across this stone slope is faster than the way through the woods," remarked Sandy. "This is pretty rigorous stuff."

"Not faster, just easier. The amount of time it takes to get here is probably about the same either way. It's just that you have the choice of beating the brush or bouncing around the boulders."

"I suppose you're right. Stuie's been *both* ways, and if he says this is the better of the two, then I guess, um, did you say 'the amount of time it takes to get _here_?'"

Erik rose and turned to gaze down at his friend. Bending at the waist and bracing his legs in a wide, balanced stance, he extended his arm— palm up—and gestured a 'come-along' with his fingertips.

Sandy placed a booted foot against the stone and reached toward the boy. She felt his warm hand close firmly and confidently about her wrist bone as he assisted her up to stand beside him on the lichen-encrusted surface. She didn't *need* any help getting to the top of that rock. She knew that, and so did he. But she took his hand anyway.

"Aleksandra Loye LeMaster," Erik announced formally, sweeping his free hand in an introductory way, "I give you…the shanty."

Dusk was bathing that grassy opening with a sleepy, salmon-colored half-light, and far, far to the east—where indigo hours patiently await *their* turn with the world—the myth and magic of the night's first brave little star poked a pinprick in the deep, cool blanket of Appletonian sky.

Spruce boughs luffed non-synchronously to a wind song composed on the faraway cold, snowy ridgeline of the Cascade Mountain chain; a melody orchestrated by the shapeless route ways of the Kennawack River. Lyrical content for this 'Sundown Overture' was provided by a solitary killdeer—the songster bird whose sad remarks on the dying of the day drifted windward; over invisible Crow highways to the heart struck ears of two Scalawags, standing on a rock, watching shadow phantoms crawl across a mountain meadow…holding hands.

*

The information was confidential, as a whole lot of police information usually is. The report had been filed by the F.B.I., in cooperation with the Securities and Exchange Commission—the United States Government agency charged with enforcing laws which regulate the availability, purchase, and sales of publicly offered stocks.

Complicated stuff.

'Big Suits' in Washington, D.C. *and* the Pentagon apparently had been monitoring the activities of an individual who may (or may not) have been involved in an 'insider trading' scheme—purportedly with an overseas business entity which was currently cultivating 'growth opportunities' in America. (Hollis would "dig it," now wouldn't he?)

The person being investigated retained a permanent residential address in the town of Appleton, Washington; and what the Bureau agents wanted to know was: Did the office of the Kennawack County Sheriff's Department have anything in their files—current or otherwise—regarding the gentleman in question which might be of interest or of use to the F.B.I. in assisting the completion of its investigation? Of a certainty, they did not. But yes, of course, the Sheriff's Department would be *very* happy to comply with the Bureau's request for full cooperation, and would furthermore immediately commence implementation of a directive authorizing a small-scale, covert monitoring and data-gathering surveillance.

Big drama comes to Little-Ville.

What it really amounted to, in a nutshell, was little more than keeping on one's toes a bit more, and paying closer attention to the kinds of small stuff which may well look suspiciously as if it could add up to something bigger than its initial appearance would indicate at first glance.

The deputy assigned to the case was, of course, Officer Carlos Santiago. The overseas 'business entity' being watched by the F.B.I. was the Japanese microchip manufacturer, Mikatsu Enterprises.

And the individual whom Deputy Santiago was assigned to keep a watchful, if distant, eye upon was none other than Lieutenant Colonel Harding Corbett Tattenger; "Hard-Core" Tattenger, U.S.M.C.

*

All right, then.

Gotta big night shapin' up. Lotsa stuff happening at the same time, in different places.

Officer Carlos Santiago is studying an F.B.I. directive empowering him with the seldom-granted authority to shadow a respected citizen of his community, just in case the fellow is, say, harboring plans to blur the line between legal and illegal business transactions.

Erik and Sandy are hand in hand, someplace where they probably really shouldn't be. And just 15 scrawny minutes *before* Erik had gentlemanly assisted Sandy in scaling the viewpoint rock above the meadow, two figures departed the shanty, and made their way across the stone wreckage, in the *opposite* direction from which the two wayward Scalawags were approaching.

YOU SAW THAT HAPPEN, CROW.
AND CROW <u>ALSO</u> SAW <u>SOMEONE</u> <u>ELSE</u> FORGET TO LOCK THE SHANTY DOOR.
<u>YET</u> <u>AGAIN</u>!
CROW LINGERS...WAITING IN LEARNTIME.

And all of *this* while, not so very far away, at the pool party...

*

"Justin! For Pete's sake, why don't you take a break—even a short one?" Debbin Ramsay's unutterably blue eyes took on a gem-like quality; clearly evidencing her borderline giddiness over the success of the afternoon party. "Go grab yourself a sandwich and a soda, you ol'rock star. We're going to start a water polo tournament; girls against 'one-handed' boys. We can go back to the music after the first drowning!"

She giggled happily at the thought of her own joke, and zipped off to announce the rules of the water game. She was having the time of her life. And why shouldn't she be?

Little Appleton's adolescent population never had it so good. Her parents (even her sister, Megan!) had put their shoulders to the task of constructing, collecting, and assembling the wherewithal for a super bash of memorable proportions. There wasn't a teenager anywhere on the Ramsay ranch who wasn't 'livin' large' that sunny afternoon in early August.

Scalawags included.

Justin was whipping through original and standard musical compositions that had virtually *everyone* on hand dancing together (*pool-dancing,* no less!), tapping their toes, or singing along with uninhibited good humor. Kelsea looked pretty as they come in a near perfect-fitting white toga with a slender gold lamé rope belt about her waist. Her mother had plaited her shiny, black hair and had arranged a dainty tiara of sweet-smelling rock daphnes that encircled the crown of her head. What a cutie!

Boys took notice. But if Kelsea *noticed* them *noticing*, she didn't let *them* notice it.

Stuart took a different tack altogether in his assemblage. Slung about his pudgy frame in a devil-may-care fashion was a pale blue, cotton bedsheet patterned with hundreds of tiny cowboys brewing coffee over campfires. The loosely slung 'toga' (if you could call it that) was cinched about his tubby middle with a brown extension cord whose prong-end hung down like snake fangs along the outside of his leg.

Rather than opting for sandals—like his authentically dressed counterpart—Stuart's choice of footwear consisted of black, high-top sneakers with neon orange laces and tie-dyed socks. Whew! Accessorizing _that_ with a fake pair of horn-rimmed glasses, a neck-tie shaped and patterned like a sockeye salmon, and topped with a Seattle Mariners ball cap and, well, the boy had created for himself a fashion statement of blinding contrasts and _horrifying_ originality!

Like everything else at the party, Stuie was a _hit_!

The badminton players had pretty much opted out of the water polo tournament in favor of continuing their activity. Volleyballers and barbecuers had already either flung themselves into the drink, or were gathered poolside to watch the _Water War of the Ages_.

A boombox was loaded up with popular soft-rock tunes, as Debbin explained the "handicapping of the boys" to eight gently bobbing contestants. She then turned the refereeing responsibilities over to none other than Stuart LeMaster who, by virtue of a whistle and his professional sports headwear, was uniquely qualified to "call 'em as he saw 'em."

Then Debbin motioned for Kelsea and Justin to join her, and she began strolling across the enormous well-manicured lawn, away from the whoops and laughter of her guests. The two exchanged quizzical glances; Justin arching an eyebrow, giving a tiny, almost imperceptible shrug of his shoulders. He had placed Woody carefully in the guitar case (like he _always_ did when he was going to be more than two steps away for any length of time), and the two of them joined their hostess, making her way toward the pastures and barns of the Ramsay ranch.

"I just wanted to thank you guys for helping to make the party so much fun for everybody," Debbin's voice was earnest, sincere. Gone, for the moment, was her air-headed goofiness that so-often came across as insincere prattle. She hugged them both, smiling with her eyes, and warming them with her words. "No wonder the whole town loves you guys," she remarked. "Pops is right on the mark when he says, 'You _Scalawags is the fizz in Appleton's soda!_'"

Kelsea and Justin chuckled at the joke—made even better by Debbin's paraphrasing of one of Pops' standard lines. It was kind of odd to see and hear her speaking and acting with such polished generosity. Odd, and very nice! The two of them were beginning to understand a side of Debbin's personality that didn't usually express itself.

Maybe she wasn't as one-dimensional as people generally assumed?

"Well, thanks, Debbin," offered Justin. Kelsea may have been caught a little off-guard by the girl's complementary tone, but Justin—comfortable with kings and carpenters—accepted the niceties with grace and gratitude. "I reckon there's *some* folks around town who'd take exception to your opinion of our group o' people."

"Oh," stated Debbin cursorily; un-hesitantly. "Rodent, Patch, and Deep Thoughts, right? The flies in our soup, the dirt in our butter."

"The water in our gas tank," assisted Kelsea.

"The worms in our apple," added Justin.

"The wretch in our wretched-ity," attempted Debbin.

They laughed together at the utter folly and *waste* of the whole 'Ratpack' concept.

Then Debbin knocked a hole in the conversation; big enough to ride one of her horses through, sideways! Raising one leg, and resting a sneakered foot on the lower rail of the fence, gazing across the low, rolling pasture greenery to the horse barn, she said, "You know, that awful, skanky Pat Cheney works at the City Pool with me on certain days. And I can't prove it but, guys, I think that creep for some weird reason or another has been stealing lipstick from my purse."

*

Time flies when you're having fun; it has a bad habit of slowing to a crawl when you're not. Sometimes things get too weird for words, and time just stops altogether. Dead in its tracks. Justin and Kelsea shared just such a crystalized moment—frozen, ice-like—suspended in a splinter of awareness (about a breath's breadth); consisting of equal parts blind luck, startling discovery, and staggering surprise.

Kelsea was the first to recover from the shockwave of Debbin's off-hand remark. By then, Justin's entire presence had taken on an almost unearthly quality of otherwhere-ness; like his mind had retreated into tracts of reckoning and reflection, and a portion of his physical being had followed suit. He almost *wasn't there*.

"Well, what do you suppose he would want with someone's lipstick?" Kelsea, cautiously inquiring, hoping the nervous excitement she felt wasn't showing. "I mean, is it just an immature way of getting your attention, or does he see himself as some kind of um…gangsta thief?"

"I'm sure I can't imagine," sighed Debbin with a trace of resignation. "But I've gone through three tubes in the last month or so…they're really expensive, too! And all I know is that they seem to disappear whenever I'm at the pool. Of course, *now* I lock everything up but, like a dummy, it took the loss of *two* of them before I wised up enough to figure out *where* they were disappearing *from,* and to start taking some precautions."

Justin hadn't made a peep, and, for all appearances, seemed to be preoccupied with some ordinary-looking cloud formations chuffing along overhead.

"Well, it takes all *kinds*, that's all *I* can say," continued Debbin, "and with the life he's had to live, I suppose you can't blame him for being kind of a screwed-up kid."

Then she added, almost sympathetically, "He could have turned out worse, I guess."

"Mm-hmm," Kelsea's thoughts had begun racing down remote paths of speculation, not at all unlike those being internally explored by her guitar-toting friend.

"OK, the horses are all present and accounted for," said Debbin. "Let's head back, and count the lifeless bodies in the pool."

The trio turned, and began making their way back to the party; the conversation sidelined for the moment as each entertained thoughts on personal levels. They were almost poolside before Justin blinked twice, stopped and turned; staring in the direction of the pasture. "All horses are accounted for?" he asked uncertainly.

"Hmm? Oh, yeah. I have to check on them once in a while, especially when we're not in sight of them for any length of time."

"Whatever for?" wondered Kelsea.

"'Cause people, kids, I suppose, have been sneaking through the fence and taking them for, shall we say, little joy-rides? Can you believe it? Hopping on somebody's horse, and riding off just big as you please?"

Kelsea was nonplussed. "You mean you've actually *caught* people...*borrowing* your horses? Out there in your pasture? Who's crazy enough to pull a stunt like that?"

"Kids, I would guess, like I said. Not pointing any fingers, and, really, I'm only supposing, but it very well could be school kids around the age of your little sister."

Kelsea blanched at the thought of Jayme even *considering* such a thing.

"No, no!" insisted Debbin, quickly sizing up the stressed looked on Kelsea's face. "I didn't mean to imply that your sister was caught messing around with our animals. I only meant to say that, you know, third, fourth, and fifth graders, they're all very curious, and interested in horses. *Every*body wants to own a pony when they're that age, but very few kids actually do, so-oo..."

"So they slip into the Ramsay pasture for a little cowboy/cowgirl adventure every now and again," finished Justin.

"That's my thought," agreed Debbin. "The thing is, if they'd just let us know they wanted to ride, we'd probably stop whatever we were doing and *take* 'em. We *know* how much kids like horses, and either Megan or I wouldn't mind going with them and showing them the way it's done. But to sneak in and just make off with them. I mean, my gosh, what if one of the horses was injured? What if one of the *children* was injured? The possibilities are just too awful to ponder."

"Does that kind of thing happen very often?" asked Kelsea.

"Yes," Justin quickly butted in, "when <u>was</u> the last time one of your horses was ridden without your permission?" He looked straight across the field in the direction of the horses; cropping grass, and whisking their tails through thin clouds of tiny, flying insects. His eyes narrowed, and he spoke with the slow deliberation of a sleuth about to reveal the identity of a long-sought criminal.

"Well...only once. And it's been quite a while now, about three weeks ago. But we like to stay on our guard just the same. We definitely *don't* want anyone to get hurt."

"Are you pretty sure about the time frame?" insisted Justin. He was chewing thoughtfully on a piece of straw and looking *hard* at those horses now.

"Actually, I am," assured Debbin. "You see, 'Summer'—the mare; the spotted Appaloosa out there," she pointed while shading her eyes with her other hand. "She was unshod at the time. She had some hoof problems which were being medicated. We weren't riding her at all, and we wanted to be sure she stayed in the pasture where it was clean and dry."

"Mm-hmm." (Think, think, chew, chew.)

"So I came out *super* early one morning, just after sunrise, as a matter of fact, and there's 'Summer,' standing by the feed trough, wet to the flanks. *Someone* had taken her out in the pre-dawn hours for a little yahoo time."

Justin surveyed the adjoining fields stitched together with barbed wire fencing. The Ramsay spread was pretty sizable. Lots of room for riding without even leaving the ranch. "Do ya think they took ol' 'Summer' off the property altogether?"

"Had to. The creek that feeds our pond is a foot wide, and just inches deep. It's no more than a rill. And the pond is fenced off, as you can plainly see over there, so the animals can't even get near it. As I was telling you, my horse was soaked up to the belly, and a little past. Mud up over the fetlocks, too. And not only did I _barely miss catching_ the '_borrower_,' but I can tell you with almost 100% certainty where she was taken on that sunrise ride."

Justin eyed Kelsea; understanding and bitterness shone in his smoke-blue eyes. Kelsea waited, unsure what was coming up next, but certain of its relevance to Justin's recent problems.

"Forbes Creek," he said. "Deep water—soft, muddy banks."

"I'd bet a stack of paychecks _this_ high on it," said Debbin, holding her hand up, thumb and index finger in the shape of a three-inch 'C.'

It was Kelsea's turn to glare, narrow-eyed at the patiently grazing horses. She clenched her teeth and balled her hands into fists at the thought: Of course, 'Summer' was wet and muddy from her early morning 'romp.' Forbes Creek was the closest place to Debbin's house where she could have gotten muddied up so quickly before being returned to the farm. And Forbes Creek ran north and south, just about halfway between the Ramsay Ranch and the quarry site.

Debbin's horse had to have been used as a _getaway vehicle_ the morning the hate message was written on Justin's bedroom window. But Debbin Ramsay had been neither the rider of the horse, nor the writer of the message.

"Patch," she breathed. "Maybe it's been Patch all along."

Justin said nothing but continued to silently wonder.

_"What _was_ it he had seen?"_

*

"Kee-ripes, what a mess. It's worse than Stuie described," Sandy LeMaster was cautiously picking through the scatterings of chip bags, pizza boxes, magazines, and soda cans. "Guys," she announced with finality, straightening her back—arms akimbo. "Guys have gotta be hangin' out here. Girls would never be part of a pigsty like this."

Erik was willing to concede the fact, but he was *more* interested in doing some top-flight detective work, and getting out before they were (God-forbid!) caught trespassing.

"This isn't *our* shack," he reminded her, "and we probably should wrap this up *fast*. Like we talked about." Then, as a footnote, "If Justin knew we were right here, right now, he'd have a shit-hemorrhage."

"It isn't *'whoever's'* shack either," she retorted. "And *they* probably shouldn't be goofing around here *either*. But since someone *is* meeting here, and they furthermore happen to be in possession of a very *criminal* brand of lipstick, I think that gives us the right to take some pre-emptive measures in self-defense."

"Maybe," Erik was being conciliatory, "but all *I* know is that Justin would take a pretty dim view of our going behind his back, even if we *do* have his best interests at heart."

"Noted," said Sandy professionally. "But sometimes the groupthink method just doesn't get the job done. Sometimes it's best to step *outside* the confines of the circle—to follow a hunch, you know? And just because we've taken independent action *doesn't* mean we're subverting the decisions of our friends."

Erik was giving off tiny signals indicating his discomfort with the situation. He was put out with himself for not appearing braver in Sandy's eyes, but he was also worried; mostly about what Justin and the others would think of the two of them if they found out they had resorted to a plan of action which directly countered a decision made by the group.

"Well, here's the lipstick and there's the slate with the list on it: 'Glass, trash, float, wood, bark.' Still doesn't make any sense, and nothing's been added or changed that I can see," Erik's nervousness was growing. "I don't see anything else that could be thought of as damning evidence, do you, Madame Sherlock?"

"It's *Mademoiselle,* Erik. But that's OK. And no, there doesn't seem to be anything of value or suspicion in here. Let's scout around the perimeter a few meters before we head home. Maybe something will turn up that we overlooked coming in."

ASH BLACK BIRD.

CHIP-BEAKED, BLUE-EYED CROW.

YOU WATCH THE SOLITARY FIGURE APPROACH THE CABIN, WADING THROUGH WAIST-HIGH WEEDS; RETRACING HIS TRAIL TO THE SHANTY—FROM WHICH HE (AND <u>SOMEONE ELSE</u>) HAD DEPARTED ONLY MINUTES AGO.

OLD MAN SUN HAS BEEN DOWN FOR OVER AN HOUR, AND HE HAS BECOME VERY ECONOMICAL WITH THE REMAINDER OF HIS LUMINESCENCE. THE FOOTFALLS OF THE RETURNING LONGLEGS ARE HURRIED, HASTY; HE MISSTEPS IN THREE-QUARTER LIGHT, ALMOST STUMBLING, CATCHING HIMSELF, AND SWEARING UNDER HIS BREATH.

A DRY BRANCH CRACKS LOUDLY UNDER A HEAVY BOOT HEEL, AND THE SOUND ECHOES ACROSS THE SHANTY MEADOW LIKE RIPPLES WRINKLING THE FACE OF A FOREST POND.

CROW SENSES SHOCK, SURPRISE, AND PANIC AS IT EMANATES FROM THE INTERIOR OF THE SHACK IN OVERWHELMING WAVES OF GUT-LEVEL FEAR. FOR IT MATTERS VERY LITTLE IF YOU ARE DEER, BEAR, CROW, OR LONGLEGS; TO BE CORNERED, TO BE BOXED IN, AND CAUGHT IS TO EXPERIENCE TERROR ON A VERY FUNDAMENTAL LEVEL.

WAVE AFTER WAVE OF DISTRESS SIGNALS ARE BROADCAST FROM THE TWO WHO ARE AWAITING THEIR FATE WITHIN THE CONFINES OF THE OLD CABIN. CROW EYES DILATE AS THE SHOCK LEVELS INTENSIFY; GROWING EVER MORE SOPHISTICATED— BECOMING UNENDURABLY SUBLIME—AS AWARENESS AND REALIZATION SINKS ITS ROOTS DEEP INTO THE YOUNGSTERS' SHARED THOUGHT:

"WE'RE TRAPPED! <u>NOW</u> WHAT?"

THE FEAR-WAVE SENSATIONS BECOME EXCRUCIATING— INTOLERABLE—AND YOU SET WINGS TO WIND, LEAVING TWO SCARED, STRANDED TEENS TO PLAY THEIR CARDS EXACTLY AS THEY HAVE BEEN DEALT. CIRCLING THE GRASSY OPENING ONCE, TWICE; APPREHENDING MORE PULSES OF MOUNTING ANXIETY BENEATH YOU WITH EVERY FLEX OF FLIGHT MUSCLE, YOU CLEAR THE TREETOPS RINGING THE MEADOW SHANTY, AND SET

Sandy drew a sharp, deep breath. But before she could utter her cry of panic, Erik sensibly clapped an open hand across her mouth. His arm enveloped her shoulder, and he held her close to him; protective, and at the same time restraining her from the slightest movement which could result in a noisy betrayal of their presence. He shook his head rapidly, and his eyes delivered the clear message that, until further notice, breathing and pumping blood through veins and arteries were the only activities allowed.

Understanding registered in her expression, and she nodded her head indicating that it was OK for Erik to uncover her mouth; she wouldn't make a sound. But the girl rested her head upon his shoulder, wrapping her arms around him, and lacing her fingers together just above his hip. It was definitely _not_ OK for him to stop holding her.

Not yet.

The shanty door was open several inches, more or less the way they had found it when they arrived in gathering dusk. A tall, thin rectangle of diffused light bled into the room, and spilled across the roughhewn floor where the two sat cross-legged, garnering courage from a cache of shared body warmth. Foot thumps could be clearly heard as somebody (sounded like a guy, they would later agree, judging from the heavy-sounding tread and long gait) drew closer to the cabin.

Very much against her will, Sandy began to tremble lightly. The tremors triggered a similarly unwilled response in Erik, whose insecurities all at once began to subside in a wash of barely contained anger. He felt heat in his face and neck; felt it resonate through his shoulders, arms, and legs—spreading the word to every muscle of his lean frame that a fight was in the making and that, come hell or high water, his body was poised and ready for whatever comes.

What_ever_ comes!

Boots clump closer. Boots scuff the sod. Boots trample grass and wildflowers.

Boots reach the cabin door.

Erik thinks, *Here we go. We're into some pretty stuff now, man! Hand is on the door. Showtime! What's it gonna be?*

Erik's body has spontaneously morphed into a 138-pound, coiled spring; potential energy straining to explode into kinetic chaos—fueled by fury, propelled by passion.

Boot kicks the door. The enemy has arrived. Muscles scream in protest of restraint.

CROW FEELS IT OVER HALF A MILE AWAY, AND PLUNGES INTO A DOWNDRAFT TO SKIRT THE TRAUMA WAVE.

Boot kicks the door again, harder! And slams it closed! Hand slaps a padlock through the hasp.

Click!

Erik and Sandy breathe and listen, listen and breathe; hearts hammering beneath ribcages; hammering in furious protest over the undelivered promise of confrontation. Isolated, together, they strain to identify a voice that melts into the deaf night muttering oaths and curses; lost within the lonesome swirl of wind stream swooshing among evergreen boughs.

*

Evening darkness collected in pockets and pools. It seeped from unlit niches—inky, viscous—collaborating with furtive forms of shadow and shade in twisting dissymmetry.

The indigo ooze dispersed, encroached, covered, and filled to spilling. Unencumbered by ambient light that amounted to not much more than a flicker of a candle flame, the expanding black shape-which-has-no-shape poured itself over, amongst, around, and through everything. Through existence itself.

Darkness is only the absence of light. But Erik and Sandy were rapidly surmising that, before this evening—before they had become locked inside their ramshackle, dim-lit prison—neither of them had ever *truly* encountered a reality this devoid of recognizable familiarity. And that darkness of *this* nature, my friend, was darkness of a new dimension.

"Do you think he knows we're in here?" Sandy's voice was little more than a hoarse whisper. *(What is it about dark surroundings that hushes the conversation?)* "Do you think he locked us in, and walked away on *purpose?*"

"I dunno. Maybe we should have yelled out. I'm thinkin' an all-out fight-to-the-finish would have been preferable to *this*," Erik was up, scrounging in the fast-fading light for anything he might use to crash against the cabin door; anything heavy and durable with which he could bludgeon their way out.

"Yes, but Erik, maybe there were two or three or even more of them out there, too. They might have had *weapons*. We have no idea what kind of people we are dealing with. They could be desperate men on the run from the law for all we know." She strode across the junk-strewn room to stand beside him, touching him lightly on the arm.

"We did the right thing, Erik," she said. "We got ourselves into a bit of a spot, admittedly, but we did the right thing. We did the *safe* thing."

"Could be worse, I guess," offered Erik. Marching over to the cabin door, he braced himself, raised his right leg high as he could, and pummeled it with the sole of his boot till his face turned red and his breath came in great gasps. "Man, oh man!" he moaned. "They don't make doors like *this* anymore, do they?"

"Well, like you said, Mr. Remarque, it could be worse."

"F'rinstance?"

(F'rinstance, when the fear factor pegs your sanity needle to the max, the last resort in survival mode is often, human <u>humor</u>; goofballing your way through a tap-dance with terror. Crow would have noted an appreciable change in the nature of the vibes zapping from the cabin at about that time.)

219

"F'rinstance, the cabin could be filling up with water."

"Or sewage."

"Ee-yew, Erik. That's gross. Or, um, we could be running out of oxygen."

"Or running out of toilet paper."

"Erik!" Sandy giggled. "Would you kindly *clean it up a little?*"

"Hard to clean up a room full of sewage with no toilet paper, Sandalita."

"I'm giving you fair warning, buster," Sandy scolded playfully. "Either play nicely or go home!"

"That's just what I intend to do, m'lady. I'm goin' home, where there's no sewage and always plenty of toilet paper."

"And how, if you please, do you plan on accomplishing *that* feat of derring-do, Baron von Remarque-able?"

"Oh, any number of ways, fer shure. Listen and learn: Solution #1," Erik, squatting, fetched up a piece of notebook paper lying on the floor. "I will simply fold this ordinary sheet of paper exactly in half, and then tear it gently, carefully, into two perfectly…equal…pieces."

"And?" said Sandy, with *no* idea *where* her friend was going with *this*.

"It's so-oo *simple*, Sandy. Two halves make a 'hole,' see? I'll just crawl *out* that 'hole' and go *home*."

"Ba-dump, pssht," Sandy, with the sound of a snare drum and cymbal; indicating the lounge act quality of Erik's joke.

"Not amused? OK, OK, I got more."

"That's kind of what I was afraid of."

"How 'bout this?" Erik began wadding a potato chip sack into a tight ball which he then handed to his friend. Taking a few short steps backward in the darkening room, he assumed a 'batter's stance' and instructed Sandy to pitch the crumpled 'ball' to him.

"What'll *that* accomplish?" insisted the girl.

"You pitch, I swing and miss. I give you the 'ball' back. You pitch again, I swing and miss again. We do it one last time, same results."

Sandy stood, staring.

"C'mon, Sandy!" he implored.

"Oh! I get it, now," she laughed. "Three strikes and—"

"I'm _out_! Brilliant, no?"

Sandy shook her head in mock contempt. "This is going to be one long ordeal," she declared. "Lord, give me patience and strength. Better yet, strike me deaf, or lacerate his vocal cords."

"This one is sure to get yer approval," prompted Erik.

"You probably mean my wrath, don't you?" teased Sandy, clearly enjoying watching Erik show off for her.

"We both start running around the perimeter of the room, around, and around, and around as fast as we can possibly go until…"

"Until? Until, what?"

"Until we've completely worn ourselves _out_, of course! Whatcha think? Which plan suits your taste? No, no! Don't bother thanking me! It's all in a night's work for a genius of my ilk."

Sandy had to save the applause for later because the explosion that rended the Appleton air sent a concussive shock that found its way all the way to the meadow shanty.

"What the…?" began Sandy after the surprise of the jolt subsided.

"Sounded like an M-80," stated Erik.

"What's an M-80?"

"Military explosive device—small scale. Kind of like a humongous firecracker. They don't cause much damage, they just make a whole lotta noise. I think they use them for detonating purposes, actually."

"Well, I don't know about _you_, but for _my_ money, that sounded like it came from the direction of…"

"Yep, I know," responded Erik worriedly. "From the Ramsay Ranch, right?"

"Spot on, Sparky."

"Wanna know what?"

"What?"

"Despite appearances, *we* may be in *less* trouble than the *others* right about now."

Sandy took his hand in hers and moved close to his side. "I hope you're not right, Mr. Visionary Genius," she said quietly. "Not this time, anyway."

And *that* was pretty much the *end* of the comic relief for the rest of the evening.

*

YOU...POSSESSING ENDLESS FIDELITY TO PURPOSE AT HAND. COMPELLED BY RAVENRILL DIRECTIVE; PROPELLED BY REVERENCE TO CROW-LIFE-PLAN. CLEAR MINDED, SELF-ASSURED, DILIGENT, AND JOYOUS IN YOUR TASK WORK.

YOU...IN CLUTCH-WITH-TALONS TIME; TO GATHER, TO GLEAN, AND, IF NECESSARY, TO INTERVENE—SPARINGLY, SPECIFICALLY—ON BEHALF OF A CLUTCH OF DISTANT KINSMEN.

SCATTERED BELOW YOU ON A THREE-QUARTER ACRE CARPET OF PLUSH, GREEN, NEWLY MOWN LAWN, CLOSE TO 60 YOUNG LONGLEGS—MOSTLY 17 AND 18 YEAR-OLDS, BUT WITH A SMATTERING OF LITTLE ONES AND ADULTS—RANGE IN A FREE-FORM MOSAIC OF ACTIVITIES. BARBECUING, HORSESHOE-TOSSING, SWIMMING, BADMINTON, AND BOARD GAMES; POOL PARTY! IT REGISTERS UPON YOU THAT THIS IS A LAID-BACK GROUP OF SOON-TO-BE-GRADUATING SENIORS AND UNDERCLASSMEN. THAT THEY DEFINITELY KNOW HOW TO ENTERTAIN THEMSELVES IN MELLOW FASHIONS.

CROW ACKNOWLEDGES, SYNTHESIZES, COLLATES...AND MATURES.

It was only 8:00 pm; dusk—"in the gloaming," as Sandy would say...as Sandy *was* saying...to Erik, as a matter of fact, miles away in a meadow shack (where Tamarack Mountain summons the shadows earlier than one experiences a bit further down, on the valley floor). Early evening; past Debbin's projected "end-time" though it was, this patently non-rowdy group of party-goers was finally beginning to ease down. Energetic and enthusiastic as they were, it had been a long,

222

wonderful, sunny day of good, rockin' fun—one for the memory books—and a peaceful mood was inching its way over the farm site, cleverly disguised as the shadow hush of nightfall.

The fatigue was well received *and* well earned.

Consider: 40 pounds of hamburger, over 120 hot dogs, eight cases of soft drinks, six cases of sunburn, a sprained ankle, a split lip, 12 large sacks of chips, one broken heart, two newly discovered love interests, one bee sting, eight embarrassing moments, 12 stolen kisses, six pies, four gallons of ice cream, over a hundred rock 'n' roll CDs, three videos on a large outdoor screen, one bruised ego, six practical jokes, eleventy-four swear words, three full garbage cans of party refuse, almost eight straight hours of non-stop laughter, one broken guitar string, and an explosion down by the horse barn that brought everyone to his senses, and to their feet in about a New York Second.

YOU HAD BEEN WATCHING FROM THE ROOFTOP OF THE RAMSAY HOME WHEN THE SUDDEN COOSH OF VIOLATED AIR RUSHED THROUGH YOUR FEATHERS. THE THRUM OF THE AIR QUAKE VIBRATED IN YOUR BREASTBONE FOR ONLY A MILLISECOND, BUT YOU SENSED ITS OUTBOUND, RADIATING INFLUENCE EVEN AS YOU SOUGHT THE SAFETY OF DARK, LOFTY WIND.

YOU HAVE "LEANED IN" LONG ENOUGH FOR THIS APPLETON DAY.

NEST-WARD FLY YOU, CROW. QUARRY-BOUND.

The blast came precisely at the end of a very slowed-down, almost introspective version of '*She Loves You.*' Justin had no more put the last, lilting touch to Woody's strings—a sweetly smiling, semi-sleepy audience just beginning to bring hands together in quiet, appreciative applause—when windows rattled with the force of the blast.

Mr. and Mrs. Ramsay were out of the house and en route to the source of the noise—the horse barn—in a split instant; Megan and Debbin hard on their heels. *Everyone else* dropped his activity, and raced behind the Ramsay family in the direction of the pasture; boys up front, in case there was trouble, girls just a step behind and sticking close together. Justin, again, took the time to slip Woody into the guitar case and close it up before racing to catch up with the others. Emergency or no, old habits, *good* habits are difficult to break.

When they reached the post-and-rail fence, Mr. Ramsay turned to the youngsters and raised his hands for silence. "Everyone, listen up," he said calmly. "I think it was probably just a cherry bomb; somebody's *idea* of a *fun* thing to do. Honey? Is everybody here? No one's off somewhere alone, are they? No? Good. Kids: keep together for just a few moments while we check things out. Don't go wandering off just yet. Whoever the *joker* was, he's probably long gone by now, and won't be back. He's had his little show, so I'll just take a couple of you boys down to calm the horses, and look things over. Donovan, you and Seth hop through the fence and come with me, please. You too, Bryan."

The boys—substantial football players, one and all—quickly followed instructions; happy to have been chosen to perform a small task of heroism for the family of their classmate. A short investigation of the area pretty much confirmed Mr. Ramsay's suspicions. Pranksters had probably thrown the gigantic firecracker toward the barn from the near side of the dirt road which crossed the property to the ranch. No damage had been done, outside of some spooked animals. And after having taken care of business, everyone returned to the house to begin clean-up in earnest.

It was generally understood that the party was over.

Justin retrieved his guitar case, shyly accepting gratuitous remarks from dozens of people for his contribution to an outstanding evening. The mood was remarkably upbeat—despite the sudden ending to the festivities—and Justin headed for his bike, whistling for Kooper, whom he had not seen for quite some time by then.

"You don't think the explosion frightened him off, do you?" worried Mrs. Ramsay, drying her hands with a dishtowel and scanning the property. "He's such a good old dog. I'd hate for anything to happen to him."

"Naw, don't worry about ol' Koop," assured Justin amicably. "He wandered off a couple of hours ago. Probably got tired of hearin' me screech, and decided there were better things for him to do elsewhere. Happens all the time," he added. "He'll show up tomorrow mornin' when he's as pooped out as these here party people."

"Sure you don't want a ride back to the quarry, son? We can toss your bike in the back of the pick-up and get you there a lot faster than leg power can," Mr. Ramsay knew the answer to the question even as he asked it. No. Justin preferred to pedal his way home under the quiet blanket of Appleton stars; thinking about the evening, thinking about his simple good fortune, and marveling at the power of music to knit people into a fabric of friendship.

Later that night—whisking wind-tousled hair from his eyes, his thoughts lit with star fire from the short, solitary ride home—Justin would remember every detail of the party's final moments. The noise, the impact, the rush of bodies, confusion, concern, relief, residual frustration at the intrusion, the trespass…the insult.

Why? he thought. *Why?* But it was not a "why" worth asking. For the "because" that prefaces the answer is the kind of "because" that spins your reasoning in circles, tips your logic on its head, and leaves your sense of common sense reeling with the sheer absurdity of it all.

"Better off not to go there, Mr. Bench," he said aloud (to no one there). "Sing yerself a nighttime melody before ya turn in, an' things'll look better in the mornin'."

Justin knelt, unsnapping the latches of Woody's case and flipping the top up and back. What he saw made him sit back on his heels, sucking in his breath as he wrestled with a yellow, sickening feeling that crawled through his body like an infection. His eyes brimming, he suddenly remembered leaving Woody in the case—lid closed—and rushing to join the others near the horse barn. No one, *no one* had remained at the house after the explosion occurred; an explosion that Justin *now* knew had been meant only as a distraction for the evening's *real* act of vandalism.

For his beloved six-string Yamaha lay in the carrier—crushed almost beyond recognition.

Woody was forever ruined.

Woody was no more.

The music…was over.

*

Clots of mud-colored clouds crept sluggishly over the summit of Chapman Butte, flowing and falling partway to the Valley floor before mashing into a toneless, pallid bank of monochromatic mush. And though the billows looked moisture-laden to the power of ten—threatening to burst at any moment into a deluge of Biblical proportions—this was not usually the case. For these were the clouds of August—the month of 'dry lightning.'

Most folks around Appleton know all about the 'Dry Lightning Month,' which typically runs its course in just over two weeks. But firefighters with the U.S. Forest Service (mostly college kids home from school, but including itinerants from all over the west) look forward to the first fortnight of August as their prime money-making stretch.

Dozens of lightning strikes touch off countless mini-fires in the dry undergrowth of the Kennawack National Forest in early to mid-month. Most of the would-be wildfires remain non-spreaders; manageable, owed to trace amounts of rainfall which typically accompany the ground strikes. This has a dousing effect—as it were—culminating in what amounts to little more than a fourteen-day run of highly manageable 'smokes' in most cases. Manageable, yes. But also very *profitable* from the standpoint of *'By Gawd'* firefighters; youthful, and eager to shore up their bank accounts before encroaching winter weather dries up the opportunity to 'make hay.'

August 'smoke chasing' paid top dollar as flame stompers hopped from 'fire' to 'fire' around the clock for 15-20 days tamping out sparks and collecting hazardous duty pay in the process.

Good work, if you could get it. An entire summer's worth of fire-free inactivity (not good, from a college kid's financial point of view) could be compensated for with a good 14-day run of dry lightning activity. And a year's worth of college tuition could be garnered in time for September classes if the entire season happened to be a busy one. Appleton's very own Tim Crowl was among many home town boys who had, over the years, financed the completion of his college degree solely on paychecks earned from summer firefighting on Kennawack National Forest lands.

Justin was not thinking about fat, ugly clouds full of electricity. He was not thinking about 20-some-year-old firefighters or glasses of beer or rising prices at the gas pumps. He was not even really thinking about Kooper, who had failed to show up from wherever it was his bad doggy imagination had propelled him. (OK, he _was_ a _little_ concerned about Kooperdog since he should have been _back_ by now.)

But mostly, he was sitting on the porch swing listening to the phone ring, and not answering it. He was listening to his CD player—silent—since it had been neither loaded nor cranked up all morning. He was listening to the sound of Woody's voice…mellow and bell-like; _ringing in his head_ since last night's hoot.

The night his music had been ruthlessly destroyed.

Justin was listening to no one; stupefied and fixated on nothing. He was brain limp and muscle weary; yearning for home, while at home he sat. He was listening to the sound of thunder rumble, somewhere off in the wherever. And to the sound of heart shatter, from distant points within.

The first week of August, 1992. And Justin Bench was cloud-hidden at the quarry site; like an islander—closed and reclusive—entertaining ashen thoughts on the first of many lusterless days to come. Anesthetized by his own dull response to loss and bitterness, the young man was only dimly aware of the approach of a tall, imposing figure swaggering up the hill to the cabin. By the time his reverie had eclipsed, and he had returned from somewhere in his own head—returned back into his body proper—he was surprised to find that he had been joined on the cabin deck by Colonel Tattenger and that the man was regarding him in a most off-hand way.

"Well there, young man," remarked the colonel, stroking his chin contemplatively.

"You gave me a bit of a start, so you did," he leaned forward some, scrutinizing Justin with the half-smile of a country doctor pulling a rose thorn out of a little girl's doll.

"Looked almost like you were in kind of a trance or something. Are you feeling all right?"

"Yes, I'm fine," Justin lied. "Just tired, that's all. I, uh, played at a party last night and got to bed kinda late…" He let the explanation hang, glancing at Woody's empty guitar case.

"Well, that's good. You look a little pale, that's all and, well, I'm not going to bother you with a lot of idle chit-chat. I've got phone calls to make and you've got some rest to catch up on, obviously. Heh, heh. I just wanted to check up on that offer I made to you some time ago, the offer to purchase the quarry land?"

"I…"

"Have you given any thought to the idea? No? Now, there's no rush on it, son, not at all. The offer hasn't got a short shelf life, and it's not set to expire at midnight tonight. Heh-heh."

"…"

"But I do have to say that, as you know, I've got a tremendous amount of work that I need to complete before I can begin what I like to think of as the next important phase of my life, uh, my *family* life."

"It's just that…"

"So take some more time, if you need to; why, you've still got plenty of time to make up your mind on this *gold mine* of an opportunity. Heh, heh. But I'll tell you what. I'll need to have some kind of assurance from you in the next two weeks that you're *at least* mulling the whole thing over. How does that sound to you? I'll be in touch in two weeks, why just about the time this old dry lightnin' stuff fizzles out, eh? Yes, and you can let me know at *that* time if the proposition is *real* for you or no."

"…"

"If it's still *real* for you by then, why, we can talk it over a bit, and I can even give you some *more* think time, if you like. But, if you decide that, 'no by gosh, this just doesn't seem like the deal I want,' why I'll begin searching for green pastures somewhere else. Sound good? What could be better, eh?"

"Mmhmm…"

"That's the spirit! Something tells me that you've already begun to size up just what a sweet opportunity this can turn out to be, ah, for the *both* of us, uh, and, and my *family* as well. Yessir, it's got the makings of a real *win/win outcome*, and there's nothing the colonel likes quite so much as a deal that pans out well for everyone involved. Don't you agree, uh, Justin?"

"I'll maybe…see ya in a…coupla weeks," Justin, offering a hand, off-handedly.

"Yes. Yes," enjoined the colonel, accepting gingerly with a lukewarm grip. Justin noticed that the Hollywood eye twinkle and toothy smile had momentarily relaxed.

The man stood abruptly as if on cue, brushing down his slacks and shirt in trademark military fashion. Then, quite unexpectedly, the seriousness dissolved from his expression, and Tattenger rekindled his charm, like a flashlight whose dim illumination is rectified quickly enough with a swift bap against the heel of your hand.

"Almost forgot to ask you," he mentioned as he descended the steps of the cabin deck. "Did you hear about Erik, is it Remarque? Yes, Erik Remarque and the LeMaster girl?"

"What? No. What about 'em? Is somethin' wrong?"

"Why, they've gone missing. Yessir. Been missing since about this time yesterday. Pretty near the whole town is out looking for them. I'm surprised no one has called to inform you about it, you being so close to them and all. Well, I have *got* to get going. Time is money. No rest for the wicked, heh, heh. You get yourself some rest, young man. You're as pale as a bedsheet."

*

Consider an ant nest.

Nicely mounded and rounded, it is constructed from millions of pine needles and tiny twig-lets; painstakingly dragged to the nest site by God-alone-knows-how-many busy, dedicated insects. It is a study in the virtue of patience, simple engineering, and single-minded 'stick-to-it-ish-ness.'

Now, if one were to tap that nest lightly with a long branch, one would observe the entire earthy clump leaping to life, crawling with countless throngs of the creatures, all adhering to an instinctive imperative ("Security Mode Alpha D," or some other similarly agreed-upon plan of action) genetically encoded for measures of Homeland Security.

It is mesmerizing to watch this rippling, frenetic, tightly organized chaos as hundreds of thousands of insects, each one indistinguishable from all the others (Where's Waldo?), scurry over and around each other in high, blind, random pandemonium to save the *ant*-dom.

With *that* image in mind, you've got a pretty fair idea of what the little burg of Appleton looked like from a *Crow's eye view* early that morning. Every business in town—excepting the hospital, post office, and gas station (p.o. and g.s., meaning…'The Queen')—was closed until further notice. Citizens of all ages—_all_ ages—were swarming, scurrying, walking, biking, driving, and skateboarding every which way at the same time; combing the community and the surrounding woodlands for the two missing youngsters.

The search was understandably panicky, feverish, omnidirectional, and rocket-paced.

Interviews were conducted and re-conducted: Mr. and Mrs. LeMaster quizzed Justin, Justin quizzed Kelsea, Kelsea quizzed Mr. and

Mrs. LeMaster, and on and on. The Kennawack River was being scouted from the Falls all the way to Chapeeka with prayer being heaped upon quietly whispered prayer that nothing would turn up on the bottom sands of the never-resting waters.

An all-points bulletin had been issued from the headquarters of the Kennawack County Sheriff's Department in Weston, but the focal point of the rescue mission was the Middle Valley where folks refused to relinquish the hope that two tired, hungry kids would soon be found, and that an explanation for their disappearance would be forthcoming.

It was simply a matter of time. The Herculean efforts of those townsfolk—so deeply imbued with a sense of common purpose—eventually would have been rewarded.

Someone would have finally broken through the buckbrush to the meadow; would have found the old shanty, and rescued its grateful inmates. Erik and Sandy would have been *dis*covered and *re*covered by Pops or Justin or Hollis or any number of community members if somebody else hadn't gotten there first.

*

All things considered, Erik and Sandy spent a pretty comfortable night in the meadow shanty. The sleeping bags had been sufficiently warm, despite their sorry, neglected condition. There was food and drink, if you could call it that; a few unopened sacks of corn chips and a six-pack of (ugh!) creme soda, but neither of them felt inclined to consume very much. Plus, <u>no</u> litter box for *these* cats (if you get the meaning). But they managed to 'hold on' all right. With no windows to admit the morning light, the kiddos had only scant illumination from cracks and fissures in the aging structure. It was enough to *see by* (barely), but they really had no idea what time of day it was, or how long they had been entrapped since *nobody* was in possession of a wristwatch.

Furthermore, they had lain awake for the greater part of the night—side by side—rolled cocoon-like in their bags; talking their way around the uncertainties of their predicament. When they finally awoke, stiff and bleary-eyed from the hard floor, they had no way of knowing that it was already 11:00 am, _or_ that the entire town was out looking for them.

"Mornin', Ace," mumbled Sandy. She was lying in a semi-curled-up position on her side with her back to him. "How'd you sleep?"

"The management of this establishment is going to hear from me about _these_ accommodations," said Erik, half-teasing, half-testy. "As a five-star hotel, this simply does _not_ pack the load. And room service! Where is the freakin' _room service_ I read so much about?"

Sandy raised herself to a sitting position and faced her friend. She smiled drowsily, and half-heartedly attempted to comb some fingers through impossibly sleep-tangled curls. Her warm brown eyes regarded him with a heavy-lidded kind of softness that made him instantly aware of the fact that he had never seen anyone or anything so beautiful in his entire 14-soon-to-be-15-year-old life.

He crawled over to her on his hands and knees and rested a palm gently on her shoulder. "Sandy," he began, "I'm really sorry about this whole thing. Not only are we gonna be in _big trouble_ with a lotta people when this is over, but jeez, no tenth-grade girl wants to be locked up overnight someplace with a stupid freshman guy. I just—"

The kiss lasted exactly 100 perfect years.

Scores of thousands of miles deep—silken, sonorous powder-blue—it bridged the Milky Way from one star-lit end to the distant-most other.

It was as featherlight and translucent as butterfly wings…with an impact measurable in kilotons.

It turned time inside out, and made colors vibrate and ring with audible clarity.

It was Erik's very first honeyed taste…of rose petals.

Floating—bodiless, and buoyant as gossamer—helpless to steal even a slit-lidded peek at the scatter-haired perfection that brushed his brow, he breathed through his heart and could have ardently sworn that he was hearing the sound of angels sighing.

He was annihilated. And Sandy—for her part—felt her love-longing awaken for the first time.

That's when the hateful, metal lock became *un*locked.

The heavy door of the meadow shanty creaked open, bathing the gape-mouthed, saucer-eyed couple in banana-yellow light.

Blinded and blinking in the intrusive burst of sun-glare, long seconds passed before they fully recognized the figure outlined in the cabin doorway. It was just too unlikely to be true—too awful to be really happening.

Sandy could only numbly whisper. "Oh, no."

The gargantuan shape pointed to the couple—sitting on the wooden floor of the shanty—paralyzed and awestruck—and spoke the first words anyone outside the Ratpack could ever recall having heard him utter.

"Don't even *think* about leaving," remarked Deep Thoughts. "You're in a *world* of hurt."

*

The remainder of the Scalawags—along with parents, families, and friends—eventually gathered at Appleton Park late in the afternoon to try and tease some meaning from the latest developments. With nearly a thousand people scouring every inch of Appleton and its surroundings, it was decided that an hour or two of 'think time' was probably in the best interests of everyone concerned. Or, as Justin poignantly put it: "Let's all sit down an' see if we can make some *head*way with our *heads* instead of our *legs*."

With dozens of townspeople milling and discussing in groups of varying sizes, Kelsea, Justin, and Stuart retreated to the park bench to mull things over. It was then and there that Justin made public a thought which he had been privately entertaining since the incident at the Swimming Hole.

"I been thinkin' long and hard on this," he began, clearing his throat and stuffing his hands deep into the pockets of his blue jeans. "Long enough to see that whoever wants me outa my house isn't likely to ever take 'no' for an answer."

Silence greeted his remarks as Kelsea and Stuart held off to see where their friend was going with this.

"Could be that takin' Colonel Tat's offer to purchase the property may just be the best thing I could do."

"Oh, no! Justin, you can't *mean* that!" Kelsea, shocked with disbelief. "That place is your *home*, it's Kooper's home, my gosh, it's, it's practically *our* home. You can't sell it off and run away. That'd be even more criminal than the stuff that's been *done to you* this summer." The color is drained from her cheeks. "Besides, you slammed the lid on *that* notion _days_ ago. We _all_ did, remember?!"

Justin's eyes grew damp and he fought to control the tremor in his voice. "Kels," he said shakily, "I can't help but wonder if the disappearance of Sandy and Erik is somehow connected to this whole mess. And if there *is* a connection; if this *is* another part of somebody's scheme to kick me outa the valley, then I'll tell you what, they have finally gotten my attention. 'Cause I'm not gonna stand by and let *anybody* put *my best friends* in harm's way. Not for *any* reason, understandable or otherwise."

Kelsea is sobbing now, arms around her middle and rocking gently. Stuart's lower lids are filled to brimming; he's studying a leaf scrap hung up in a bit of grassy whatever, unable to make eye contact with anyone.

"I haven't made a hard, fast decision either way," pronounced Justin. "But I told him I'd talk to him in a couple of weeks' time, and let him know if I thought the idea had merit." He lowered his voice and spoke as reassuringly as he could, "I just didn't wanna have to spring it on you all at once, that's all. I just wanted you to know that it's a serious option, and I'm givin' it some serious consideration."

"Well, what if you *did* sell?" enjoined Stuart, drying his tears with his shirttail.

"What if the captain bought the quarry lands from you and, and then, the same stuff started happening to *him*? Maybe some whacked-out freak cult of some kind wants the woods for their *own* screwed up purposes and there's just no end to it, no matter *who* owns it. You would've given up your home when it wasn't even *you* they were targeting."

Justin paused, eyeing his young friend very carefully. "C'mon, Stuie," he said quietly. "Do you honestly believe that I am *not* being targeted here? Stu? Honestly?"

"And it's *colonel*, not captain, Stuie," Sandy spoke gently. "But that's all right."

You have *never* seen three bodies spin around so fast in all your life. Well...maybe *once* before (Remember?) Why, the wind created by that trio of whirling dervishes could fling a Crow from here to Patterson's Falls without the need for so much as a single wingbeat.

There they stood! Sneaked up on ol' Justin and the 'Pool Two'— half the town, really—as distracted as they all were with their serious strategizing. But there they stood nonetheless. Erik and Sandy— scratched, dirty, grinning, and damn glad to be home.

"Wha, where have you, are you, are you two, the whole town...we've been...do you guys even... What the hell?"

"We'll tell the whole thing later...and believe me, we've got *plenty* to tell!" Sandy was businesslike, despite the circumstances. "Justin! Quick! Where's Kooper?"

"Why, I don't rightly know, Sandy. He wandered off from the pool party just about the time you two musta done your vanishing act. He hasn't been back since, and I'm gettin' kinda worried."

Sandy took Justin's hands in hers and held them tightly. "Justin," she said, "we have *got* to find Koop just as fast as we possibly can. He is in *serious* danger."

"What? Serious, *how*?"

Sandy flicked a glance in Kelsea's direction, before returning to Justin; her eyes lingering only long enough to deliver the unspoken answer.

"Uh-oh," she broke off.

"Here come Mom and Dad. And am _I_ ever happy to see _them_!"

"Woh, looks like most of the town is comin' with 'em," echoed Erik. "Man, it looks a little like a hangin' party," he joked. But there were tears of relief in his eyes as he raced across the short distance between them and melted into his father's arms.

*

The search for Kooper didn't get underway quite as quickly as the Scalawags had hoped. Two-handedly munching sandwiches, apples, and/or granola bars, the newly-turned-up "missing youngsters" were intercepted by authorities, just moments following their unexpected appearance in the Park. *Authorities,* in this particular case, refers solely to Officer Carlos Santiago, who joined a gaggle of highly agitated and very worried parents who were in a big hurry to unload a couple of bucketloads of tears while simultaneously securing the answers to nearly a dozen hour's worth of questions.

It was like the Spanish Inquisition, but without the torture.

How much to tell and how much to keep to themselves? Tough decision. No one wanted to betray the trust Justin had placed in everyone's assurances that his problems over the course of the summer would be addressed privately. But moms and dads who have been forced to face the possibility of enduring a reality made up of some of their most deeply held fears were *not about* to let up without getting some *really sound* explanations about "what the devil was going on."

The kids were on a very slippery slope here. And it all went down more or less like this:

"Locked inside a cabin? What cabin? Where is it?"

(Short explanation of location with a brief description of cabin appearance.)

"Who locked you in? Why didn't you let them know you were inside?"

(Panicked, didn't know what to do, it all happened so fast, felt guilty about trespassing, etc., etc.)

"What were you doing out in that part of the woods anyway?"

(Just exploring, hiking, looking for adventure.)

"Looks like you found the <u>adventure</u> part all right. How did you get out of the cabin?"

(Deep Thoughts came by with a key.)

"<u>Deep Thoughts</u>? What's <u>he</u> doing with a key to an abandoned cabin?"

(Ratpack is using it for, like, a clubhouse or something. That's why the sleeping bags, and all that stuff is up there.)

Lecture, lecture, lecture, hug, hug, lecture, lecture, scold, threaten, hug, hug. HUG!

(Apologize, promise, hug, hug, assure, reassure, apologize, apologize, promise.)

HUG...*HUG*!

It was decidedly *difficult* to convince Messrs. and Mmes. Crowl, LeMaster, and Remarque to allow their youngsters to embark upon the hunt for Kooperdog. For even though the scare was over, a lot of adrenalin was still at work in those shook-up, grown-up parental units. Even so. "All is well that endeth well," and upon Phillip LeMaster's suggestion, the adults agreed to organize a "car search" while the Scalawags resumed on bikes.

Carlos Santiago fingered his mustache thoughtfully. "Anything else you'd care to add to your explanation?" he asked. "Anything about, anything? No? Really? OK, then. Case closed. Right?"

Mumbles and shrugs.

Convincing? Well, maybe. Somewhat. Sorta kinda.

Santiago wrapped things up. "Guess I'd better check up on the 'packers,' and find out what it is they're up to. Deserted or not, I don't think it's a good idea for anybody to be hangin' round that mountain shack. It's a recipe for trouble, as we've already found out."

Smiling (thinly), the deputy left them there—huddled, mute, and conscience-stricken from their unspoken, agreed-upon suppression of certain facts. He wheeled his cruiser in a wide circle and headed down Frontier Street, waving as he passed. The LeMaster automobile, with all the adults, followed suit and for long seconds, there was nothing to see but a thin film of dust filtering through declining, leaf-broken sunlight.

Nothing to hear but the non-stop sound of the letter 'S'...as mountain air tickled the stiff needles of the park's evergreen trees.

Nothing to think about except *Why is this happening? Where is Kooper? What is this all about?* And...

"What was it that Justin had seen?"

*

"Listen, you two. Before we go any further, there's something you need to know about," Kelsea looked to Justin for support, and received

238

his gravely nodded agreement. "Justin has been hit again. It happened at Debbin's party, right at the end. There was a cherry bomb, an' it went off down by the horse barns. It was used to create a distraction so that someone, someone who was hiding close by, could get a hold of Woody and…"

"And what?" asked Sandy, dark eyes slitted in anticipation of hard news.

A long quiet moment.

"And _what_?" she repeated. "Get hold of Woody while no one was looking and _what_?"

Super pregnant pause. Then.

"Smash 'im into a thousand pieces," finished Justin; voice shaky. "_Somebody_ out there hates me more than ever. And I'm thinkin' about foldin' my hand an' lookin' for another game, if you get my meaning."

"Damn!" whispered Erik, his voice constricted; venomous.

"Justin," cautioned Kelsea, "you promised us that we'd _all_ take the time to brainstorm _that_ problem the next time we circled up. Keep your word, and let's stick to one issue at a time."

"You're right," he allowed. "First things first. Let's get on with findin' Koop. _Then_ we'll talk about what to do with the colonel and his offer on the quarry."

Kelsea, Justin, and Stuart made ready to grab their bicycles. But Erik and Sandy remained motionless—hesitant and indecisive—staring hard at one another with an uncertainty that rippled the space between them, and heightened a sense of awareness.

"All right, guys," Stuart spoke lowly, slowly. "Something's up. Let's have it."

"Better give 'em the information now," suggested Erik. "We _gotta_ find Koop, but they gotta know about _this_, first."

Sandy's thoughts were moving at light-speed. _What to do? What to do?_

"Sandy…" urged Erik.

"Well…?" pried Justin.

Sandy LeMaster drew a deep, unsteady breath. "I'm going to make this explanation fast," she blurted. "Not all of it makes sense, but I'll tell you what we know, and let Erik fill in any holes I leave along the way. Then, for cryin' out loud, we have _got_ to go find Kooper!

"Now, you already know that the one who finally unlocked the meadow shanty was…"

*

"…Deep Thoughts!"

"Don't even _think_ about leaving," he said. "You're in a _world of hurt_."

What scares _you_ the most?

Looking down from high places? Thunder? Cold water? Bats? Snakes? Algebra? Educational TV? Uncle Irv?

How about being locked up in a deserted mountain cabin? How about all those weird _night sounds_? What _is_ that stuff out there? Maybe you don't really _want_ to know.

How about a _huge_, dark, hairy, creep of a kid who hangs out with the town trouble-making punks? Mysterious, secretive, brooding. Sinister-looking. Whose only words you have ever, _ever_ in your whole freakin' life heard him utter are for _your_ ears only; directed solely at _you_:

"You're in a _world of hurt_."

Would you find that bothersome?

Maybe not. Maybe you feel adequate to the task of defending yourself in situations that smack of peril. Perhaps you are trained, or gifted, or are in possession of abundant quantities of _damn good luck_ and can somehow summon courage and resourcefulness whenever and wherever you find it necessary to save your sorry, skinny carcass from impending doom. If so…good _on_ yer! Erik was _not_ so predisposed.

Erik and Sandy were both (to put it _very_ mildly) scared spitless.

They sat there on the shanty floor; cotton-mouthed, and electrically charged with fear so compelling, so completely constricting that any and all thought of 'fight or flight' was subsumed—immersed and dissolved in a shared understanding that the only path to survival lay in strict compliance, total obedience to the boy doing the talking; the boy who had *just now* informed them that what they had procured for themselves was…a "world of hurt."

Deep Thoughts left the door ajar. He took two enormous strides and slid smoothly and effortlessly into a cross-legged sitting position directly in front of the pair. He considered the two of them for some moments as if studying their predicament, and what it must mean to them. Or perhaps weighing his next move against all the alternatives.

Who knew what was going on inside that mind of his? The silence congealed; gained mass as well as momentum.

From somewhere outside came the keening cry of a solitary Crow.

Elapsing time became measurable in audible heartbeats and quiet, shallow, rapid breaths of air. Erik felt as though his pulse might at any second rupture the veins in his wrists. His fear began to lose its point of focus; transforming its own quality and quantity, as it suffocated what little strength his hope had left to offer. He felt nauseous.

He couldn't look at Sandy for fear of compounding his own stress and anxiety (and doubling hers in the process!).

Deep Thoughts allowed them to simmer in the elixir of their shared misery.

Brushing lengthy, dark hair from sad, even darker eyes, he finally broke the unnerving silence.

He spoke.

And his audience listened very closely.

"People fear what they do not understand," his voice possessed an attribute that was curiously engaging and adult-like. "You're afraid of me because you don't understand me, and you don't understand me because you've never…taken…the time…to even…*try*."

Erik attempted to swallow and found that he could not. Sandy fought phantoms of queasiness, with limited success. They both felt light-headed and dizzy; a surreal condition like someone had blindfolded them, spun them in circles for a good five minutes, and then forced them to walk backward on a moving carousel.

"Deep Thoughts," began Erik. But his voice—parched and arid—made it sound more like "Eep Thoss," feeble and hoarse.

Deep Thoughts held up his hand for quiet. "Here's the news," he said straightforwardly. "Hot off the press." The giant of a boy bored eyeball holes through the both of them; not lethal, nor even mean-spirited. But in much the same way a mildly disgruntled store owner would confront two small children whom he had just caught swiping apples from his shop. "I'm not much of a talker. Better listen good."

And so he told them what he knew…beginning at the beginning.

*

First and foremost, Deep Thoughts did *not* think of himself as a Ratpacker. Sure, he spent a considerable amount of time hanging around with Rodent and Patch. You probably would too, if nobody else would have anything to do with you…if everyone in town went about life collectively assured of the presumed and mutually agreed-upon contagion that you personified.

Never mind the fact that he spent hours heaped upon hours in the public library; his nose glued between the pages of literary works that most Appletonians didn't even know existed. Overlook, if you wish, the fact that he had never *once* been busted for violation of even a *single* city or county law or ordinance; never once been accused *of* or implicated *in* those kinds of activities.

But he was also *never* above suspicion.

Why *was* that?

Because he was huge? And quiet? And kept to himself? Because he didn't turn over his personal choices for other people to make for him?

Because he went his own way and reserved comment on what anybody might think about it? Not exactly an airtight case for tossing him into the category of 'outcast.' But he played those cards just the way they were dealt, and he asked no favors.

So, Appleton hadn't exactly *shafted* him, but they hadn't rolled out the red carpet or offered the services of the 'welcome wagon' either. Whatever. It was neither here nor there to him. Deep Thoughts went about his solitary ways, all his solitary days. To the people of the community, he was a potential threat on a multitude of levels, even though the nature of those threats or the weight they supposedly carried were impossible to define. It was just an unspoken 'understanding' and everyone stayed vigilant.

To the Ratpackers, he was an unknown quantity; occasionally with them in body, but never really with them in spirit. Rodent and Patch were still waiting on him to make up his mind to start raising some hell with them. Deep Thoughts was in their company often enough to know plenty about the anarchy they were always brewing. But he didn't know *everything,* and his status was still officially considered to be that of an initiate; a *potential* 'Packer' rather than a full-on member of the clan.

Deep Thoughts cut off his narrative; withdrawing into a silent, reflective state that endowed tiny bits of time with the heft of concrete blocks. The dark boy fixed his captives with a look that communicated, what? A question? Something sought? But without the use of any words. Whatever it was, that unspoken expression was more _dis_arming than _a_larming, for Eric and Sandy were suddenly awash with the unmistakable feeling that they were no longer on the threshold of being shredded (or eaten!) alive.

Sweeping aside a Papa Tony's pizza box, Deep Thoughts picked up the whiteboard square upon which the cryptic list was still scrawled. A short, quick puff of breath issued from his nostrils, accompanied by a barely audible grunt; Deep Thoughts' version of a fit of laughter.

"Did you guys ever figure out the meaning of this little, 'To-Do List?'" he asked.

He fingered the edges of the slate gingerly, like a teacher focusing his ideas and preparing an explanation for some very young, very simple-minded children. "Because that's what this is, you know, a To-Do List."

"We *had* thought of that," ventured Sandy.

"Well, you're on the right track then," returned the boy. "What did you come up with?"

An errant breeze found its way into the meadow shanty, bearing scents of pine pollen and warm earth. From a growth of vine maple at the base of the rockslide, a Stellar's jay broadcasted on and on (and on) about conditions which he found to-be or not-to-be to his liking. Inside the shack, hearts settled back into their proper places beneath respective ribcages, and *every*body waited for *some*one to say *some*thing about *any*thing.

Deep Thoughts sighed. "I haven't got the whole thing figured out," he said. "But obviously *you* don't have the *slightest idea* what's goin' on. So I'll tell you what I *do* know, why I know that you're all in a world of hurt at this point. The rest, you'll have to figure out for yourself because, frankly, nobody in this town has given me a reason to give a tinker's damn one way or the other.

"Somebody wants Justin Bench outa that quarry cabin, pronto. Surely you must know *that* by now. Yes? Good. I mean, that's a given, right? All right. Now, exactly *who* is it that wants him gone? I dunno. You dunno. Am I wrong? I thought not. And *why is it,* exactly, that somebody *wants* him gone? I dunno that either, and neither do you, right? Uh-huh. Am I goin' too fast for you? Fine."

That voice.

One would never expect a voice that mellow—that mature—to come from a silverback gorilla like Deep Thoughts. It was actually kind of a *settling* experience just listening to him speak. It lended plenty of credibility to the idea that *truth* is often much stranger than *fiction.*

"So let's assemble our facts, and see if we can pour anything worthwhile out of the blend. **One**: Justin is on *somebody's* hate list.

Two: _This_ place is _their_ place, and I don't have to explain to you who _they_ are, do I? No? I didn't think so. How long have you been shut up in here now? Just overnight? You're lucky. Could've been for the whole weekend if I hadn't showed up, quite by a _whim_, you can bet. And how you got trapped without anyone seeing you is _anybody's_ guess. Rodent, or Patch, whichever, must have been in a _big_ hurry to have locked the place up without even looking."

"I _knew_ it!" Sandy exploded. "I just _knew_ it would be _them_ using this place for something _despicable_. Them and…"

"…me?" Deep Thoughts finished what was obviously on her mind. "Them and that creepy freak, Deep Thoughts? Sure. Fine. What…ev…er."

He left the self-indictment hanging, and Sandy felt her face flush; wishing she had engaged her brain before putting her mouth into gear.

"At any rate," he continued lightly. (He actually seemed more bemused than angry with Sandy's near-hurtful misstep.) "The Pine Hideout is Ratpack territory, for good, for bad, or for otherwise."

Erik fought the impulse to offer a scathing remark about the most-likely intended use of the cabin by the 'Packers.' But he had learned a clear enough lesson from Sandy's close call. Better to remain silent and be thought a fool, than to open his mouth and remove all doubt.

"So-oo, **three**… Rodent and Patch occasionally show up in town clutching in their sweaty fists a crisp, one-hundred-dollar bill. Rodent is unemployed and Patch works _part-time_ at the Pool. It begs a question, does it not?"

It did. Where is that cash coming from?

Deep Thoughts placed the white slate on his thigh; the writing toward the Scalawags who, by this time, were entertaining a completely reconstructed opinion of a guy they suddenly realized they had never even given themselves a chance to get to know.

"Now, **four**: None of us, myself included, knows who wrote this list. _Oui? Mais, certainement, mes amis._ And the meaning of these words is obscure, until you start linking them to specific events which have already occurred."

Erik and Sandy looked at each other, and back to Deep Thoughts. "OK," said Erik steadily, "we follow, but we haven't got anything to add to what you've said so far. Go ahead."

Mr. Thoughts, becoming solemn, continued at a slightly slower pace. "Think figuratively," he suggested, "and prepare to make some inferences as well."

They nodded.

Deep Thoughts pointed to the first word. **"Glass,"** he said. "Where did the first incident with Justin Bench take place?"

Sandy's eyes became as round as silver dollars. "Justin's bedroom window," she breathed. "A message written in lipstick, on **glass!**"

A nod of encouragement—a curt acknowledgment, before indicating the second word. **"Trash,"** he said gravely.

The shanty buzzed as Erik and Sandy began verbally testing every word they could conjure to make meaning of the clue: Junk. Garbage. Refuse. Crap. Spoils. Waste. Midden.

"Midden?" queries Erik.

"Never mind," admits Sandy. "Not widely used."

Deep Thoughts shook his head. "That's what *I* did when *I* first saw the list. Wrong, wrong, wrong. You've got to think *figuratively*. C'mon, Sandy. I hear you're supposed to be pretty good at this." He gave her the faintest hint of a semi-smile that might *even* have plucked a string on her heart's harp if she wasn't currently dancing to the tune of *'What A Cute Guy That Erik Is.'*

She knitted her brows, thinking furiously, attempting to make sense of the one-word riddle, while simultaneously rising to the challenge of Deep Thoughts remark about her intellectual reputation. She wasn't getting anywhere at all, and Erik appeared as dumbstruck as she was.

"What happened next?" offered Deep Thoughts. "What happened to the quarry cabin? Think back. Relate it to the word, and for Pete's sake, don't be so *literal*."

"Trash!" boomed Erik suddenly. "Justin's house was ***trashed*** while we were all at Kelsea's barbecue!"

"Of course!" echoed Sandy. "That's it, isn't it, Deep Thoughts? They wrote down **'trash'** because the next thing they wanted to do was 'trash' the place!" The girl paused only briefly before pointing to the next word and uttering, "**'Float!'** Erik! We know what *that* means, right?"

"That day at the Swimming Hole! The day the little raft *floated* by with another warning message!" Erik's expression showed the storm that was building inside him. "I can't *believe* this crap!" he bellowed. "This whole thing was dreamed up by *those* two; planned in secret, and carried out according to a *timetable* following this *stupid, damn list* right down the line!"

"Hold on just a second," cautioned Deep Thoughts. "All we know for *certain* is that this list," he held the slate up, tapping it with his forefinger, "is right *here* in the 'Pine Hideout'—Ratpack Manor, so to speak. We do _not_ know if Rodent or Patch or both of them *authored* it. We do *not* know if they are the 'go-betweens' for another party who is carrying out the dirty work. We don't even know if the money they have been waving around has been provided as payoff for, shall we say, 'services rendered?'"

Erik slumped; chastened, convinced of the wisdom of Deep Thoughts opinions.

"All we really know for sure is that all of these things are interconnected somehow. But before you go jumpin' the gun, you'd better make darned sure you've not only got *all* of the facts—and I mean _all_ of 'em—but you've got 'em all lined up and arrow-straight as well."

He stared out the door of the old shack, allowing himself a respite from the task of 'speaking with strangers.' "You jump up now and start barkin' like a brain-scabbed coyote, and you very well could blow the whole thing before some *real* justice can get done."

Sandy chuckled softly, "You're beginning to sound a lot like Justin." Only she didn't *say* it, she ***sang*** it—to the tune of '*It's Beginning to Look a lot Like Christmas.*'

In that instant, the embracing, brown-green wall of earth, stone, and wood surrounding the meadow shed hummed with unabashed, youthful innocence. 'Fear' ducked his hoary head and—horror-stricken—fled the first strains of the 'New Music'…those heart born harmonics forged in the refining fires of honest risk. Time, alone, knew if patience and persistence could polish a fledgling friendship from this unlikely and wholly unanticipated emerging awareness…created near 'SunHigh time' in a mountain meadow shanty.

But this much was certain: some erroneous ideas finally lost their relevance, and a new way of thinking about people and situations and the misinformation risk inherent in first impressions began to bloom and grow the day that Chase 'Deep Thoughts' Reed threw his shaggy, dark head back, looked at the cabin ceiling, and _laughed_ full out.

"I'll take that as a compliment," smiled the boy, dabbing a mirthful tear from the corner of his eye with a beefy finger. "Not *because* of your musical voice, Sandy," he grinned, "but *in spite* of it."

"Careful, man," warned Erik, dripping drama. "If you rile her, she may sing *again*! Haven't we got *enough* problems without adding eardrum injury to the list?"

Sandy feigned umbrage, and whopped Erik a good one on the upper arm. "You ain't heard nothin' yet, my non-Ukrainian pal! Just for that remark, Mr. Remarque, the next time Justin does his bit with Woody, I'm gonna do just that!"

"That brings us to the fourth word on the list," reminded Deep Thoughts. The incandescence of the moment was extinguished by a sudden return to solemnity; indicative of a return to the business at hand. "**'Wood'** is the word. Did the sound of the explosion make it this far west early last night?"

Both of the youngsters stiffened. Deep Thoughts sure knew a lot of stuff about a *lot of stuff!*

"Well, I don't have a ton of *details* on *this* one. Alls I can say is that I overheard 'the boys' talkin' about an M-80 and Justin's guitar."

"**Wood!**" exclaimed Sandy. "Erik, they were talking about Woody!"

"And the noise from the detonation came from…?"

"Debbin Ramsay's pool party, exactly," finished Deep Thoughts. "The picture isn't very clear, but I think we can guess the rest, right? And just remember, the only connection that links *all* of this to the Ratpack is this." He hefted the whiteboard, shrugging his shoulders and shaking his head.

"Incriminating," agreed Sandy thoughtfully, "but not enough to prosecute."

"Not yet, anyway," growled Erik. "I'll keep my accusations to myself, but I gotta tell you right here and now. This stuff smells like Packer work, and it always has. Right from the start!"

"**Bark,**" mused Sandy quizzically; moving to the last word on the list. "Kinda goes with **'Wood,'** doesn't it?"

"Trees," attempted Erik. "The quarry site is covered with trees. It could mean anything, really. Bark, trees, limbs, wood, timber, forest. It could even be a reference to a specific *type* of tree, like pine or spruce; it's just too wide-open."

"Unless I miss my guess," offered Sandy, "'**Bark**' hasn't happened yet. Am I right, Deep Thoughts?"

"Probably not."

"Then if we can *infer* from the previous clues, maybe we can *predict* what the next move is going to be," Sandy's hopes were rising.

"And maybe instead of simply *stopping* the event," suggested Erik, "we could lay a kind of a trap and snag, *whoever it is*, right in the act, and put an end to this garbage once and for all!"

"Problem is," cautioned Deep Thoughts, "we don't know *where* or *when* it's gonna take place."

"Or even *what* it is, yet," added Sandy. "Do we?" She scrutinized Deep Thoughts carefully, thoroughly. "Well, Monsieur Thoughts? Do we?"

Deep Thoughts folded his massive hands in his lap. The look on his face was one of unresolved questions, about the Scalawags, about Justin's problems, and about his *own* stake and role in the unfolding drama. "Do you even know what my name is?" he asked mildly. "My...*real* name?"

Sandy and Erik looked sheepishly at one another. "Well, um, it's Reed, uh..." pausing here, coloring visibly, "I don't think *anyone* does, really. Um, do they, Erik?"

"Is it...is it...'Chad? Chad Reed?'" Erik, with nothing to add, shaking his head, feeling suddenly foolish and embarrassed. So *much* about the character and personality of this big guy had been taken for granted. There he sat—cross-legged before the two of them—polite, intelligent, *revealed* and yet, still so aloof, with layers and layers of undisclosed attributes, like the pages of a book, waiting to be discovered, understood, and shared.

"Well, you're half-right. My name *is* Reed," he said simply. "*Chase Reed*." He rose—loose, stretching—heading for the door of the cabin. "Ya better get on your bikes and ride, people," he said over his shoulder. "Because I'm not terribly bright about these things, but *if* I'm reading my clues correctly, then **'Bark'** refers to <u>dog</u>. And, if *that's* true, it means that Kooper is in *real danger*...right now. Like I said before, 'yer in a world of hurt.'"

Then, over the shoulder as off he goes, "Lock up when ya leave, will ya?"

*

Sometimes things occur in threes. Not always. But sometimes. As Hollis Greenwood would say:

"Dig."

There are the three branches of our state and federal governments, and three colors on the American flag (*lots* of tri-colored national flags, for that matter).

There are elementary schools, middle schools, and high schools (three, see?) which teach (among other things) readin', writin', and 'rithmetic. *All* matter exists in one of three states; solid, liquid, or gas, and is furthermore constructed from protons, neutrons, and electrons. There are three parts to each day; morning, noon, and night; with a meal for each—breakfast, lunch, and dinner; dinner often being sub-divided into an appetizer, an entrée, and a dessert. And while we're on the subject of time, don't forget about the past, the present, and the future.

Stories (like, for instance, *'The Three Little Pigs,'* *'The Three Bears,'* or *'The Three Musketeers'*) are composed of three readily identifiable components; a beginning, middle, and ending. N'est-ce pas?

'Three Blind Mice.' *'Wynken, Blynken, and Nod.'* Yes sir, yes sir, *three* bags full. Birth, life, death. Before, during, and after. Melody, harmony, lyrics. Rock, paper, scissors. Trilliums, trimesters, tripods, tricycles, triceratops. Tic-tac-toe, three in a row.

You and me and baby make *three.* *Third* time's a charm. *Three* periods in a hockey game. *Three* goals to make a hat-trick. *Three* retired batters to an inning.

Three strikes, and *you*, my friend, are *out.*

Kooperdog has been lost for *three* days by now.

Let's pick up the strand right here.

Dig?

The Scalawags were hunkered together. They were listless; neither sullen nor depressed, but reflective and adrift in private thoughts too over-watered by recent events to bear fruit. They were tired. Tired of hashing and rehashing the connecting links of Justin's sad circumstances. Tired of searching and re-searching every weed patch, alley, and field for Kooper. Tired of having to work so damned hard at having a fun, worry-less summer. School is going to resume in *three* weeks, and Woody—Woody went out with the trash *three* days ago.

Justin was working on a poem; an attempt, however half-hearted, to twist negative mental energy into something productive and beautiful. He knew that pain, grief, and anger were the wellsprings of creativity, and his gentle spirit guide was overseeing the struggle; thought by thought, feeling by feeling, line by line, and word by word.

Stuart was immersed (or so it seemed) in _All Quiet On The Western Front_. His fascination with the idea that Erik was named for a famous author had inspired him to purchase a copy of the 1928 novel, and he had been plowing through the text at every quiet opportunity; mirroring the book-loving behavior of his sister more with every passing day.

Shiny-haired Kelsea, sproingy-haired Sandy, and clipper-haired Eric were methodically employed with kitchen chores. They were making sandwiches and lemonade; trying to enjoy an hour or two of azure August noon-ness before splitting up and continuing the hunt for Koop.

At that same time…

SOMETHING DRAWS THE ATTENTION AND THE TRUST OF CROW. AND SO YOU ALIGHT, POOFING A TINY CLOUD OF FINE DUST JUST METERS FROM THE WOODEN DECK OF THE QUARRY CABIN.

DANGER-<u>IS</u>? OR DANGER IS-<u>NOT</u>?

CROW WAITS IN LEARNTIME AND, QUICKLY SURMISING THAT DANGER <u>IS-NOT</u>, YOU HOP CLOSER. AND CLOSER STILL. YOUR PRESENCE REMAINS UNNOTICED; MINDS ARE CURRENTLY OCCUPIED FIVE DIFFERENT WAYS ON A SINGULAR PROBLEMATIC ISSUE.

UNTIL…

<u>THREE</u> WING STROKES LIFT YOU <u>THREE</u> FEET ABOVE APPLETONIAN TURF, AND YOU PERCH IN CLUTCH-WITH-TALONS TIME ON THE DECK RAIL, FOR <u>THREE</u> SECONDS.

And in those three seconds: Kelsea and Sandy take notice of you and smile. They <u>love</u> animals; <u>love</u> Nature. Erik regards you with a mixture of puzzlement and mild interest.

Having only recently immigrated from an urban environment, he has never really seen a wild bird of your size this close up before. Stuart spares the briefest of glances in your direction. Even though he is the closest to your clutch spot, and should have been startled by the flap and flutter of your arrival, he is back to the book in a shredded second; burrowing into his ever-accelerating preoccupation with great literature.

Justin quietly lays his pencil across the notebook, and watches you, Crow, watching him. "I keep seeing you around, don't I old fella?" he says.

The sound of a spoken word implies possible danger-Is to Crow, who quickly becomes otherwhere!

"Crows have gray eyes," Justin, expanding on the thought. "That's just the way things are."

"True enough," agreed Stuart over the top of his novel. "Black feathers and gray eyes, one and all. They don't have much choice in the matter."

"Not if they wanna be _crows_, anyway," chuckled Eric.

"Indubitably," pronounced Sandy.

Three more seconds of silence. Then: "Well, just as sure as you're born, _that_ one had _blue_ eyes. Blue as any blue you could ever hope to see," he said. "And a chipped beak, as well."

"Hmm. Imagine that," offered Stu. But he was already back between the pages, and he really wasn't imagining much of anything at _all_ that the author wasn't putting _into_ his head _to_ imagine.

Kelsea paused—having overheard that particular discussion; the one finishing up just a few feet away—and stared out the kitchen's glass-less summer bug screen at nothing in particular; a wistful expression of semi-remembrance on her tan-smooth face.

It had been two years since the near-tragedy of the Silver Creek Fire. The pain and peril. Isolation and survival. And of equal importance, the subsequent dreams that continually recurred over the intervening years. Dreams which were always perceived with an undeniable 'fantasy feel' attached to them—as if witnessed through a pair of eyes that were _not her own_. For in her sleeping mind, Kelsea collated her past, present, future life/lives through the lenses of...

BlueCrowEyes.

She was _certain_ of _that_ much. Almost. Almost certain...

Kelsea Kathleen Crowl, smiling faintly, not knowing why; shaking her head to nobody, and returning to her sandwiches. Dream feelings were always warm; comforting. And even if she couldn't quite *understand* them, she felt as much a *part* of them as she could feel to/of/with life itself. She risked a quick peek at Justin, who was still lounging on the pine deck. He was deeply considering...

A blue-eyed crow...blue eyes.

...Eyes...

*What **was** it he had seen?*

*

August 10th. Justin's birthday.

Light snacks were being prepared to mark the event...*and* in preparation for a return to the possible long haul of continued 'dog search.'

The Scalawags were munching; small-talking. In general, trying to kick back. Paying careless inattention to the stack of frustrations that lay smoldering and unresolved on the back pages of their collective 'to-do' list.

Justin didn't know it, but his four friends were vamping; languishing in a 'waiting mode.'

They were waiting for someone.

For someone carrying something.

Carrying something for him.

The waiting is the hardest part. But waiting is as waiting does, and the whole 'Waiting Thang' eventually drew to a symphonic conclusion when Officer Carlos Santiago pulled his patrol car into a parking spot of the old quarry site, and began hoofing it up the slope to the wooden deck; smiling broadly, and carrying a guitar case with a single word embossed in large letters on the side.

The word was 'Yamaha.'

Happy birthday, Justin.

*

After the laughter, the tears of joy, the heartfelt hugs, the delirious, delicious, dancing feeling of surprise and exhilaration, Justin settled into his favorite chair (*favorite*...with the possible exception of a certain green, park bench) and ran the palm of his hand over the smooth, blonde soundboard of his new guitar.

The instrument had been well-loved; it had been previously owned by someone who had played it a'plenty. That much was obvious from the lightly engrained brush marks across the pick guard. A couple of bump dimples near the bottom of the soundboard, and, my gosh! A small scratch mid-way up the back of the neck in just about the same spot Woody's was! This guitar was an almost *perfect* twin to Justin's old 'friend!'

Now, one would think that a shy, self-effacing kind of guy like Mr. Bench would be overwhelmed and speechless at a tender moment such as this. Uh-uh. Quite the contrary. The wind full-billowed in his vocal sails, so to speak, and Justin's excitement over the generosity of his friends spilled out in wallops of disconnected blatherings.

Such as...

"There ain't but two cents worth of difference between this guy an' Woody, now is there? I mean look at this design around the sound hole. Will ya just *look at that*? Is that Woody er <u>what</u>? An' check out the action on the fretboard. Well, never mind, I know you don't play. But trust me! It feels *just like playin' Woody*! I mean, it's incredible! The similarity is just, just impossible to describe! Where in the world did you find him? You guys are just too much! Do you know that? Just too much! Look at that scratch right there! Will ya look at that? Did you put that there to make 'im look more like Woody? I mean there's even a doggone scratch right where Woody's was! Oh, man!"

"Um, Justin?"

"Man, oh, man!"

"Justin?"

"This is *great*, guys!"

"Oh, Juu-uuss-tinn..."

"Huh?"

"Don't you think you oughta name him?" inquired Carlos.

"Yeah," encouraged Kelsea. "And then it probably wouldn't be a bad idea to get on with some music, doncha think?"

"How about that poem you've been working on this morning?" asked Stuart. "Think you can set it to a tune?"

Justin began slowly closing the floodgates on his high-octane enthusiasm. *(Settle down there, Hoss.)* "Well, sure!" he responded. "I've already got a name picked out for 'im."

"So soon?" asked Sandy. "That sure didn't take long. What is it, then?"

"Well, this here Yamaha is such a knock-off of Woody, in just about every possible way that, shoot, it's just Woody all over with just a couple of minor differences."

"Yes? And so, your point would be?"

"Heck, just swap the 'W' and the 'D,' change 'Woody' to 'Doowy,' an' the deal is done."

"I get it!" said Eric. "It's like Dewey, D-E-W-E-Y only it's Doowy, D-O-O-W-Y!"

"Word up!" agreed Kelsea. "I like it. It makes sense, and it fits his personality."

"Works for me!" added Officer Santiago.

"Well, get on with it then!" urged Eric. "Doowy sure isn't gonna play *himself*, now is he?"

"Yeah, c'mon Justin! Let's put ol' Doowy through some paces before we head out this afternoon. Whatcha gonna play for us?"

"Not *this* one, that's for sure," Justin slid aside the poem he had been crafting, stood, and slung Doowy's strap over his shoulder. "Too dark. Too brooding. We need to _rock_ in a big way! Doncha think?"

"Amen, brother!" exhorted Stuart, tossing his book on the table. "Do it, Doowy! And don't spare the horsepower!"

Justin exploded into a *trio* (things in _threes_) of energy-fueled pop songs; vocal *and* string-shredding versions of *'Things We Said Today,'*

'*I'll Cry Instead,*' and '*Hide Your Love Away*'; Beatles standards with a rough-hewn edginess built into the delivery from years of Scalawag practice and revision. Doowy was, in a word, 'brilliant!' His voice was deep and resounding, with brand new bronze strings that brought forth crisp high and mid-range tones.

It was a *fun*tastic workout! The new guitar was a dream come true, and the wooded foothills encircling Appleton Quarry became bathed once more in hip-swinging, foot-stomping, finger-snapping, sweet, sweet, *sweet* music.

The way it was *supposed* to be.

The way it was *meant* to be.

The way it *needed* to be. Especially since everyone—Justin in *particular*—desperately needed a reason to stop agonizing over Kooper's whereabouts, if only for the duration of *three* songs.

And *that* was the *first* of *three* important things that happened on Justin's twentieth birthday.

So…

*

Many years ago, a movie was made in Italy starring a little-known American actor named Clint Eastwood. It was a low-budget, 'B' movie; a western saga with plenty of sub-plots involving war, gold-lust, and the alliances made, broken, and re-made in stroking up some petty obsessions and the baser human instincts. The movie was a runaway hit, spawning an entire cadre of lookalike 'spaghetti westerns,' and catapulting Mr. Eastwood to international stardom.

The name of the movie was '*The Good, The Bad, and The Ugly.*'

Three. Again.

Allow an old Italian movie script to serve as a metaphor for the events which befell Justin Bench on that day. His birthday. The surprise gift—'Doowy'—purchased by the Scalawags in a Weston-located secondhand store, and presented by Officer Santiago; the embodiment of "The Good."

The third singalong rock number had just ended. Justin's entire face was radiating swaths of pure sunlight across, over, around, and through his 'troops'—his lemonade-swigging deck mates. There was a hint of promise in the air. It was palpable. You could *reach out and touch it!* Everyone present was reelin' with the feelin' that a corner had been turned. That better times were steppin' up to the plate, and that the next ball pitched was goin' right over the left-field fence, Jim.

It was 'The Good,' man. 'The ***Good***!'

But, how quickly things can turn.

Hollis Greenwood came slowly up the hill to the quarry cabin. He had news for Justin and the others.

And *this* was 'The Bad.'

*

He just stood there. Just stood; his breath coming in short, quick spasms—trembling—as saltwater rolled down his cheeks, and dropped into the dust of the old Appleton Quarry. He sniffed loudly—repeatedly—and the wet, rattling sound that he made was clear evidence of the fact that he had been crying for more than just a few moments. Crying long and hard.

Shifting his weight from leg to leg, Hollis struggled to speak, his voice no match for the burden he bore. It cracked and broke, forcing him to clear his throat repeatedly; snorting back the contents of his runny nostrils. He was the ultimate picture of grief and despair writ large; a dark angel of despondence arriving just as the promise of levity was being semi-rekindled amongst the Scalawags.

No one knew what to say. No one knew what to do. But somehow, everyone knew what was coming next.

CROW KNOWS. DON'T YOU.

A premonition of misery doesn't *completely prepare* one for the actualization of its occurrence. It is but a *glimpse* of a thing to come; like *knowing* you will be a ninth-grader in a new home, in a new town with new friends next year, but *not knowing* for certain what that will *mean for you*, or for your *happiness*. Could be 'thumbs up'...could be 'thumbs-not-quite-so-very-up.'

Ya just gotta *get there,* or you'll never ever know for sure.

Justin fixed his hipster friend with a level gaze. When he spoke, his tone was quiet and kind. "Hollis," he said, "where's Kooper?"

Hollis stared vacantly at the tan-brown soil under his sneakers. A thin, clear drop of snot hung suspended from the tip of his nose, and he unselfconsciously wicked it away with the back of his hand.

"Hollis, my friend," he repeated. Placing his hand on the boy's shoulder, he squeezed lightly, reassuringly. "Where's my dog?"

Hollis took Justin's right hand in his own. Twisting his wrist and opening it, palm up, he retrieved, from his shirt pocket, a locket of long, coarse, blonde fur—tied in the center with a short piece of green ribbon. He placed the snippet in the center of Justin's hand, closing the young man's fingers over the top; all the while holding those hands with his own and bleeding his grief in streaks of tears.

"What I found, I buried," he said; a huge effort to stem the heaving. "He'd been poisoned, and what I found... what I found was not for you to see, man. So I buried him and brought you this. In case... in case you..." he trailed off, unable to continue.

A cruel silence hammered the quarry site. Made the ears ring. Made stomachs turn upside-down. Forced minds to accept the unacceptable and to believe the unbelievable.

It pounded without remorse at hearts already cracked and ready to split apart at the seams. Pummeled away at denial and strafed the senses with a soundless, lifeless feeling of unbearable loss and outrage. And for a brief instant in time, love itself was drained of color, and nearly ceased to exist.

SHAKEN BY THE SUDDEN, NUMEROUS, UNEXPECTED GRIEF QUAKES ECHOING THROUGH QUARRY SPACES, YOU RETREAT TO THE NEST SITE; WAITING OUT THE DAY—ENDURING. CROWMIND INTUITS: THE WAITING IS THE HARDEST PART. BUT CROW COMPLIES. CROW ABIDES; LEARNING IN WAIT-TIME.

"Was it," stammered Stuart haltingly, "an, an accident? Do you…" He lowered his voice, double pianissimo, "Do you think he got into something, accidentally?"

Hollis Greenwood shook his head sadly. "No, man," he managed between gulps. "It was no accident. I seen *this* kinda stuff go down before. I saw what was left of what he'd eaten." The boy swallowed hard. "He was *baited*." His red-rimmed eyes sought Justin's, and with the remaining ounce of courage at his disposal, he murmured, "I'm sorry, dude. I am so, <u>so</u> sorry." He paused again, garnering strength. "Old Kooperdog was poisoned," Hollis sounded a sob of pain so visceral, it seemed hardly human. "Some sick freak killed your nice old dog, man."

Kelsea and Sandy collapsed upon one another, releasing torrents of angst and anger.

The boys, tear-streaked and shaken, huddled around Justin fumbling to build a buffer of solidarity and comfort, attempting to fashion some kind of hastily assembled demonstration of support.

But Justin Michael Thomas Bench was no longer of this world. Ashen-faced, expressionless, he resisted the entreaties of his comrades—gingerly fitting Doowy into the black guitar case, folding the strap neatly underneath, and closing the four latches one after the next with quiet little clicks.

"Go home," he mumbled dully. "Go on home everybody, an' I'll give you a call after I've unplugged for a while."

The Scalawags looked at Justin and at each other, uncertain as to what exactly *was* the right course of action. They were used to sticking together, come hell or high water, and the idea of splitting up—of retreating in the face of a mutually shared catastrophe—was unconscionable, unthinkable. They needed *each other* **<u>now</u>** more than ever.

Didn't they?

Clearly, Justin did not agree.

A change had come over him—with such devastating unexpectedness—that the guy was, in some subtle, but very profound ways, no longer recognizable. Even to himself.

He spoke no more to his friends that day (or the next, or the *next*, as it came to be).

Hollis encouraged the troupe to respect Bench's wishes and so, one-by-one, they filed by the silent, stricken figure—delivering hugs and murmuring assurances, heading for their separate homes and the pale quiet that awaited them there.

A thin rain dropped apologetically, moistening little more than a vagrant breeze breath which swirled its clueless way; lost and looking for a wooded hollow in which to expire unnoticed. Justin, disconnected from AnyHereNess whatever, wordlessly pronounced himself dead, and began going about the sad mental business of divesting, *severing* his every interest in happiness from his existence.

Poor Justin.

He had no idea what kind of mistake he was making. Reveling in his abandon and isolation, he was systematically (if unknowingly) compromising the power of his clear, pure heart by cleaving himself from the very souls who fueled his strength and resolve.

He had allowed the Scalawags to become sundered, dissipated. *That* was his unwitting crime. And the chain of *friendship*—a crucial tool of survival in a world which, sad to say, simply cannot be trusted—now lay abandoned in five useless, non-interlocking links.

Waiting on rust to finish the job.

Justin, trying so hard to make it on his own. No longer willing to risk infecting anybody with his misery and problems. Making every effort (however ill-conceived) to spare all of his friends the burden of bad karma that'd been his lot to accumulate over the summer. Not even open-minded enough to entertain the idea of getting some help from Carlos Santiago, whose profession it was to protect and assist folks who find themselves in just such a predicament.

People can be strangely stubborn sometimes. Especially if they are frightened, or if they are hurting inside. Or when they feel *alone and isolated* (If you *think and _feel_* that you are isolated, but you really *aren't*…are you isolated?).

YOU, CROW…YOU INTUIT THIS; THE DARK, POWERFUL HUMAN PERCEPTION OF CRUEL, SENSELESS WASTE. WORSE, THE ACCOMPANYING UNDERCURRENT OF SURRENDERED DEFEAT. LIKE YOUR WINGS HAVE BEEN INJURED; BENT OR BROKEN.

AS A COLLECTIVE SORROW WASHES THE VALLEY AIR, YOU ARE SPIRITUALLY RENDERED INCAPABLE OF FLIGHT. AND YOU AWAIT THE DARK APPROACH OF NIGHT WITH A TENTATIVE FEELING OF DISSOLUTION; IN COMMISERATION WITH THE SCALAWAG-LONGLEGS.

But, in the meantime…

Not 20 minutes after the departure of his quarry mates; still slumped in a deckchair—stunned and staring at the tiny lock of Kooper-fur— Justin experienced the *third* event of the day; the arrival at the cabin of Colonel Harding Corbett Tattenger.

'The Ugly.'

*

"What do you _mean_ you shook hands on it? Did you _sign_ anything? No? Well, we can thank your lucky stars for _that_!"

Kelsea Crowl had finally reached the point of ignition, and the fury she vented was both surprising and a little alarming to her unsuspecting friend. Justin sat formless, like a creature lacking a skeletal under-build. But his pupils dilated and his eyebrows arched at the intensity of her verbal barrage.

"Kels," he attempted, "I just can't *do* this anymore. I can't go *through* it, and I can't put anyone *else* through it either."

Kelsea struggled to control her emotions, as well as the decibel level of her voice.

After 72-ish hours of nerve-shattering silence from the quarry cabin, she had taken it upon herself to pedal up the hill and make an effort to break through Justin's self-imposed isolation. Come what may, she could not suffer him the depraved, lonely pleasure of devouring himself in loss and loneliness.

"Selling the quarry woodlands to Colonel Tattenger is **_not_** the answer, Justin! Why can't you understand that? Why, you haven't even *attempted* to get the authorities involved with this, this *mess* we've found ourselves in."

Justin shook his head; his mouth a tight, straight line cut across a careworn face. "It ain't *our* problem, Kels. It's *my* problem, and I aim to keep it that way." He gave her the weakest facsimile of a smile. "You'd do the same if you were in my boots. You'd protect the clan. You know you would."

"Like _hell_, I would!" Kelsea, instantly hoping that the words didn't *sound* as venomous as they *felt* when they came flying from her mouth. "I'd have Officer Santiago crawling all *over* this case! And I'd make *damn* sure I kept myself locked in *tight* with the people who share my heart song. That's **_us_**, Justin Bench, in case you've forgotten. We've *always* stayed together for one another. *Always*!" She eyed him with a curious mixture of sympathy and contempt. "I'd let the _clan_ protect _me_! And _you_ should be doin' the same damned thing."

Justin closed in unto himself; hid his mind and heart within the self-willed confines of a thick-stoned catacomb of numb surrender. Anesthetized and only partially aware, he caught about every third or fourth word of his friend's admonishments, which sounded to him something like: "I'd. Officer. All. Case. And I'd. Locked. Share."

His body ached. He was shaking all over. He was sitting in the armchair of the quarry cabin, on one of the last days he would be able to call that place his home, and he was shuddering—defenseless and out of control. The tremors—regular and repeated—increased in intensity until he felt like a ragged flag flapping and flailing in a late summer squall. Tossing and quavering—was this an epileptic fit? Or an anxiety attack?

Neither.

It was Kelsea.

Kelsea Crowl was the reason for the body quakes. She had grabbed him by the shoulders and was, for want of a better phrase, 'shakin' the shit outta him,' cutting off his retreat into self-pity, and rousing him back to reality—painful and disorienting as it was.

"Justin!" called the girl. "Justin! Snap *out* of it, will you? *Justin*! Listen to me. **Listen. To. Me!** I can't do this alone. I'm going to get the gang. Justin! Do you hear me? Everyone is at the Swimming Hole today. I'm gonna go get 'em and bring 'em up here, and you're gonna get the support you need whether you *like* it or *not*."

The girl relaxed her grip as Bench's eyes seemed to un-cloud, and he showed signs of a slack kind of semi-focused attention. "Justin," she continued, "when is Colonel Tatt supposed to show up with the paperwork? Look at me, Jus.' Look here," she swiveled his head to bring his eyes in line with hers. "When's he gonna bring the papers up here?"

A shake of the head was all she got.

"Justin, partner, I'll be right back, OK? We're all gonna work our way out of this thing, all right? Just **don't sign _anything_**! All right? Justin? Don't sign! We don't know but that old fart may be part of all these problems. Really! I'll be back with the gang in a couple of hours," she paused at the cabin door, pleading once more to know when the colonel planned to return, and seal the deal on the quarry site. Then she softly closed up, padded down the hill to her mountain bike, and made for the river beach.

"He's due here in about half an hour," mumbled Justin distantly, to mute cabin walls.

"Please hurry, Kels."

It *is* possible to exceed municipal speed limits while bike riding.

And breaking the law is breaking the law, whether driving an automobile or riding a mountain bike.

Kelsea Crowl was *burning* down Quarry Road, where the legal limit for *all* moving vehicles was posted at a safe and sensible 35 miles per hour. Night black, windblown hair—hints of sunlit cinnabar woven within—flew straight out behind her like the incoherent mane of a wild animal. She bent her slim strong body low to the bar cafe racer style—to cut the wind drag and increase her acceleration.

At first glance, one might think that all those tears she kept shedding and wiping, shedding and wiping were due to the smack of rapidly moving air across her lightly-freckled face.

But we know better than that.

Kelsea top-ended at right around 48 miles an hour. Had Officer Santiago been on the scene he undoubtedly would have: 1) lectured her on traffic safety, 2) presented her with a warning ticket, and 3) gone over every square centimeter of that bike with her—imparting information on brake cables, chain tension, lubrication specs, and loose or missing parts.

And at the very moment, Appleton's pretty, young heroine was earnestly and urgently *bending* a minor county traffic ordinance…

YOU RISE!
RISE!
UP HIGH ENOUGH TO MAKE THE KENNAWACK RIVER LOOK LIKE A BENDY, BLUE RIBBON ON A BACKGROUND OF PLUSH, GROWING GREEN. RISE UP—SMOKE LIKE—AND TRAIN YOUR EYESIGHT FAR DOWN THE VALLEY. THERE. THERE IS THE DEPUTY SHERIFF'S PATROL CAR COMING UP THE HIGHWAY, JUST ABOUT HALF A MILE THIS SIDE OF WESTON. OFFICER CARLOS SANTIAGO IS BEHIND THE WHEEL, AND HE'S DRIVING AT A PRETTY GOOD CLIP.
CROW SEES, AND FLIES FAST; RIDING ON THE WIND.

Curious, and coincidental. (Remarkable, really.) Kelsea Crowl and Officer Carlos Santiago, both in a big hurry (Kelsea, mostly) to get to (as it just so happens) the very same place—ultimately and eventually, the quarry lands—Justin's cabin. Two different people, of two different genders, and two different ages, working around the traffic laws (a little), employing two different modes of transportation in a simultaneous rush to eventually get-to-the-same-somewhere-sooner-rather-than-later.

Adding to the interest is the fact that…

Carlos' squad car comes up low; that is to say, a rear-passenger tire is low on air pressure, and the gas tank is low on fuel. And darn the bad luck, because *that* is just *bound* to slow him down a little. For *her* part, Kelsea is praying not only for strong tires, but strong legs as well. Hoping like crazy that *neither* will give out before she can make it *back* to the quarry…with her friends in tow.

Time is at a premium. Time is of the essence. There is no time to lose and no time to spare. Time is getting short. Time is running out. Gotta beat that clock, 'cause it's a race…against…time.

Below the threshold of conscious perception, Kelsea is the Crow.

Her leg muscles are wing muscles, and with every reciprocating stroke of bike pedal, she churns blood through sinew and flesh; an orchestrated body song propelling her in ground-level flight over the undulating Appleton terrain.

Her mind—focused and singularly pinpointed—knows velocity for velocity's sake. Every WhatEverElse is secondary; something to be addressed later, when time allows. Seconds and minutes curve and crush; subordinating their value and relevance to all-encompassing momentum. Subliminally aware of the stares she encounters from gape-mouthed gardeners, and small-town OutForWalkers, **Kelsea Crow** cleanly splits the breezes; joyous in her pain-stricken, noiseless, arrow-like pursuit born of unconditional loyalty to a high purpose, and a just cause (a Justin-Cause).

She arrives at the River Beach—sweat-drenched, wind-beaten—lungs lunging like surf on a faraway shore. Road dust whirls, settles and clings to her heat dampened T-shirt, and her breath comes in bruised gasps; huge and unladylike—sucking oxygen down, in and away from the crowns of surrounding trees, wherein sits a solitary, blue-eyed Crow with a chipped beak…leaning in, in LearnTime.

There is no one here. The sunny sandbar is vacant. She has arrived too late, and everybody has left for who-knows-where.

"Oh, Justin!" she moans.

And she begins to cry.

*

When a meddlesome crow (or another winged intruder, for that matter) inserts itself, whether accidentally or purposefully, into the nesting space of smaller, highly protective, easily agitated birds—such as a group of starlings—the resulting cacophony can be alarming. The squawks, kraws, and skrees can be heard over a considerable distance, and inter-aviary episodes have been known to become dramatic and prolonged; gaining the attention of pretty much everyone within earshot.

Debbin Ramsay was rousted from her semi-slumber by just such a wing-borne clamor erupting in the treetops towering over the Swimming Hole. She had arrived in the mid-morning hours, relishing what she hoped would be the opportunity to snag some solitary sun time on the beach, and she had tucked herself away unseen behind a small dune about 60 meters from where Kelsea stood astride her bicycle—weeping and inconsolable.

Lying on her back, propped by her elbows in a half-reclined position, and having satisfied her curiosity that the bird scare was nothing to get into a bunge over, Debbin was easing herself back to full-on supine mode when her split vision recorded the sight of Kelsea at the road's end.

Uh-oh, she thought. *That doesn't look good.*

Folding her sunglasses, and hooking them pistol-like through the hip strap of her bikini swimsuit, she brushed the damp sand from her bottom and ambled over to see what the trouble was. Kelsea—mind-blurred and preoccupied with a *load* of *heart-wrenching* questions; percolating thus in a brackish broth of unattractive options—didn't hear her approach until she was nearly within touching distance. Then...

"Hey, Kelsea? What's wrong, kiddo?"

Kelsea started at the unexpected sound of a voice on the 'deserted' beach. "Oh my gosh! Debbin!" she stammered. "Whew! I thought I was alone here. Jeez, you are really, um...*stealthy* aren't you?" she managed to finish with a weak, well-intended chuckle.

"Well, it *is* a beach, and sand doesn't make a whole lot of noise when you walk across it, right? Besides, unless I miss my guess, you're pretty involved with some grim private *distractions* right about now. I don't think you'd hear a train approaching, would you?"

Kelsea produced a weak giggle and smiled politely. "Probably true," she replied. "I've got a lot on my mind today."

"Anything I can do to help? I'm just soakin' up some sun before my shift starts at the pool."

"No, not really, Debbin. I, um, well, you didn't happen to see Erik or the LeMasters here this morning, did you? They told me they were going to be here early."

"Sure. They just left. I—"

"*Just* left? Are you <u>certain</u>? When? *When* did they leave?"

"Well, my gosh, Kelsea. Um. I'd say about, you know, maybe five, six minutes ago. How long have you been standing here? You couldn't have missed them by more than a couple of minutes, tops. But what's..."

Kelsea's mind raced at breakneck speed. "But I didn't pass them coming here from town. What's up with that? I should have met them on the way here. Unless—"

Debbin read her mind correctly. "Yeah," she said. "I overheard them say that they were going to take the long way back to town."

In unison, they blurted, "Around Ptarmigan Loop!"

"Exactly," beamed Debbin.

"Indubitably!" echoed Kelsea. "ThanksATonDebbinSeeYa!"

"Um, yeah, bye. I...guess?" Debbin, uncertain. "And, um, you're welcome...ish?"

Crow flies north.

Crowl flies south.

Time flies.

*

Rendezvous (n.) A meeting. An assemblage. A coming together.

Simultaneously (adv.) Two or more things happening at the same time.

What happened next was that on that warm day in mid-August, _three rendezvous—three_ comings-together—occurred in Appleton. And as you may have already guessed, they occurred simultaneously—at the same time.

Deputy Carlos Santiago who, having remedied his minor auto disability, pulled into the Appleton office of the Kennawack County Sheriff's Department, across from the park on Frontier Street. He wheeled into his designated slot, grabbed an attaché case full of paperwork, and strode confidently across the tiny parking lot; a look of concentration and readiness etched upon his handsome, suntanned features.

Inside the modest, two-room station, _three_ 'Suits' were waiting for him.(Yeah, _three._). They were, in a word, _dark._

Each was dressed in _dark,_ formal/professional attire. They wore _dark_ glasses and carried _dark_ briefcases (O.K., _black_ briefcases) loaded to the brim with important-looking paperwork. They were grim-faced and uncommunicative. Strictly business, if you don't mind. Strictly business, even if you _do_ mind. They all looked as if they hadn't had a good laugh (or even a good _bowel movement_) in at least a year.

Nature of the job, no doubt.

Carlos took a seat opposite the *dark,* taciturn gentlemen. Two of them remained standing—flanking the third—who, after removing his sunglasses, set about retrieving mountainous stacks of classified documents. A tedious session of explanation, review, and signature signing followed. For Deputy Sheriff Santiago, this was uncharted territory; this particular brand of police action was not commonplace in pastoral, thinly populated regions like Kennawack County. This constituted some pretty big stuff where *his* experiences with law enforcement was concerned.

Deputy Santiago was alert, but neither worried nor nervous. He had performed in an exemplary fashion in this investigation. His professionalism in conjunction with the Federal Bureau of Investigation was worthy of merit, and he was to be duly recognized for his assistance in drawing the case to a successful close.

So saith the 'Suits.'

Meanwhile, as all the 'Rendezvous I' legal eagles busied themselves with bureaucracy ("Crossing their eyes and dotting their tease," as our Stu would have shamelessly punned), 'Rendezvous II' was commencing just about 50% of a mile south of the Kennawack River's locally famous oxbow lake.

Like a bullet to the bull's eye, Kelsea Crowl had her target in sight, and was all but creating a vapor trail en route to hooking up with her confreres.

What ensued was a stepwise, rapid-fire, rat-a-tat-ism of facial expressions, extravagant gesticulations, and animated dialogue as the Scalawags were overtaken by the hyper-ventilating, super animated Ms. Crowl.

First, the register of pleasant surprise—smiles and bright-eyed hugs.

("Yo, Kelsea! This so too cool! Glad you found us! What's the big rush?")

Next, following the brief, breathless explanation, the look of alarm—jaws dropped wide open, eyebrows ascending to the scalp line atop very, _very_ round eyes.

(**"No way! Justin _can't seriously_ be thinking of selling the quarry lands! When did he decide on _that_? We've gotta _do_ something!"**)

Finally, the lickety-split problem solving with a shared look of steely-eyed seriousness.

(**"Let's finish out the Loop. We're already too far around to go back the way we came. We'll figure out what to say to him on the way. _Let's just get there, immediately, if not sooner!"_**)

Despite the fact that there was a less-than-zero chance that Justin's biker buddies could pedal past any speed limits (the way to Justin's cabin was all uphill from where they sat), their adrenaline-fueled mercy mission was still a triumph of determination over the limitations of physical strength. Make no mistake about it: Those kids were _movin!'_

And now. Rendezvous III.

Have you guessed where _that_ occurred?

Justin Bench, seated at his dinner table; not looking at all well. Pale, defeated—lots of other adjectives come to mind. None that one would ever have expected to apply to such a bright-souled and compassionate person as himself. The light had truly gone out of his eyes and yet...

What was it he had seen?

"I can tell by the look in your _eyes_," remarked the colonel, "that this is still weighing heavily on your conscience, my boy."

Eyes?

"But like most real estate transactions," he continued unimpeded, "the risk can sometimes _appear_ to be substantial at first, yes." The colonel handed Justin a ball-point pen and gestured with his hand to the line on the page where he wanted him to sign his name.

"Having lived here a year or two, with land values appreciating the way they have—and do—why, even the shyest, most skeptical investor is invariably forced to admit to the shrewdness of his _own_ financial wizardry, um...when a financial opportunity of this sort turns up."

Justin stared blankly at the pen in his hand. *Eyes? Something about eyes? What was it?*

"Believe me, young man. With the whopping profit you're getting from this uh, shall we say, win/win transaction, heh-heh, why, you'll be able to set yourself up just about any way you choose. And you will look back someday and say, 'You know, that old colonel really knew how to swing a deal both ways.' Yes, sir! 'I owe that old soldier a lot,' is what you'll be telling yourself; the uh, signature goes here, here, and again right there, and right... over... there, my boy. Yes."

Justin put the pen to the paper.

"Right on the line, Mr. Bench. Yes. Write right on the line. Heh-heh."

'J'

Eyes.

'u'

What was it he had seen? Eyes. What about 'em?

's'

Eyes eyes eyes eyes eyes eyes eyes eyes eyes eyes eyes eyes eyes eyes...

't'

"Very good. Very good, indeed. Just, finish up here and perhaps we'll enjoy a little toast to ah, celebrate our mutual good fortune. Yes."

'i.' 'i's?' 'eyes?'

Eeeeeeeeeeeeeeeeyyyyyyyyyyyyyyyyyyyeeeeeeeeeeeeeeeeeeesssssssssssss ssss!

"Do you care for champagne, Mr. Bench? I hope you don't think it presumptuous of me, but I, uh, brought a bottle of the bubbly along to mark the occasion. Yes. As a matter of fact, it's chilling on ice in the trunk of my car as we speak! So, ah, if we could, uh, just finish up with the formalities, yes, that's right."

Revisit the morning, Justin.

The pre-dawn hour when you were awakened by the sound of a light tapping upon your quiet, darkened bedroom window. Go back, Justin, as you have gone back so many times in days gone by. Because there is something crucial that you've missed on your every return to that early morning summer dawn. Something there that you Just. Can't. Quite. Put. Your finger on.

But this time, this one last time, let your understanding of events unfold through one of Kelsea's memory dreamscapes…

Through the sight and insight of a blue-eyed Crow.

That persistent semi-recollection won't leave you alone, will it?

Here it comes again.

Watch closely now!

CROW IS IN CLUTCH-WITH-TALONS TIME, LOW IN A PONDEROSA PINE WHOSE LIMBS SEEM TO EMBRACE THE QUARRY CABIN LIKE A PROTECTIVE MOTHER HOVERING OVER HER SLEEPING CHILD. THE FIRST FAINT HINT OF COLORED ILLUMINATION HAS CRACKED A HOPEFUL LINE OVER THE EASTERN RIDGES, THOUGH CROW KNOWS THAT THIS IS 'FALSE DAWN;' THAT THE TRUE SUNRISE IS STILL A GOOD HOUR AWAY. THE WORLD—THE KENNAWACK PART OF IT—SLEEPS ON.

THE LONGLEGS APPEARS ON HORSEBACK IN THE FRINGE OF SPARSE VINE MAPLE, ACROSS A SMALL MEADOW—70 METERS FROM JUSTIN'S HOME. HE TETHERS HIS MOUNT—SECURING HIS INTENDED MEANS OF ESCAPE—PULLS A BLACK SKI MASK OVER HIS HEAD AND SLIPS THROUGH STRUGGLING QUARTER ILLUMINATION; SILENT AND MENACING.

HE MAKES SEVERAL QUICK CHECKS INSIDE THE ROOM WHERE JUSTIN RESTS PEACEFULLY; UNAWARE, TRUSTING, STRONG-HEARTED. FISHING THE LIPSTICK FROM HIS RATTY JEANS POCKET (AND, AT THE SAME INSTANT, UNWITTINGLY DRAWING AND DROPPING A KEY), HE MAKES HATE A READABLE THING.

NOISELESS, DESPICABLE MERCENARY OF DARK HOURS AND DARK PURPOSES. CROW COMPREHENDS YOUR MOTIVATION; KNOWS WHAT DRIVES YOUR PATHETIC AGENDA.

CROW PERCEIVES THE SINISTER NATURE OF YOUR ACTIONS, AND KNOWS THAT THEY ARE BORN OF HUMANKIND'S BASEST FLAW OF CHARACTER—GREED.

CROW OBSERVES, UNOBSERVED.

BE THE EYES OF THE CROW, JUSTIN.

WATCH CLOSELY NOW—WITH YOUR MIND'S EYE—AS CROW ILLUMINATES WHAT BEFORE WAS ONLY DIMLY REVEALED TO YOUR SLEEP-MUDDLED AWARENESS.

Greasy, blonde hair sticks out from under the woolen ski mask like dirty, dry straw. Fingernails—filthy, untrimmed. Coarse, calloused hands working their way over the smooth surface of your window. And there! Very high on the left cheekbone! Barely visible through the eyehole of the mask is... The Scar! The identifying mark that can belong to only one person in this Valley!

"Patch!"

"I beg your pardon?" asked Colonel Tattenger.

"Patch. The scar. The message, and probably _all_ of the messages. It was Pat Cheney all along," Justin, whispering; wonderstruck with the revelation.

"Justin, ah, I don't see what you're getting at with this type of, uh..."

"And if Patch is the guy who's been on my back all this time," Justin slowly raised his eyes, and met the colonel's bewildered gaze, "then you can darn sure bet that Rodent had a hand in it, too."

"Now, now, son! It's very plain that this, ah, business venture of ours has got you in a dither. Yes. Well, Justin, my friend, there's no reason why we have to, ah, rush to finalize things. No sir."

Justin's piercing stare was hawklike; withering. The color had risen in his cheeks and his expression had taken on a self-assured quality; growing with the awareness and understanding of his own victimization.

Colonel Tattenger continued to fluster. "I only thought that, ah, at this time you were ready to take the steps toward, ah, securing your own betterment, your future, ah, quite the same as I, and well, it seems as though you're—well, perhaps you are just fatigued. What with that Cheney kid poisoning your friend, uh, Kooper and all."

The ensuing silence could have smothered a silverback gorilla. Then…

"How do *you* know *Pat's* the person who killed my dog?" asked Justin, his tone strained *with* restraint.

Tattenger squirmed uneasily. "Why, ah, everyone in town knows of your misfortune, Mr. Bench. It's common knowledge that he, ah, that is you, well *you*, yourself just uttered Pat's nickname, did you not? And that must have struck a chord in my thoughts, so I…my knee-jerk reaction was to, ah, repeat *his* name with respect to the recent misfortune which befell, uh…Kooper, your fine old friend. You see…"

"I don't think so, colonel," remarked Justin. "I really don't think so," he paused, scrutinizing the man to whom he had nearly sold his sanctuary; his home. "And just how aware have *you* been of your *son's* checkered relationship with Patch lately?"

"Now just one minute, young man," began the colonel in self-defense. "If you are suggesting in the least way that I—"

The cabin door banged open with sudden ferocity; Scalawags stumbling and tumbling in breathless abandon. Justin, registering modest calm at the unexpected crash and chaos; smiling in a sly, knowing fashion through the yelps and exhortations demanding that he **"not sign anything!"**

"Don't worry," he reassured his frantic friends, "I didn't…" eyeballing the colonel, now. "And I *won't*."

Colonel Tattenger, bright-faced with barely contained rage, and in desperate need of an alternate plan of action, attempted to draw out a lengthy rationale for postponing the signing ceremony to a time "more attuned to the appropriate needs of my, ah, junior partner, Mr. Bench." Having said as much, and gathering up his paperwork and windbreaker as he spoke, the man bid a terse, military "good afternoon" to the quarry clan and began to make his exit when…

"Colonel Harding Corbett Tattenger, I am F.B.I. agent Thomas Castle. These are agents John Telford, Andrew MacIver and Sheriff's Deputy Carlos Santiago. Sir, you are under arrest for violation of

Federal Trade Commission rules regulating the unlawful communication of information regarding securities and trusts. You have the right to remain silent. Everything you say, can and will be used against you in a court of law. You have the right to an attorney. If you cannot afford an attorney..."

That's pretty much the way things finally went down on _that_ August day in Appleton, Washington, U.S. of A., just north of town at the wood-hidden wilder-land of the old stone quarry.

At Rendezvous #3.

*

Deputy Santiago spent a good portion of the afternoon explaining to Justin and the others all the details of Colonel Tattenger's doings, and _un_doings. It was a pretty convoluted story, with plenty of twists and subplots. But in the end, it was easiest and best understood as just another tawdry depiction of human prejudice and unbridled greed.

Having given a life's worth of meritorious service to the Marine Corps, Colonel Harding Tattenger had begun to harbor internal resentment at what he considered 'lackluster compensation' for his years of devotion to his country and the Corps. As the end of his career approached, he became increasingly vexed by the tonnage of American corporate CEOs who had found slick ways of 'pulling a few strings,' and walking away from their short professions with a cornucopia of bonuses and perks; _mountainous_ in comparison to his military retirement compensation.

He chafed. He festered. _"His resentment grew unrestrainedly," as Sandy would aver._ And he finally concluded that all he had given of himself in the service of American interests around the world could only be repaid **_in kind_** if he was strong enough, intelligent enough, and _man_ enough to get it _all_ for himself. Nobody _else_ was going to do that _for_ him.

Willingly, he had paid whatever price was asked in order to advance the cause of his own career arc. No task or risk was too great for Harding Corbett Tattenger. And fixing his sights on a bright, future, the colonel knew all too well that someday, it would be pay up time.

As Colonel Tattenger's rank and authority rose, his power and influence began to spread, and he took pains to become well-networked with a select cadre of cherry-picked industrial captains across the U.S. But it was his assignments in Japan that introduced him to the more shady and questionable business practices which would eventually color and define his post-military life plan.

There, he met Masahiro Ishiguro, a star player in the fast-growing microchip industry.

Ishiguro was a self-serving shark who had learned and become well-versed in every backroom, rule-bending scheme ever known to generate a yen. Ruthless, brilliant, and insatiable in the gross pursuit and accumulation of capital wealth, Ishiguro's factories and plants were flung across the globe, generating hundreds of millions of dollars in yearly revenue.

All legally operated—at least, on the surface—for appearance's sake.

Together, Colonel Tattenger and Mr. Ishiguro had collaborated on a variety of projects; the colonel bringing his considerable military influence to bear in slick, tricky ways which his Japanese counterpart—via some additional managerial and fiscal legerdemain—could abracadabra into fat profits. Profits with a substantial kickback.

Hard-Core and Masahiro—runnin' between the legal raindrops all the way.

Kennawack County tax laws were almost continually being reshaped and refashioned in order to make the fiscally struggling region more appealing to investment interests; domestic or foreign. *This,* the colonel knew, was an open secret. Relying on 'insider' information, supplied by his good friend and associate in Japan, Colonel Tattenger hatched a scheme whereby he would secure a large tract of land for development by Mikatsu Enterprises. This for the purposes of developing a cutting-edge techno-research facility, and sprawling administrative campus. It was an investment worth hundreds of thousands of dollars, and expected to recoup millions in yearly profits given the time and proper (iron-fisted) tenure.

A description of the potential land site he had selected proved to be of extreme interest to Mr. Ishiguro, who enthusiastically 'fronted' the colonel a considerable amount of currency with which he could purchase the land at slightly above market price. Mikatsu Industries would then repurchase the acreage from the colonel, who would reap a tidy profit from the quick resale. For his part, Ishiguro would get another toehold in U.S. big business with a *major* new satellite whose prospects for the generation of capital were just short of mind-boggling.

"Well, why wouldn't Mr. Ishiguro just make an open offer for the land site?" wondered Sandy. "Why all the subterfuge and under-the-table dealings? Why resort to clearly illegal undertakings, when an above-board deal seems to me to be a real possibility?"

Carlos explained that, in this instance, leveraged action—legal or otherwise—was truly the *only* way that the lucrative transaction could go down; for *three* reasons. First, Mikatsu Enterprises, ravenous in its desire for expansion, desperately *wanted* the parcel of land which had been scouted and offered by Colonel Tattenger. Kennawack County tax shelters were, literally, a gold mine for global-conscious corporations like M.E.

Furthermore, the size and location of the land site were tailor-made for Mr. Ishiguro, whose particular needs and interests leaned toward small, rural settings; regions that possessed long histories of job and revenue fluctuation. Counties and communities hungry enough to offer plenty of business incentives while 'looking the other way' whenever asked to do so by the Chief Executive Officer.

Second, the colonel—hellbent in his lust for the heady feeling of self-esteem which all too often accompanies the accumulation of wealth—was motivated enough to bring the better part of *three* decades of military expertise and experience to bear in order to 'press' the issue, and ensure delivery of the property into his possession.

"It's all about generating bigger profits the further up the chain you go," summarized Santiago.

"'At's right on, Depu*tay*!" agreed Hollis Greenwood, who had arrived on the scene as if by magic. (Good future attorneys-at-law can *always* sniff out where the action is!) "I think I can *dig* how the whole sys*tam* gets oppa-ray*shown*al, my dudes and dudettes. Ya see, the FatCat BigBoss—that be the Microchip dude—he get in cahoots wit' da man wit' da muscle, that be Corporal Flatulence."

"You mean *Colonel Tattenger*!" laughed Sandy.

"I like it better *his* way," offered Justin.

"What*evah*!" replied Hollis coolly. "The whole deal make a little cash at the bot*tom,* a little mo' money in da mid*dell* an' a whole whoppin' boatload at the top. Dig: Ratpack get chump change from the colo*nel* for makin' Jus*tan* jumpy enough to wanna sell. Am I right Offi*sair*? Uh-huh. See? This ee*say* as pie, once you start put*tan* it all toge*thare*, ba*bays!* So now, Mistah Bench here, he does all right by sel*lan* what he own at some kinda percent *above* market price, dig? Soun' good? Mm-hmm. Well, then the colonel, why he make some pret*tay fine* coin when he get a lip-smackin' check from the FatCat by signin' the deed o*vare* ta him."

"I think I get it now, Hollis," attempted Sandy. "If the land had a fair market value of, let's say $200,000, and Justin sold it for $275,000, why, everyone would say that he made a pretty shrewd bargain, right?"

"Right," interrupted Stuart. "The colonel could afford to buy Justin out because he knew all along he was gonna resell it to a prearranged corporation for, what? *Double* the price!"

"And Mikatsu could pony up *that* much cash because, in *real* terms, the parcel was worth millions, *yearly!*" finished Carlos, shaking his head. "Like I said, the further up the line you go, the bigger your take in profits. If Mikatsu had attempted to do business *directly*, Justin would have been immediately aware of the *true* net worth of the quarry lands.

Its rating as commercially _and_ residentially zoned property would have sent the price tag skyrocketing, and that's something."

"...some_thang_ that my daddy, the numero uno attorney in the coun_tay,_ would _never_ have let go down. Dig: my daddy an' Jus_tan's_ uncle wuz, like, tight as knots, right on! The on'y way FatCat gonna get inta rippin' off Kennawack County wuz by sneakin' in through the back door. All that insi_dare_ informa_shown_ I be tellin' you 'bout some time back? Tha's the stuff the colonel was hip to. Tha's how he hope to make his 'big-time money.' Tha's how FatCat hope to make his 'bigger time money.' That kinda activity is ill-damn-conceived, ill-damn-advised, ill-damn-legal, and turn yo' brains to cottage cheese. Dig it."

"The Feds have been following the business dealings of those two for a long time," offered Officer Santiago. "Timing was very important to making the bust, one that wouldn't be so easy to slip out of with a little legal maneuvering. Even now, we can't be completely certain that a really clever team of attorneys won't find a loophole that'll let every one of them off scot-free. But we do know this: that microchip factory would have been worth millions to Ishiguro when it went online and reached peak production. And the way he chose to get there, by communicating information which unfairly favors _some_ investors to the exclusion of others is a violay_shown_ (winking at Hollis) of Federal law."

And really, if anyone had stopped to consider things in the light of all these newly-revealed facts, the _third_ reason that the quarry transaction _had_ to be undertaken by dealing dirty was the simple fact that Justin Michael Thomas Bench would never, _ever_ have given up his home in the woodlands north of Appleton. Not to Colonel Tattenger. Not to Mikatsu Industries. Not to anyone. Not without a genuinely compelling reason.

Such as fear.

*

That was Rodent's job—to induce fear.

Rather, it was Rodent's job to *mastermind* a crockpot full of dirty deeds (which he himself was too fainthearted to carry out) in order to 'soften up' Justin, and lubricate the purchase offer which would eventually be made by the colonel. Patch, of course, was only too happy to put his shoulder to the task of carrying out each piece of the plot to harass and harangue poor Justin...all the way into submission.

For their troubles, Rodent's father quietly and regularly greased their palms with a crisp one-hundred-dollar bill—courtesy of Mikatsu, Ltd. The colonel had only a rudimentary idea of the framework and timetable which his son had engineered, and which Patch ("That *loathsome lizard*," as Sandy was overheard to remark) was charged with carrying out. He didn't *want to know* the details. Details had *always* been someone else's job; that and the *mop-up*.

No, what the colonel was interested in was *outcomes*—primarily, successful ones.

And as long as trepidation was growing in the heart of that misfit up at the quarry, Tattenger didn't care squat about how his henchmen went about accomplishing their duties. That's what it boiled down to: unconditional, unswerving allegiance to duty.

Allegiance to him. Military-style.

So Patch secured part-time employment at the city pool. (Gotta help pay the bills <u>some</u> way.) While he was there, in the near vicinity of the well-groomed Ms. Ramsay, the idea was born for using her lipstick to write some threatening messages to Justin. It was a weirdly perfect idea for instilling the initial feelings of fear. And besides, the evidence, if carefully analyzed, would only lead back to Debbin. Same thing with using her horse for the quick getaway during the first of the intrusions. Any clues uncovered would simply point—curiously, but convincingly—to Debbin. Again. Very confusing for the Scalawags, yes?

However, once the pitch was made (and rejected by the reluctant Justin), the ante had to be raised. The injurious nature of the assaults not only had to increase in frequency but had to intensify; so that fear, fury, confusion, and a growing sense of hopelessness was forced into his day-to-day activities. The destruction of his beloved Yamaha guitar nearly put him beyond the limits of his endurance. But it was the loss of Kooper—an unprovoked act of unconscionable hatred—that broke Justin and coerced the abject surrender of everything else he valued in life; including his friends.

Or nearly so.

Agent Castle and his associates with the F.B.I. had been monitoring the comings and goings of Colonel Tattenger (as well as those of his partner, Mr. Ishiguro) for the better part of nine months. They had, furthermore, secured the services of Officer Santiago in an inter-agency investigation aimed at slamming the lid on the 'big dogs' involved in a *string* of insider schemes—of which the Appleton Quarry case was merely one element.

But the success of the operation relied heavily upon the abilities of *teams* of law enforcement personnel—networking and compiling evidence from all over the world.

That kind of work takes time.

And the big worry was that Justin's nerves would crumble and collapse from the onslaught of indignities and assaults. To bust the Ratpackers for their many substantial offenses against Justin would be to save him from further victimization, at the expense of letting Tattenger and Ishiguro off the hook for criminal acts on a global scale!

Essentially, the colonel had *used* his own son, not only to carry out the grunt work for his maligned plot, but to serve as a *warning device* and, ultimately, the *fall guy* in the event of a criminal investigation. Tattenger could pass just about any lie detector test by testifying, with a large amount of truth, that he did not know what Rodney and Patch were up to. Rodent's deep-seated fear of his father—as well as a rigid upbringing; deeply steeped in codes of honor, and violent discipline—virtually assured that he would never disobey or blow the whistle on his father. And Patch was simply too angrily muscle minded to know whether to fart or wind his watch.

Insubordination appeared not to be a risk. No threat from the flunkies.

So the F.B.I., the Kennawack County Sheriff's Department, Justin, the Scalawags—everyone—had to sit tight and wait it out; each in their own fashion. The hammer of the law had to hold off for its light to strike, and Justin was forced to endure much.

The waiting is the hardest part.

*

A couple of more 'getups' came and went.

Something on the order of a routine was re-established. Old, familiar ways of going about things were rediscovered, dusted off, and slipped back into like your favorite pair of beater shoes.

The long, strange summer was nearing an end. School would start up in ten days for *three* new tenth graders (and one new 'niner'). But the weather! The weather was "posilutely fantabulous" (as Pops would say)! Warm, cloudless days were lined up like bowling pins; just waiting to be knocked down by the unfettered, revitalized, re-energized exuberances of high-school Scalawags.

Things were looking up.

According to the very latest news from Agents Castle, Telford, and MacIver, Colonel Harding Corbett 'Hard-Core' Tattenger would very soon be court-martialed.

Heavy-hitting techno-business exec Masahiro Ishiguro was cooling his heels in a colorless, cold Japanese penitentiary which he would find over the years to be, understandably, very much to his disliking.

Some of the mysteries of the recent past were finally dragged out into the light of day by virtue of the fact that the Scalawags—with plenty of assistance from Officer Carlos Santiago, simply pulled the drawstrings taut, so to say, and began connecting a loose array of barely discernible dots. That Patch had been pilfering Debbin Ramsay's top o'the line cosmetics was an easy one to prove. That he had also been the guy who rode off with Debbin's unshod horse on the morning of the first offense, was cleared up when Justin had *finally* remembered to remember that he had seen the scar on Patch's face—just inside the eyehole of the ski mask that he wore that morn.

And it only took Stuart one trip to the city pool to uncover the fact that Pat Cheney, and everyone *else* employed there, had been *sent home at noon* on the day of the 'raft message' misadventure: a pre-scheduled closure for filter maintenance!

"Patch'd had *plenty* of time to set that flotation device in the water, and then beat feet down to the swimming hole before it came bobbing around the bend to us," Sandy surmised. "All they had to do to escape culpability, was stay frosty and feign mild interest in what was occurring...*the reptiles!*"

"And who wants to bet that Patch or Rodent...or *both,* were lurking somewhere near the park...waiting to plant a thumbtack in Justin's tire...delaying *all* of us from getting to the Swimming Hole ahead of *them*...while giving *them* the time to contact Patch before the *pool* closed so that *he, Patch* would have *no* problem getting upstream from us with the float note...and yaddah, yaddah! All pretty damned easy to see *after* the facts finally scurry out to whack us out of our 'numb-nicity.'"

As for anticipating the whereabouts of the Scalawags at all times; securing the knowledge of their comings and goings so as to fit them in with Rodney's evolving plans of attack, well...Appleton *is* a small town. It really isn't all *that* difficult to keep a fairly intimate, hidden watch on people without them discovering *your* whereabouts *or* your nefarious notions. You can hide in a city, but not so easily in a village.

Craven-At-Heart-Rodent had buckled quickly under interrogation by 'The Suits,' who wasted no time dropping hints a' plenty of mitigating his soon-to-be-determined court sentence...in exchange for a full confessional. Rodney sang like a proverbial (jail) bird; incriminating himself *and* Patch in a lengthy list of transgressions including, but hardly limited to, breaking and entering, destruction of private property, and harassment on a grand and criminal scale.

Rodent and Patch would soon be sent 'down the river' to take up what was expected to be the better part of a two-year residency at Kestler Hall—the Kennawack County reform school. Most Appletonians *could* have said, with all honesty, that they saw it coming for the Ratpackers from the very beginning.

And most of them probably *did* say it.

Mrs. Tattenger, poor woman—very little of her self-esteem left intact—opted to return to her own little hometown in mid-state Indiana. She had some family living there; some old friends, too, and she hoped to pick up the pieces of her crushed life. To somehow begin again. Appleton wished her well in that regard.

So!

"Oh, man!" exhorted Justin on the last weekend of the eighth month of the year. He inhaled deeply, and let it go like a little kid on his first-ever trip to the town bakery. "I smell the sweet scent of freedom blowin' in the breeze. What're us quarry cats doin' hangin' around the cabin? Summer's expiring in 4/4 time. Let's get our rockin' _be_hinds out to the Swimmin' Hole while the sunshine still allows!"

And that is *exactly* what the Scalawags set about to do! A sack of apples was fetched, and some power bars were discovered and divvied up. Justin got Doowy loaded and ready. Sunscreen? Check. Snacks? Check. Reading material…for Sandy? Check!

Check!

"Check, already! For cryin' out loud, let's get this camel caravan rollin'!"

THIS MIGHT HAVE BEEN UTTERED BY YOU, CROW, IF YOU COULD BUT SPEAK THE LANGUAGE OF THE LONGLEGS.

Then… comes a visitor.

Up the hill marches Hollis Greenwood; grinning from ear to proverbial ear. Exuding an aura of undiluted sun glow, Appleton's future pro basketball player/attorney-at-law swaggers his light-footed way to the quarry cabin, arms tenderly folded around… a ***puppy***!

"Well, I'll be dogged," muttered Justin, a slow, radiant smile spilling across his features.

"Kinda looks like it, bro," said Kelsea, hinting at knowledge previously obtained and secretly mothballed.

"Sunrise in *Justanville*, man! Ain't it grand? Dig it!" quips Hollis.

The girls were **_all_** **_over_** the pup—cooing and oohing, tickling and stroking—all to the little dog's wiggling pleasure. Then, he was in Justin's hands—held aloft—up against a backdrop of impeccable mid-valley August sky; the young man turning a slow circle, grinning up at a furry scamp, squirming happily in the gentle grip of his new owner. The little guy was hugged and patted, groomed and laughed over, then hugged again, and yet again.

Justin and his friends had all died, and gone to dog heaven.

"Hollis, man, you are too much," exclaimed Erik happily.

"He's beautiful, Hollis," gushed Sandy. "My gosh, he even *acts* a little like Kooper, in a laid-back kinda goofy way."

"He doesn't much *look* like him," mused Stuart, "but he's definitely got that 'KickBackKooper attitude' all right. Hey, wait a sec. Don't you have a dog, Hollis? A *female* dog?"

A smug look came over the expression of their street-savvy friend. "That's correcto-mundo, my man. And that ol' rascally Koo*pare* spent many a roman*teek* hour at my place, courtin' the lovely lady dog who resides in my back yard. But, dig: I know whatchuall thinkin', an' uh-uh! My dog been to the vet, see, an' ain't *no* chance of *her* gettin' in a family way, if you see what I'm on 'bout."

"Well, if this isn't one of Kooper's pups, then, who is it, and where'd it come from?" Kelsea, pressing for information, scratching behind the little guy's ear (like Kooper used to enjoy).

"Naw, babe, I did not *say* this pu*pay* dude was *not* one of Koo*pare*'s offspring. Dig. In point of fact, he most cert*aynlay is* one of Koop's little boy-os. The one in the whole litter who takes after his daddy's slow-goin' ways the ab*s*olute…posi*teeve*…most. Dig it. But he come from a place across town, man. As a gift from a sort of a shy type, you know, who don't exactly like showin' up an' lettin' people make a fuss aroun' him an' all. Dig?"

"I can dig it, Hollis," said Justin, continuing to stroke the pup's glossy brown coat. "But are you at least allowed to tell us the name of the person? I'd sure like to find a way to thank him."

"Sure thang, man," Hollis flashed that billion-dollar smile. "You can thank that dude anytime you gotta mind to. Guy who own the female that had Koo*pare's* pups is Chase Reed. *Uh-huh*! 'At's right, an' by the way, babe…He said to tell you in advance, man, that, like, '*You're welcome!*' Dig it!"

"Deep Thoughts!" marveled Stuart.

"Wonder upon wonder," added Kelsea.

Sandy reached for Erik's hand, standing there side by each, smiling in the sunshine—sharing some private bits of information to which only *they* were privy.

"A name. Do I hear a name?" barked Stuart. "Dog's gotta have a name or he darn well won't show up when ya go to call him."

"His name is just so obvious, Stu D. Baker," Justin admonished, winking.

"He's got a name *already*," surrendered Erik. "Why am I *not* surprised?"

"Let's have it, man!" hooted Hollis. "Can't start the trainin' too soon! You *do* dig, do you not?"

"Well," began Justin, trying to build a little suspense into the mix. "He's a carbon copy of Kooper. Well, manner-wise at least, so…"

"I got it! I got it!" yelled Stu, as Justin paused to politely to allow him a guess.

"It's gotta be like what you did with Woody and Doowy. Ya just leave the ending—the last syllable—alone, and reverse the first and last letters of the first syllable, right?"

Kelsea thought for a moment, and then caught the wave of the idea and squealed, "He's on it, isn't he? Stu figured it out, didn't he Justin?"

Justin Bench smiled broadly and nodded, securing the pup inside his bike basket and closing the wire mesh cover. "C'mon, 'Pooker,'" he said happily. "We got cool places to go, and cool things to do."

"Like *where* and *what*, may we ask?" inquired Kelsea, tapping her foot—arms folded in an unmistakable '*I-deserve-an-answer*' kind of stance.

Justin, feigning total surprise at the question. "Why, to the Swimmin' Hole, of course. That's where we were off to just a moment ago. Have you forgotten?"

"Well, what about 'Pooker?' Are we taking him on his first road trip so soon?"

"Not so much a road trip, Kelseroo," advised Justin. "More like, um, shall we say… swimmin' lessons?"

"Water-ward!" that's Kelsea.

"Surf's up!" that's Stu.

"Gonna sure enough do some doggone dog paddlin' today, man. Dig it," Hollis, right?

"Indubitably," laughed Sandy, squeezing Erik's sun-warmed hand.

"In-double-dubitably!" returned Erik, holding her gaze.

And their eyes communicated the rest.

*

YOU ARE THE CROW; BLACK, GLIDING INHABITANT OF LOFTY, WHIRLING AIRSPACE.

LONG SEASONS AGO, YOU EMERGED FROM YOUR EGG—GRAY/EYED, AND NOT YET CHIP BEAKED; WET FEATHERED AND BLINKING—TO TAKE YOUR PLACE AMONGST THE SUBTLE SPLENDOR THAT IS THE HALLMARK AND DOMAIN OF ALL CREATURES BORN OF THE KENNAWACK LANDS.

YOUR TIME, THUS FAR, UPON THE EARTH AND WITHIN THE SKYWAYS OF THIS PLANET HAS BEEN RICH, DANGEROUS, UN-CONCEITED.

IMMERSED IN TRUE-FREE-JOY. AND ALWAYS, ALWAYS WAITING IN LEARNTIME.

NOT UNLIKE THE VALLEY RIVER, TIME FLOWS ONWARD, DOWNWARD; FORWARD TO THE GREAT COLLECTION OF EVERY-ALL-NESS WHICH IS, AT THE SAME TIME, ITS SOURCE AND ITS DESTINATION. AND NOT UNLIKE THE OXBOW LAKE THAT COUNTERS AND CONFUSES THE DRAIN AND DIRECTION OF STREAM WANDER, SOMETIMES TIME FOLDS BACK UPON ITSELF IN DIRECT SELF-CONTRADICTION—DEMANDING THE IMPLAUSIBLE AND PERFORMING THE IMPOSSIBLE. AND YOU, BLUE-EYED CROW...YOU EMBRACE THE COMPLEXITIES OF TIME ON A VAST (BY LONGLEGS STANDARDS), ALMOST UNIMAGINABLE SCALE.

BELOW YOU, ALONG FRONTIER STREET, ACROSS FROM THE LIBRARY, IN APPLETON'S LITTLE TOWN PARK, YOU SPOT THE MAN ON THE PAINT-PEELED, OLD GREEN BENCH. THE GUITAR IS ON HIS KNEE, AND HE CROONS SOFTLY IN THE SHELTERING SHADE OF LEAFY TREES WHOSE STORIES, IF THEY COULD BE TOLD, WOULD FAR TRANSCEND APPLETONIAN LIVES AND TIMES; WOULD OUT SHADOW EVEN CROW UNDERSTANDING OF THE SUPERIORITY OF LOYALTY AND LOVE OVER THE BRUTE ENERGY OF GREED, AND THE INFLAMMATION OF SENSELESSLY ASSERTED POWER.

YOU SEE THE SMALL DOG, SLEEPING UNDER THE BENCH BETWEEN THE MAN'S BOOTS, AND YOU THINK TO YOURSELF: "THAT IS NOT 'THE' DOG." BUT YOU PAY NO FURTHER NOTICE. THE CATARACTS OF THE HIGHLANDS TUG AT YOUR BLOOD, LIKE MOON TIDE.

AND YOU ARE COMPELLED TO COMPLY WITH A LIFE PLAN WHICH WAS EMBEDDED IN YOUR MIND, SPIRIT, AND WING MUSCLE UNRECKONABLE EPOCHS AGO.

RAVENRILL...

O RAVENRILL!

THERE, TO WEAVE INTO THE TAPESTRY ALL THAT WHICH YOU HAVE SHEPHERDED, BUNDLED, AND AMASSED. AT THE SAME TIME, TO ABSORB AND ASSIMILATE THE REFINED AND BURNISHED, EVER-EVOLVING, EVER-REVEALING NARRATIVE OF THAT-WHICH-IS.

YOUR TIME, YOUR LIFE SPAN NEAR THE LITTLE TOWN OF APPLETON—SO QUIETLY SPREAD ALONG AND ABOVE THE STONY BANK LINES OF THE BEAUTIFUL KENNAWACK RIVER—IS LONG, FAR YEARS FROM ITS ENDPOINT. OF THIS, YOU HAVE NEITHER

DOUBT, NOR CONCERN. BUT WITH ITS EVENTUAL TRANSCENDENCE, YOUR BODY WILL FEED THE SOIL ACROSS WHICH HAVE TRODDEN UNCOUNTABLE NUMBERS OF DREAMERS, DRUNKARDS, FREEMEN, AND FOOLS—ALL SEEKING THE LOVE AND WARMTH OF THEIR PEERS, AND A NOOK IN THE SHADE WHERE THEY MIGHT ONE DAY LAY EVERYTHING DOWN AND PEACEFULLY CEASE TO BE.

On the first day of school, in her tenth-grade year—on the afternoon of her 15th birthday—Kelsea Crowl was using a mirror in the girl's restroom to adjust her hair clip. She was surprised to discover that— somehow, over a short period of time—her irises had changed from rain gray to river blue, and that a tiny brown dot of a mole was emerging on her upper lip...in the same general location where the beak of a bird had once been broken.

She smiled the smile of a person who has been graced with a secret; one which has been locked so protectively inside her animal spirit self that even she cannot decipher the breadth and scope of its deeper meanings.

Well.

What do we, any of us, really know about our inner-selves anyway? Hmm?

Of Acorns and Oak Trees

Readers (including myself) sometimes ponder various sourcing questions, such as: "Where did that writer get the inspiration for that particular project? What got the ball rolling for him/her with regard to that idea? What was the "ah-ha," defining moment that convinced that author to dive in and push that particular theme to completion?"

Speaking strictly for myself, when I compose a song, a poem or a short story I can state categorically that I am very seldom aware of just *how* any idea takes shape in my mind. So, here and now, I would like to extend a generous dollop of gratitude to my Muse; my Guide who, given to taking *plenty* of breaks and sabbaticals, nevertheless consistently supplies me with a plethora of working possibilities on a more-or-less regular basis—presumably from out of the aether.

Thanks, ol' friend, whoever you are!

But once in a very great while (think "Blue-Moon-ish-ly") I have a clear and focused remembrance of exactly what it was that galvanized my creative impulses, and placed me on some well-defined and dedicated literary path, *"Appleton Quarry/Appleton Crow"* is one such example.

Sometime near the end of the 1990s, I stumbled across some bits of free verse that I had composed ten years earlier, and an idea took root in my imagination. How or why these experimental efforts with various poetic formats directed my thinking along the lines of a full-on manuscript is still a mystery to me. But energize me, they did. And if my reader cannot grasp the connection between my verse and the completed novel, then at least he can reckon himself neither more nor less in the dark about it than I.

In posing the question, "Where did the motivation for the novel come from?" The answer would be: From two of the poems, I composed in the mid-80s. But this merely begs another question: "Then where did the motivation for the *poems* come from?" Well, the first poem, *Crow Eye*, was inspired by *another* poem that I read in *Harper's Magazine* in the very early 1980s. Sadly, I can recall neither the name of that poem, nor the name of its author. But having read it, I began entertaining the concept that God *could* be keeping tabs on his Earth through the eyes of an innocent, unassuming bird:

Crow Eye

Crow Eye
Up on high pine limb
Follows him.
Quick flick,
Little, gray bead
Catches every deed done
In new morning sun.
Blackwing rustle;
Every muscle senses a beat
Replete
With the flotsam
And jetsam
Of human imaginings.

Feathers clasp unseen motion;
Windborne.
A flutterspun descent
With little intent
But swirly flight.
Alights,
Hop-dancing on spongy earth.
Peck-tap at paper cup;
Mindless significance.

Senses grasp invisible moments;
Time.
Assured of worth
By design
Encoded in Crow Life Plan.
Instinctively thinking:
"It is. I am."

Flits alongside
(for a time)
With no thought to following.

Little Watcher.
Eye of Crow.
Mind of God.

In the second poem, _Len,_ I wrote about a young man who, despite laboring with a number of physiological challenges, had a heart of solid gold, and possessed the ability to engage in some terrific guitar work. That composition came out of my reaction to an anecdote told me by Sam Willsey, a lifelong Central Washington friend of mine. Years ago, Sam regaled me with the story of a real enough small-town acquaintance of his, who had a similar, though not exact, set of circumstances. The idea resonated with me, and became fodder for later writing:

Len

Len's sittin' out there again
on that wooden bench
they put in front of the Post Office
years ago.
You know the kind of bench I mean;
the kind with wood slats,
and a curved back,
and green paint
that's half-peeled-off/half-not.
Year in
and year out,
that bench looks exactly the same;
like it's peeled off all the paint it's gonna,
and is finally comfortable
with the balance.
That's one reason
I believe in Magic.

Ol' Len,
(We call him "old,"
but he really isn't.
Around 30, I think.)
he's kind of a spooky guy;
weird guy.
See:
He was originally cross-eyed
as a cuckoo.
Then he lost an eye somehow;
his right eye,
I don't remember how.
And now, his left eye
is all he has left.
And that old eye just kind of
looks at his nose all the time.
Or maybe at that blank spot
where his *other* eye *used* to be.

And his back is kinda funny;
not really a hump-back,
but *almost.*
Like a baby-hump
that you just *know*
is bound to grow bigger and *bigger*
as time goes by,
and no more paint peels off
that curve-backed bench
he sits on all the time.

His right leg is way shorter than the other.
I mean
__*way*__ shorter.
I think that's why
he sits on that doggone bench
so much.

It requires too much effort
to walk,
what with him throwin' his whole body
like he does,
and hardly seein'
where he's goin'
anyhow.
And his teeth…
all crooked-y
with a funny color
to 'em;
sort of grey-like.

So you see:
This guy, Len…
he's no Romeo.
No, sir.

But really,
more than the way he looks,
the thing about him that's sorta the spookiest
is the way he laughs.
Not really *how* he laughs,
but *when*.
He always laughs at things
that nobody else laughs at.
And when everybody *else* laughs,
he is strangely silent.
I tell you:
it's kinda weird.

But despite the timing of his humor,
despite his cock-eyed eye,
despite his baby hump,

despite his short little-leg,
despite his crooked-y/grey teeth.
I have never,

<u>NEVER</u>
heard a harsh word
pass his lips.
And I have never
heard him complain.
And that's another reason
I believe in Magic.

Now,
I'm 14 years old.
And some of my friends
can be downright mean
to ol' Len—
call him names,
and make jokes about the way he looks.
But not me.
And he smiles at me,
and winks with that deep-dented
no-eye socket
(You oughta see *that!*),
and picks up his guitar.

I say,
"Don't sing, Len."
(He sounds like a ruptured beagle.)
"Just play today."

And when he plays guitar…
and when he plays guitar…
and when he plays guitar…
that's yet *another* reason
I believe in Magic.

"Crow" and Justin Bench were born of these two examples of my early verse. One thing can lead to another, and *Appleton Quarry/Appleton Crow* emerged as my *own* response to my *own* previous poetic experimentation and effort. If you are able to spot any "acorns" within these two poems, then perhaps you can visualize how the "oak tree" evolved from the planting thereof.

This is also why I *never* throw any literary scribblings away. One simply never knows…does one?

For readers seeking a deeper, more substantial, eyebrow-arching and oftentimes smile inducing study of corvids in general and crows in particular, I invite you to "lean in… in LearnTime" with _In the Company of Crows and Ravens_ (2005, Yale University Press) by John M. Marzluff and Tony Angell.

—JMW

COLD CUSHIONS OF ALPINE AIR EVERUNDER YOUR WINGS…RISE, FLY! HAPPY EXPLORING!

—CROW

CPSIA information can be obtained
at www.ICGtesting.com
Printed in the USA
LVHW082003090622
720900LV00003B/143